Keys to the Garden

EDITED BY AMMIEL ALCALAY

CITY LIGHTS BOOKS
SAN FRANCISCO

10 9 8 7 6 5 4 3 2 1

Cover artwork by Jack Jano
Reproduced by courtesy of Jack Jano
Cover design by John Miller / Big Fish Books
Book design by Robert Sharrard
Typography by Harvest Graphics

See page 372 for an extension of the copyright page.

Library of Congress Cataloging-in-Publication Data
Keys to the garden: New Israeli Writing / edited and with an introduction by Ammiel Alcalay.
p. cm.
Translations from the Hebrew and Arabic.
ISBN 0-87286-308-5
1. Israeli literature—Translations into English. 2. Jews Oriental—Israel—Intellectual life. 3. Sephardic authors—Israel— Interviews. 4. Jews—Middle East—Literary collections
I. Alcalay, Ammiel.
PJ500599.E1K48 1996
892.4'08—dc20 95-24516
CIP

City Lights Books are available to bookstores through our primary distributor: Subterranean Company, P.O. Box 160, 265 S. 5th St., Monroe, OR 97456. 541-847-5274. Toll-free orders 800-274-7826. FAX 541-847-6018. Our books are also available through library jobbers and regional distributors. For personal orders and catalog, please write to City Lights Books, 261 Columbus Avenue, San Francisco, CA 94133

CITY LIGHTS BOOKS are edited by Lawrence Ferlinghetti and Nancy J. Peters and published at the City Lights Bookstore, 261 Columbus Avenue, San Francisco, CA 94133.

CONTENTS

ACKNOWLEDGMENTS

Much of the work on this book was done from 1991 until 1995, a period in which I found myself quite involved in the situation in former Yugoslavia and Bosnia in particular. As I write this, Žepa, one of the so-called "safe havens," is under attack. Srebrenica fell several days ago and Sarajevo continues to be shelled daily. I can only imagine what will have taken place by the time this book appears. Living through such times, even at this remove, has only confirmed what I have come to value regarding the connections between cultural work and the world—not in any abstract sense, but within and through relationships to people and places.

Like the work on Bosnia, *Keys to the Garden* has also been a collective endeavor. Despite this, I often found myself working alone and relying primarily on my own resources to do the kind of work that, ideally, should be carried out within the framework of an institution, with all the amenities, support and legitimacy that fully functioning institutions can provide. There is, of course, a certain freedom in working outside such a framework, but it bears an almost parallel quotient of exhaustion along with it. Having mentioned the solitary nature of much of this work, I would also be the last to wish to hold a monopoly over my vision of it and I remain most eager for others to participate by offering alternative readings that lead in new and different directions.

Before beginning what can only be an inadequate and incomplete list of debts, I must also offer a disclaimer. *Keys to the Garden* is not, in any way, meant to be a definitive anthology, a canonization of any kind. Certain writers do not appear—most obviously, for example, Sami Michael and Amnon Shamosh who, for all intents and purposes, should be natural inhabitants of such a garden. In their case, my decision not to include them rested on the fact that—although not readily enough available—their work has been translated and published before in English. Other obvious choices would include two writers who continue to write in Arabic, Itshak Bar Moshe and Shalom Darwish. Then, of course, there is the playwright Gabriel Ben-Simhon; the novelists Eli Amir and Noga Treves, the poets, some more well-known (such as Maya Bejerano, Peretz Dror Bannai; Shlomo Zamir; Herzl and Balfour Hakak), and others who might not be so well-known (Yosef Ozer, Eli Bekhar, Moshe Benarroch, Ella Bat Zion, Orit Cohen, Rachel Atalia). These are only a few names that come to mind among so many others whose work needs and deserves to be translated and examined within a wider context. My hope (in addition to opening up the truly diverse and rich spectrum of Israeli writing to American readers), is that by simply providing an introductory offering, I can whet the appetite of others to delve deeper and further into realms that have remained inaccessible for far too long.

Obviously, my primary debts are to the writers themselves. Some I have known for quite a few years, while I have gotten to know others more recently. Throughout the process, they have made Israel an even more intense place than usual to be. Since many of the writers included here have not, given their circumstances, been so easy to find out about, work on this anthology has also involved an intricate chain of references.

I would never, for example, have known of the work of Shoshannah Shababo had I not met Professor Yosef Halevi, whose research has been instrumental in her rediscovery. I would never have met Professor Halevi had it not been for Professor Ephraim Hazan, whom I have known through our common interest in the full corpus of Hebrew poetry written throughout the Mediterranean, North Africa, Yemen and the Balkans following the expulsion from Spain. Professor Halevi was also kind enough to put me in touch with Orna Levin who, in turn, was kind enough to provide me with a picture of her mother, Shoshannah Shababo. This kind of connection was also made when I contacted Josette d'Amade in Paris; she was kind enough to provide photographs of her sister, Jacqueline Shohet Kahanoff. And I would not have known of Jacqueline Shohet Kahanoff's work were it not for Nissim Rejwan; nor could I have gotten a hold of certain texts had it not been for Eva Weintraub, whom I would again like to thank for assisting me. In turn, again, I believe that I originally was referred to Eva Weintraub by Professor Sasson Somekh, a constant supporter of my various activities. It was also through Nissim Rejwan that I met Yosef Dehoah Halevi, the editor of *Afikim,* one of the longest standing *mizrahi* cultural institutions in Israel; it was through Yosef Dehoah Halevi that I discovered the work of Simha Zaramati Asta, as well as many other Yemenite writers that, unfortunately, I have been unable to include here. Through Shelley Elkayam, I got to the work of Yehezkel Kedmi and Uziel Hazan; through Avi Shmuelian, I got to the work of Jack Jano whose art has been used for the cover. Through my friends Meir Bar Asher and Arieh Kovsky, I met Shlomo Avayou; and through Asher Knafo, I met Erez Bitton. I am sure there are many more such connections.

Many thanks are also due to Shimon and Gila Ballas; Sami and Shelley Chetrit; Yitzhak Gormezano and Shosha Goren; Tikva Levi; Samir and Vicki Naqqash, and Ronny and Liora Someck; thanks also to Amira Hess, Ronit Matalon and Moshe Sartel. Many, many thanks to Eli Hamo for providing photographs that visually capture some of the climate out of which these texts have emerged; Eli has also, over the years, been a reliable and accurate reader of the *mizrahi* scene, providing me with vision from within. Many thanks to Anton Shammas for his unflagging support and continuing sanity; thanks to Mira Rima Eliezer, as well as to Charlie and Jakob Abutbul.

None of this would have been possible without excellent translations. The task of translation, a perennially under-rated and underpaid but often mystified art, were quite daunting in this case. I owe very special thanks to Marsha Weinstein who, although listed as a translator, often did the work of a collaborator. I found her editorial advice impeccable and her eyes and ears fully attuned to the nuances of the formidable texts she managed to transform into American. Many, many thanks also to Susan Einbinder, whose fully realized and subtle translation of *Iya* by Shimon Ballas I use with her permission. Thanks also go to Yaffa Berkovits, Yonina Borvick, M. Joseph Halabi, Henry Israeli, Nava Mizrahhi, Betsey Rosenberg and Hannah Schalit. Special thanks also go to my colleague, Professor Ali Jimale Ahmed of Queens College and the CUNY Graduate Center, for guiding me through the truly perplexing and formidable Arabic of Samir Naqqash, as well as to Ruth Naqqash for her Hebrew translations of some of those same texts.

Thanks also go to editors and journals where some of this material has appeared previously. Walter Cummins, the editor of the *Literary Review* at Farleigh Dickinson University, enthusiastically accepted and supported my proposal to guest edit an issue on *mizrahi* writing which was then followed by an issue on new writing from Beirut. Here, I felt a spirit that clearly paralleled my own and the issue proved to be the stepping stone upon which the legitimacy of this work came to be grounded; for that, I am extremely grateful. Thanks as well to Jill-Menkes Kushner for her fine editorial support during the preparation of that issue. Thanks also go to the poets Aleš Debeljak and Leonard Schwartz for first suggesting that I contact the *Literary Review.* Thanks to Ben Benani at *Paintbrush* for featuring an early selection of texts; to Ken Brown and Hannah Davis at *Mediterraneans;* to Jenny Seymore at *Tribes;* to Joe Stork at *Middle East Report;* to Burt Kimmelman at *Poetry New York;* to Aloma Halter at *Ariel;* to the *Painted Bride Quarterly* and the *Melton Journal.* Thanks also go to Ruth Siegel and Jayana Clerk, as well as Mary Ann Caws and Christopher Prendergast, who used previously published material in *Where the Waters Are Born: Modern Literatures of the Non-Western World,* and *The Harper Collins World Reader.* Many, many thanks to Deborah Harris, Galia Licht and Beth Elon of the *Harris/Elon Agency* in Jerusalem, for their friendship, support and permission to use the work of Dan Banaya-Seri, Avi Shmuelian and Albert Swissa. May other American publishers be so bold as to finally give us more than a glimpse of these truly stunning writers.

While support for my work has been more covert on the East Coast, it was Marcella Harb of the St. Marks Poetry Project who asked me to participate in an evening of readings by translators working out of the classical and modern languages of what we call the Middle East: Hebrew, Arabic, Turkish and Farsi;

I thank her for that and the opportunity to meet two kindred spirits, Murat Nemet-Nejat and Peter Lamborn Wilson, both of whose works and concerns have been of great value to me. It was with support from the West Coast, however, that this book was born. Beginning with the insistence of Gil Anidjar and Ruth Tsofar to have me speak at Berkeley, the generosity of Professor Aron Rodrigue to have me at Stanford, the enthusiasm of Ron Nachman to have me read at Small Press Traffic, and Bob Sharrard's invitation for a book party at City Lights, my varied roles as poet, translator and scholar finally got a chance to address the same audience. I consider this a turning point in my own work and, in addition to those I have mentioned, would also like to warmly thank Etel Adnan, Norma Cole, Juan Felipe Herrera, Mustapha Kamal, Semadar Lavi, Laura Moriarty and Michael Palmer for helping make such a coincidence possible.

At Queens College, I have had the good fortune of having a captive audience of students through whom I have been able to constantly test the intentions, the successes and failures of much of this material, both in Hebrew and English. Some of the writers included here (Ronny Someck, Sami Shalom Chetrit, Tikva Levi and Shelley Elkayam), have even been our guests, giving students a very intimate look at their work. Of these students I would, in particular, like to mention Pazit Algazi, Nurit Antman, Tali Barukh, Avia Brobeck, Micole Galapo, Noa Goldman, Ayelet Hen, Ruth Kroll, Robin Levitt, Vanessa Merlis, Ami Neeman, Morane Schwartz, Ganit Steifman, Haya Tsafeer and Kalman Vidomlanski for their insight and dedication, and for being repeat offenders. There are many, many others whom I do not mention by name that I would also like to thank.

Thanks are due to The Lucious N. Littauer Foundation for their support at an earlier stage of this project; I also have had the good fortune to be the recipient of two PSC-CUNY travel grants which have been immensely helpful.

Before ending, I would like to thank Bob Sharrard for his immediate, unequivocal and continuing support for this project. He has been a true pleasure to work with and, having, as it were, cut my teeth on the Pocket Poets Series, I find it quite fitting that this collection be published by City Lights; my heartfelt thanks to everyone there who has been involved.

Finally, I would like to note that this project has been carried out under the auspices of *NUR: Fire & Light,* a collective of *mizrahi* artists and activists with members in the Middle East, Europe and the United States.

And for everyone that I am sure to have forgotten in each category, my sincere apologies.

FOREWORD

We are too often lulled into thinking that texts in translation come to us simply because of their "intrinsic" worth. Nothing could be further from the truth. We should never forget that texts and the cultures out of which they emerge enter our common vocabulary by circuitous navigation through a variety of institutions, whether those be actual functioning institutions or institutionalized assumptions and expectations, modes of thinking that determine what we deem plausible and what we deem outlandish or unlikely. There is no intimation that availability of certain texts might have something to do with the production of a receptive space through the political and economic relationships that exist between countries and that migration itself, of both people and goods, is socially produced by those very conditions and relationships.

Unlike France or Great Britain with their colonial histories (or even Spain with its Islamic and Jewish past), the United States has had no direct or long-standing symbiotic contact on a large scale—regardless of how conflicting such an encounter might have been—with Arabic and Middle Eastern culture. The only exception to this can be seen in Iran, following the CIA-backed overthrow of Muhammad Mosaddiq in 1953 after his nationalization of the Iranian oil industry. Although the Shah remained in power for twenty-six years before being deposed by the Islamic revolution of 1979, one would be hard-pressed to compare the U.S. policy of domination by remote control with the experience of generations of people from France, for example, who settled in North Africa, not to mention the enormous effects of wars of liberation and decolonization on the society and culture of former colonies *and* colonial powers, the effects of which are still very much with us today.

Regarding contemporary Israeli writers, we are given to accept the fact that translation of more popular writers somehow already implies or guarantees the importance of their work. That many Israeli writers are readily available in translation (as so many triumphant and self-congratulatory critics are all too ready to point out with surrogate pride), is a state of affairs that can only have come about, presumably, because of the quality of this work. The idea that the availability of such texts might have as much to do with institutional relationships between Israel and the United States and everything that goes along with such relationships, including the politics of publishing, is a subject better left undiscussed. Why aren't, for example, Iranian, Lebanese, Turkish, or Moroccan novels available with such immediacy? Why aren't the few works that appear from such countries more prominently reviewed or distributed? And even more to the point, why are only some Israelis translated and published abroad? The idea that contemporary Israeli writing might be a highly contested field, a place where social and political struggles occur, is never even broached as a possibility. Yet, Israeli culture—and writing in particular—clearly is a highly polarized and contested field.

In addition, knowledge of Israel—at least until very recently—is filtered through an extremely narrow spectrum of political assumptions and institutional structures that are quite pervasive in the media, the academy, and popular culture. Even in specialized contexts, the overwhelming emphasis remains on the Eastern European experience, the Holocaust, Zionism, and the Israeli/Arab conflict from an Israeli or American rather than an international perspective. This is significantly different than, for example, in France, where a large Middle Eastern Jewish and Arab intellectual presence has had such a significant impact on the common vocabulary of French culture. Nor does general knowledge or the particular study of Middle Eastern culture in America directly link up to a flourishing intellectual emigre community as in Great Britain or France. Such knowledge, where it does exist, is still primarily used to feed into the production of demonic imagery and the perpetuation of a reductive analysis of "the threat of Islamic fundamentalism." Even the defense against such assaults often employs the same reductive discourse, shrinking very complex and dynamic situations into static dichotomies of "us" versus "them."

The twenty-four writers gathered in this anthology encompass an enormous diversity of experience, yet access to the worlds now and once inhabited by these artists is consistently deterred by a lack of historical context, various forms of misrepresentation, and a host of false assumptions. Much of this has to do with the fact that the peoples out of which these writers emerge have been able to exert little or no control over the discourse produced about them within Israeli society. Lacking political autonomy, economically and culturally subordinated, they have had to witness the socialization of successive generations into a society that has either fundamentally denied or severely restricted the deepest recesses of their personal and collective geography and culture. As the novelist Albert Swissa has written: "In the cauldron of the generation that founded the state, whole cultures melted into oblivion, were eroded, vanished—life experiences, gestures, customs, sights, smells, sounds, languages, people." Yet, far from accepting the status of victim, Swissa also goes on to note that "as a result of sudden changes in their social and economic behavior patterns, those who were arbitrarily thought of as 'backwards' were suddenly thrown into the very heart of a class struggle when they were 'naturally' placed at the bottom of the ladder. Overall, it fell to the Oriental Jews to fight on all fronts of Israeli society, to fight against this society itself, and to fight against the image Israeli society ascribed to them—and I am not sure that this was such a bad thing." For even a rudimentary grasp of the seemingly contradictory nature of this situation, at least some background is needed.

The conflicting pressures that have shaped the fate of Mediterranean and Middle Eastern Jews have, indeed, been quite intricate and complex. Despite many ups and downs, the Jews of the Levant and the Islamic world remained a people distinctly empowered by the light that only recognition can nurture and provide. Historically, this recognition was legal, communal, covenantal, linguistic, spiritual and, at root, unconditionally common. Regardless of whether things got better or worse during periods of natural and human catastrophe, enlightened or autocratic rule, the Jews of the region remained *ahl-al-kitab,* "people of the Book." This acknowledgment had never been granted in the Christian world, where fundamentalist warlords and inquisitors ultimately extricated *both* Jew and Muslim from the common history of a Europe in which each had been native for close to eight hundred years. The expulsion of the Jews from Spain in 1492 coincided with even greater waves of terror and expulsion directed against European Muslims, the Moors. This suppressed chapter in European history came back with a vengeance only during the Enlightenment and colonial periods when an imperial curriculum succesfully managed to ethnically cleanse any references to semites—Jews or Muslims—that might indicate them to be both posessors of an autonomous history and inextricable partners in the creation of "European" culture.

It is in this crucible that Levantine Jewry struggled to come of age in the late 19th and 20th centuries—between the push and pull of competing nationalisms (Arab and Jewish); universalism (in the form of communism); colonialism (as the minority of preference); and the world of the law (through rabbis desperately struggling to maintain communities under duress from every quarter). It is also in this context that the traumatic encounter between Eastern European Zionists, ideological heirs to the most retrograde 19th century assumptions about the "Orient," and Middle Eastern Jews took place. As many of the texts included in this collection attest to, the scars of this encounter still remain open wounds, once the surface had been scratched and the old forms of identity and recognition (communal, cultural, and covenantal), were scrapped for the newer national, ethnic, and class markers.

During the 1950s and 1960s, over half a million Mediterranean, North African and Middle Eastern Jews came to Israel with little more than the clothes on their collective back. For all intents and purposes, the majority of these people remained hostages to the culmination of greater political forces that had already begun to play themselves out both within the region and in their communities over the past one hundred years. Completely dependant upon state institions intent on remolding them in their own image, choices were limited and autonomy, except in the most private sense, was unimaginable: assimilation, denial, active and passive resistance were all modes of coping with the utterly alienating circumstances they faced. Active resistance often took the form of social and cultural movements and it is within these movements that a *mizrahi* consciousness developed. Originally a component of the pejorative label used to institutionally categorize non-European Jews (*benei 'edot ha-mizrah* / "the offspring of the Oriental ethnic communities"), the word *mizrah* ("East") and *mizrahi* ("Easterner") gradually took on qualities of pride and defiance as the *mizrahim* (plural: "Easterners") came to describe themselves. Although long a majority, the *mizrahim* continued to be treated as a minority, yet their culture and presence had come to fully transform the official parameters of Israeli society.

From the 1970s on, there was a veritable explosion of creativity emerging from *mizrahi* consciousness—in writing, music, theater, art, and popular culture. Not surprisingly, the mainstream Israeli critical establishment, composed of a proportionally tiny elite weaned on the narrowest ethnocentric, political, and cultural assumptions regarding Israel's place in the world, consistently ignored, maligned or, at best, misinterpreted this work. What can, for want of a better term, be called "Zionist discourse" (with its hybrid Enlightenment, romantic, revolutionary, and colonialist legacy, as well as its attendant assumptions regarding Jewish history and the diaspora), has permeated almost every aspect of modern Jewish culture. While an earnest critique of this legacy and these assumptions has begun, modes of discourse that can only be called paternalistic, ahistorical, and inadequate have proven particularly resilient in the study of literature and language since the revival of modern Hebrew forms such a deep component of the ideology itself. More insidious, embedded in gaps and silences, this discourse relies on exclusion or partial accomodation as a means of asserting truth and maintaining control. The maintenance of these borders between "us" and "them" has carried quite easily overseas so that American "scholars" of Israeli culture and literature can, without compunction or recourse to a counterposition, make statements such as this: "From a Middle Eastern perspective, then, all Israelis, even those of Moroccan or Persian or Yemenite origin, are European; their literature is European; their outlook is alien or external to the Middle East."[1]

While the absurdity of such a statement might seem self-evident, the extent to which such fictional constructs are typical and remain unchecked is truly remarkable. All of the anthologies of Israeli literature available in translation, for

1. Warren Bargad and Stanley F. Chyet, *Israeli Poetry: A Contemporary Anthology* (Bloomington, 1986), p. 3.

example, systematically exclude the work of *mizrahim*. The rare exceptions to this only seem to prove the rule. This, in turn, greatly effects what publishers and editors are even capable of *imagining* to be part of Israeli culture. Again and again we are told, inexplicably, that "Hebrew literature, though now created preponderantly in the Middle East, resolutely remains a Western literature, looking to formal and even sometimes stylistic models in English, German, and, to a lesser degree, Russian, French, and Spanish."[2] The fact that writers such as those included in this anthology might look to a diverse variety of Lebanese, Iraqi, Egyptian, North African, Palestinian, Turkish, or Greek writers as models and contemporaries remains a nonissue, just as their relationship to the extremely significant but largely unexamined emergence of Sephardi/*mizrahi* modernity in the late 19th century, along with its ongoing practice in the present, remains unimaginable.

Keys to the Garden: New Israeli Writing is the culmination of close to fifteen years of attempts at getting the work of *mizrahi* writers published in the United States. Before the publication, in 1994, of a special issue of the *Literary Review* that I guest edited, and where some of this material first appeared, the results of my efforts amounted to the acceptance of not one novel or substantial prose work and the appearance of only a handful of poems in small magazines. But the proverbial jinn is, clearly, out of the bottle. There is little doubt that some of the most vital contemporary Israeli works have emerged precisely out of the *mizrahi* problematic, with all its attendant concerns about identity, memory, language, and minority/majority relations. In fact, a case could be made showing that many of the major trends of Israeli culture as a whole are the result of the initial and ongoing process amongst *mizrahi* artists in reassessing their past to create a unique new culture. Indeed, the kinds of complexities involved in recreating identity and transmitting different versions of the past and present puts the work of *mizrahi* cultural figures very much within the terms of current debates taking place globally. In this sense, the intersecting nexus of elements that characterize the writers included in this anthology (and others who, due to lack of space, could not be included here), is quite akin to, amongst others, the ongoing, emerging and reinvented Arab, African, Indian, African-American, Latin American, and Caribbean literary traditions. Ironically, the writers included here simply make more sense when put in the context of these global trends than when they are read alongside their own mainstream Israeli contemporaries. When placed against more well-known Israeli writers who are widely translated, the work of these writers seems to come from an entirely different imaginative

2. Robert Alter, *Hebrew & Modernity* (Bloomington: Indiana University Press, 1994), p. 7.

and experiential realm, one that people are quite unfamiliar with. The language, conventions, assumptions, characterizations and references are all significantly different than what people "naturally" assume to be "Israeli." One of the reasons for this is that, as the musician Shlomo Bar has pointed out, the *mizrahim*—being brought up as Israelis—have learned mainstream Israeli culture and then gone back to repossess, rediscover or even deny their own culture. In terms of creative possibility, this would seem to give the *mizrahim* a distinct advantage over those who have chosen to negate or ignore the Middle Eastern elements that, by now, constitute part of every Israeli's cultural formation.

The writers included here identify themselves in various ways: at least, among so many other things, as Jews, Levantines, Arab Jews, *mizrahim,* and Israelis. While many feel comfortable within the company this anthology proposes, some may not. There are both deep connections here, and fragmentation that almost defies logic. While working on the *Literary Review* and then on this collection, it became clear that many of the writers were completely unaware of the work or even the existence of many others I had included. Some even encountered the work of their contemporaries for the first time in translation. In such a highly centralized society as Israel, where access to publishers and reviews, not to mention education itself, is so often contingent upon ideology, party affiliation, or simply who one knows, this astonishing fact can serve as an indication of just how marginalized many of these writers are. It is, in some sense, a crowning irony to the ideology of the ingathering of the exiles that this group of writers—heterogeneous in a way that is quintessentially Israeli—should find their works published, recognized, and commented upon in an even more remote exile, in English, so far (geographically, emotionally, and intellectually), from the sources of their inspiration. But instead of glorifying one fashionable condition or another—whether it be the "post colonial" or the "post modern" — to justify their marginalization, these writers remain acutely aware of the power struggle involved in being dispossesed at home; as Sami Shalom Chetrit writes: "When, for once, will our/translated poems be able/to breathe in Hebrew?

In reading, analyzing, selecting, editing, translating, and teaching these texts over the years, I have come to appreciate their power and uniqueness all the more. Although this work emerges from the entirely new conditions of Israeli society that these writers inhabit, the work does form part of an enormously rich and diverse legacy that both spans and refers to a millennium of life in the Levant. More important, its allegiances point to the future. Because *mizrahi* Jews were not immigrants to Israel by choice but by necessity or lack of choice, their indebtedness to Zionist ideology is only skin-deep. This has allowed them to break many of the taboos about memory and the past that ruled and reigned in Israeli culture and society for so long. Although much of the writing included here might *seem* conventional at first glance (at least in relation to the formal pyrotechnics that have come to characterize an international postmodernism),the fact that the humanity of these writers has been so abbreviated in such a highly contested cultural sphere imbues their work with a deep but subtle innovative quality. One gets the sense that the innovations achieved in these works are not technical but have more to do with incremental and sometimes radical changes and differences in consciousness. So unlike much of what seems, at this point, made-to-order "multicultural" fare, one also gets the sense that there is great personal and social risk at stake in this work. Despite the candor of enormous pain, tremendous loss, deep mourning, and a pervasive sense of irony, the work is also permeated by acute absences yearning for articulation. This yearning is intimately connected to a public possibility that is ever-present in the work, to an unequivocal sense of belonging to the region, to the interior and exterior geography and topography, not the political borders of the Land of Israel but the greater space and culture that land forms an indivisible part of. Thus, the work of these writers has, and continues to have, a tremendous impact on the direction Israeli culture as a whole can take, an impact that cannot be measured by opinion polls but one whose true implications have barely been recognized or acknowledged.

Finally, there is an implicit and sometimes explicit sense in the work of these writers that they have been called upon to take testimony and serve as witnesses during a time of great cataclysm. The poet Yehezkel Kedmi speaks of "the idea of perpetuating something. I had a stake in creating a document, a literary document that would serve as testimony for this generation, of this time and of these events because the work was written on the great historical moment of the redemption of the Jewish people. But right alongside this were the darkest moments possible, that is, daily life in the state and, most importantly—the phenomenon of class segregation." In another interview, Moshe Sartel speaks of being a "poet-historian" who writes today, "but not *for* today." Most eloquently and provacatively, Amira Hess states, "Even if I was sentenced to the hell of distancing myself from the home of my parents and reliving the death of all those who were burned in every ghetto there ever was, I would still come through to tell of it." Here, the full power and deeper implications of the work of these writers becomes apparent. By remaining connected to the sources of their own particular pain and experience, these writers refuse to accept the universality of what has, ideologically, come to be construed as Jewish "fate," applicable to all Jews, in all places, at all times, sooner or later. Most paradoxically, this refusal is expressed through insisting on the fact of exile, both personal and collective, within the promised land, within the space of return itself. While the ideology of the ingathering of the exiles would see the creation of a Jewish homeland as a return *into* history, the chance to be a nation like any other nation, many of these writers—having been the victims of that very ideology—cannot muster such confidence. What they see is precisely the opposite: To embrace the collective would be to accept the mass production of false consciousness, to negate the distinctiveness of local knowledge and particular history, to obliterate the very texture of their own memory. As Mr. Pazuelo, a character in Albert Swissa's *Bound* remarks: "Exile! There is no other path. Exile in the Holy Land itself. At a time of dispersion one must congregate."

As an antidote to this, they have done everything in their power—often against great odds—to use the materials of the personal and collective past and present to create new memories of the future, alternatives to versions of history that reject a multiplicity of identities, that banish different parts of the self and others to separate realms where there can be no intimacy or ambivalence, love or jealousy, respect or common destiny; where the full range of complex emotions, intentions, conscious and subconscious traces inherited through a long life lived together will simply be shelved in the name of some impersonal and polite forms of "cooperation" or, perhaps even worse, just deemed unimaginable. Any relationship to Israeli culture must include a relationship to the Middle East and its diverse cultures that is informed by knowledge and the sympathy of a shared fate. To make enemies by building layers of hatred through false assumptions and dichotomies, misrepresentations and ideology presented as history is to commit the most atrocious acts of self-destruction, for we are all multiple and cannot pretend to be exclusively this or that. My own Hebrew first name and Arabic last name tell me as much. The writing of *mizrahi* Jews offers us intimate passage into worlds we need to know more about, and I am very grateful to have been and continue to be a channel through which access to these journeys can be provided.

—*Ammiel Alcalay*

SHOSHANNAH SHABABO

SHOSHANNAH SHABABO was born in Zikhron Yakov in 1910 to a family that had lived in Safed for many generations. Her father's origins were from Cordoba, while her mother's family was from Iran. Her father had been invited by the Baron Rothschild to teach at the Zikhron Yakov school which, for a period, was under the direction of the writer Yehuda Burla. Shababo studied there before going on to the Levinsky Seminary in Tel Aviv. She spent most of her life in Haifa where she died, relatively unknown, in 1992. Her first novel, *Maria,* was published in 1932; this was followed by *Love in Safed.* In addition, she published many short stories; these have not yet appeared as a collection. Amongst these are a series of remarkable animal fables. Certainly some of the neglect of her work can be accounted for by the harsh judgement of her teacher, Yehuda Burla, who characterized her work as trivial, melodramatic, and sensational. Shababo's prose displays an uncanny use of colloquial language and contemporary usage, not to mention the diverse society of Christians, Muslims, and Jews that she depicts. Her work is also characterized by a keen sense of dramatic detail and psychological insight. As the slow process of rediscovery begins, the primary debt for this renewed appreciation must be paid to Professor Yosef Halevi of Bar Ilan University; singlehandedly, through extensive research, Professor Halevi has provided a context in which a truer reading of Shababo's work and its historical importance can take place. While all of Shababo's work remains out of print, a monograph on her by Professor Halevi, *New Daughter of the East,* including a selection of her short stories and animal fables, has recently been published in Israel.

SIMHA'S WONDROUS SPELL

"Thoughts" knocked at the portal to the heart of Yael, wife of the Scholar; they knocked, they pounded with the fierce, fraught longing to cradle a warm babe, to feel his soft breath, hear his laughter, the laughter of angels. This day, like every day, motherly yearnings coursed through her, fluttering and wondering in her heart spent of hope—for the Scholar was as barren as a tree that would not bear fruit. This day she was visited often by the storms in her soul, tormented as if afflicted, pitching and rolling between despair and the hope brought by the wondrous spells Simha cast for her, for luck.

The "thoughts" that so depressed her—wrapped in a new veil, hidden from the eye—vexed her sevenfold sore this day, making her tremble with every move. These four years "the Scholar's wife, she who feasts on almonds and sugar ," had been consumed with the sorrow of the childless; wherefore then had these "thoughts" come to plague her this of all days?

She determined to distill the "thoughts" to their essence, to know what she would do. She determined to eradicate them—but then despaired. First she clasped them close, then dropped them with a start, like one who has grasped hot coals.

Abashed, Yael wandered between the walls of her house, her eyes averted. She feared the keen eye of the Scholar, lest he read the secrets in her heart, lest he discover the strange musings that flitted through her mind this day, which would bring tragedy upon her and her house. The Scholar was most wise; he need but look at her once, and once again, to know the logic of her heart from beginning to end. He would understand what had this day darkened her heart, what had made her blood boil under the influence of the spells; he would say to her, and rightly: "What is this disgraceful abomination in the heart of the Scholar's wife?" In so saying, he would speak the truth.

Fearing the keen eyes of the Scholar, Yael busied herself cleaning the house in preparation for the holidays, her eyes ever downcast and her face pale. When the Scholar turned his searing eyes on her, as was his wont, they burned her like the rays of the sun. The Scholar loved to gaze upon her always; he derived great pleasure from the gentility of the young woman he had wed at the end of his days, to warm his bones. Proud and haughty was his heart, and he felt himself to be as King David. He loved to watch her as she bent over the wash basin or washed the floor; when she ate, he hungered for her pale, tired fingers. He craved her black hair, her milk-white skin.

And this day she pleased him greatly, seeming more lovely than ever before. Why the timid modesty after four years of marriage, as if she had only now come under the wedding canopy? What was the rosiness that fleetingly crossed her cheeks, flushing them as the cheeks of a maid? He marveled. He read without reading, prayed without praying, murmured without murmuring. His eyes leapt from his books to the woman, from the woman to the letters and back to the woman, as if, comforted by this girl-woman, he had forgotten the heavy sorrow he concealed from her—the heavy sorrow of his barrenness—so warm and lovely was she whom he had wed to warm his heart in old age.

Indeed ". . . her price was far above rubies."

When she brought the coffee on its shiny, gleaming tray, as she did every day, he grasped her soft hand, laughing and blushing and wondering aloud: "What has come over you, Yael, that you are so bashful today?" Startled, she lowered her eyes lest he read what was in her heart. She tried to avoid him. When the young student, "the Skeptic," came to drink coffee with the Scholar as he did every day, she flushed to her earlobes in panic, and fled for her life to the kitchen.

This day the Skeptic startled her more than ever—as if he had not always come to drink coffee and converse with the Scholar; as if she had only now noticed his strong features, his sturdy arms.

The Skeptic sat, as usual, beside the Scholar, alternately sucking in his coffee and sighing sighs of pleasure. He talked of worldly affairs and told of the marvels of government. Yet the voice was not his voice, as if it, too, was changed this day; it made her limbs tremble.

A silliness came over her. To the Scholar's amazement, she began to jabber and prattle and laugh with the Skeptic like a drunken maid. Her eyes were intoxicated, her lips intoxicated, her heart intoxicated with passionate yearnings. She gazed at him, studying his form as if seeing him for the first time. When her imagination presented him to her at night and at dawn, he was handsome, captivating. Yet what was he to her, this youth who had dealings with the "nations," who spoke in their tongue and acted as they? What to her was the part in his hair or the scent of his cologne or his worldly dress, so different from that of the other townsfolk? No, he had never pleased her. Who could please her after the Scholar? What about him could please her? Was he her brother? Her cousin or kin? Her savior?

Shame covered her face. The wife of the Scholar—the most honored of men—and the local Skeptic, who spurned belief and had ties with the nations?

Yet again the same strange thought rose in her heart. This time when it rose it was more familiar, less foreign, more reassuring. She would do it for *him,* for the Scholar. In *his* name, lest it be forgotten . . . may the Lord bless her intentions. Would Yael dare commit a deed that would cause the Scholar, the dust of whose shoes was eagerly sought by the townsfolk, to grow pale? No one would ever know . . . within a year she would be cradling a son in her arms, feeling his soft breath and hearing his laughter, the laughter of angels. The other women would no longer dare to sigh loudly or prick her heart as she passed them in the women's gallery at synagogue.

Yael smiled in anticipation of the joy to come and gazed into the eyes of the Skeptic—large eyes, their lashes black, their gaze deep—so unlike the eyes of the Scholar. The Scholar revered the soul, and the Skeptic the body.

Her heart's musings made her wild and her dreams made her ill; she was as a deceptive maid, baring her neck, donning her prettiest dress, adorning herself with jewelry, laughing aloud: all for him, for the Skeptic. Were he to arrive suddenly—not at the time for coffee—she would redden and pale by turns, like a demure bride before her groom.

The next day, Simha came to finish her "work," fervid women's magic spells to appease the womb: Three times must the barren one pass by three slaughtered sheep, and three times return; strange and various beads; fish bones; the blood of a dove; the hair of a nanny-goat. A bevy of wonders. Signs drawn on the naked belly. Charms tested and tried: More than once had Simha succeeded, more than once had a child been born.

Simha seated the naked Yael in the wash basin, pouring magic waters over her head and whispering the names of phantoms and witches, spirits and sons of spirits and strange shadows never before heard of. With oaths and without oaths, with vows and without vows, beseeching and not beseeching she commanded the angels of evil and destruction to thrice recite the names of the holy patriarchs, Abraham, Isaac, and Jacob, over Satan's head, to bind him with magic cords and break his neck so that he not harm the woman's womb. Run and race, servants of the womb; hurl yourselves down in supplication before the matriarchs until a seed be sown in the womb of this young woman, Yael daughter of Sarah—a good daughter, granddaughter of our matriarch Eve, wife of the Scholar.

Hearing the names great and awesome, Yael's hair stood on end as Simha with a whisper cast out all of the evil spirits.

Between one spell and the next, Simha told Yael of the Scholar's first wives.

Boussa-Rivka of Izmir endured trials and tribulations before, at long last, being blessed with the "luck" of the Scholar. Pretty as the pristine moon . . . the women of the town came to see her, all of them, as one, coveting her strange modern dress. Mazal-Tov the orphan was the second wife. Stubborn and bitter, she did not love the Scholar from the day of their marriage. But Simha had doubts: "Truth is buried with the dust." How could the Scholar, most respected of men, not be beloved? Rachel of Muscovy, the third wife, blue-eyed and rosy-cheeked, worked the magic spells of her countrywomen. Some say she conceived by the Scholar, but the child died and she with him, for a curse had been placed on her womb since her youth—of dubious virtue. With her own eyes Simha had seen the child—born yet unborn, a strange creature touched by the hands of evil spirits.

Yael heard: The Scholar's 'luck' is hard, but Simha herself would come and with her spells invoke the angels for the purpose of the great reward. Alas, all three wives died. Because of her beauty, Boussa-Rivka was stricken by the evil eye cast by the envious women of the town. Mazal-Tov died during the famine, during the war. And Rachel's child killed her. All three went to the world of truth, to placate the willful curse that tainted the seed of the Scholar. Now Yael had come along, the fourth wife, to win the great reward.

These stormy whisperings and enchantments raised a tempest in the young woman's heart, inflaming her desire. When the work of the wondrous spells had been completed, when the spirits were ready for their task, the heinous thought ripened in her mind, making her drunk.

★ ★ ★ ★ ★

Returning from the ritual bath, Yael somehow lost her way, finding herself at the young student's doorstep. She stood there for a moment, listening to the pounding of her heart, to her doubts and regrets, as if hesitating.

A dull apprehension overcame her, an awesome fear of the Scholar and of the Skeptic, of the townsfolk and of all of the town's houses and streets and gossip. Thousands of eyes stalked her from every corner, staring at her from the dark, narrow alleys, from the cracks in the buildings, from the breeches in the fences. The eyes saw her, the wife of the honorable Scholar, as she stood, quivering, outside the home of the Skeptic, renouncer of belief and wisdom.

The wind blew open the door, which was never properly closed; the Skeptic stood opposite, bewildered and ashamed. The courage of the wondrous spells took hold of her, and she entered. She looked about, bidding herself seem tranquil.

"I was passing by your house and thought to see if you had the Scholar's prayer books in your possession" —she found an excuse for her arrival and tried to appear as if she were looking for something— "I know he lends them to you, and the holidays are at the doorstep."

"What a great honor this will be taken to be, the revered Scholar's wife coming to my home" —the Skeptic stammered, unsure what to do, he was so excited and happy. While he searched hither and thither, arranging the prayer books on the table, Yael sat on the bench, pale and trembling, her eyes glowing with a strange radiance. The Skeptic turned as if looking for something lost, seeking cause to converse with her. With a female passion she came to his aid, employing her coquetry, her wan movements, her laughter and the smile that danced in her lovely eyes. Soon he forgot that it was the Scholar's wife before him. The barrier between them melted. He asked about her past and about her life, thirstily drinking in her soft, warm words, hungrily devouring her intoxicating eyes, her passionate glances, which burned into him with both modesty and exhortation. A moment later, it all suddenly became clear to him. A frenzy overcame him, and he trembled with awe and rapture. He loosened his collar, like one who is stifling.

The home of the Skeptic was far, at the edge of town. The way seemed long to every traveler, but brief to Yael. Radiant, fresh as the good earth whose seeds have been quenched by rain, Yael hurried home. It was the eve of the Sabbath, and she had to send the *hamin* to be baked. The Scholar saw that her cheeks were flushed and her eyes glistened, and he laughed with pleasure. He came close to her and pinched her cheek, as was his wont: "Let me pinch a red-cheeked damask-apple."

The Scholar went off to greet the Sabbath and Yael stood to bless the oil lamp, her soul singing within her, singing and humming like a flock of cooing doves, her heart like the glimmering wick that flickered and danced before her. The new life for which she had waited and hoped night after night, day after day for four long years now coursed in her blood.

Yael was intoxicated, and in her intoxication acted wantonly. One moment she sang and the next she cried, hugging everything that came to hand, or clinging to the Scholar like a little girl. Once she even forgot herself and hugged the Scholar in front of the Skeptic, embarrassing them. The Scholar's amazement grew from day to day: "What has become of my wife?"

Yael wept a spoilt-child's tears. She was full of mischief. She wept and laughed and prattled to the warm babe, to his tiny hands and his rosy lips . . . he would clasp her neck and doze on her breast; every night his breath would brush her face . . . His eyes would be like hers and his hair like hers; he would have the Scholar's wisdom, and he would be great in all Israel.

She jabbered on in her intoxication as if talking to herself. Her face was like a red rose, but the face of the Scholar grew ever paler, as if the blood had been drained from it. He tried to deny what his ears heard, but again her voice rang with the laughter of angels . . . and he swooned.

For many days the Scholar lay ill. In the meantime, three mysteries took place, making the town simmer.

★ ★ ★ ★ ★

The first mystery was the sudden disappearance of the Skeptic. One said he had gone to Jerusalem on matters of government, and another that he had gone to Tiberias on matters of real estate, while still others believed he had retired to his own company. He was sorely missed, for the townsfolk relied on his help to petition the government in the languages of France and Arabia, or to draw up requests and documents in his fine calligraphy. He was also a wise scholar and great reader, even though he renounced the beliefs of the others because of the "European spirit" that had seized him. The Scholar loved him for his razor-sharp wit when arguing about the miracles, which he explained away as natural phenomena, and for representing him before the authorities; the Scholar paid no heed to the slander of others.

Yair the scholar sought him out to ask that he petition the government for him in his lovely calligraphy—but he found no one. He asked after him—but none knew his whereabouts.

The second mystery was joyous: Yael had conceived a child by her husband, the Scholar—though most of the women of the town doubted it. The Scholar was old and barren as a tree that would give shade but bear no fruit. All benefited from the shade of his wisdom, but none hoped to reap its fruits. Yet there it was! The women knew that Simha and her wondrous spells had had a hand in the matter. Simha herself wandered among the houses to tell the women of the news, in all its detail. The joy in the town was great. One guessed Yael would bear a girl as pretty as her mother, while another swore she would bear a boy, as wise as his father.

But the greatest of the mysteries struck the townsfolk like thunder.

They argued and debated among themselves, some siding with the Scholar, renowned among the multitudes, and some siding with his righteous wife, most modest of women. Every mouth spoke and every brain labored to solve the mystery. But the Scholar had made up his mind and would not be moved: He would divorce his wife, without returning her marriage contract.

Things were wondrous strange. Wherefore was the Scholar divorcing his beloved wife? Now, after four years of marriage, when at last she had conceived by him, by good luck? Would he cast her out without a marriage contract—like a harlot? It must be that she had committed a sin, done a deed that must not be done. Could it be otherwise, if her pregnancy brought the Scholar grief? Unless it was the Skeptic—he who drank coffee with the Scholar every day—who had sinned and led the Scholar's wife astray. Perhaps he had thought it over and fled for his life "one night, when the light of the moon did not shine," dragging the whole town down in disgrace.

And so the emissaries of the court came, and with them the scholar Shlomo Ganon—a young student who was to take the Scholar's place—bringing the bill of divorcement, according to the law of Moses and Israel.

★ ★ ★ ★ ★

Yael's spirit was broken.

Four years had passed since her wedding day, four years of tribulation and pain that had gnawed at her heart; at last she had made peace with her fate, with the "black luck" decreed the day she was born. Then the wondrous spell had come, stirring her spirit and riling her blood, making her dizzy until she was as if intoxicated. Indeed, it could not be that she had strayed to the home of the Skeptic! Who had brought her there? Whose were the legs that had led her to his doorstep? Who could have pleased her, after the Scholar? Who was the Skeptic to her; what was the Skeptic to her? She would swear that she had neither seen nor known him outside the walls of her home, where he had sat with the Scholar discussing the affairs of the world and the marvels of government. Was he not like a brother to her? A cousin, or kin? A savior?

She would make amends with the Scholar, and the Scholar with her. She would tell him of the long nights when she had lain in her bed and gazed at the stars in the sky, the "tear on her cheek." She would tell him of the women's sighs, which had cut her to the quick, like a dagger. She would tell of the envy that had blazed in her heart like Rebbe Shimon's bonfire. She would tell him of the mosquito that had pricked her wounded heart, of the *dybbuk,* the deceptive *dybbuk* of that woman—Simha's—wondrous spells, which had entered her . . . and the Scholar would understand. He would not accuse her. Mercifully, he would take her back as if bringing home a strayed lamb. He would forgive her. After all, it was he who had filled her with false hope when he told her of his wife Rachel, who had conceived by him—hope that had brightened her soul when she pleaded with him not to keep the fruit of her womb from her. Had it only been to quiet her and brush away her tears that he had said what he had said, sworn what he had sworn? It was in him she had trusted when she'd sought the deception of the spells, to win the "great reward," to gladden his heart, to establish his name and an heir.

Yael recalled her marriage to the Scholar. She a young girl and an orphan, he forty-eight years her senior. In her poverty she had married him, for she would rest from the toil of her life, from its spareness.

Yael did not complain. Her life with him had been comfortable and tranquil. The Scholar had pampered and spoiled her, and all the women had respected her. She had had a seat at the front of the women's gallery in synagogue, and her home had been open for all and to all, like the home of a lady.

Now all rose against her. The Scholar . . . the townsfolk . . . where could she take her shame, where could she flee from its countenance?

★ ★ ★ ★ ★

In sorrow she did the deed, her death her atonement.

On the morning of the divorce, the women harkened to her desperate, keening cries. They saw her burning like a giant torch, leaping about like a madwoman, beating her flesh to put the fire out, the wind fanning the flames.

The women at last extinguished the flames, and she collapsed. The child fluttered within his dead mother's womb, fluttering and dying, and the women pounded its head, beating and beating the seed of sin, to destroy it.

— Translated from the Hebrew by Marsha Weinstein

from MARIA

In the Convent, 1923

That year, she entered the convent.

In her piety and austerity, she was an example for the other nuns. All day she murmured prayers, kneeling before the holy icons of Jesus and the Virgin Mary.

- Holy Mother—she whispered in awe—take me unto thee, strengthen my spirit, in these times.

On entering the convent she denied her body with fasts, chastised her spirit with castigation and remorse, in an effort to cleanse her spirit of the sins of her past, to be worthy of the Holy name, Maria.

No one could explain her turning to the nunnery.

Not even her family could divine the true and real reason for Maria's withdrawal from life. They were chastened before those who offered solutions to the riddle.

Her father was greatly wounded by his daughter's dangerous step, which she had taken of her own volition. In public, he was forced to seem pleased. He thought much, took counsel with his friend Habib, but could conclude nothing.

Only one soul—one wretched soul—the aged Najma—knew the whole truth.

The day her charge Maria had left home, she, too, had left the Jedda family. From that day on, none knew what had become of her. Rumors abounded as to Najma's fate—in the main, that she had lost her mind the day Maria entered the convent. For proof they took her ridiculous stories of a son, light of her life, born to her in old age.

Such tall tales captured the imaginations of the curious for some months. But in the end, all stilled their tongues.

For what was poor Najma, a pitiable nurse, in the rush and flutter of life?

There were those who said that her neighbors had heard a baby's cry coming from her house. But this, too, was mere speculation.

★ ★ ★ ★ ★

All knew to tell of the day she went to the convent.

It happened on the fifth of the month of May, 1923. That morning, Maria appeared at the French convent, dressed in black.

The sisters wondered at the appearance of one so lively of spirit within the convent's dead walls. What could she want here? So lovely, she could not have come to take the vow. . .

Instantly they surrounded her, admiring her stature with awe and reverence as if she were a creature of a higher order who in error had strayed down to earth. They whispered among themselves intently.

- Where is the Mother Superior, Sister Elizabeth?—asked Maria, her voice quavering.

- At once!—some answered in chorus.

A moment later she stood face to face with Mother Elizabeth.

Just then the holy sister had been at prayer. Her pursed lips had slowly formed the words, her small eyes darting over the pages of the open book. When she had heard the steps, she had risen from her chair. Coldly she invited the visitor to come, her glance indicating the empty chair. Hands gnarled with bluish veins removed her glasses. She examined Maria from heel to crown. After looking her over several times, she said drily:

- Reveal your face, child!

Maria removed her black scarf.

Mother Elizabeth opened her eyes wide in astonishment.

- Stately, stunning—she thought to herself spitefully.

For several moments, they stared at one another. Maria saw before her a withered, dried face, a sharp mouth shut tight, and tiny, cold blue eyes. Startled by the flower of youth standing before her, Mother Elizabeth was humbled.

- What could you want with a convent—she asked with expressionless laughter—your beauty does not suit our walls. Here, your place will be lost to you. Go, daughter, go back to the living.

Maria froze on the spot.

- Look, young lady. Here—the nun pointed to the garden—you see this garden. Look how lovely the flowers are. Inhale the heady scent. Bask in the sun's glory. Lift your eyes to the Carmel, so lofty and proud. All this, child, is forbidden to us.

Despite her pride, the nun could feel herself being taken in by the girl's divine beauty.

Maria did not move. Calmly she heard the nun's efforts to tempt her away from her desire. Quietly she averted her eyes, and waited for the nun to finish.

Just then a pair of swallows alighted on the grill of the window. They bobbed and circled one another in joyful song. . .

- Freedom, liberty, love—Mother Elizabeth smiled derisively.

- Holy Mother!—Maria cried aloud—I have made my decision. I will be a nun, come what may!

Her magnificent face paled. . .

Her words bore witness that great torment had led her to decide what she now sought. Her sculptured face blanched, all tranquility leaving it. A sharp furrow appeared on her smooth brow. The expression of sorrow on her face was so natural that the Holy Mother took pity on this proud one who chose humility.

- Very well, young lady—she said—I will not keep you from taking this step! But I will give you three days' reprieve. Think it over, seek the counsel of others. . . on Sunday, bring me your answer. I hope, young lady—she added, arching her brows—that you will not regret my having granted you this extension. Good-bye till Sunday then!

Maria hurried out.

The Ceremony

On the first of February 1923, a Sunday, the induction of a novitiate took place at the French convent.

Maria, near fainting, mumbled inaudibly.

- There is no other way; thus I shall be purified. This is from God.

The morning was bright; the rising sun pushed away the darkness. The church bells began to chime.

- I must go early—she cheered herself—she has promised to accept me. Can I really hope that she will grant my request?—she thought as she stood at the Exalted Mother's doorway—my request is one of those who abstain. But I must try.

With a shaky hand she knocked on Mother Elizabeth's door. Pale and trembling, she waited impatiently for the nun's call.

The nun with the pursed lips and cold eyes stood in the doorway. With a slight nod of her head, she hinted to Maria to come inside. Then she shut the door.

- Exalted Mother—Maria began—hear my petition.

- Speak, child!

- Will you grant me the permission—she said softly, regretting that she had begun thus—No . . . Yes . . . as you know—as she spoke, her wrath was kindled against herself—today the ceremony will take place.

- Yes—Mother Elizabeth interrupted.

- Well, then—she bowed her head in anguish—I would ask Your Grace . . . Mother . . . Exalted . . . her voice quavered.

- What is it then?—the nun was startled—Do you relent?

- No, not so—she said, shaking her head impatiently—I have decided. But I have another request. Just once a month. Once only . . . if I could have permission to leave the convent. Please, holy virgin, have mercy . . . I know this is difficult, but . . . on my soul . . . he . . .

Mother Elizabeth's face went white. Maria was overwhelmed.

- Don't turn me away unanswered—she pleaded—please know that your mercy will never, ever be forgotten.

Their faces filled with both anger and grief.

Mother Elizabeth was surprised by the young woman's astonishing entreaty. At the same time, her pity was aroused to see such a proud woman cloaked in humility. She understood that this stranger harbored a deep secret. In her heart, she was glad to fill the maid's request. Maria piqued her curiosity.

She promised her liberty for three hours a month, beginning the following week.

- Miss Jedda, permission is granted!—she stated, the coldness never leaving her eyes.

Maria grabbed the nun's hands and clasped them to her heart.

- Oh, many thanks, Exalted Mother . . . a thousand thanks, Holy Sister. At peace, heartened, she returned to her room.

- I have no need of life—she laughed—if only I can see my child! I will find joy with him, even if only once a month. I will know how to use the three poor hours which have been granted me. I have succeeded. I have been victorious. I was only overcome, because it hurt so . . .

A tear of joy and longing froze in her eye.

* * * * *

A clear day dawned on the city.

The giant sun softly caressed the grape vines twined in the convent garden. The bells rang out with glee. Flowers spread their petals, their scent wafting heavenward. Only in the convent was the light shut out. Outside the larks sang, but in the convent—dark prayer. It seemed that two separate worlds had awakened to their weighty tasks. The world—to the jubilation of life, and the convent—to its anguish. Now and then a few strands of light stole into the nun's cells, as if to mock their mourning. Sometimes white doves would rest on the windowsills, cheerfully flapping their wings, as if against the maids' torment. All these were messengers of the outside world. But inside, nothing could be seen of this world. Only the mournful sound of a sad song echoed within the dark walls.

At the seventh hour the nuns donned their black robes and picked up long candles wrapped in black paper. The ceremony would take place in the great hall.

Father Gregor prepared himself for his holy task. Two priests cloaked in priestly garb attended him. Before them stood a statue of the Christ child swathed in his Mother's arms.

- They are coming—one priest whispered to Father Gregor.

Father Gregor straightened a bit. With his writing hand he smoothed his beard, and passed over his white silk cassock. He grabbed his great gold cross and pressed it to his heart. Father Gregor was filled with emotion. This was the first nun he himself would bring under the Church's wing. He knew the order of the ceremony well.

- She is a Jedda!—the priest whispered.

Father Gregor paled. For years, this name had aroused his veneration. Now it stunned him.

- A Jedda—he whispered with quivering lips—a relative of Eveline Jedda, perhaps her sister . . . perhaps Eveline herself. Ah, but no—he laughed, relieved—she is dead.

A chill went down his spine.

A soft rustling came from the next room.

Father Gregor made an effort to be still. He watched his two assistants with small, deep eyes. With an unsteady hand he took the basin of holy water, swung it lightly, and put it back in place.

- They are coming—he whispered to his assistants—let us pray!

A procession of women entered the hall.

At its head strode Maria Jedda, dressed in a white wedding gown. She walked barefoot. Her small toes showed under the folds of her long gown. Her long black hair hung loose, covered with a white veil. Beside her walked Mother Elizabeth, her face solemn. The nuns walked behind them in silence.

An awesome stillness filled the hall. Only the whispering of the priests rasped. It seemed as though this were a wake for the dead.

Maria looked like a white lily, her large eyes sunk in their sockets, their dark lashes lowered. She stepped silently in time to the piano. For a moment, she recalled the wedding of her friend Rachel Rojas, the Jewess. She, too, had been dressed thus . . . a wedding gown, a white veil, bows, strings, lace . . . Though she had worn shoes on her feet. How jubilant Rachel had been . . . And she, so sad . . . Bitterness clouded her heart.

Suddenly her eyes lit on the black candles. She was surprised. Why should these be carried on her wedding day?

She turned her eyes to the latticed windows. The sun shone there, the birds sang, the city hummed. Life went on beyond them as usual. As if the day of her terrible wedding would not change a thing . . . again her thoughts turned to her friend's wedding. There had been gay laughter, cries of joy, the music of dancing. There young men and women had danced, even she had danced at the wedding of her friend.

Suddenly she felt all alone, lost within the horrid hallways of the cloister. Her parents, her brother, her relatives—none were present at her happy event. Everyone stared at her with the eyes of vipers. She would have screamed, but her voice hid in her throat.

Slowly, slowly the thin voices of the sisters joined that of the piano, as if wailing a lament.

This was the marriage of Maria Jedda, only daughter, without parents, without family, without friends . . . this was the wedding of the vain Jedda girl, her father's pride, his hope.

This was what Fate had decreed for the beautiful Jedda girl, the glory, the crown of her family.

★ ★ ★ ★ ★

The procession stopped in the center of the hall.

Maria walked forward alone and stood before Father Gregor. Silently she prostrated herself on the cold floor, her face resting on his feet. Then she arose. Willfully she lifted the veil from her face and lay bare her curls.

Father Gregor took a step back.

With shaking hands he held the cross out for her to swear her oath. She clasped it, vowing to withdraw from life, to abstain from all the pleasures of the world.

The nuns murmured in prayer. Mother Elizabeth made the sign of the cross several times; the piano droned thickly, heavily, sadly, as if sighing at the magnitude of the sacrifice.

- I swear, and will keep silent forever—Maria whispered to herself. She swore she was a virgin, though she was a mother.

When she saw that the priest was overcome with emotion, she urged him: "I am ready, Father!"

Father Gregor was calmed. She was someone else . . . a Jedda, but not the beloved, the dead Eveline.

With a wave of his hand he motioned to his assistant, who handed him a pair of scissors.

- Quickly, quickly!—cried Maria aloud, frightened by the gleam of the scissors as they neared her locks.

- I am cutting—he assured her, catching hold of a thick strand of hair.

A hushed prayer was sent aloft; the priests crossed themselves. The nuns wailed. Father Gregor intoned his prayer.

Curl after curl was cut and fell earthward.

The nuns looked with pity on the long hair ruined, fallen.

Maria sighed—my hair, my curls, my beauty . . . All is lost . . . Jesus, Mary, pardon me! God Almighty, give me strength. I am lost. . . I am mad . . . people, hasten. My hair . . . my hair falls. Merciful hearts, save me.

As her hair was shorn she felt boundless pain. Tears of rage froze on her lashes like diamonds. Her face paled and reddened by turns. Her chest rose and fell quickly.

How she had loved her hair. For years she had grown it! For years she had combed it! For years she had delighted in it, gloried in it! Now it was being ruined, mercilessly.

- Finish your deed, Father!—she cried.

- I am finishing—he answered, full of compassion.

- Enough. Enough. Enough!—she shrieked, shaking her head—You are hurting me, enough.

- Just one lock more.

- All is destroyed—she moaned in lament—nothing is left, even the last lock has been shorn.

- Finished!—Father Gregor pronounced, handing the scissors to the priest beside him. Slowly, slowly he brushed his hands of the shorn hair, lightly brushed his wide silk sleeves, ridding himself of the remnants with disgust—as if brushing away repulsive insects.

Maria began to laugh. Her laugh was terrible, awful, penetrating, vengeful. Her face took on an expression of horror, her nostrils flared like those of a beast panting for the fight. Her lips drew back, baring the rows of her teeth, and her eyes flashed.

Father Gregor was alarmed.

- Thank you so much, my Father!—she added with a bitter smile.

She turned toward the startled nuns, and strode at their head toward her room.

★ ★ ★ ★ ★

It had been the custom that, after taking her vows, a novitiate be placed in a coffin prepared especially according to her measurements. While the custom had been banned in most convents, the French convent carried it on, according to tradition, until that very year. Thus it was that they placed Maria in a coffin, and closed the door to her room.

- Naked and bare . . . naked and bare—murmured the poor wretch during the 24 hours she spent in the coffin. Naked and bare . . . though I have seen it with my own eyes, I do not believe . . . how will I ever adjust to the cruel idea that I must remain bareheaded? Naked and bare . . . naked and bare—she continued to moan—I don't want to believe it. Chills shake my poor scalp . . . I am empty, weightless . . . the warmth and comfort I felt when my locks covered me, my head, my ears . . . where is their soft caress on my bare shoulders?

She opened her eyes, and a shriek of despair escaped her lips:

- O, what darkness, what blackness . . . I would do better to lie with my eyes closed. . . This is the Shadow of Death. The darkness frightens me. Have I gone mad with misgivings? O, nuns, sisters, people—hurry, take me from my prison! The darkness kills me . . .

She tried to move, to raise her right hand, but she could not. The coffin was narrow and close, and she could not budge. There was only one small, round opening, in the coffin lid, through which she could breathe.

- What is this?—she jumped, the terror of madness gripping her—Am I dead, that I cannot move? What has happened to me? I wanted to touch my hair, but I cannot. Has the end come? I must feel my pulse . . .

Again she tried to move her arm, but could not.

- Father! Mother! Jacques!—she cried with all her might as cold sweat covered her body—Save me, I am dead . . .

Her voice was smothered by the coffin. Only a dull echo reached her ears. For a moment she was silent, listening . . . perhaps she would hear an answer to her call . . . she thought she heard someone on the stairs—but the steps grew distant and vanished.

- It must be that you wish me dead—she spat angrily—or mad. But I will not give you the satisfaction! I will not be mad . . . But if I die, it may be better for me, and for you . . .

The first hours seemed to her as days. In the end, she did not believe she would get out of her prison.

With the coming of evening, her mind clouded over, and she again began to plumb the depths of her soul:

- What have you done, Miss Jedda? Have you gone mad? You've sacrificed your life, your happiness—for what? Is this the way for a proud Jedda to act? You've fallen, given in, abstained from life, from happiness, from love. Is it really so evil, love? Have you not been filled with joy in the arms of the young man who is your husband, father of your child? Did you feel disgust when you gave your breast to your child? Have you really given all these up of your own free will? No! No! But for them, the proud Jeddas, your own family . . . It was them you feared . . . you did not fear yourself . . . What have you to do with them? Let them be shamed, make what excuses they may—as long as you find rest and peace with your beloved and the glorious fruit of your womb . . . But what have you done? You have destroyed everything in one hour. . . Oh, Maria, I pity you. . .

Repentance and regret hounded her to death.

She sighed and whimpered—great God Almighty, pardon me. Mary, Jesus, take pity on me. Answer me, with your Grace! Pardon me, Savior! Or grind me to dust, crush me under the weight of my sin. See how poor I am, Holy Virgin. Absolve me in Your mercy, save me from suffering. Send me Death, the Redeemer, O Sweet, Holy Mother.

As she sighed she felt the bitterness dissipate, leaving her.

Then, as if to comfort her, she heard in her heart: The world of the Spirit still exists—a world of goodness and justice, of righteousness and truth . . .

- Here I will go—she whispered, drained and weak—I am going to the world of the Spirit, the world of goodness and justice, righteousness and truth . . .

The next morning they found her in a swoon, the shadow of a heavenly smile on her thin lips . . .

—*Translated from the Hebrew by Marsha Weinstein*

JACQUELINE SHOHET KAHANOFF

JACQUELINE SHOHET KAHANOFF was born in Cairo in 1917; her father's family originated from Iraq, while her mother's family was from Tunis. She left Egypt for America in 1940–41; there she studied, worked, and began writing in English. In 1946, she won the *Atlantic Monthly* award for best short story as well as the Houghton Mifflin Fellowship for *Jacob's Ladder,* a novel depicting life in Egypt between the two world wars and appearing in 1951 under her maiden name, Jacqueline Shohet. Soon after, she returned to Egypt before going on to Paris where she spent some time prior to settling in Israel. Her language being English, she remained somewhat on the margins of the Israeli cultural scene despite her reputation as an important and challenging essayist. Through a circle of friends, among whom was Nissim Rejwan, she was introduced to Aharon Amir, the prolific translator, novelist and editor of the journal *Keshet.* There her essays began to appear regularly before being collected in a book, *From the East the Sun,* that appeared in 1978, a year before her death. Ironically, although most of her essays appeared in Hebrew, they have never been published together in the original English. By the late 1950s, Kahanoff had already formed her personal and then almost unique vision of Israel as an integral part of the Mediterranean or Levantine world, a vision that was very much an intimate part of her life. From growing up in the privileged class in colonial Egypt to sweeping floors in America to support herself; from having the revolutionary and future president of Algeria, Ahmed Ben Bella, sheltered as a house guest by her parents to her increasing isolation in Beersheba and Yad Eliyahu, the range of Kahanoff's experience presented an almost unfathomable paradigm to the assumptions reigning within Israeli society of the time. As one member of her circle put it: "When Jacqueline wrote about Levantinism, she wrote about us. Jacqueline was a cultural option." Poetic and analytical, Kahanoff's work reflects the conflicts of a generation undergoing drastic change. The selections below are from her novel, *Jacob's Ladder,* her collected essays, and from a piece about

her father's death, "To Die a Modern Death," often used as a text on bereavement in Israeli nursing schools.

from JACOB'S LADDER

"Rachel! It's time to go home!" Miss O'Brien called from the end of the enclosure in the Ezbekieh Gardens reserved for English nurses and their children.

"Yes, Nanny, I'm coming!" Rachel answered, and scampered off with the other children who obediently abandoned seesaws, swings, and sandboxes to join the nurses, busy folding their stools, collecting their knitting and thermos flasks. Before she had had an English nanny, Rachel reflected, she used to play in the part of the gardens where all the people went who weren't English. There Anna would chase after her, and she would slip away when she was caught, until they were both laughing and out of breath, but now it was "Yes, Nanny," all the time. In the morning, she did not run after her mother while she gave orders about the house, nor did she stay chatting in the kitchen while the cook spread out his marketing, and pedlars came with baskets full of oranges, but every morning at nine, she came to this same place. She didn't go to see Nonino and the girls in his store, or to Uncle Joseph's house on Saturday afternoons, or eat things good enough to give her indigestion. She didn't speak Arabic, Italian, or even French any more, but only English, even with Papa and Mamma. She never did things that made her feel happy, only sometimes on Nanny's day off, when she was left with her mother, she became again Caline, who spoke French. The other days were sad and ugly, like the old sewing basket in Nonina's house, but today was Wednesday and perhaps Mamma would take her to the shop belonging to the Indian gentleman with a turban like a big onion on his head. He would let her choose the pyramids of incense she liked best, and they would light them up in the enameled burner. Meanwhile Mamma examined vases, ivory statues, and cashmere shawls, saying, "Wouldn't these look wonderful at home, darling?" Rachel also looked at gauze scarves like rainbows. So shiny and light were they, she could never be sure she had touched them. Then she liked to pass her finger over Buddha's astonishing round bronze tummy. But on Thursday, it was as if there had been no Wednesday, and she wondered if Mamma still loved her, because she, too, wasn't the same any more.

"Here I am, Nanny," Rachel said dispiritedly, noticing that even if the day were hot and dusty, making Nanny's face very red, her uniform, the grey dress with the starched white cuffs, collars, apron, and veil were spotless, and so stiff they could stand up by themselves.

"My, you do look a sorrowing little imp. What ails you, child?"

Miss O'Brien, kind, worried, smiled at the child. She had been with Rachel five months. A bright little girl, she thought, so quick in learning English, eager to please, gentle—too gentle, that was the trouble. The more fluent their conversations, the less she understood the child. Training was all very well, a pup must be housebroken, but not lose its bounce and kick. The child's face was wistful, and her green eyes, fixed on her with too deep a melancholy, seemed to conceal some mysterious life flickering behind their quietness. Miss O'Brien's gaze followed Rachel's and fastened on a nurse who scolded and cuffed a little boy, "Time and again, morning, noon, and night, I've told you not to scratch like a monkey."

"It itches," the child whimpered.

"Don't be rude. Don't argue," the nurse said sternly. Miss O'Brien blushed, catching the flash of rebellion in Rachel's eyes. The younger children suffered from prickly heat rash, and it was unfair to blame them for it. The nurses should sponge them, keep their tender skins dry and cool with a soothing powder rather than scrub their poor little hides as if they were the brass buttons on a soldier's uniform. She was never harsh with her child, and yet Rachel sometimes gave her the same quick, hot glance. Something must be amiss, and she must put it right, skilfully as the little girl was hiding it. To see a child's misery and think she might be the cause of it was something she would not endure.

"Come, let's wash your hands," Miss O'Brien said, her arms around the little girl's shoulder, guiding her to the clubhouse.

Rachel's nostrils puckered with distaste at the pervasive smell of carbolic soap and disinfectant in this little house where all the armchairs were covered in blue, like at the YWCA, with three daisies sticking out of a little brass vase on every table, and Mrs. Sawyer, fussing above them, always talking of flies and microbes. Rachel did not like her, but greeted her politely, thinking, as she washed her hands with the harsh, smelly orange soap, that it was a wonder the woman's pale hair and eyes did not run off her face like water from the tap. Mrs. Sawyer, even more flustered than usual, was telling Nanny all about the *khamsin* that was coming, the air was so still and heavy; she had lived in Egypt long enough to know, good gracious, and in this heat, one must be so particular about the things one ate, and never, never touch native food, and always be after the servants, a filthy, unreliable lot. Rachel was sure all Mrs. Sawyer said wasn't true, and she sighed to think of the tea they had in her clubhouse. Even the little pink cakes were made with butter that came from a country called Australia, at the other end of the world, and it was so salty it tasted like carbolic soap. Rachel smiled, imagining the faces the Smadjas would pull if they had to eat them. Nonino would spit Mrs. Sawyer's cake right out, and if he did it with all the nannies around, it would be so funny! She burst out laughing, and Miss

O'Brien looked at her, surprised. The child's gaiety was as disconcerting as her moody, silent spells.

Once her hands were dried, Miss O'Brien brought the blue muslin veil gathered around Rachel's white panama hat down over her face, and tied it at the back of her neck, telling her, "Now, don't let it get in your mouth, all wet and dirty. Breathe through your nose."

Rachel did not argue, knowing it was useless to say she hated breathing through the veil, there was not enough air. She liked to see things in their real colors, and would rather breathe real smells, flowers, orangepeel, even the bad smell of animal droppings, and she liked to feel the dust prick her eyes rather than have this awful veil, but the nurses liked fresh air only when it was English.

"Goodbye, Mrs. Sawyer," Rachel said sweetly, and marched off with Nanny firmly holding her hand, clumping along like an English soldier, one, two, one, two, not looking right or left, only in front of her, and never stopping, as the other nurses had told her one must do in Egypt. Rachel dragged her feet and cast longing glances at the people sprawled in the real Ezbekieh Gardens that were for everybody, where pedlars went about with circles of crusty *semeets* standing on poles around their baskets, which mothers bought for their children, who then ate them with good, strong *Kashkaval* cheese. The Arab women laughed with their pretty, painted eyes, nursed their babies, and all the colored glass bracelets on their arms made lovely music. She would have liked to roam about, to talk to people, and when she and Miss O'Brien emerged into the street, Rachel inhaled through her veil deeply, to catch a whiff from the branches of apricot blossoms a peddler offered. All these things were like punishments, worse than being spanked or standing in a corner, but she obeyed, to please Mamma and to be the kind of little girl she wanted, so that her Mother should never think of getting another baby. But why did Nonina and Aunt Renée keep asking what she liked better, a brother or a sister? She didn't want either, and since she had kept her promise and been good with Nanny, Mamma must keep her promise too.

She forgot her woes once they had crossed the street and she caught sight of a band of beggars hardly older than herself, their bodies showing through torn rags, besieging passersby, fighting among themselves in their hunt for cigarette butts, scattering quickly when a *shawish* descended upon them with his stick, except for one who never ran away before he bit and kicked the *shawish,* who boxed his ears and beat his head. This one never begged from Nanny or anyone else who was with her, Rachel had noticed, and unless he was engaged with the police, he stopped to see her go by, and smiled at her just as she smiled at him, a little bit only, from the corner of the eye. But now, with the blue veil, she could not even do that, Rachel thought, and her heart sank because he wasn't there among the others today. The little beggar was more handsome than her cousins Henry and Claud, with his flashing white teeth and black eyes, and far braver, and she felt happy when she saw him. She thought of him when she caught sight of street urchins digging for food in garbage pails, or sleeping curled up against a wall, wondering if he were hungry and cold. After saying her prayers, she ran away with him in her imagination, ran away from nurses and *shawishes,* and when they had safely escaped together, she fell asleep. She loved him even more than Mamma, and she thought he loved her, too. Always, when she saw him fight the *shawish,* Rachel told Nanny she had a pebble in her shoe, or a stitch in her side, to lag behind and make quite sure he had escaped the *shawish's* clutches, but Nanny didn't believe her, and walked on just as usual. Rachel waited and worried, sometimes for two or three days, until she saw him again, afraid that the police had caught him this time and locked him up in the government prison-school which, Mahmoud said, was worse than death.

Her eyes scanned the street, and Rachel's heart beat like a drum to see him, a *shawish* holding him by the neck with one hand, while he blew his whistle with the other. Another *shawish* was running up to them, and as she passed the lad, furiously fighting back, his eyes blazing, she shouted, "Run! Another *shawish* is coming!" He freed himself and raced away with the two policemen on his heels. Rachel had time to observe his escape, and sighed with relief.

"What has come over you, Rachel? This is no way for a little lady to behave," Nanny scolded, and as they turned the corner, Rachel couldn't be certain the little beggar hadn't been caught, and wondered how long she must wait to know he was safe. She didn't want him ever to be locked up, because he was brown, as she was, and they were together against *shawishes* and pink people who spoke English. Rachel thought she was wicked to think this of her Nanny, who never beat her as the *shawish* beat the little beggars, never was nasty to her as the other nannies were with their children, who was Irish, not English or Scotch. Nonino and Aunt Renée's skins were fairer than Nanny's, but it wasn't the same thing, they must be brown inside, and she loved brown people, not the pink and pale ones, like Mrs. Sawyer.

Miss O'Brien had felt the child's hand stiffen in hers, and Rachel's unseemly interest in a beggar boy moved her. The child might be loved and spoiled, but she must be unbearably lonely if she cared for such a dirty little scamp. At first when everything in Egypt was strange, new, and often shocked her, Miss O'Brien had followed Alice's instructions and the advice of other nurses that children must be kept away from all that smacked of native life, but now this seemed cruel to her.

She observed Rachel nodding to the owner of a pharmacy standing on his doorstep, and on an impulse, she entered it, although this was not the place she usually patronized. The owner tended to her needs in person, and when they had done, he handed the child a packet of American chewing gum, recommending, "It's clean! It's good! Hygienic! Sanitary! American!"

Rachel looked at her questioningly, and Miss O'Brien said, in spite of all the nurses' warnings about how very careful English women must be over the sly advances of native men, however innocent they might appear, "Yes, you can take it, Rachel."

The child thanked her and thanked the man, and when they were in the street again she said, "You know, Nanny, the Syrian gentleman always gives things to children." Her voice was so eager that Miss O'Brien was sorry not to see if she was smiling beneath her veil.

"How do you know he's Syrian?" Miss O'Brien asked, puzzled. Except for the lower-class Arabs, she could not tell people apart, and it had intrigued her not only that Rachel knew these things, but that there were so many fine shades of familiarity, respect, condescension, in her manner of saluting people in the street; more than once, when in her own unavoidable dealings with natives, servants, and such, Rachel had acted as interpreter, she had instinctively modeled her conduct upon the child's.

"Everybody knows," Rachel said excitedly. "Now Stavros, the hairdresser, he's Greek. Before, he always spun his scissors round his thumb, very fast, when I said hello, and Soliman the florist, he used to give me a flower. The narcissus was gorgeous," Rachel said, pleased to use a word she had just learned.

"Did you know many people in the street?" Miss O'Brien inquired. She felt sad that the barber no longer twirled his scissors to amuse the child, that the florist no longer gave her a flower, and as she passed them, she nodded, with clumsy friendliness, although she had hardly noticed their existence before. It made her think of Palm Sunday, this procession the child must have gone through in the street, and yes, come to think of it, if she had been horrified by the brutality, filth, and indecency, by seeing beggars turn up their rags over their heads in the rain, revealing their nakedness, there was something about their fine limbs, the sweet innocence and wonder of their faces, that made her think the people who had listened to Christ, who had loved Him and believed in Him, must have been just like these she saw in the Cairo streets. Rachel, too, was like one of those children of long ago, with thoughts and feelings that were not of this age.

A LETTER FROM MAMA CAMOUNA

To those of us who were born in the communities of the Orient, the names of places that were once familiar—Baghdad, Damascus, Cairo, Tunis, Algiers—are now the faraway places in that mythical geography of hearts and minds, where distances do not correspond to those on maps. And I wonder sometimes how the cousins, "shlish be'shelishi" ever got to places like New York, Montreal, and São Paolo, when for countless generations their families had been rooted in the ancient communities of the Orient. Even before the establishment of Israel precipitated a mass exodus, our grandparents or great-grandparents suddenly packed up and left their ancestral homes. Cairo, Paris, London, then Jerusalem, and now New York became crossing points of these caravans pursuing their peregrinations through space and time.

Gathered around our festival tables here in Israel we rejoice to see the increasing number of grandparents and even great-grandparents living with their children and grandchildren. Perhaps to them the ring of our faces constitutes that fortress which in childhood appears impregnable. But together with the rejoicing, a sadness, a kind of anguish, creeps in as we remember those who are no longer, who rest in abandoned graves in lands we cannot visit. And somehow we would like these children descended from them, wherever they now are, to remember those who sat at the head of the table when we ourselves were children, in other lands, in other times.

The parents whom we, of the middle generation, knew in their full vigor, and against whose authority we often rebelled, are now these frail old couples who look so much like the pictures of their own parents that decorate their rooms. We feel an immense, aching tenderness for them, our parents, no longer strong and powerful, more often vulnerable and dependent. We become aware that they, and we, and the pictures of the old people on their walls belong together to a world which those who are now children can only know about by hearsay, if they are prepared to listen.

These old couples are all the more defenseless since they came to Israel at an advanced age. It isn't only a question of finding their way in unknown surroundings, but that we, their adult children, have become their only link with their past, and feeling disoriented, they project us backward into their own world. That can be unnerving, particularly when, as immigrants struggling to build new lives in Israel, we feel we ought to concentrate our energies on a present open to the future. Nostalgia for the past appears a luxury we cannot afford. We know there is no going back, nor really do we want to. From that point of view, Tel Aviv can be just as much an exile for the aged as Ottawa or Montevideo.

When my parents came to Israel from Egypt after the Sinai Campaign, and we lived in a two-room apartment that was not even paid for yet, I'd become annoyed as I cooked our meals over a kerosene burner when my mother, unpacking her suitcases, would call to show me dresses she had worn at various family weddings back in the 1920s, or photographs of her parents, or of my sister and myself as children, or would insist on reading to me one of those famous letters Mama Camouna used to write, and which were always read aloud as we all gathered every "Motza'ei Shabbat," in Uncle David's house. I didn't want to remember the time when we were this huge, exuberant family, quarrelsome and gay that assembled in my grand-uncle's house, because it hurt more than I could admit.

All her life, Mother had kept all the letters she had ever received tied up in little parcels, which went into boxes, bearing the names of people who had written them, sometimes over a period of fifty years. And the cupboard that held this huge correspondence, more than anything else, was what delayed her and my father's departure from Egypt. It had been difficult to carry on my own correspondence with them through third parties and I had been torn between two conflicting needs: on the one hand to transmit correct information about life in Israel, and on the other to make sure that this information should never point to Israel so clearly that Egyptian censorship might give them trouble with the political police.

Mother would write, "I'm going through all the letters in the big cupboard in the hall. With every letter I read, I remember the best years of our lives. Every letter I tear up is like tearing my heart away. I'm going through the correspondence so that I can later select the strict minimum I want to take to our new home. I also found a box of letters from your friends. Would you like me to keep it for you?"

I'd write back via Paris or Rome, with someone changing the envelopes so that the postmark "Israel" would not figure on the letter. "Our apartment is a small one with absolutely no storage space. Nowadays people live with the bare essentials. Don't keep any of my letters. Burn them. Nowadays it's best to travel light."

I had kept this correspondence with friends who had studied or married abroad, or rather, had left it at home, and being very much my mother's daughter, it hurt to give it up. But I thought that only by sacrificing my treasure—the record of our generation, really—could Mother be encouraged to prune hers more severely. She wrote a letter so tear-stained I could hardly read it of the auction sale at which all that had been our home had gone for nothing like its value, and I could see Mother and Father wandering in this big empty apartment with the bare minimum left, and Mother still sorting out the letters and pictures she could not bear to be separated from. As time passed, our correspondence became more frantic, and prudence was thrown to the winds. A German-born friend of mine in Tel Aviv urged me: "You must push them harder. It was just the same with my people. They couldn't bear to leave their home. It seems that the more the outside world threatens, the harder older people cling to the illusory safety of memories. It is a form of paralysis. My family got out on the very last ship that left Hamburg for England . . ."

What worried me most was the thought of an illness or accident that might make it impossible for them to travel: Then they'd be completely cut off from us. Finally, after months of waiting, they were with us. Safe. For me, that was the main thing. But Mother didn't see it that way. She'd say, "Who else do I have here except for your father and you with whom I can share my memories? I only brought one suitcase of letters and photographs, and I brought them for you and your sister, thinking that you, too, would like to have souvenirs of home. But you won't understand. You've become so hard in Israel, your father and I don't recognize you at all." She'd begin to weep.

Sometimes I'd indulge her. But there was no end to the flow of memories connected with each letter, picture, or object. And during that time, of course, I wasn't getting on with the household chores, or with the articles I was writing for the Jewish Agency on integration and absorption of immigrants and the happy, happy family reunions in Israel. It hurt too much to write about happy family reunions in Israel, if I allowed myself to think of what had been home sold at an auction, or about the fun we used to have in Uncle David's house, a band of cousins skating down the immense corridor, or playing savages with great war whoops, or running to be fondled by our grandparents sitting in the big room. And as I typed stories of people I interviewed in Dimona, Ashdod, or Kiryat Shmona, who often had been crying their hearts out—although the photographer managed to get them to smile for the cause—I'd think angrily, "As if the people who left their villages in Poland or Ukraine to settle in the Lower East Side of New York, or the South Side of Chicago did not have their hearts break, just as my mother's does now, at the tearing apart of this organic tissue called a family". It was on such occasions that I would recall the big, jerky, clumsy alphabetic characters filling the letters Mama Camouna used to write.

Mama Camouna was a great power of a woman, and totally illiterate. How was it then that she could write letters? Well, that's the story.

My grandmother had lost her mother in infancy, and her father, my mother's grandfather, had remarried. This second wife was Mama Camouna. She was a "Tunshi," a member of the local Jewry that spoke a Maghrebi dialect, and which the upper-class Tunisian Jews, who claimed to have hailed from Livorno and who spoke Italian, looked down upon as distinctly lower-class. Mama Camouna had many children and it was said she had been rather rough on my grandmother. Nevertheless, families are families. When my grandfather and his brother and their families left Tunis to settle in Egypt where they opened a department store, Mama Camouna suffered to be separated from her stepdaughter, whose family had become hers. She found it intolerable to have to rely on the goodwill of others to write what she had in her uncommonly strong head to say. So Mama Camouna, watching her grandchildren in Tunis doing their homework, got it into her head that if those little brats could write, so could she. It was simple: they'd teach her. They teased, "How can you learn to write, Mama Camouna? You don't know how to read and you hardly know any French." But Mama Camouna said she didn't need all that. All she wanted was that they teach her the "signs that show the sounds." My grandmother's half-sisters with whom their widowed mother lived in turn, would write to us in Cairo describing those epic lessons. The grandchildren would get impatient as they guided the old woman's hand on the paper as she learned to write her name, and they'd run away. She'd chase them, catch one of them by the scruff of his neck, plunk him down by the table and warn, "You aren't going to play until you've taught me to write the sound "SSSS." And so it came about that Mama Camouna learned to write her Judeo-Arabic dialect with French letters. Her letters were incomprehensible to those who did not know the Maghrebi dialect, and the writing was so completely phonetic that it made no sense until read aloud. She wrote exactly as she spoke.

So, one Saturday afternoon, in Uncle David's house, there'd be this tremendous excitement when my grandmother would say, "Guess what I have in my handbag?" and we'd all exclaim, "A letter from Mama Camouna!" Even the small children would drop their games, as rolling with laughter, or with tears in our eyes, we all listened as Mama Camouna expressed her feelings in her rough-simple way, in that impossible jargon of hers. For the best part of thirty years we were truly thrilled to receive those few lines that took Mama Camouna hours to write.

She died in her nineties, during the Nazi occupation of Tunisia. Of grief perhaps. What made her slip out of the house in a cold winter night we cannot know. She was found dead in the morning on a park bench. Jeannot, her favorite grandson, had died in the meantime somewhere in the Libyan desert after having joined the Free French Forces. Jeannot had been the grandchild she had battled with most, until he understood what it meant to this old woman to write and taught her, not because he was forced to, but willingly, moved perhaps by that sense of justice which made him join not only the Free French but also the Communist party. And because he had taught her as a little boy, she had been able to write to him, and to other members of her brood who left Tunis, one by one.

A short time before his death, Jeannot had turned up on leave in Cairo, and of course, was feted by those enormous couscous meals we used to have, and he brought with him one of his Muslim comrades in arms who, like him, had joined the Free French full of hope about the world that would emerge after the war, bringing independence, freedom, and justice for all. I was in New York at the time, and Mother had written to me, telling about Jeannot's visit. Grandmother was dead, so was Uncle David, but the family still met every Saturday afternoon in the house of Uncle David's widow, and there Jeannot read to the assembled families and his comrades what must have been one of Mama Camouna's last letters.

I remember Jeannot from the days when we went from Egypt to Tunis for the marriage of one of my aunts. We must both have been five or six at the time, and we immediately fell in love. Some branches of the family were well off, others poor, but it made no difference. There was such warmth and gaiety as every family in turn feted my aunt and her fiancé. Jeannot and I considered ourselves engaged as we exchanged cigar rings as wedding rings and in a family where so much of private emotion was in the public domain, everyone called us "Les Petits Fiancés." This embarrassed me greatly in later years when, after much writing back and forth, our dispersed tribes would meet for a glorious orgy of familial affection in some alpine resort, I'd be asked, "Don't you remember Jeannot, your little fiancé?" But Jeannot's family was too poor to come, so I never saw him again after that memorable visit to Tunis, where together we had discovered something about the relationship of light and love. During the hot afternoon hours, we'd play in a darkened room, where just one ray of light with millions of tiny specks of dust dancing in it passed through the nearly-closed shutters. We played at capturing the sunray in the palm of our hands, and offered it to one another. We began to dance, spontaneously as children do, drinking in the light, and when it fell on my face, Jeannot would steal a kiss, and sometimes I'd dodge, and sometimes I didn't. Of course, we were caught at it and scolded. We didn't feel we had done anything wrong: After all, we only kissed the light.

So, many years later, Mother wanting to read me letters from Mama Camouna seemed determined to pull me back into that region of the mind that is still, where time is abolished, where separation, sorrow, death do not exist. But time abolished by its very immobility foreshadows death, and we must live, all of us, in the world as it is, where no love, be it as strong as Mama Camouna's, is as innocent as that which Jeannot and I felt for one another dancing in the pure dancing light.

On occasion I'd tell my mother, by way of consolation, "In Israel, so many people lost so much more than we did, we must consider ourselves lucky in comparison. So you left your sisters, brothers, nephews, nieces, and innumerable cousins. But you'll see at least some of them again, someday. Think of those families who perished, whole families with so few survivors left."

I didn't really believe it but that was what most people said.

Mother, stubborn in her sorrow and sensible in her way, didn't take to that line of argument at all. "I suffered to be separated from you and now I suffer to be separated from them. And please, don't tell me we are lucky in comparison to people whose families perished in concentration camps. Do you think those survivors would not prefer to suffer being separated from those they love than to forbid themselves even to think of them? How can you accept what happened in concentration camps as if it were a normal condition of life? I refuse to. I never shall. The normal thing is for families to be happy when they are united, sad when they are parted. But we, we are always torn."

Our neighbours, who had just arrived from Poland, treated my parents when they met in the staircase as something infinitely precious and fragile, as if made of spun glass. My father was rather uncertain on his legs, and when the children raced up and down the stairs, our neighbours would hold them back and help him. One of the women said "Our children will never know what it's like to have grandparents. In Poland, life was too harsh for our old people. Almost none survived. You are blessed to have them, blessed to have been able to save them. There's nothing more beautiful than old age. They say Israel is the only place where a Jew can live fully. May it be the place where Jews live to become old, surrounded by their families."

With the passing of years, a few members of the family settled in Israel; others, including my sister, came to visit. There were times when the feeling of exile was unbearable, and times when Israel was a link between us in our dispersal, increasingly part of the fabric of our lives. Among the most memorable of these visits was that of my father's favorite sister, whom he had not seen for twenty-five years, when she had last visited us in Egypt. She had married in Manchester a good half-century back. Aunt Rose had a dream, imperatively ordering her to visit her brother Joseph. So she came, accompanied by her daughter, Amy, whom I hadn't seen since we were both toddlers on one of our visits to Manchester. Amy looked incredibly British, and behaved with old-style Victorian decorum, when very formally shaking hands, she said, "How do you do?"

Aunt Rose said, "Really Amy dear! Don't you remember your cousin? When they stayed with us in Manchester you pushed Jacqueline down the stairs!"

"I'm so sorry. That was very naughty of me," Amy said. There was that twinkle in her eyes, so much like that of her grandfather—and mine—when he teased, and we both laughed. It was fascinating, this extraordinary family resemblance we came to discover, not so much in looks but rather as something very deep in our natures, which made us react almost exactly in the same way and share the same likes and dislikes. Amy and I went on a few excursions, but

Aunt Rose saw nothing of Israel. That was not what she had come here for. Every morning, from her hotel, she'd take a taxi to see my parents, and they'd talk, remembering.

It was in this way Amy and I had heard how our grandmother had gone to Egypt with the smaller children after our grandfather had set up a proper house for them in Cairo. He had crossed the Syrian desert in a caravan, but grandmother, after visiting one of her sisters in Basra, went all the way round the Arabian Peninsula up to Port Said, on one of those famous British Peninsular and Orient liners. It was a long trip. She was ultraorthodox, and it was out of the question that her family should eat in the ship's dining room. Grandmother had come on board with a Primus stove, a sack of rice and one of lentils, among other provisions, and every day she cooked "Medjadara" on the deck, the only cooked food they ate on board. Father, who was almost seventeen at the time, rebelled and went to eat in the dining room. He found the nonkosher food delicious, but it made him very sick. After so many years, those two old people with their dark brown faces, white hair, and thick white eyebrows shook with laughter as they revived that old Primus stove on which their mother had cooked that long ago "Medjadara" on the ship on which they had made their crossing to the western world.

Then Sammy came to visit from New York. His father, my father's nephew, had wisely put him on the immigration quota to the United States some time before "the events." Sammy, whom I picked up at his hotel, had a Ph.D. in economics, worked for a big investment firm, and talked expansively about finances, American-style. He was mad about the United States, contributed to the U.J.A., attended Bond dinners. He had "integrated" fully. He was trying so hard to be ultra-American. Yet, when he saw my father not only was he moved, but the old patriarchal tradition in which he had been brought up spontaneously expressed itself. He kissed my father's hand and received his blessing, exactly as it had been the custom in the house of his great-grandfather who had left Baghdad to settle in Cairo. So we began to talk about the numerous branches of the family now settled in the United States. Most of those in their thirties had managed to get university degrees while they worked, and had eventually brought over their parents, and cared for them. "There's a time they decided things for us, now we decide for them," Sammy told me in an aside. And the younger girls, those in their twenties were all going to college, doing well, even brilliantly. They were five generations removed from the ultraorthodox and illiterate old lady who had cooked "Medjadara" for her children on the way around Arabia. We told Sammy the story, and he said he'd tell it to his sister's children, so that they remembered. Of course, he spoke of Aunt Rose's visit and exchanged the latest news about the branch of the family in

England. Then Father told Sammy he wanted him to write something down. It was this: our family had moved from a town called 'Ana to Baghdad 735 years before they left Baghdad to settle in Egypt, which was in 1911. He wanted those in America to know. Sceptical, I asked my father, "How can you know without any records? Seven centuries is a long time." And he said that nothing written could be more exact, give or take a few years, than oral tradition. People might cheat with written documents. But when the head of a family knew he was approaching the end of his days, and passed on what he wanted his sons to remember and in turn pass on to their sons, he was careful to calculate exactly, and one must not cast doubt on what was thus solemnly transmitted from mouth to mouth, throughout the generations.

I asked Sammy if he saw much of his cousins in New York, and he gave an answer that was typical. "When our parents wanted to force us to, because it was the family, and hold us by the old rules, we wouldn't have any of it. But actually, some of us see a great deal of each other, guided by a natural affinity and common interests, something which draws us together. On the whole we've made quite a society of cousins. It's strange. There's something deeper than the culture we acquire from the countries we live in. We adapt to them, of course. But there's a kind of kinship that's hard to descibe but that seems to persist, no matter what." "Kol Israel Haverim," my father answered, recalling the motto of the Alliance Universelle Israelite, which had been instrumental in bringing about the emergence of the old communities of the Orient into the western world.

Not long after Sammy's visit, my father died after a long illness. My mother's sorrow and mine was compounded by the fact that there were not ten men who had known him in his life to stand by his grave and recite "Kaddish" for him. Seeing we were so few, some strangers at the Holon cemetery visiting their own dead did the "mitzva" of coming to recite "Kaddish" for this Jew they had never known. This was the time when we felt that Israel can be exile most bitterly and cruelly. But telegrams and letters poured in from so many places in the world where father's brothers, nephews, and grand-nephews lived. In New York and in Manchester there were enough of them to gather in his memory and do things the proper way, as he had done all his life for others. And when some of them now come to Israel, and ask to visit his grave, there is a more gentle sorrow, a kind of peace over the fact that he is remembered by them. Sometime, I go alone, and this loneliness seems incredible when once we were so many.

Then I remember my grandmother telling me when I was a child how Mama Camouna and the other women would take the children to the Jewish cemetery in Tunis, so that the dear dead ones would not feel lonely. "At first we lamented and tore at our cheeks, and then we'd settle down for a collation, and the children would play hide-and-seek among the graves. And we'd remember what our dear ones had said and done and told stories about them. Oh, we'd laugh so much remembering your great-uncle Fragi, because he was so gay, always playing pranks, and at weddings he'd compose songs, honoring the bride and groom and their families, with funny refrains about everybody." Then grandmother and her daughters would remember those weddings in Tunis and what everybody wore, some of the women still in their traditional dresses, wrapped up in big white silk shawls, and those who already dressed in the style that was "modern" before the First World War. Their infectious laughter sometimes seems to echo among the cold rectilinear alignment of the graves in Holon, and they all seem to be there, and I the surviving witness of something marvelously warm, vital, and alive, which I knew but no longer is. Nowadays, even the dead seem regimented in these straight-lined cemeteries, so different from the old ones, where families kept together, in death as in life. And yet, somehow, life continues, reasserts itself, and some of the old ways still survive. After my father's death, my mother stayed some time with my sister in Paris, where she saw many of her cousins, some who had left Egypt after the Sinai Campaign, and some who, in the meantime, had left Tunis and other North African cities. Then she stayed with my father's relatives in England, and each of his nephews and nieces brought their children and grandchildren to see her, exactly as it was done in the old days. She wrote: "They still cook the same dishes, some of them, at least for the holidays."

She returned to Israel having seen them all, appeased. In Paris, her cousins, the daughters of Uncle David, who are now old ladies, still meet every "Motza'ei Shabat," and read the letters they have received. Anyone who passes through Paris joins the circle. The younger people sometimes come and sometimes don't. Perhaps this will be the last generation to keep up the custom, but in the meantime it holds.

And so it was that Gerard, a great-grandson of Uncle David, called me up one day from his kibbutz. A little mockingly, he said "Grandmother said that if I don't see your mother while I'm in Israel, she'll never forgive me. So when can I come?"

We make arrangements for his visit. He arrives, a handsome boy of eighteen, a student who, trying to look serious, tells me that he, too, paraded with the black flag of anarchy during the student riots. We laugh. With his long blond hair he looks very much like a beatnik and his pink outfit is very dirty.

"Would you like to wash?" Mother suggests.

Gerard looks scandalized. Then his eyes begin to rove over the pictures hanging on her walls and he recognizes some of the old people he knew when they were still young, and of some he asks "Who is he? Who is she?" For a brief moment they live again as part of our lives, mixed up with what we say about the Six-Day War, and what Gerard tells us of his kibbutz, and the family in Paris and the student riots. And Gerard tells my mother, "Aunt Yvonne, you should have seen the crowd that came to hear your letters being read. Aunt Louise called us all up, and said "A letter from Yvonne!" and we all went. We heard all about your visit to Jerusalem. It was very moving. But your letter about the visit to the Golan Heights drew crowds three Saturdays in a row! It was a masterpiece. You can't imagine what it means now, to have family in Israel."

Mother was very pleased. "I'm only an old woman. I just wrote about what I saw and what I felt about it, and wanted to share it with those I love."

Gerard knits his eyebrows and asks, "But how did it happen that for the last three or four generations we've been constantly on the move? And it's not finished yet. How did it all begin?"

So mother tells Gerard how in her family it might have began. "You see, your great-great-grandfather had an oil press in Monastir, a small village in Tunisia. The oil was stored in big jars, like those in the tale about Ali-Baba and the forty thieves. One jar was kept for ablutions. There was of course no running water in those days. Well, one day, after he had worked hard and sweated and felt very hot, he had the jar filled with cold water and stayed in it too long. He died of pneumonia as a consequence. Times were already changing, and your great-grandfather, my Uncle David, the eldest son, decided to try his luck in Tunis, the big city, and gradually he brought the whole family over to Tunis. That's how it all began."

"Well," Gerard said, "It's not given to everybody to have had an ancestor who died taking a cold bath in an oil jar. I'll have to tell the cousins in Paris about it. I wonder why grandmother never did."

"Perhaps," Mother said at once gentle and reproaching, "because you never asked. How do you want us to tell, when you young people nowadays are really not interested in those old tales, when you can't really be bothered with the past, because the world they live in is so different? So it's wiser to wait until they ask." She glances at me, a little slyly. "Isn't it so, my daughter?"

I say yes and I think it's always the same caravans crossing and recrossing. Perhaps memories are like water in a well, that well Rachel uncovered for Jacob when he came to his Uncle Laban. Perhaps that is when it all started, and since then it is only the means of transportation that have really changed.

—*Jacqueline Shohet Kahanoff*

from TO DIE A MODERN DEATH

I recall how one Passover, on my grandfather's one-hundredth birthday, we were all gathered round him to celebrate. He had a cold and was slightly feverish, but he conducted the Seder as usual. At night he said: "I am full of years. My hour has come. This is my last Passover." He died that very night, after having blessed us all. That was a dignified, old-fashioned death, a death we can all understand and accept. But the death of his son, my father, who died at eighty-three after months of agony, in a room not his own, a bed not his own, in clothes that did not belong to him, alone among strangers—that kind of death is something I can neither accept nor forgive, although I don't really know whom nor what it is I can't forgive. My father died in what is politely referred to as a "hospital for chronic diseases," although that type of place is more like a concentration camp with full care where we dump our old folk, out of the way, out of sight, when they become infirm and senile and when we no longer can, or are simply unwilling to look after them at home. Here the victims are not an ethnic or religious minority, but a most defenseless group—the aged. My father was an old-fashioned man who died a modern death.

In that hospital I spent with my father the Passover that I hoped would be his last. Bent down, trembling, dribbling, the patients were wheeled, dragged, pushed, pulled, like mules to water, to sit blank-eyed at the table. Their unsteady coarse hands spilled food on their worn clothes, which had been picked up at random. Some spat on the floor, others had a tube hanging down the opening of their trousers. A wizened old couple kept squabbling, whining and groaning, not listening to each other. Here and there, middle-aged children helped their parents with their food. One caring son carefully picked up the slop from his mother's hairy chin. With an unsteady hand he conveyed a twisted tin spoon loaded with gefilte fish from the plate to that forlorn port, his old mother's mouth. There were no forks or knives. He was reading from the Haggadah.

I also had my father's Haggadah with me. "Wouldn't you like to read a bit?" I asked.

"No," came the firm reply, "I would not." As if to reassure me that he was not angry with me, he took my hand and we held hands for a while.

From time to time I placed a spoonful in his mouth, forcing myself to eat with him, because he ate better that way. Happily, the TV was switched on. There was Cairo, a view of the pyramids and the Nile. The Good Son was reading aloud: "For I have taken you out of the land of Egypt . . ." This hurt almost unbearably. Father's mind was lucid enough to understand that to him and to these old Jews around him death in Israel would spell mental and physical torment.

★ ★ ★ ★ ★

A dying animal usually finds a place to hide. Not so man. Four hopelessly sick old people watched father's agony. They were frightened, during my father's terrible moments of lucidity, between the long and merciful spells of dozing, or sleep, just as when they watched the agony of those who were there before him. There was quite a turnover in Father's room, and of the ten or twelve old men I knew during his five months at Beit Miriam, only one actually walked out and returned home. Father once said to me: "I have had a long life, but only now have I learned something about it." We learned together with him.

We went to the hospital the night we heard that Father had died. The night porter let us in when we rang the doorbell. There, on the desk in the tiny hall, on a piece of paper with his name on it, lay Father's wedding band. They gave it to Mother, but we didn't quite understand why. We asked to see him, but the night porter said: "We've already sent him to Ichilov hospital. He stank. We can't keep them here."

For some reason I had assumed there would be a room that guaranteed privacy during these last moments. In fact I lacked the courage to ask. Poor Mother! For years she nursed this sick old man until he fell and broke both hips and, although we tried for two months, it was no longer possible to look after him at home. Only a few weeks before his death she had brought a cake, flowers, and some wine to the hospital to "celebrate" with Father their fiftieth wedding anniversary. Now she stood there, twisting the wedding band between her fingers, groaning bitterly: "They didn't even let me stay with him in the afternoon. I so wanted to stay with him to the end, to close his eyes. But he died alone."

★ ★ ★ ★ ★

Oddly enough, that night I slept like a log, the peaceful sleep of the just, the kind that had eluded me for months. I was no longer haunted by that nightmarish dream in which my father, an old man I had brought over from Egypt to Israel, got up from his hospital bed hobbling on crutches, crossing the fields to look for me. He grew taller and taller as he came nearer, until he found my house, my room. He then collapsed before my eyes, dead, and his ghostlike figure, with arms outstretched, lay sprawling on the ground. That night, as in the nights that followed, I no longer woke up in a cold sweat wondering: Is he awake? Is he suffering? Is he calling while nobody comes . . . how helpless they all are . . . Father may have fallen off the bed again and hurt himself. . . . It often happened because his broken hips made it so difficult for him to turn around in bed as he tried to get into a more comfortable position, and when he finally succeeded, he often fell to the ground. I slept because at long last he was deep in merciful sleep. Everything was finally over. Father had found peace.

★ ★ ★ ★ ★

Let me make it quite clear: I do not regret my father's death at the age of eighty-three. All I felt when he died was a sense of relief, because his suffering had ended, and so had mine. He should have died sooner, at eighty-two, for instance, when he caught pneumonia. I can say these things about my father because he was the man I loved most and without question for the longest time, and even Beit Miriam could not totally destroy the bond between us. Yet I cannot remember him without thinking of Beit Miriam. I try to remember him as he was in my childhood, how he used to whistle when he came home, how I used to run along the hallway to meet him. I try to remember the frail man he was here in Israel. But the memories of an entire lifetime cannot erase the images of Beit Miriam.

Feeding him I sometimes could see through the live green fence dividing Beit Miriam and the neighboring garden, a small girl skipping on a rope. Away from those human wrecks warming themselves in the sun, among the fruit trees, the little girl skipped her rope over and over again, without a thought for death. I was thankful to that girl for reminding me that I too knew a time when death did not exist. I remembered our garden at home in Egypt. I was seven or eight. It was my birthday and my grandmother was coming up the path, swaying on her delicate, tiny legs, because she was so fat. Angrily I thought: "I'll never let myself grow old and fat. Never. Never." I went on skipping the rope. Such innocence protects children. How else would they find the strength and faith to grow and reach maturity and old age? The sight of the girl dispelled the foul hospital smells as the contents of each spoonful slid into father's desolate mouth.

That wreck was my father and little by little I could find less to say to him. "Tell me something amusing," he told me once. I searched my mind, but couldn't think of anything to say. He actually found ways to convey and express the mysterious grace of love. I felt it in the squeeze of his hands, the way he put my hand to his cheek when I kissed him good-bye, the way he guessed when I could no longer stand the smells, the sights and sounds of Beit Miriam, the taps that never closed, the lavatories which were never properly swilled. Then he would say: "Go, smoke a cigarette outside," and when he himself could no longer bear what was going on in his room he would say to me: "Now go home . . . and thank you for coming."

I must confess, I fled twice. It was more than I could bear. But sometimes, when the patients in Father's room could walk, or when they were in the dining room and we were left alone, he talked with amazing clarity, although his voice was weak.

He once asked me: "What are the happiest days of our lives?"

I gave him a quizzical look.

"The happiest days." He answered his own question resolutely. I didn't understand, the sentence seemed to be incomplete.

He said: "Once I had an argument with my brother Salim. He asked me 'What are the happiest days of a man's life?' I replied: 'The happiest days'."

"What are the happiest days?" I asked impatiently thinking he was losing his mind.

"Simply the days you feel happy. There are no rules. I remember these days, all of them and there were many, too many to list here. Now, do you remember that day when . . ."

As it happened, we both recalled the silliest of happy incidents. It occurred to me that more than defending him as best I could against the grim reality of this world of gloomy struggling semi-corpses, he was trying to protect me with the brittle power of his love. The happiest days did exist, in some specific, flimsy, and timeless sphere we are able to salvage, just like those wrecked bodies moving and feeling their way through the long long hospital night. Father could no longer experience comfort, bitterness, fear, resentment, guilt, and compulsion, yet the last thing he clung to was the memory of those happiest days.

Oddly enough, Father, whom I knew to be earnestly religious and devoted to Jewish tradition, never once pronounced the name of God since the day he entered Beit Miriam. That summer I brought him peaches. Saying *"Shehehyanu"* was always a joy to him. He began reciting it, but when it came to *"vehigianu lazman haze"* he shook his head in protest. He refused to say Amen. It was quite impossible to guess what thoughts were passing through my frail father's mind—though I believe that he was trying to say that nothing mattered except what people did to each other. Not God, but human tenderness, that was what really mattered.

* * * * *

On the Saturday before his death I rocked my father in my arms as if he were my own child. I sat a little while on the edge of his bed, stroked his head, held his hands which clung to me with his remaining forces. The nurse came to change his linen, pushing under him another pillow that he had removed. I saw that tormented skeleton with its crooked hips, covered in a thin layer of dry skin, grey and paper-thin. You could almost pass your hand through the hole in the hip bones. His whole body was covered in sores and the stench was dreadful. But when his wandering eyes focused on me, they were my father's eyes, brimming over with tenderness. Weak as he was, it was his smile, despite the gaping pit that was his mouth, and that bluish and transparent hand which found strength to bring my cheek closer to his—it was my father's hand. We held each other tight, but I could not stop the tears, despite the four frightened old men watching us and knowing that their time would also come.

I asked the nurse whether I could stay the night. "His heart is strong. It can last another three or four days," she said. "Go now, my dear," Father whispered. "Let me rest."

That evening I told Mother: "It is the end." The next day we went together, and I was furious that they had put Father in an easy chair. Couldn't they simply leave him alone? The thought that it might last another three or four days seemed intolerable. I suddenly remembered his walking stick. It was gone. Another patient had taken it, one who had been moved to another room. I hurried to Shimon. "I want my father's stick." He came with me to the room where that patient was lying. I almost snatched it out of his hand as he held on to it crying: "But it's mine, mine." I was on edge. There was something urgent I had to do and I had to rush back to Tel Aviv. Seeing my great anxiety, Father gave me a mischievous smile, saying: "Aren't you going to give me a kiss? Won't you say good-bye?"

I gave him a quick kiss and said good-bye. It was the last time I saw him alive, the last important event in our lives at which I did not receive his blessing. I didn't wait for it. I fled. Mother and I agreed that she would come over to our house that afternoon. Instead, she went back to Beit Miriam to see him. The phone there was out of order. I was nearly out of my mind with worry, and when she arrived hours late I scolded her angrily: "You should preserve your strength. It can last another three days. How much can a man suffer?"

"I had to go," she said. "I couldn't leave him. But they wouldn't let me stay. So I said good-bye. I said: 'God bless you my darling. God bless you. Can you hear me?' And he said: 'And how!' He closed his eyes and said: 'Now go home, my dear. I'd like to rest a bit.' "

Soon enough a call came through from Beit Miriam to say that it was all over. All I felt was tremendous relief. It was all over at long last. We cabled my sister and she called the following morning. I asked her not to come from Paris, I didn't want to delay the funeral for even an hour. "We must care for the living," I told her. "The dead are at peace, they no longer need us. . . . I asked Mother to go and stay with you for a while, you'll help her get over it all."

At Ichilov hospital they let us take a look at Father. I cannot say that he looked peaceful. The bearded man in a black cloak refused to let us give him a last kiss. Religion forbids it. His face was covered with a piece of black cloth. My mother sobbed bitterly as they poured earth over the black cloth in the grave into which they lowered Father's body. Strangers came to join a quorum for the Kaddish at the Holon cemetery. But all I saw was the sand, the skies, the glorious wreath, the colorful flowers I ordered for him, so that he would, at least, not die like a pauper.

All I heard of the prayer was: "May he rest in peace in Paradise." I could smile again. His pathetic body has been returned to the dust where it should have gone long ago, but Father's delicate spirit, its purity, its selfless love, was free, free at last. And so was I, free, free to live and to remember him not only at Beit Miriam but also in the "Happiest days," of which this was one.

— Translated from the Hebrew by Hannah Schalit

SIMHA ZARAMATI ASTA

SIMHA ZARAMATI ASTA was born in the Yemenite Quarter of Tel Aviv and died in 1993. Her books include two novels, *The Kite-Maker* (1982), and *Without A Rainbow* (1984); three books of poetry, *Late Rain* (1982), *From the Cloud on the Mountain* (1986), and *Evening West* (1991); a book of short stories, *Neighborly Album 'A'* (1992); and two biographies, *The Life of Yosef* (1987) and *Avshalom* (1990). At her death, she had been collecting material for a book on Yemenite women. Her condensed prose often deals with issues of racism towards *mizrahi* Jews as well as the more particular social, economic, and cultural problems faced by *mizrahi* women. As in the text included here, her work often deals with characters in transition; her language, as well, reflects a rich mixture of usage from Biblical and traditional sources along with a sharp ear for the colloquial. Of her work, Yosef Dehoah Halevi, the editor of *Afikim*—one of the most important and longest-standing *mizrahi* cultural institutions—has written: "Her stories allude to many of the negative phenomena appearing in our lives here following Independence—discord amongst brothers, as well as between the community and individuals; the tendency to pursue immediate gratification rather than take into consideration the human and social aspects of the nation as a whole, in all its diversity; the quest for easy and meager forms of seduction; the relentless pursuit of material goods and get rich quick schemes; cheap and slavish cultural imitation—all of these things have blurred the distinction between what is essential and what is secondary, between positive commandments and prohibitions, as the content of our lives fades off in their tracks to become arbitrary and devoid of substance . . . In *Neighborly Album,* for example, the author surveys a varied gallery of captivating characters that, on the surface, appear "small." Yet, in reality, they are great in themselves, possessed of particular and distinctive qualities. With such characters, one can soar to ethical, social, and human heights."

THE DOWRY

No one troubled himself to learn why the body of Nadra, whose name means light, was found on the railroad tracks near Musrara.

They all made do with the official printed and broadcast announcements prepared by the police, which said that the young woman whose body was found had been in the first months of pregnancy, and that anyone who knew anything about a missing woman should report immediately to the police station nearest his home.

The people of the neighborhood muttered that this wasn't the first incident; insufficient lighting and neglect had taken the lives of many residents. But who heeded the grumbling of the neighbors? Sometimes it seemed they existed solely for the sake of the census.

There were those who knew about Nadra's disappearance: her father, her stepmother, her husband and her mother-in-law. They also knew why she had disappeared; surely they also knew that her death hadn't been an accident. Surely they knew that Nadra had done it on purpose.

That's why no one bothered to go and identify the body; as if the father and mother-in-law had made a pact to keep silent. Actually they had no contact, despite their being related.

Nadra's father had the fortune not to have to endure the hardships of the transit camps of the state's early days, thanks to Nadra's mother, who before her death had given Nadra her jewelry, an inheritance from her grandmother. Thanks to Nadra's prudent decision at the airport in Aden not to hand over the jewelry to the emissaries of the Jewish Agency—emissaries who took the jewelry of the guileless and never returned it—and thanks to the relatives who had turned the jewelry into lira, he had the fortune to live in the neighborhood.

Nadra was magnificence; her voice made hearts tremble. The elders of the neighborhood courted her with their eyes, but had to admit she was too young. Nadra's father did not think so though; more than once he had wondered aloud how it was that none had come to offer him a dowry and take her to wife.

The elders of the neighborhood told him that such was not the custom of the Land of Israel. We have learned to act according to local custom, they said, and not as we did in exile. In Israel, dowries had lost their place and purpose. But Nadra's father would not hear their counsel; he continued to wait for the one who would bring a dowry.

Nadra went out to work and discovered another world, though inside she knew she had not yet learned the customs of the Land of Israel. She differed from the girls of the neighborhood in her way of speaking, in her way of thinking, yet none of her flaws prevented her from aspiring to become part of the life of this country, which seemed to her decent and good. She turned her entire salary over to her father.

Nadra loved going to work. At the home of her mistress she would sing as she toiled, lovely songs that her mother had sung to the drone of the grindstone, and by candlelight. Her delicate voice made the whole building tremble. She would stop singing whenever she heard the neighbor's son playing an instrument that was unfamiliar to her: a piano. The sound of his playing was pleasing to her ears.

The melodies carried her far away, back to the land of her childhood, a land of songbirds, streams, and the tinkle of the bells of the herd that wandered the hills and dales in landscapes of pink sunrises and red sunsets.

When he would stop playing, her clear voice could again be heard as it wafted through the air.

Nadra loved her mistress' home, and she tried to be like her. When her mistress went off to work, Nadra would try on her high-heeled shoes, her revealing, rustling dresses, and her feathered hats, delighting in her reflection in the mirror framed by electric lights.

In her dreams the image of herself as it appeared in the mirror would come to her; in her dreams she would walk coquettishly down the sidewalks of the city, her dress rustling, the tassels of the belt at her narrow waist swaying to and fro to the rhythm of her step. To that rhythm she would sing of a woman in love who conjured the image of the young man she awaited—*dakik, al-hisr*—a slender young man who'd come down to the stream to water his horse.

Nadra did not know that dreams were uttered in vain, that reality was always different.

She would tell her dreams to her friend, a girl from the neighborhood who, though she had lived there a long time, had not learned the customs of the land—though this did not keep her from winning her father's love and the love of her intended groom.

The day Nadra's father received the dowry he was overjoyed. At first he promised his daughter he would buy her jewels and clothes to cheer her, lest she leave his house empty-handed. But once he had clasped the hard coins in his fist, his heart, too, hardened, and kept him from giving his daughter her due.

Nadra was not happy on her wedding day. The week of the wedding she did not cease crying. The day the woman who was to be her mother-in-law came to make promises to her father, Nadra had felt her fate was sealed. Her father sent an emissary to see if the woman spoke the truth, and whether there would be enough to live on; he found her words to be true. The groom sat at the entrance to a small shop while his mother fetched and carried. Nadra's father doubled the sum of the dowry he had meant to ask.

When the woman heard Nadra's father's demands, she herself doubled the dowry: If the father was asking so-many dinars, then she would give double so-many dinars. On the day appointed for the ritual bath, the woman came bearing a copper tray laden with gifts, as was the custom in her land; but not even the sight of the tray could stop Nadra's tears or her pleas that her father change his mind. Nadra thought: My father has not heard my words; will he hear my song? In the words of the poetess of Yemen she sang:

My father, my mother how would you sell me?
Sell the sheep and the cattle
As ransom for me.
Know that if rain falls at night
It is but my tears;
Know that if thunder and lightning you hear
They are but the pounding of my heart.

But neither did the song penetrate her father's heart. He was proud of the generous dowry that had found its way into his pocket. As was Jacob on his wedding night, so was Nadra on her wedding night.

Even with the first caress the groom's immense hand groped at her tiny face; Nadra shuddered, but his thick hands did not stop groping her body, pawing each and every limb as he groaned with pleasure. He would not leave her be; when she'd try to evade his touch he'd seize her, bellowing, "Where are you?"

Only at sunrise did she discover that her bridegroom was blind. His strong body was full of vigor, but his wide eyes were sightless.

Dread filled Nadra's heart. How could it be? Was this why such a great dowry had come into her father's hands? Was this why her mother-in-law had brought a tray so laden with gifts? It must be that father had been deceived! He could not have known—for he sent an emissary to see the betrothed. The emissary must not have seen that the clients feared her husband's blindness more than they feared his mother's watchful eyes.

She felt choked, felt she would suffocate. While she was yet trying to comprehend who this was who now stood before her, hand extended, his mother entered bearing a tray piled high with a sumptuous breakfast and proclaimed: "Good morning, young lovers!" Lovers? Her body ached from being bitten and squeezed all night.

He moved closer to his mother, groping at the tray, inhaling the food without pause. Nadra lifted nary a crumb to her mouth.

She hoped that, in the morning, he would go with his mother to the store. But he stayed riveted to his chair, his hands groping at her body. He did not stop making "love" to her. Her body cried out for rest, but he would not desist, not even on the second or third day. Finally, on the morning of the first day of the new week, when his mother asked that he assist in the store, he went, only to quickly return. Nadra took advantage of these few minutes and fled to her father's house. All the anger, the fear, the humiliation of her husband's house gushed from her mouth in a torrent of screams. Bemoaning her wretched fate she cried to her father, asking over and over: "Did you know? Did you know? This man knows only the flesh, the ways of the flesh are his rituals, he won't let me be, when I bathe he asks that I leave the door open! Does he see my nakedness through his blindness? Or does he delight in the sound of the stream of water, in the scent of the soap—as he says? For these things can be sensed just as well through a closed door! He keeps me from the company of others. I asked him if I might go to the cinema with my girlfriend. He knew she was my only girlfriend and he liked her, the mute girl who could not scream even when the neighbor's son raped her, even when in the throes of labor. She could not scream like other women, but I am not mute. He forbade me to go and sent my friend away in disgrace.

"I can talk, I can scream, I am screaming, I will scream. You will hear me my father. Father, I do not want this marriage. Father, he has the strength of lions, he will not let me be, he never tires. He does not go out, he sits at home. He does nothing. His mother runs everything, she buys, prepares, and serves. I am only a body to be lain with."

"Sit down. We will see what will be. But remember, you are a married woman," her father replied.

Not more than two or three days had passed before the mother and her son appeared at Nadra's father's house bearing food and drink—essential goods in those days of austerity, the first days of the state. Before she could sit down the woman said: "Don't forget that we've paid a dowry." That very night Nadra returned to her husband's house. His mother used flattery, but did not forget to remind her, "After all, we've paid a dowry for you; we've brought you honor." Nadra had not even set down her things when he'd firmly clasped her thin wrist and roughly pulled her toward him, pressing himself on her with his full weight. An unquenchable fire flared in his body. He was deaf to her cries, her pleas, her moans, her screams.

Then she made up her mind: She would vanish, forever.

Several days passed, but they were just like the nights. The dreams of happiness that had once sustained her soul now turned to nightmares.

She began to feel ill, even though she did not eat the rich food that the woman tried to ply her with. She began to vomit. Her sparkling eyes lost their luster; her face became pallid as death. During those few days even the smell of the house made her nauseous. How much more so the smell of her husband's body?

The weaker her body became, the stronger became her resolve to leave and never return.

One night before he came home, she carried out her plan. First she bathed her body, washing off every trace of all that had clung to her in that house. Then she put on the best of the dresses she had brought from her father's house, donned the traditional *gargush* and, like a queen, strode toward the railroad tracks, singing as she walked a song she recalled from her childhood days, a song her mother had sung, one she had not understood until that very moment. The closer she got to the railroad tracks, the louder her voice became; the closer the clacking of the wheels, the higher her song rose, becoming a scream:

She who suffers in life is hardened;
Death for her is peace and rest.
Even the stone becomes silent
When on the pathways grow
Only thorny bushes,
Flowerless.

Nadra's voice stilled, her body on the tracks, the train rushing on in a din.

The customs of the Land of Israel, too, are blind.
They do not see what goes on in the soul.

— *Translated from the Hebrew by Marsha Weinstein*

NISSIM REJWAN

NISSIM REJWAN was born in Baghdad where he began writing for the *Iraq Times* while managing the Al-Rabita Bookshop, a meeting place for many prominent contemporary Iraqi writers. After coming to Israel in 1951, he studied at the Hebrew University and joined the staff of the *Jerusalem Post,* a widely read English-language daily. There, for over forty years, he has done book reviews covering a dizzying range of topics and interests as well as feature articles on the Middle East and Israeli culture. He also worked, for a number of years, on the Arabic section of the Israel Broadcasting Service; from 1959 to 1966, he was editor of the Arabic daily *al-Yaum.* A journalist, historian, and political commentator, Rejwan's works include *Nasserist Ideology: Its Exponents and Critics* (1974), and *The Jews of Iraq: 3,000 Years of History and Culture* (1987). He has contributed articles to a wide range of collections on the contemporary Middle East and also written for journals such as *Commentary, Midstream, Present Tense, Dissent, New Middle East, Le temps modernes, L'Arche,* and *The Jerusalem Quarterly.* A remarkable synthesizer of information and ideas, Rejwan's unflinching honesty, seering irony and acerbic wit have made him a consistent voice of sanity in Middle Eastern affairs for the past four decades. He presently lives in Jerusalem, where he is at work on the completion of a number of projects, including *Passage from Baghdad: A Memoir 1924-1951; Israelis and Arabs: A Post-Zionist Appraisal; Arabs Face the Modern World: From Afghani to Sa'dun Hammadi,* and *Modern Predicaments: Currents in 20th-Century Arab Intellectual History.*

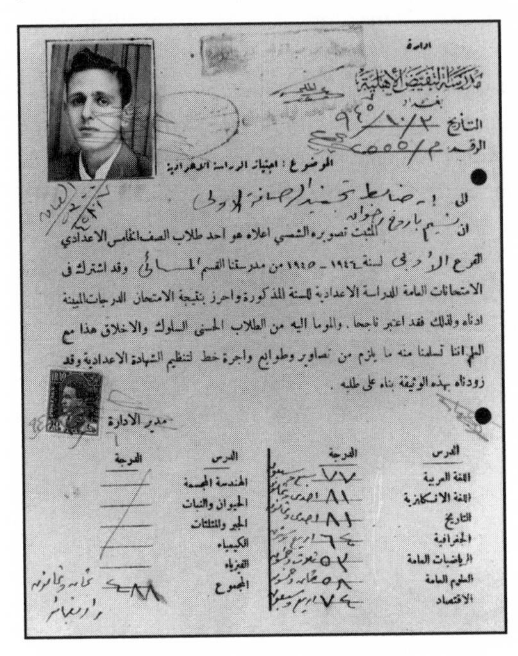

الادارة

مدرسة التفيض الأهلية

بغداد

التاريخ ٢/١٠/٩٤٥

الرقم

الموضوع : اجتياز الدراسة الاعدادية

الى :

ان ... المثبت تصويره الشمسي اعلاه هو احد طلاب الصف الخامس الاعدادي
الفرع الادبي لسنة ١٩٤٤ - ١٩٤٥ من مدرستنا القسم المسائي وقد اشترك في
الامتحانات العامة للدراسة الاعدادية للسنة المذكورة واحرز بنتيجة الامتحان الدرجات المبينة
ادناه ولذلك فقد اعتبر ناجحا . والموما اليه من الطلاب الحسني السلوك والاخلاق هذا مع
العلم اننا تسلمنا منه ما يلزم من تصاوير وطوابع واجرة خط لتنظيم الشهادة الاعدادية وقد
زودناه بهذه الوثيقة بناء على طلبه .

مدير الادارة

الدرس	الدرجة	الدرس	الدرجة
اللغة العربية	٧٧	الهندسة المجسمة	
اللغة الانكليزية	٨١	الحيوان والنبات	
التاريخ	٨١	الجبر والمثلثات	
الجغرافية	٦٤	الكيمياء	
الرياضيات العامة	٥٢	الفيزياء	
العلوم العامة	٥٨	المجموع	[illegible]
الاقتصاد	٧٤		

from PASSAGE FROM BAGHDAD

BOOKSHOP DAYS

At some point my mind began to wander—I cannot say exactly when. I was sitting there in this university auditorium attending a very special and exclusive seminar given by one of the most distinguished historians of the modern Middle East. The subject was Arab-Jewish relations, the position of Jews in Medieval Islam, and "anti-Semitism in Islam." The main lecturer was speaking about what he called "the myth" of Spanish Islamic tolerance towards Jews and how it had been fostered precisely by Jewish scholars in Europe in this century, allegedly using it as a stick with which to beat their Christian neighbors. Muslim-Arab scholars in our own day, he was saying, particularly delighted in ascribing the virtue of tolerance to Spanish Islam.

And so on. It was round about this time that the lecturer all but "lost" me, and I began to think of a more recent period and a more personal recollection—Baghdad of the mid-forties and my own experience within the largely Muslim-Arab milieu in which I grew up to consciousness and found the nearest thing to emotional and intellectual maturity and fulfillment. What with the difficulty of organizing one's thoughts in such circumstances, I caught myself flitting from scene to scene, person to person, and place to place—and I finally managed to concentrate on those formative years of the second half of the forties, some of my peers and elders at the time, and the general atmosphere of "tolerance" in which we moved, read, loved, and just plain lived.

The lecturer was still splitting hairs about tolerance, and how "the myth" of Spanish Islamic tolerance furnished an interesting example of the pitfalls and ambiguities of history and the writing of history. He was talking of two kinds, at least, of tolerance—tolerance as the absence of discrimination and tolerance as the absence of persecution. It was when he began to elaborate and allocate marks that I ceased to listen altogether and started reconstructing the faces and scenes involved in the launching, thirty-five years previously almost to the day, of my career as an assistant bookseller.

Some of my fondest memories of Baghdad, in fact, have to do with my work in Al-Rabita Bookshop, an offshoot of a cultural association of the same name that was founded by a group of intellectuals with leftist political leanings though stopping short of being card-carrying Communists. The association's secretary and honorary treasurer, a genial and engaging man by the name of Khaddouri Khaddouri, had asked me to help with the establishment of the store, which was to deal almost exclusively with British and American books. I then had a short interview with the association's chairman, Abdel Fattah Ibrahim—and in what seemed to be no time at all, a place was found, books were ordered from individual publishers, shelves and desks were set, and the shop opened. Except for the more specialized works on sociology, economics, and history, which were chosen by Abdel Fattah himself, I had a completely free hand in making the orders, and my various literary predilections and inclinations played a decisive role in establishing the character of the bookshop and the type of clients who frequented it. I recall clearly that on opening day and during the week that followed a large ad was placed in a local paper listing what purported to be "Ten Books that Changed the World" —all of which were available at the new store at fairly low prices. The books included Plato's works and Darwin's *Origin of Species,* Marx's *Das Capital,* and Freud's "basic works" — in the Modern Library Giants series; but it also included Tolstoy's *War and Peace* and James Joyce's *Ulysses.*

The bookshop, which opened in the spring of 1946, soon became a meeting place for intellectuals and bookworms of all kinds—and although I had already had my own circle of friends and fellow literati, some of my best and most lasting intellectual friendships and associations had their origins there. Baghdad of the mid-forties was a comparatively provincial little place with a rather limited number of people who actually read foreign languages with ease or for pleasure. Even among the Jewish community, foreign languages—mostly English and French—were the languages of commerce and trade, and rather useful if you wanted to get a job in one of the foreign banks or firms. There were, to be sure, three or four bookshops before Al-Rabita, all specializing in English and French publications. However, although they offered works of the classics and some topical political books, contemporary works of literature—the novel, poetry, and criticism of the thirties and forties—were practically unknown. As my friend, the late Elie Kedourie, used to say rather disdainfully of certain members of our generation, "English literature, for them, ends with Oscar Wilde." The novelty of Al-Rabita bookshop, and of the circle of literary aspirants which it helped to create, was the introduction of what was considered to be the last word in literary fashion—in poetry, the works of T. S. Eliot, Ezra Pound, Auden, MacNiece, Spender, Barker, Edwin Muir; in fiction, the works of Joyce, Kafka, Mann, Koestler, Orwell, Greene, Warren, Trilling, and Bellow—not to speak of the host of little magazines fashionable at the time—*Partisan Review, Sewanee Review, Kenyon Review, Hudson Review,* and *Politics* from the United States; *Horizon, Scrutiny, Cornhill, Life,* and *Letters and Polemic* from Britain.

Among the young men whose acquaintance I made through the bookshop was Buland el-Haydari, a true bohemian and an as yet immature poet who was to become one of Iraq's leading pioneers of "the new poetry." Buland was born in the Kurdish province of Arbil in 1926 and came to Baghdad when a little boy. At the age of about fifteen, under the influence of Hussein Mardan, a fellow bohemian who taught him that the family was "the great killer," he left high school in midcourse and lived the life of a real tramp, roaming the streets during the day and sleeping in public parks and under the bridges of the Tigris at night. Feeling the gap in his education, he used to go into the public library and read anything that came to hand. At one point he "specialized" in psychology—so much so that he became a laughingstock among his friends as "Mr. Psycho."

Eventually, Buland published his first collection of poems, entitled, typically enough, "Heartthrob of the Mud" *(khafqat el-teen).* The book came out in 1946, when the poet was just turning twenty. It is impossible to say now whether he preceded everyone else in pioneering the practice of free verse in Arabic; but one thing is clear: Of the young Iraqi poets who started the fashion—and it was undoubtedly in Iraq that the fashion started—el-Haydari was in the forefront, together with Badr Shakir el-Sayyab, Rashid Yasin, Akram el-Witri, and others. It must be pointed out here that the introduction of free verse into Arabic amounted to a veritable literary revolution, and that such a development would have been unthinkable had these young men not come under the influence of modern and contemporary European poetry. To appreciate the significance of Buland's work in the development of modern Arabic poetry, I will point out here that the modernist movement was ushered in when he and his contemporaries shifted to free verse. For reasons which would be too academic to go into here, this shift to *vers libre* represented a radical movement in Arabic letters as a whole, ending as it did a tradition of rhymed, rhythmic poetry of some fifteen centuries' standing. Buland el-Haydari himself relates how he and his friends used to gather together and read aloud some of the works of contemporary British and American poets. In the Beirut weekly *Al-Usbu' al-'Arabi* of June 23, 1975, he confesses in an interview that, with their English being what it was, he and the others read these works usually in the presence, and with the help, of one whose knowledge of the language made it possible for them "to grasp the poetic dimensions of those experiments." He mentions the names of two of these early mentors: Jabra Ibrahim Jabra and Najib el-Mani.' His account, as printed in the Lebanese weekly, includes these remarks:

> During this period I came to know Jabra, who played a leading role in transferring the poetic experience to us. Also, my relations became closer with Najib el-Mani,' Hussein Hadawi, and Salman Mahmoud Hilmi. We used to frequent Al-Rabita Bookshop, where we met a Jewish intellectual by name of Nissim Rejwan, who used to make typed copies of any book of poetry that reached the store and sell it to us at a cheap price. Among those books I remember T. S. Eliot's *Four Quartets.*

I regret to say that here the poet's memory simply fails him. No one had the time to make typewritten copies of books or even of individual poems. What happened was that the books were sold at full price, and Buland and his friends were apparently willing to forgo a meal, a movie ticket, or even a visit to a brothel to purchase them.

Buland was one member of an intimate circle of young men whose friendship was based mainly on a shared interest in things of the mind. During endless hours spent in Café Suiss on Baghdad's main street in winter evenings and in open-air coffeehouses and restaurants on the banks of the Tigris in summer, some of the latest literary "discoveries" were endlessly discussed and analyzed: Orwell's *1984* and *Animal Farm,* Kafka's various works in their recent English rendering, the latest issues of *Polemic* of London or Dwight Macdonald's short-lived *Politics,* Pound's *Cantos,* Eliot's poetry and plays—and of course the mysteries of James Joyce's *Finnegans Wake.* Local developments, literary as well as political, were also a subject of long debates and discussions. Essentially, however, we tended to be apolitical.

When late in 1947, following adoption by the United Nations of the Partition Plan for Palestine, and the mass convulsion in Baghdad in reaction to the Portsmouth agreement between Iraq and Britain, Palestine again became the main subject of discussion and agitation, Buland composed two lines of traditional verse which fairly reflected the mood then prevailing in our circle—both among the Jews and the Muslims. (As far as I can recall, there were no Christians in that circle—except for Jabra, who later came to Baghdad as a refugee from Jerusalem.) It is highly difficult to render Buland's lines into English, partly because they are interspersed with colloquial idioms, words, and expressions. But this is a fairly faithful rendering:

> Do let the Jews have it, and good riddance!
> Our patience it has sorely tried,
> Depriving us of faith and all guidance.
> For far too long we have been plied
> With its troublesome palaver.
> Will this stranglehold go on forever?
> For how much longer will it hold us in thrall?
> By God we are sick and tired of it all!

During this troublesome period, just following the Arabs' defeat in the war of 1948 with Israel, a young Briton made his appearance in Baghdad. His name was Desmond Stewart, and as a kind of identity card he brought with him an English rendering of one of Plato's *Dialogues.* He worked in the English section of the local radio station as well as getting a job teaching English. When the authorities discovered that he broadcast talks that no one had authorized, he was given the sack but managed to keep his teaching job and stayed on in Baghdad for some time. Stewart, who in the meantime has written a number of books on the Middle East as well as a recent study of Theodor Herzl, was an anti-Semite in the classical Western sense of the term. Out to capitalize on recent events in Palestine and what he judged to be growing Arab resentment against Jews, he started discreetly to circulate a little pamphlet he had brought with him from England. It consisted of eight or so pages and contained the text of a long poem of his that seemed to contain all the conceivable anti-Jewish sentiments and allegations constituting the main gist of the anti-Semitic doctrine current in Western Europe in the nineteenth and early twentieth centuries. The poem, composed in an old-style epic vein, included crass statements such as "And Jews are the descendants of the Devil . . ."

Stewart's poem, of course, was meant to be addressed precisely to the kind of young educated, English-speaking Arabs who were part of or frequented our small circle. But he had a little unforeseen problem on his hand: The circle included two or three Jews who somehow seemed to be quite at home in it and shared a high spirit of friendship and camaraderie with the Muslims. Finally he found a solution. He gave copies of the pamphlet to the Muslim members of the circle, beseeching them not to show it to me and extracting a promise from them accordingly.

But the ploy didn't work. After reading the broadsheet in verse, one at least of my Muslim friends, Najeeb, told me all about it and gave me the pamphlet to read. I never confronted Stewart with this; it just seemed of so little significance, especially since the poem had no influence whatever on the people around us.

As a matter of fact, all the seemingly world-shaking events of the times—the United Nations Partition Plan for Palestine, the Portsmouth Treaty between Iraq and Britain, and the popular convulsion in the streets of Baghdad which came in its wake, the dispatch of an army to Palestine and its defeat there at the hands of "the Zionist bandits," and the wave of persecution and harassments to which the Jews of Iraq were subjected subsequently—all these and many more developments occurred without relations between Jews and non-Jews in our circle being affected in the least.

Not that there was an attempt to ignore these events or gloss them over. Quite the contrary. Sometimes, indeed, there developed some fairly heated discussions over the rights and wrongs of the Arab-Jewish conflict in Palestine. These debates were conducted due only to the fact that two of our members held what was taken then to be the Pan-Arab and Arab nationalist position and were really perturbed by what was happening in Palestine. Khaldun Sat'i al-Husri, eldest son of the man who is considered to be the founder and leading ideologist of modern Arab nationalism, was then teaching at some high school or college in Baghdad and was endlessly preoccupied with the problem of Palestine, following events in the Holy Land day by day. I myself was not really interested in "politics," although when it came to the subject of Jews and Palestine I had my own, admittedly amateurish opinions. I remember one quite fierce discussion with Khaldun, who was discoursing in his quiet, soft-spoken way on the injustice done to the Palestinian Arabs by the decision to partition their land and establish a Jewish state there. When he spoke of the role of the Jews or the Zionists and how they had managed to "take" the land from its rightful owners, I remember arguing in reply—not very profoundly I am afraid—that it was not the Arabs of Palestine that the Jews fought and took the land from, but the British. Now, with the advantage of hindsight and the experience of thirty-five years, I consider that argument to be shaky and the remark positively vicious. But I recall very distinctly that no one among my listeners, not even Khaldun, took it amiss, and we habitually turned to the other, more interesting topics of our usual discussion.

The last I heard of Khaldun Sat'i al-Husri was that he was working as lecturer at the Arab University of Beirut and wrote a number of books—one of them, in English, is about the fathers of the modernist movement in Islam. The other Pan-Arab nationalist in the group was 'Adnan Raouf, with whom I shared far too many interests— including literature, and just plain companionship—for him to allow his political views to interfere in our friendship. To be sure, there were the usual differences of opinion about the subject of Palestine and the Jews. I remember giving him John Hersey's *The Wall* to read and that he was deeply touched by it. (It had then just come out.) But we were definitely more interested in exchanging pleasantries and jokes than in engaging in futile discussions about the topics of the day.

I don't know exactly what has happened to 'Adnan by now. But in the late sixties, he worked for his government in New York as deputy ambassador at the United Nations. Knowing of this from the papers, I decided to establish some sort of contact with him, however indirectly. I found an occasion in the winter of 1969. Ronald Sanders of *Midstream*—which was then edited by the late Shlomo Katz—had asked me to write an article depicting a composite profile of an East Jerusalem intellectual; and as the subject appealed to me greatly I did this promptly, and the piece was printed in the February 1969 issue of the magazine ("The Chequered Career of Gassan Hamzawi," pp. 3–20).

Knowing 'Adnan was in New York and out of harm's reach—for how would I have a Jewish Agency publication sent to him at the Foreign Ministry in Baghdad?—I asked Sanders to send a copy of the issue to him at the UN Headquarters. He did—and in a letter dated February 20 and addressed to me, Sanders wrote: "I sent a copy of the February issue, as you requested, to 'Adnan Raouf, and today we received from him the following letter, which I quote in full: 'Thank you for your letter of 13 February 1969, and for the February issue of *Midstream*. I should like to thank Mr. Rejwan directly for his kind attention, and I would welcome your advice as to how this could be done.' I of course sent him your address, and I presume you'll hear from him soon."

Interestingly enough, Sanders added the following story:

"The next day after sending out the 'marked copy' to him, Shlomo (Katz) had begun having second thoughts. He feared that we were perhaps getting somebody in trouble (we had sent it, of course, in care of the Iraqi UN delegation—now we have his home address, which I will give you below), and I was inclined to agree. Everything seems Okay now, however, and Shlomo has suddenly become very excited about being in touch with a real live Arab diplomat this way . . ."

Giving me the home address, Sanders added he thought I should use it rather than the U.N. one—and concluded: "Let me know what happens."

Well, nothing happened! For one thing, owing to reasons which cannot be listed here, I refrained from writing to 'Adnan, much as I wanted to do so. So there was no communication. For another—and here lies the real reason why he never came around to writing me personally to thank me—I had asked Sanders to continue sending 'Adnan new issues of *Midstream* as they came out—and as luck would have it, the very next issue of the magazine, the March one, carried an article of mine on the notorious hangings in Baghdad involving a number of plainly innocent Jews who chose to stay and work in Iraq after the mass exodus of the early fifties. Among those hanged was an old friend of mine, and my article was of course condemnatory of the massacre anyway. It so happened, too, that precisely at that juncture 'Adnan was finally appointed Iraq's ambassador at the U.N., succeeding Adnan al-Pachachi, who was said to have resigned his post in disgust or despair at his government's behavior in general. It was therefore quite out of the question to expect 'Adnan to write a letter to an Israeli address, and I respected his reticence and did not want to embarrass him in any way. I explained this in a letter to Sanders dated March 17, adding: "Incidentally, he has accused Israel of organizing a worldwide campaign against his country—so I am afraid that when he reads my article in the March *Midstream* he may see it as part of that campaign. He should know better though."

Khaldun and 'Adnan were really exceptional in holding Pan-Arab convictions, at least in the circles in which I mixed. My nominal boss at the bookshop, Abdel Fattah Ibrahim, was a social democrat by conviction and had little respect for the kind of xenophobia that then went by the name of Arab nationalism. George Orwell used to call the ideology he believed in "democratic Socialism," and (as Bernard Crick relates in his excellent biography) used to insist on writing it with a small "d" and a capital "S." This is exactly how I would today describe the political position of Abdel Fattah.

When I started working for the bookshop he had for some time resigned a very senior government position (as director-general of the Ministry of Education) because of differences of opinion with the minister and also because he was dissatisfied with the whole system generally. Shortly after opening the store, he initiated the formation of a political party and started a daily—both leading the party and editing its newspaper. Neither lasted for very long, and when the party was banned, the paper had already been ordered to stop publication. I remember, with some embarrassment I must admit, that when he made an appearance in the bookshop the day he learned about the ban on his party, I said something to the effect that perhaps one should congratulate him on the occasion. Seeing he was not amused, I asked seriously whether he was sad—and why. "You don't seem to understand," he said with real sadness. "How should I put it? It's like the death of a baby you've begotten, tended, and cared for for a certain period of time."

I was, of course, extremely touched and left it at that. Not that there had not been differences of opinion and heated discussions between us. I recall one occasion on which I debated with him the whole subject of democracy and whether it was "practicable" in Iraq in the circumstances. Again I am afraid it was basically a half-baked idea of mine, but I remember clearly arguing for hours with Abdel Fattah about it. My "stand" was that, although I wholeheartedly agreed with his views about the desirability both of democracy and socialism, I was not sure Iraq and the Iraqi people were "mature for democracy." Endlessly he reasoned with me on this point, explaining with exemplary patience that there was no such thing as a people unfit for a democratic system of government. Now in retrospect, having seen how democracy and parliamentarism can be manipulated and prostituted in the best and most "advanced" of societies, I tend to agree with his viewpoint. Indeed I have come to believe that, whether illiterate or educated, wild or civilized, the so-called man in the street tends to have a kind of "gutsy" healthy instinct about regimes and rulers that is not always displayed by the politically sophisticated members of the society.

There was of course no trace of anti-Jewish feeling or prejudice in Abdel Fattah Ibrahim. Shortly after the rout of the Arab armies in Palestine in 1948, however, I thought I began to detect in his talks with me a feeling of sadness—which bordered on resentment sometimes—about the turn things were taking. "The Arabs have a very long memory," he said to me one day when news from the front finally indicated that the Arab armies were not making any headway. "They are not likely ever to forget this humiliation." He always spoke of "them" when referring to the Arabs, never of "us." I am certain this was by no means an attempt on his part to dissociate himself from fellow Arabs and coreligionists. It was simply that detachment which one usually finds in the true intellectual. And he said what he said neither with anger nor bitterness—nor even with a sense of real involvement. It was, rather, a kind of warning, a grim prophecy concerning the shape of things to come. It must also have been a subtle comment on the way in which I myself reacted to those events, making no attempt whatsoever to hide my pleasure and satisfaction at the course of events.

I don't think Abdel Fattah was an anti-Zionist. (Nor, of course, was he a Zionist.) But he had a great deal of empathy for the Jews and the Jewish problem. "You Jews," he said to me on another occasion, "are the salt of the earth. How do you think you are going to manage to live in a state of your own—all cooped up together in one place and having solely yourselves to deal with, depend on each other, earn your livelihood one from the other?" Then, no doubt reflecting on the trouble he himself was having with his own government and his own people, he said in a gesture of mock-desperation mingled with his typical good humor: "All right! Have it your own way! Have a bloody state of your own! Come to think of it, why should we be the only sufferers? You will soon discover what a burden it entails!"

Abdel Fattah was especially eager that I personally should know what I was doing when I took the decision to leave Iraq permanently and go to Israel. "If," he said to me on one occasion, "if you imagine for a moment that you are nearer, in outlook and temperament, to a Jew, say from Germany, Russia, or Poland, than you are to me or to Iraqis in general then you are quite simply mistaken. You just don't know what you are in for!" But I remained coolly unconvinced—and after that he quietly gave up trying.

★ ★ ★ ★ ★

AL-RABITA AND AFTER

One morning in summer 1948, some six weeks after the first truce was proclaimed in the first Arab-Israeli war, a letter was brought to the bookshop by special messenger. Addressed to me and marked "personal," it read in full:

Dear Rejwan,

Owing to the prevailing depression of business I find it necessary to cut down our expenditure on editorial contributions. It is with regret therefore that I have to inform you that as and from the end of this month we will be unable to publish book reviews and we will also have to stop film criticism.

You will appreciate that I did not wish to take this step but am forced into it by the fact that business is so bad.

With kind regards,

Yours sincerely,

G. Reid Anderson, Editor.
The Iraq Times

The letter was dated July 24, which gave me a mere week's notice. Needless to say, no radical change was noticeable in the business of *The Iraq Times* to call for the use of the term "depression." Moreover, my immediate reaction—an offer to write for lower remuneration or contribute fewer reviews or both—was politely turned down. With the situation of the Jews of Iraq worsening day by day, my suspicions grew, and these were eventually confirmed when Anderson's secretary Marcelle, a friend of sorts, told me that the letter was dictated to her by telephone from the British Embassy, where the editor paid regular weekly visits on Saturdays (the paper did not appear on Sundays).

I never could find out whether this urgent action was taken as a result of the house search to which I was subjected by error or by the fact that the powers-that-be at the embassy had decided it was unwise for *The Iraq Times* to have a Jew as its sole book and movie reviewer. Be that as it may, the last contribution I was to make to the pages of *The Iraq Times* was a special assignment made by the editor a few months after my services to the paper were terminated—a full-page survey of the year in contemporary Iraqi literature that appeared in the special Christmas—New Year number in December 1948.

The piece was well received, both by members of our circlre, many of whom figured in the article, and by outsiders including the young Englishman who was then director of the British Council in Baghdad.

For almost two years following the termination of my work for the *Times* I continued working with Abdul Fattah and the Al-Rabita Association. In addition to the bookshop, Abdul Fattah had planned to establish a printing plant and a publishing firm and we were then busy ordering the machinery and building the plant. I did all the correspondence and the bookkeeping involved in these operations as well as running the bookshop, ordering books and periodicals, keeping the accounts, and acting as sole salesman.

As 1950 came along, the machines at hand and the plant firmly erected, Abdul Fattah started having second thoughts about the bookshop. He thought, rightly, that the business was no longer paying its way—or just about doing that and nothing more. The fact was that, with a completely free hand and little thought about the business side, I was ordering almost anything that caught my fancy and there was simply no market for such books, either for lack of interest or lack of money. To confound the situation, Abdul Fattah himself ordered books rather indiscriminately—weighty, expensive books whose only merit was that they were "good" or "important" or "essential," regardless of whether they were salable. The result was that by the end of 1949 we had on our hands a variegated stock of books of history, philosophy, sociology, science, literature and poetry that few individuals could afford to buy and whose only potential purchasers were libraries and academic institutions. Abdul Fattah decided to transfer the books to the new building so that he could manage the printing and publishing as well as the book ends of the enterprise from his office. This left me with precious little to do and, since by that time I had already been toying with the idea of emigration, I declined an offer to work on a part-time basis and left Al-Rabita at the end of March 1950.

It wasn't long after my departure from Al-Rabita that I and mother went to the *Mas'uda Shemtob* Synagogue in *Bustan el-Khas* which was volunteered by the Jewish community temporarily to house the offices and officials dealing with Jews who wanted to surrender their Iraqi nationality and emigrate to Israel. Simha, my sister, had safely arrived in Israel by then and just over eight thousand Jews had registered for emigration. It was shortly before the stampede caused by the bombs thrown or planted in Jewish institutions and resulting in quite a few injuries—bombs no one knows to this day precisely who planted though some continue to claim the Zionists were the real culprits, attempting to cause panic and accelerate the exodus.

The synagogue was fairly quiet that morning, with no long lines and only a few Jewish activists from the movement offering counsel and guidance to those who came to register for emigration. It took us just a few brief moments to sign the necessary documents and get the makeshift certificates that allowed us to leave the country for good. I still have those two documents and I often wonder at the ease and speed with which the whole fateful "transaction" was finalized.

NAJIB AL-MANI' AND SCOTT FITZGERALD

Sometime in the late 1980s, having read his byline in the literary pages of the London based Saudi daily *Al-Sharq al-Awsat* and learning that he was working for the paper as a freelancer, I made bold to write a brief note to Najib al-Mani' saying hello and seeking to establish contact with him. The letter, sent care of the paper, was never answered, either because it never reached Najib, reached him with the inevitable office gossip that he was getting mail from Israel, found him bewildered and possibly a little frightened that such contact could be established—or for all these things put together.

Of Buland el-Haidari and 'Adnan Raouf I have already written elsewhere. But it was really in Najib that I found the most intimate and satisfying intellectual and emotional match. Gentle, somewhat shy, wise for his age and extremely receptive to ideas, Najib was an insatiable reader and had somehow picked up a knowledge of English, by no means common among our group. We could talk about Kafka, whose books we read concurrently, for hours on end—or about Sartre's *Nausea* which had just come out in English, making analogies between what was described there and our own situation as some sort of caged intellectuals. It was a period when many landmarks in contemporary literature were coming out—Orwell's *1984* and *Animal Farm,* the English translations of *The Stranger* and other works by Camus, renderings of Rilke, the poetry and plays of Lorca, and Thomas Mann's *Doctor Faustus;* Cyril Connolly's *Horizon* was still coming out and *Partisan Review* was in its heyday; in all these and many other intellectual treasures I and Najib shared. We pondered them, discussed and analysed them for hours on end sitting mostly in an open-air cafe on the Tigris not far from where I lived. I have no idea how Najib found the time, in the end, to prepare his lessons or even how he managed to graduate from the Law College where he was studying. Shortly before I left Baghdad, he wrote me a long letter, full of sweet sentiments and very appreciative and sad—a sort of farewell letter that I took with me to Israel, where it somehow disappeared from where I knew I had put it. I often think that some idiot from the Shin Beth, Israel's internal security services, took it as evidence of my alleged Communist affiliations—or even worse—after secretly searching our tin hut in the Talpiot transit camp.

It was only in the late 1960s that I finally heard from Najib. An Iraqi Jew who came to Israel shortly after the Six-Day War, a journalist, brought me regards from my old friend, who was then working for the Ministry of Foreign Affairs. From time to time I had seen Najib's name in certain periodicals published in Beirut, sometimes as the author of a short story, a book review, or a critical essay—and on the rare occaisons when I was abroad I always had the urge to call Baghdad, to see if I could find him at home or at work. But the situation being what it was then, I always resisted.

One day, in the summer of 1971, while chatting with Mahmoud Abu Zalaf in his office—he was then editor of the East Jerusalem daily *Al-Quds,* I spotted a slim paperback lying on one of the side desks. It was one of the famous Egyptian fiction series published monthly by *Dar el Hilal* in Cairo, but the book struck me as something I wouldn't have expected a series like that to care much about. The Arabic title was *Gatsbi el-'Azeem* and it took me a few seconds to link it with the original work—Scott Fitzgerald's masterpiece, *The Great Gatsby.* My curiousity was certainly piqued as to who might have taken the trouble to translate it and how it came to pass that a series like *Riwayat el Hilal* decided to publish it. When I picked it up and looked at the title page, I read: "translated by Najib al-Mani' and edited by Jabra Ibrahim Jabra." Naturally, I asked Abu Zalaf if I could borrow the book.

I was curious about the quality of the translation and in going over some passages found it quite good—something of a feat, in fact, considering the original. There were also two biographical notes, one for the translator and one for the editor. I had known that Najib was born in a small town near Basra but I didn't know he was two years my junior. The back cover mentioned he was a graduate of the Law College, that he had a special interest in English and French, that he wrote "a number of short stories and articles in Iraqi and Arab periodicals," that he was a Foreign Ministry official, and that he was presently at work translating a selection from the speeches and letters of Abraham Lincoln. This meant that during an interval of more than twenty years, Najib hadn't yet managed to publish a book of his own.

This didn't surprise me, knowing how fastidious Najib would be about anything he wrote. Eight years later, though, I finally did stumble upon a book of his at the Muhtasib Bookshop in East Jerusalem—a novel with the striking title *Tamas el Mudun,* a fairly untranslatable phrase which I would render as *A Proximity of Cities* or *Cities Chafe.* I thought it was artfully done, written with taste and economy. It dealt with a period not known to me—the fifties and sixties—but I still thought I could detect some of the characters and identify the places in it.

After nearly ten years during which I heard nothing either from or about Najib, a friend sent me photocopies of parts of *Al-Ightirab al-Adabi,* a literary quarterly published in England and devoted to the works of writers and poets living in exile, mainly Iraqis who found they couldn't do their work in the suffocating atmosphere of Ba'ath dominated Iraq. To my shock and grief, the first several articles were tributes by friends and fellow emigre writers and intellectuals to the work and personality of Najib al-Mani', who had died suddenly of heart failure one night in his flat in London, alone among his thousands of books and classical records.

Feeling the urge to know more about my unfortunate friend and seeing that Najib's sister Samira was *Al-Ightirab's* assistant editor, I wrote her a long letter of condolence, asking her to tell me more about her brother's years in exile. Did he die a happy man? Was he married? Did he live with someone? Did he have any children? All I could learn from the tributes was that his room was scattered with books and records and papers. Damn the books, I murmured to myself, being then right in the midst of a colossal operation aimed at getting rid of some two-thirds of my private library.

Samira's reply was as prompt as it was touching and detailed. "Dear Nissim Rejwan," it read in part, "The name I heard Najib mention so often. I also saw the photograph of you two together in a cafe on the banks of the Tigris in Baghdad in those long gone days . . ." The story she had to tell about Najib's fortune and fate seems typical of so many other Iraqi writers and intellectuals who had gone into exile. After spending most of the 1950s and 1960s in relative comfort, occupying high official positions—including director general of the Ministry for Foreign Affairs, director of the Iraqi Petroleum Company, and others—Najib came to London in 1979 "for some fresh air," leaving behind his wife, three sons, and a daughter. Shortly afterwards, with the outbreak of the Iran-Iraq War, two of the sons were sent to the front, so Najib's wife was unable to leave for London and join her husband. To complicate matters even further, the daughter married while he was abroad and her husband left her shortly thereafter, for Holland, where he stayed. As to Najib's last years in London, Samira described them like this: "He lived alone with his lame cat in a flat in London . . . He died in the company of someone he loved, his open book on Najib's chest. Is there anyone better than Proust in situations like these?"

So it was Proust that he was reading on his last night—Proust, whose works we all got to know in the 1940s and which, at least in their English renderings, were first made available in Iraq by the Al-Rabita Bookshop. Truth to tell, I found myself regretting the scanty part I myself had played in Najib's incessant preoccupation with works of literature—apparently to the exclusion of much else by way of real life. Reading the words of appreciation written about Najib—two of which were by close friends who evoked their youthful memories of him—I found myself mourning not only Najib but that whole world of our youth which seems lost forever. I caught myself pondering the question as to how many young men and women in Baghdad today—forty-five years later—are even remotely aware of the kind of writers or literary works that so preoccupied our thoughts and consumed our spare time?

—*Nissim Rejwan*

SHIMON BALLAS

SHIMON BALLAS was born in Baghdad in 1930 and emigrated to Israel in 1951. A major novelist, Ballas has published ten works of fiction, several important studies on contemporary Arabic literature, and numerous translations from Arabic. Although he began his career in Arabic, Ballas switched to Hebrew in the mid-1960s. Since then, Ballas, perhaps more than any other Israeli writer, has opened a window onto the political and psychological life of the contemporary Arab world, both at home and in exile. Although generally pigeon-holed by the literary establishment as a "realistic" writer, his works consistently defy categorization; they include the first Israeli novel to depict life amongst the Arab Jewish immigrants of the 1950s (*The Transit Camp,* 1964), the portrayal of a Palestinian architect returning home for a visit after years in Europe (*A Locked Room,* 1980), the depiction of a community of Middle Eastern political exiles in Paris (*Last Winter,* 1984), and the ruminations of a Jewish historian converted to Islam in Baghdad during the 1980s (*The Other One,* 1991). Other books by Ballas include: *Facing the Wall* (1969), *Esav from Baghdad* (1970), *Clarification* (1972), *Downtown* (1979), *The Heir* (1987), and *Not in Her Place* (1994). His important study *Arab Literature Under the Shadow of War,* which had begun as his doctoral thesis for the Sorbonne, appeared in 1978. He continues to write critical works in Arabic, the most recent of which, *Secular Trends in Arabic Literature,* appeared with the Iraqi exile publishing house al-Kamel Verlag, in Cologne, Germany. He is presently working on a historical novel based on the life of James (Yaqob) Sanua, the Egyptian Jewish nationalist, playwright, and satirist who opened a theater in Cairo in 1870. Recent translations of his work are due to appear in Arabic in Beirut. Ballas teaches in the Department of Arabic Literature at Haifa University and also spends part of the year in Paris, where he does most of his writing. The text included here, *Iya,* is remarkable for the lengths Ballas has gone to to rethink very fundamental assumptions; told from the point of view

of Iya, a Muslim maid working for a Jewish family on the eve of their departure from Iraq in 1951, Ballas turns the accepted terms of discourse about identity, home, displacement, and exile on their head. Here, the tragedy is depicted from the point of view of those who stay rather than those who have been forced to leave. As in all of his work, the very dense and complex nature of a layered identity is woven into the narrative itself to the point that readers are challenged not only to rethink the issues he raises but also, more importantly, the very role and possibilities of "conventional" or "realist" fiction.

AT HOME IN EXILE:
AN INTERVIEW WITH SHIMON BALLAS BY AMMIEL ALCALAY

Starting with education, practically and in a wider sense, how were you formed as a writer?

One has to go very far back, to early childhood. I was always attracted to writing. I connected it to stories told at home and I used to try and write them down for myself. I was always a little reticent to show them to anyone, I was scared of criticism. I was also very drawn to reading. In comparison to my friends at school, though, I actually read less. They swallowed books, I did too, but I would think about them and contemplate things more, I would write notes. By the third or fourth grade we read a lot of translations from French. Adventure stories, Arsin Lupin, Alexandre Dumas. And also things like *Les Misérables.* Most of the translations were done in Egypt, from the 1920s to the 1940s, and most were of Romantic literature, but not always the best. That was our fare. And versions of *The Thousand and One Nights* or La Fontaine for kids. I went to the Alliance so by the fourth grade I could read French. But I didn't like the books they gave us—children's stories, or eighteenth-century stories about aristocratic families.

The question of a colonial language didn't seem to be so crucial in Iraq. When I think, for instance, of things Etel Adnan has written about French in Lebanon, or things that Edmond Jabès has written about Egypt, it seems to me that you had the freedom to say— "this is a bore, I'll go back to Arabic"—something that wasn't possible in places where the colonial language was more dominant.

For someone like Jabès, French was also the language spoken at home; it was the primary language—they didn't have an Arabic option. For me, reading Arabic was a pleasure, the material available was a lot more interesting, a lot more exciting. When I was a little older, I could read literature that I liked in French. I read world literature in French, I read English literature in French. For example, the book that drew me to the Communist party in quite a romantic way when I was fifteen was Jack London's *The Iron Heel,* which I read in French, with all the footnotes. Though my source for world literature was French, I loved Arabic and it was the language I wrote in so the situation was quite different than under more extreme forms of colonial rule.

When did you start reading modern Arab writers?

At that age, I read more in Arabic translation. When I was twelve or thirteen, I discovered Gibran. I learned whole sections by heart, I would imitate him. I read everything including the books written in English and translated into Arabic. I also read Taha Hussein. Those were the two major Arab writers for me then. I wasn't particularly drawn to Tewfiq al-Haqim, for instance. But at the same time I was very drawn to the newspapers even though they were in a pretty sorry state then in Iraq. In terms of journalism, Iraq was a province of Egypt whose dailies and weeklies came to us with their literary supplements and higher standards. I subscribed through one of the news dealers. We had a deal where I would go twice a day to take the newspapers and magazines—since I didn't have enough money to buy them all—and read them quickly before bringing them back so he could resell them at a discount. From that I went on to more serious literature. My French had gotten better, so I could read more complex works. But Arabic was the only language in which reading was a real pleasure. For those of my generation, the state of modern Arabic prose—in terms of the novel and short-story forms—was still in gestation. I think only the generation younger than mine grew up on authentic Arabic literature. We didn't have that experience, we grew up much more on translated literature, there was always this orientation towards the West, that's where the influences were supposed to come from. I didn't get interested in writers like Naguib Mahfouz until later.

What about the theater, the movies?

I used to see several movies a day, going from cinema to cinema. I saw anything that came, inevitably this meant American films from Hollywood. I went to Arabic movies more for the music. There was a time when I wanted to be an actor. There was an Egyptian actor that I worshipped, Yusuf Wahbi, very theatrical, very exaggerated in his roles, and I would try to imitate him. I even signed up with a group of theater enthusiasts that started in Baghdad then, I must have been fourteen. But nothing came of it so I went back to what I felt more secure in, sitting in front of a piece of paper and writing. In the Alliance I wrote short stories which I still didn't show anyone, but I had two friends who also loved writing and we would discuss things together. My first novel was a detective story set in Baghdad. Then we lived in the old city of Baghdad in a small house and in the evenings I used to go out to the cafes and sit in a corner and write. That's where I wrote the novel. I also kept a diary that I would conclude every year with a notebook of memories so that I could assess what I had gone through in the previous year, judging it from more of a distance.

From where do you think this need to write comes?

I think it's simply the need for expression, to see yourself, to see yourself in relation to your surroundings, to recall your experiences, to give them some kind of value simply by putting them down on paper, as if they had happened to someone else even if no one ever reads of them. I burned all of that stuff before I left Iraq and I am extremely sorry about that; it was such a long period, the period of coming to maturity, the period in which a person is formed. Now I have to try and recollect everything and I can't remember. It's all gone, cut off, just this barrier left between myself and that time.

When you finished the Alliance, did you think of going further in your studies?

I wanted to go on studying literature, history, languages, but I was already in the Party by the age of sixteen. I'm from a family that, from an economic standpoint, was quite poor, but our social standing was middle class. A middle class that was very marginalized, very far from political involvement and very far, as well, from the day-to-day life of the poor, the kinds of neighborhoods that many Jews lived in. I grew up in the Christian Quarter where Jews of a higher status lived. In effect, I was cut off from two things: There was no political life and there was little contact with the lives of plain people.

What was the role of Judaism in all of this? What kind of a Judaism do you remember from this period?

The question of Judaism was very much a part of things, but not particularly so. My father was often away from home, he was a merchant and he had a shop in the south of Iraq so he only came home to visit, once a month for a few days or a week, so we grew up under my mother's wing. And when my father came home he went to synagogue on Friday night and Saturday morning, and often took us with him. But he did this because he was used to it, he went to the synagogue because that's what was done, to see his friends, to talk. At the Alliance there was only an hour of Hebrew which wasn't counted in our final grade so we didn't really give it much thought. When I came to Israel I barely knew the alphabet because after grade school even this hour of Hebrew wasn't given. Of course on the holidays, like Passover, we read the *Haggada* and did everything we were supposed to do. But the question of Judaism or religion did not play a great role. Maybe this was because we didn't live in a Jewish neighborhood where there was a full Jewish life, and we were distanced from that kind of experience. In an odd way, I was really lacking traditional Jewish roots. As I said, what brought me to communism was much more what I got through books, the romantic dreams, the romantic hero who stands for freedom, who stands up for things. I wrote about poor people, a porter carrying a huge load who fell leaving his children fatherless, things like that. This is in the mid-1940s. The war years were very tempestuous, very fertile in Baghdad. After the failed coup of Rashid Ali, there was more freedom to be active in public—various parties got permits and the Communist party also came out into the open and I was quite involved. I even had a short stint as a movie critic for one of the new papers, but I was always in search of a group where I could express myself, where I would find people with whom I could share knowledge and ideas. And it turned out that the connection came through a friend of mine from the Alliance. One day he told me that his brother had weekly meetings with a group of people where they discussed Marxism and all kinds of things. Baghdad developed to the south and there were real villas built there, primarily by Jews. And that's where they met. I just said, hey man, I'm dying for this kind of thing, do me a favor, get me in somehow. A few weeks later, everything was arranged but the first meeting was a disappointment. I was expecting them to invite me to one of those villas, instead I was told to come to a cafe in one of the poor Shiite neighborhoods, with a sign on it saying "For Muslims Only." I got there, it was winter, the place was filled with smoke, people sitting around playing dominos and *shesh-besh* and here I am carrying my books and a copy of *al-Mukhtar* which still comes out, it's a selection of articles from *Reader's Digest* translated into Arabic! With my copy of *al-Mukhtar* —and I'm supposed to be some kind of an "intellectual" —we sat around the table, four or five people, all dressed very modestly, one was a shoemaker. They asked me some questions about my studies, about my reading. The secretary of the cell asked me to explain the difference between idealism and materialism. Materialism, I said, that's pretty simple—a materialistic person loves money and possessions while an idealist is someone who loves great ideals, very romantic. He listened and smiled a little saying, I see, you're explaining it from a poetic point of view. Who else can explain it? The shoemaker started in, explaining the difference replete with references to Marx and Hegel and here I was, the most highly "educated." I just felt like disappearing.

As a child of what you have described as the somewhat marginalized but aspiring middleclass, you discovered a different city made of different people through your political involvement in Baghdad. When you came to Israel and got involved with the Communist party, what stood out for you?

I remember meeting Meir Wilner, one of the leaders of the party in the very first weeks after emigrating and he started asking me all kinds of questions about Syria, about the people, general information, because there had just been a *coup d'état* there. This was a shock for me. I didn't understand what was going on. Here was a leader of the party, for the first time in my life I was talking to a party leader, a member of Parliament, and he was asking me, a new immigrant from Iraq, the most trivial questions. It took me a long time to figure out that, essentially, I represented a different world altogether and this somehow always obligated me to explain something. No matter where I was when something happened in the Arab world people would ask: What do you say about that, what's your opinion? This obligation pressured me into becoming informed so that I would be *prepared* to answer when people asked me, and that is how I found myself writing my first article in Hebrew about the religious leader Afghani and later on becoming the editor of Arab Affairs for the Communist newspaper *Kol Ha'am*. Again, it was reality that pushed me into fulfilling some sort of a function here, of serving as a connection to this world that was not only seen as being in a state of war and perpetual hostility but was totally and absolutely alien. And this includes everyone, not just the Zionist parties or the Right but the Communist party as well. I wrote a lot on Arabic literature and culture. I also did the anthology of Palestinian stories that came out in 1969. You begin to think that if you don't do these things then no one else will, so it becomes a role that you have to fulfill, a duty that you have to take upon yourself. And the fact is that I began writing about Palestinian literature. No one had heard of Ghassan Kanafani before my translations of his short stories. Emile Habiby was also unknown as a writer when I began writing about him. Although I left the Communist party in 1961, my political positions remained unchanged and I continued to write on social and cultural issues.

In the early 1970s you were in Paris, can you say something about that?

Finally, here was the great dream coming true. It brought back memories of those days in Baghdad, just before I emigrated to Israel when I was working as an aide to the Jewish senator Ezra Menahem Daniel. Just after making the arrangements to go to Israel, I was informed that I had been chosen for a scholarship that he had set up to study at the Sorbonne, but it was already too late. Instead of the Sorbonne, I ended up in a transit camp. This time, twenty years later, it was through a grant my wife had gotten. I was working as a correspondent for a number of Israeli papers and writing; doing anything at the Sorbonne was the farthest thing from my mind. Through a series of circumstances related to an article I was preparing, I did end up at the Sorbonne where I presented my doctoral thesis; this became my book *Arabic Literature Under the*

Shadow of War which I wrote in French and later translated into Hebrew and Arabic. That was the start of my academic career. We go to Paris often and most of my books have been written there.

Earlier you spoke about taking on certain roles, providing people with access into unknown areas. If we look at your books, in many ways each of them takes readers, particularly mainstream Israeli readers, into unknown and perhaps even unimaginable realms. At the same time, your work is curiously disconnected from the bulk of modern Hebrew literature.

I think it was Ehud Ben Ezer who wrote that *Last Winter* did not depict Paris as an Israeli but as if a Parisian had written about exiles in Paris. This is also true for *The Other One.* A number of people commented that this book could have been written in Arabic by an Iraqi. The fact that it was in Hebrew was not particularly significant. Even though I am a Hebrew writer and I write in Hebrew, I am not affiliated with Hebrew literature.

I almost see the different experiences you represent in your books as filling various pockets of empty space that exist in the Israeli imagination, or as if you were building a counternarrative alongside those pockets of empty space, as an alternative. The question of language and ideology has only come to the forefront in Israeli literature relatively recently through the work of Anton Shammas, the idea that Hebrew is simply a language that can be used by anyone who happens to be using it. But I think this has been implicit in all your work, the use of language as a tool that is simply a tool, without mystification.

And without the Judeocentrism that has characterized Hebrew literature. I also feel this but it is very difficult to pin down. I think that for me the transition to another language is crucial, the use of language as a means. Yet language is not only a tool, language is also part of the personality. That's what makes this transition so difficult: you have to literally reconstruct yourself, you recreate yourself through a borrowed language.

But your Hebrew, in its semantic structure and content doesn't carry all the baggage of people raised within the context of Zionist ideology. This is one of the reasons why your work isn't very well understood. People immersed in this context have no real way of assessing what you do since what you are doing isn't really within their consciousness as a possibility nor would it be considered particularly desirable as something to strive for or even think about.

Now we've really put our finger on it, this takes us into the realm of ideology, ideology as a world view, of Judaism, of Israel, of Hebrew, and the total identity between Hebrew and the Jews. I'm a Jew by chance, it doesn't play that much of a role with me. Zionist ideology is essentially an Ashkenazi ideology that developed in a different culture, in different surroundings, in a different world and which came to claim its stake here in the Middle East through alienation and hostility towards the surroundings, with a rejection of the surroundings, with no acceptance of the environment. I don't accept any of this, this is all very different from what I am. I am not in conflict with the environment, I came from the Arab environment and I remain in constant colloquy with the Arab environment. I also didn't change my environment. I just moved from one place to another within it. The whole project of a nationalist conception, of Zionist ideology, of the Jewish point of view, the bonds between Jews in the diaspora and Israel, all of this is quite marginal for me and doesn't play a major role, it's not part of my cultural world. I am not in dialogue with the nationalistic or Zionist point of view, nor am I in dialogue with Hebrew literature. I am not conducting a dialogue with them. If anything, I am in dialogue with language itself. On the one hand, I am trying to fend off, avoid or neutralize ideological connections or associations within the language. On the other hand, I think that I am probably trying to bring my Hebrew closer and closer to Arabic. This isn't done through syntax, but maybe through some sense of structure or way of approaching things. It is very abstract and I don't do it in a way that is completely conscious either. That's the problem, and it is extremely difficult to describe or quantify.

If you take your books and put them next to the work of Yusuf Idris or Jabra Ibrahim Jabra, for example, they make a lot more sense than if you put them next to Amos Oz or A.B. Yehoshua. Maybe this is natural, something that derives from your education, from your background, which is what we started with.

My education and also the process of transition into Hebrew. I didn't search for influences, they simply didn't interest me, because I already had all the tools for writing itself. I just wanted to understand the language. So I went to the sources, the Bible and the Mishnah, all I needed were the means, that is, the language.

Maybe the literary establishment is simply doing to you what you've been doing to it, rejecting it. They're as uninterested in you as you are in them.

The question is more complex. If the literary establishment rejects me, this simply serves as evidence that such a structure is unable to comprehend or accept a writer that does not meet its assumptions. That's the literary establishment's problem and not mine. A writer, as far as I am concerned, must remain faithful to themselves and to their work and not make compromises in order to be accepted as part of the prevailing consensus.

Do you think that what you are doing has implications for younger people, for other writers who also feel that something is not quite so "kosher" here?

That's hard to say, certainly there are younger writers who find themselves in conflict with this establishment, but there is a difference and that is the difference in age and personal experience. They grew up here and studied Bialik and so on and so forth and all of this has already been completely internalized. This is not the case with me. I came from a different world and I never denied that world. I still see myself as part of that world while at the same time being deeply involved with life in Israel. I just moved from Arabic to Hebrew; that makes me define my connection to Hebrew literature as a connection between place and language.

You are an Israeli Hebrew writer who, on the one hand, feels very connected to the place, to the language, to the necessity of conveying things to readers; you have also made a great commitment to providing an alternative in Hebrew and Israeli culture—through your writing, translations, and academic work. Yet, on the other hand, you are completely ignored as an integral part of all of this and are constantly referred to as some kind of Iraqi or Baghdadi, as a representative of something not defined in your own terms. How do you feel about this, does it bother you?

To say that it doesn't bother me would be an outright lie. Of course it bothers me, but again I would explain this through the literary establishment's lack of preparadeness and lack of ability to open itself up to works that do not meet their expectations. It is much more convenient for this mainstream establishment to refer to my work as the work of an "Oriental Jew." In other words, work that belongs on the margins, beyond the mainstream. This, however, absolves them of having to contend with my work on its own terms. I think that by operating in this way, a great disservice is done not only to the state of literary criticism itself—even as practiced by mainstream critics—but to the state of Hebrew literature. As for myself, I haven't compromised myself nor do I intend to in order to make it easier for this literary establishment to accept me, since it is not for them that I write.

—*Translated from the Hebrew by Ammiel Alcalay*

IYA

1.

"I won't." She recalled her sister's voice as she repeated her daughter's words with a satisfied smile. Her only reaction had been to nod and lower her eyes to her hands folded in her lap. She had already told her sister many times that she would not burden Muhyi by sharing the single room with them, but Naima needed to hear her say it over and over again. Her remorse was repugnant to her, and at that moment she felt hurt by the demand to evince compassion and consolation, when she was the one who deserved them. Could she have imagined that this was the way things would turn out, and that she would have to end her days at her niece's? Going back to the family—people say—like a man who departs for foreign lands and returns in old age to die at home.

Those were her thoughts as she sat on the low stool in the kitchen with a cup of tea in her hand. The kettle on the kerosene burner, turned low, gave off a thin intermittent hum. The tiny spout on the porcelain teapot mounted above it emitted a tall and lazy plume with a heavy, pungent odor. The afternoon tea hour was her daily hour of rest, an hour for introspection and retreat carefully maintained since those faraway days when her husband had forbidden her to venture past the threshold to spend time with the women tenants. Now, while the family reposed in their rooms, she put the kettle on the three-wick burner and sat down to wash the dishes and put them to dry in the wicker basket beside the sink. Before the water boiled, she turned to the inner room that served as a pantry and removed the tea and sugar canisters from her tiny wooden cupboard. The cupboard door released a mixture of scents when it was opened, dominated by the sharp odor of dried cloves. A pinch of these, crushed, would be added to the tea. Everything she owned was ordered and packed in this simple cupboard, which had aged with her and followed her through her life's wanderings since her marriage at the age of twelve.

Iya. That was what the children called her. Like all toddlers, they had had difficulty pronouncing her name, and in time it had become an endearment. She had watched over their cradles, and they had grown and matured in her care. She had no children of her own, nor had she her own home, but she had never eaten the bread of charity. Ostensibly, her status was a servant's. While her own family treated her like a stepchild, to her many acquaintances she had become a part of her adoptive family since the day she had left her sister's house and gone to live with the Jewish neighbors' daughter. A small woman, with black eyes and a tattooed dot between her eyebrows and another on her chin. Her handsome face was unwrinkled, and two thin locks of hair, henna-colored, curled on either cheek. The black kerchief which was always tied on her head was pushed back while she worked, revealing a smooth brow a shade lighter than the rest of her face.

"The house is yours," Hamida said to her, "and Jawad is like your own son." Hamida's a good girl, the great consolation of Naima's life, which had known no happiness, and Jawad is an officer in the army with a secure income. "Come kiss Aunt Zakiya's hand!" he would call to the children whenever she stopped by. "And what's more," continued Hamida, "do you think that when Muhyi marries, his wife will agree to look after Mother? Here the house is big, and I would be happy with you both." A good girl, what more can Naima ask for? Muhyi will be thirty on the Great Holiday. A quiet, shy boy who goes straight home from work, a few hours in the coffeehouse and home again. Like his father. If Jawad had not found him an office job, he would have remained stuck in that miserable vegetable shop. It's not much pay, but he's a clerk in a suit and tie, God just hasn't favored him. "The communist's going, too?" his voice echoed in her head. There had been no need for her to answer after Naima had done it for her. As if seeking to justify Farumi's actions, she said that he wanted to study, he was always sitting with his books. She hadn't thought of Muhyi's sensitivity. Lowering his eyes to his cigarette, he then said the things that angered his mother. It hurts him, it still hurts him that he did not do well in his studies and his father was compelled to forfeit his share in the store to pay for his draft exemption.

Three who grew up in her arms, but she would not rejoice at their weddings, throw sweets over their heads, see their offspring. Iya, Sophie pronounced from her cradle, smiling sweetly, and Sarah laughed: "Do you hear, she calls you Iya!" A sweet child who would stretch out her hand and try to nurse from her dry breast. So, too, the brothers who followed, who clung to her dress while taking their first steps and put their hands in hers on the way to school. Three who were like children to her and it had been decreed she would be separated from them. If a fortune-teller had predicted that it would be so, would she have believed it? Who knows the intentions of Heaven! "Hamida is also like a daughter to you," Naima said to her, "and the children love you." Four small children and her belly still swelling. She would help her with the housework, she would carry the infant to be born on her arm, an old aunt uprooted from a home that had also been hers.

She stirred the cup slowly, as if enjoying the thin ring of the spoon against the glass. Choice Ceylon tea, mixed with ground clove, which turned into a black and bitter essence half-filling the cup. To this she would add water from the kettle. She never used household tea or sugar for this hour, but bought her own with the little money she received on holidays and various occasions, because this hour was entirely hers, a small corner in a life which had known no corner of its own. She had never lived on her own, but was handed over to a violent man while still an innocent girl. He covered her body with bruises and raped her night after night. A naive girl, who only left childhood the morning she escaped to the roof and bared her head to the Lord of the Universe. "Hear this wretched woman's prayer," she screamed from the depths of her tortured soul. "Take him! Don't bring him back to me! Don't bring him back to me!" A sergeant stood in the courtyard of the house and hurried him along to join the flock of those conscripted by order of the Turkish governor, and he found an excuse to become enraged with her and beat her with the large iron skillet until its handle broke. That morning she vowed that if her prayer were heard, she would never give herself to a man. That morning she went forth to a new life, the five years of her marriage wrapped in shrouds of oblivion, like a heavy, repulsive bundle she cast behind her.

She remembered how Farumi loved to hear the story of that day. She stretched her legs out on the cold cement floor and leaned back against the wall. Small beads of sweat appeared on her brow and on the sides of her straight, angular nose. She rested the cup in its glass saucer on the floor and lifted her gaze to the mulberry tree visible from the high window, the afternoon breeze rustling its dense leaves. Farumi would squat beside her in the courtyard of the old house while she made him tea and told him about her childhood. He loved to be near her. When she broke the sugar lumps with the little axe, he would come to her to gather up the pieces in his tiny hands and put them in the big tin box. "Father says you don't love him." How old was he then? Such a skinny urchin with glittering eyes. What could I say? Love Saul? Did Sarah love him? She suffered him in silence. He was from a remote village in the south, and she from a well-connected family from Baghdad. Her father was a respected man, even though he was not rich and supported his family with difficulty. Two daughters were struck by fate: one went blind as a child and the other was disturbed. Sarah was like a flower in their midst, beautiful and intelligent, and while still very young she assisted the family by spending her days doing exquisite needlework. What could I say to the boy? That it wasn't true? Hide from him that his father took his mother's money and sold her jewels right after the wedding, when his business got into trouble? Not tell him that his father set his eye on my jewels, too, and kissed my head while he swore that nothing would happen to them? Children see and hear, and it is forbidden to lie to them.

To this day, she could not understand how she had dared to give him her golden box to pawn. Sarah was horrified when she heard, and she couldn't sleep at night. And did it do any good? Always paying off debts and sinking into new ones, until there was no way out and the police came and took him to prison. Did he learn anything? Did he mend his ways? If he had at least stopped drinking! If he had exercised some self-control instead of terrifying the neighbors by making scenes! An incurably angry man. And Sarah so refined, and her voice inaudible. She bore her suffering heroically and did not yield to her brothers' pleas that she leave him. "Take the children and go? Be a burden on my brothers? Isn't it enough that two sisters sit at home?" I took her side. A husband in trouble shouldn't be left, and it would be a pity for the children to grow up without a father. And Saul, with all his defects, is not a bad man. He just doesn't know how to manage, and the *arak* goes to his head. But he never raised his hand to Sarah, he loved her after his own fashion and respected her, and when his rage died down, he would ask her forgiveness with lowered eyes. He knew he was inferior to her, to her educated brothers who finished their studies thanks to her. Return to them in shame after her father's death? Raise the children with them? She didn't want to. She would suffer with her husband but not go back. My sister Sarah, I said to her, you are not like me, you have a husband for better or worse; he loves and respects you, and the children are your consolation.

2.

The sound of approaching steps made her stir from her thoughts. "Farumi hasn't come down yet," she said when Sophie stood in the kitchen doorway.

"I couldn't sleep, it's very hot," said Sophie, rubbing her eyes.

She gave her a long and distant gaze and finally said: "Did mother tell you about Habiba?"

"What happened to her?"

"They sold everything and the house is empty. Only the mattresses are left. But Habiba laughs and carries on with her daughters. 'We'll do farmwork,' she says, 'there it's no disgrace, women work too.' A madwoman. She always was." A smile appeared on her face as she gauged Sophie's reaction. "I thought about you. You with your delicate hands!"

"I don't think about that," Sophie shrugged.

"Even better. God is great, my daughter."

A spark flickered in Sophie's big eyes. "I think about you," she uttered after a short silence.

"You think about me," she nodded sadly, "I? what am I? An old woman."

Sophie looked at her intently. It was clear to her what was in the girl's heart. Hadn't she grown up in her bosom? She lowered her eyes to her hands and said no more.

"I'll go take a bath," Sophie said energetically and turned away from her.

A beautiful and educated girl, splendid and upright, how would she do farmwork? Like those sunburnt barefooted girls? And when would she marry? Who would give her a dowry? In another year or two here, her brothers would have succeeded in saving a little money for her, but over there? How would they marry her? And the father staying here without a penny in his pocket! She thinks about me. Naive. What is there to think about me, my life is already over—but you! How I wanted to rejoice at your wedding as I rejoiced at your mother's!

"What time is it?" she asked Sophie when she passed by the kitchen again, on her way to the bathroom.

"Three," was her answer.

Farumi is sleeping too long. Perhaps he's reading. He shuts the door and there's no knowing what he's doing inside. Since we moved here, he shuts himself up in his room and doesn't speak. In the old, small house, you could see everyone from the courtyard. And him, with his books. Stop talking, you're bothering me! Here no one bothers him, he has a room and Aziz has a room. But Aziz is not like him, they are different in every way. A big European house, surrounded by a garden. They had just started working, gone and rented this house and furnished it with new furniture. What more could Sarah hope for than this? The children had realized her ambition; this is her consolation after years of distress. She raised them with so little! Did their father worry about them? He didn't even buy them clothing, and they always wore their uncles' used clothes, which Sarah cleverly adjusted to fit. But they never cried, why do our friends have new clothes and we don't. And what did their father do for them? Sat in Shatra and sent letters. And with each visit, he filled the house with pandemonium. He would yell from the top of the street: Zakiya! Sarah! And the neighbors would rush to the windows to see him running before the porter. He would enter noisily and let loose a band of screeching chickens which dirtied the courtyard. And what kind of baggage would he bring? Stinking clothes. And so it went every year. A few days' visit and then he goes back. What was he for them? A father for short visits, and every evening the *arak* on his table. Now all that is over. He closed the store and came to dwell among his family. But his family is leaving.

Silly. He wanted to live in Baghdad, a wholesale trader with an office and a shingle. To be a bigshot. His brother, who didn't know how to write his name, didn't leave Shatra and got rich selling tobacco, while for him, who had actually studied, nothing worked out. Silly. And what kind of life? Alone all these years in a snake-infested *khan,* in a wretched room, far from his family, cooking his own meals and dining at his brother's table only on Sabbaths. Luck. If he had only behaved like a human being and didn't make scenes. And the children looked at him like frightened chicks. Have mercy on the children, don't yell! And when they grew bigger, they were ashamed of him. Only Farumi behaved impudently towards him. Hot-tempered like he was. "*Arak* on my books!" and he swept the glass to the floor. Still a boy and so rebellious! And Saul wept for wrath: my son, the fruit of my loins, treats me like this! What a wretch he was, but Farumi—no, he had no pity for him. Doesn't love him, carries a grudge. Even now he hasn't changed, ignores him and doesn't speak to him. When he does have to tell him something, he won't look at him. Sophie and Aziz never raised their voices to him, and now they are trying to surround him with warmth and make him feel he is home. Not Farumi. Treats him as if he is unwanted and unnecessary. Does not forgive, absolutely does not forgive. Remembers everything. And is it possible to forget the sorrow he caused them? The gloom when he did not come on holidays? On Passover Eve, Farumi would sit by the window in order to chime: Daddy's coming! It was heartbreaking to see his grief when daddy did not come and he listened to the voices of the neighbors reading the Haggadah. A boy wants to be glad on the holidays like all the other children, he wants a daddy who will buy him new clothes for the holiday, he wants to hold his father's hand and be proud of him. Children don't forget. They forgive, but they don't forget. Farumi doesn't forgive. And Sarah pretends not to see the way he acts, or chides him gently. She raised them and she was mother and father to them. The mother goes with the children. She won't let them go alone. The husband can stay if that's what he wants. In any case, he had never belonged. Licenses. He just talks about licenses. A merchant licensed in tobacco, textiles, grains, and not a penny in his pocket. It will be all right, I'll send you money and we'll get together in a year or two. Does anyone believe him?

Farumi. It's all because of him, if not for him they wouldn't move. He's the youngest and he draws the others after him. The communist's going too? Yes, that's how it is. Without telling anyone he went and signed up. How had Sarah guessed when he went up to his room to get his identification card? A mother's intuition. What did you do? You sneaked away to sign up? Rebellious boy. He wanted to run away from home, it's no good for him living with the family. I won't allow you to go alone, either you stay with us, or we'll all go! Mother. A mother does not abandon the fruit of her womb. What was his rush? Why does he have to be different? Always sitting with the books until one day they came knocking at the door. New friends, not from school, not from the neighborhood, how did he find them? Who got him into this? I'm going to the demonstration, if I don't come back don't worry. How did he dare? And Sarah lay sick and wept. Have pity on your mother, don't go! Did he listen? Rebellious son. How horrifying, how horrifying! And the uncles yelled at him, threatened him, and he in return. He wouldn't listen, argued with everyone, was insolent and mocked the uncles. No respect. Demonstrations. And we could hear the gunfire and trembled. And if the police had come to make a search? What was in that tin box that we buried in the kitchen niche? I shut the hole myself and filled the niche with all sorts of unnecessary things. I'll run away, don't tell mother. If I hear there is danger, I'll run away. Promise me you won't tell her. And if they take your brothers instead of you? You're killing your mother, you're killing us all! Why are you like this, Farumi, why? And now what's driving you? A good appointment and they praise you at work, the Old Man loves you like his own son and invites you to his home. What more do you need? A big house, a salon with a carpet and armchairs and sofas, all sparkling new. You've made your mother happy, you and Aziz. What drove you suddenly to abandon everything and go? To end up who knows where, to be a farmer? For this you studied? For this you sit all the time with the books? To be a *fellah?* Why? Why?

3.

After she had finished drinking the fourth and final cup, she poured water from the kettle into the teapot and put it back in the overturned lid and covered it with a rag. Sophie had already left the bathroom, and she could hear her talking to her mother; even with the silence reigning in the house, she could not distinguish a thing. She rose to wash the cup in the sink, and as she left the kitchen she looked towards the closed door at the top of the concrete stairs, then turned to the parlor in the center of the house. On the sofa beside the window Sarah was busy mending socks, and the brass-spoked fan, which stood on the table next to the radio, blew a thin strand of hair over her forehead with every turn. She stopped far outside of the breeze's range, and looked into the open bedroom, where Sophie combed her hair before the bureau mirror. "Your dress fit Hamida exactly, as if it had been sewn on her," she remembered to say with a smile.

"You saw her?" asked Sophie, watching her in the mirror.

"Naima told me."

"I have another one I don't wear."

"The collar bothers her," said Sarah without lifting her head from her work. "Only one style would suit her and then it wasn't comfortable!"

"It's impossible to take everything anyway, so why not give it to Hamida?"

"God grant your mother the strength to sew you new dresses."

"Iya is worried," Sophie smiled meaningfully into the mirror and beyond her. "She says we'll have to work on a farm!"

"Habiba's tales," she tried to show equanimity. "How would she know? Don't you know how she is?"

"And if it's true?"

"I remember how she learned to dance," she added, ignoring her question. "She hasn't changed. And the daughters carry on like she does. 'There we'll go around in shorts and won't need dresses at all!' Crazy girls. They think it's Paradise there."

"It's nice, actually, to go about in shorts," Sophie challenged her in the mirror.

"Shorts? I want you to find a suitable husband!"

"And how will you know if I do?"

"God is great. Farumi will send a letter. He says he'll send it through Paris."

"And if they confiscate the letter? Father will get in trouble."

"Enough. Don't tempt the Devil," she rebuked her in a gentle and soothing voice.

Sophie stuck the comb in the hairbrush on the bureau and turned to her sharply. "You simply didn't want to come with us! It could have been taken care of easily. Money takes care of everything. But they don't let you!"

"Why return to this now?" Sarah turned to her irritably.

"I'm not returning. I've been saying it all along," Sophie said aggressively.

Sarah gazed at her searchingly over her sewing glasses, and she smiled in embarassment. She wanted her to answer instead of her, but Sarah went back to threading the needle through the sock. What to say to the girl? How to explain things that can't be explained? She turned away and her glance fell on the four tin suitcases, which for a month now had been standing one beside the other in the vestibule by the door. The blood rushed to her head. "It's all in God's hands," she pronounced gloomily, "it's all written and decreed." She retreated backwards as if to evade Sophie's accusing gaze, and finally turned towards the stairs. "I'll go and see why Farumi hasn't come down."

She grasped the blue-lacquered railing, and began to go up a step at a time, bending only one knee because of the rheumatism in her knees and ankles. "Farumi," she called before reaching the landing, and upon hearing his answer she completed her ascent and opened the door. "You're not sleeping? Why didn't you come down to drink?"

Naked to the waist, Ephraim was sitting on the floor surrounded by books stacked in piles of varying heights. "You see," he said and spread out his arms.

Rolls of wrapping paper which he had brought back two days earlier leaned against the wall; he still hadn't untied them. "How will you make packages of all this?"

"Not all. I'm sorting. I'll only send what I need."

"And the rest you'll just throw away? You spent so much money on them!"

"Give them to Hamida's children. Give them to whomever you want."

His hair was ruffled and the slow, sad smile which made her heart beat faster spread across his face. "I'll bring you the tea," she said and turned back.

"I'll be down in a minute."

"It won't taste right. It's already been sitting on the heat a long time."

"And you'll come up again?"

"I'll come up. My miserable legs can still pull me along."

On returning to the kitchen her glance fell on the boiler furnace, which was filled with burnt papers. She had not had the heart yesterday to sweep them outside. He had burned everything. He crouched beside her and threw everything he had written over the years into the flames, all the notebooks, all the printed sheets she had buried in the kitchen niche of the old house. "Why burn it? I'll take care of them," she said to him. And he had smiled his sad smile. "I'll write other things." How hard he had worked on this! Entire days bent over the desk, writing and reading, at home and in the coffeehouse. Young people his age go to the coffehouse to play and amuse themselves, and he sits alone and writes. What did he write? What could all those burnt papers contain? And how could it not hurt him? How could it not hurt to leave behind the books and go? So much money, so much work! And if they came to search? No. I don't want to think about that. Let him go! There he won't have to burn papers and hide them from his pursuers. Let them go, let them go! Just keep them from suffering and let them live a good life. "They'll come back yet, victorious!" She recalled what Muhyi had said that angered Naima. "They'll learn to fight and will come straighten things out here!" And he laughed, enjoying his own provocation. Did he believe what he was saying? He's naive, he hears what they say in the coffeehouses and repeats it. Return? How? When? Jawad said nothing, except when Hamida told her: "You'll come to us." Then he said: "you have nothing to worry about, Aunt Zakiya." It's better this way. Everything had gone wrong, and life would not go back to what it had been. Palestine had ruined the whole world. What good were words? Disasters. Not since Rashid 'Ali had the Jews been in such a panic. To leave, to leave. But then they hadn't left, and life returned to normal, just the soul-shaking memories went on. Could one forget? How to forget that terrible night! Only Farumi was impervious, sprawled on an easy chair and sunk in deep sleep.

"I was thinking about Habiba and how she learned to dance. Do you remember?" she said with no apparent connection to her thoughts, as she offered him the tea. As a small boy, he had loved to accompany her to the dairy at the end of Convent Alley. Habiba's door was open and the neighbors came to see her dancing barefoot with her husband in the courtyard. "She took you in to dance with her. Don't you remember?"

"I remember that she was yelling the whole time that her husband was stepping on her toes," he answered with a laugh.

"He was drawn after her like an idiot. He must have been twenty years older than she was, and she was pretty and peppery," she said as she sat on a chair. "Poor soul, she burnt his heart until it killed him. Crazy. And her daughters are just like her."

She deliberated whether to tell him what she had said to her, but she doubted this was the thing to draw him into conversation, as he was ready for anything. On his own he said, "there we'll get a tent without electricity or water." He wanted to dissuade his mother from her decision. "I'll get settled by myself and you'll come afterwards. They'll still be letting the Jews leave." To run away, that's what he wanted, to leave home and go.

Watching him grasp the cup with two fingers, caught up in thought, she remembered the cellar in which the family had gathered the night of the riots. An angel of God had mercy on him and spread his wings over him. Who could close his eyes on that night? Sarah sat erect and Sophie curled next to her on the sofa; Aziz was on the second sofa pale as chalk and with glittering eyes. And the looters passing through the narrow alley, their load thudding against the door. With each thud the heart falls. Everything frozen and motionless, even feelings, like in an endlessly recurring nightmare. And the terrible, paralyzing, anticipation, and the thoughts spinning in one's head like a whirlpool, and the unceasing uproar of the looters outside. Could that night of terror be forgotten? I prayed in my heart to the Lord of the Universe: Have mercy on these children, have mercy on us and save us from the rioters just as you saved me from the hands of that beast and revived my soul! What would they have done to me if they had broken down the door and come in? Could I have screamed? Could I have stood before them as Muslims stood before them and protected their Jewish neighbors? I, a panic-stricken, miserable woman? A long, torturous silence. Only the neighbor spoke to us through our common air shaft, and passed on the news her sons heard on the radio. Boil water, she said, to pour on the rioters if they bang on the door, and in my confusion I put the kettle on the burner! It wasn't until morning that I realized how foolish I had been, and the children laughed: with a teakettle you wanted to run them off?

"You remember Nissim, mother's uncle, what he did to himself?" she asked, again with no connection to her thoughts.

Astonishment came over Ephraim's face, and before he could answer she continued:

"Just like yesterday. His head was nodding on the porter's shoulder, and his hands and legs like two rags. The porter was running ahead and the wife and children behind, wailing and pulling their hair. You don't remember? He drank a bottle of camphor. He wanted to die after going bankrupt. But they saved him. And afterward, he would tell how he didn't know where he was when he woke up in the hospital and saw the lights and his family around him. That's the way it is. God does not take the soul of someone who's still supposed to live."

"Why do you remember that now?"

"Yesterday, I met Su'ad in the synagogue. She said to me: Father did not live to go with us. I told her: he lived to marry you and your sister and see grandchildren. You should thank God for granting him more years to live, and that when his time came he died with dignity."

Ephraim gazed at her for a long moment, as if wondering what she was thinking, and did not react.

"I meet a lot of people there." And suddenly, alertly: "All these books are on communism?"

A surprised laugh escaped him. "What's worrying you?"

"What's worrying me? You ask what's worrying me?"

A melancholy shadow passed over his gaze, fixed on her, then he lowered his eyes and finished the tea without saying a word.

She watched him go back to his work, moving books from pile to pile, flipping pages a bit, hesitating, taking the pencil from behind his ear and scribbling something on a page on the floor. Scraps of paper slipped from several books and he looked at them intently and cast them into the carton by his side. What bothers him? What does he seek in these books, and for how long? Aziz hasn't touched a book since the day he finished his exams, and the same goes for all of them. And how will he learn there, in a tent with no electricity? "You see," she remembered his exultant voice as he pointed to the letters in the newspaper, "here's my name, and I wrote all this!" Not just writing in the paper, but with his name, so everyone will know. Looking for trouble. Just looking for trouble!

"You're not going to work today?" she asked after a long silence.

"I'll be finished in a bit. Tonight I'll make the packages."

"The floor is covered with dust from the books," she said, and when she got no answer, she shifted as if to rise, and finally said: "tomorrow is Wednesday."

"Yes, Wednesday," his answer was like an echo.

"I'm wondering whether to soak the laundry." When she got no answer, she added, "I don't know if she'll come or not."

"Who?" he looked up at her. "The washerwoman?"

"She said she would send her son to tell me, but it's impossible to depend on her."

She couldn't stand her. Bothersome and near-sighted, and she always had to check up on her and help. For two years now, a washerwoman had been coming once a week. The house was large and the workload great, and she wasn't at full strength. Aziz said, we'll bring a maid too, but she wouldn't agree. Weren't the many expenses of the house enough for them? "The children have grown and it's time for you to rest," Naima said to her. Yes, that was true until the disasters. How will they manage there? Sarah doing laundry? In a tent?

"What can I say, my child, what can I say? I don't know what to say," she took a deep breath and got up.

"You're going?"

"Do you need anything?"

"No, nothing. I'll be down in a minute," he held out the empty cup to her.

At that moment, they heard the front door slam, and she went out to the landing. "Father's back," she said, and began her descent.

4.

Saul was sitting on a wicker chair facing the stairs, erect, legs apart, a string of beads rolling between his fingers. He spoke quickly, and before she reached the bottom, he turned towards her with a big smile: "wish me good luck!"

"Good luck," she said in surprise.

"The permit's in hand and I've already got a partner!"

"You haven't got anything yet," Sarah retorted, reproachfully.

"What do you mean, I haven't got," he turned to her energetically. "I'm telling you I saw the permit with my own two eyes, and it had my name and my picture on it. It's all done. It just needs the Minister's signature."

"Wait 'till he signs."

"He'll sign," he raised his voice angrily and rolled his brown eyes under his thick-knit brows. "They're not making problems now. If you have a document showing you haven't given up your citizenship, you'll get it! Wherever I go, people congratulate me. You're the only one who has doubts!"

"I have no doubts," Sarah retreated in a small voice.

"Three men want to go into business with me," he continued talking to her, with a jubilant ring. "One from the Damerchy family, a decent man I've known for years, a rich businessman with a lot of property. He's offering me a third against two-thirds, not bad, eh?"

"It's fair," she answered and looked at Sarah, who had ceased her work and put on her distance glasses with the gold frames.

Sophie's short laugh sounded like a hiccup, and he turned to her irritably. "You're laughing? You'll be sorry yet that you didn't listen to me!"

"Actually, I'm happy," Sophie said apologetically.

"Yes," he nodded his head with dignity. "Go ahead and laugh. You don't want to believe it, but in a little while you'll see that I was right." He slapped the beads meaningfully and stuck his other hand into his jacket pocket to take out the silver tobacco case. He opened the richly engraved cover with his thumb and began to roll a cigarette, the beads still wound about his palm.

"The truth is," he said, with a knowing air, "there are rumors that all this business will stop. The government is about to stop letting the planes land at the airport." He licked the edges of the paper with the tip of his tongue while a small and self-effacing smile played about his mouth.

"They'll stop the departure?" asked Sophie.

"That's what they say," he said, lighting the cigarette. "They never imagined it would be like this. Baghdad without Jews? How would Baghdad look without Jews, they say to me."

"And what did they expect?" Sarah persisted.

"Could they expect there would be bombings? If it hadn't been for the bombings, this would never have happened."

"First they throw bombs and now they're sorry," Sarah retorted impatiently.

"Who threw? Do you know who threw them?" He gazed at her in sharp rebuke. "In any case, the whole business will apparently stop," he added, and drew deeply on the cigarette.

She stood in the middle of the room, looking from Sarah to her husband, and finally said: "Who knows. Just talk."

"Anything's possible," he hurried to squelch the tone of doubt in her voice. "If the government decides, everything will stop in an instant."

"And what about the money and property they've taken?" asked Sarah.

"They didn't *take* it. They *froze* it. Those who have left, have left. Those who stay will get a certificate, like I did, and their money and property will still be theirs."

"And you believe it?"

"What do I know." Suddenly, he was doubtful. He leaned back in his chair and crossed his legs. "They also say the government will fall," he added, staring at the palm of his hand as if deep in thought.

"And that's good?" Sophie asked innocently.

Silence reigned briefly, and she exchanged questioning glances with Sarah. "I'll go warm up the food," she said, but did not budge.

"It is written: 'The righteous shall live by his faith.' " He spoke heavily now and looked away from his palm. "I believe that all those who leave will return." His expression was tense as he looked at her. "You'll see yet, Zakiya, they'll return. In another year or two at the most! They're just taking a trip!" His laugh was short and unnatural.

"It's all in God's hands," she answered him mechanically and turned to the kitchen.

He says what he wishes were so, she said to herself as she put the empty cup in the sink. God help him earn a living and not need help from his brother. She bent over to light the oil burner and set the pot on top. Afterwards, she emptied the contents of the teapot into the garbage and rinsed the teapot and cup under the faucet. And who knows, maybe there's some truth to it?—she continued talking to herself while drying her hands. She also wanted to believe that it would be so; she recalled Muhyi's words but immediately dismissed them. Nonsense. People sit in the coffeehouse and spread rumors. Each man after his own heart. It's just talk. It's all in God's hands, and the eyes see what is written on the forehead. On leaving the kitchen, she suddenly felt weak. She leaned briefly against the wall, then entered the washroom and rinsed her face with cold water. The water relieved her, and she decided to go out despite the early hour. She carried the boxes of sugar and tea into the inner room, put them in the bottom of the cupboard. From the top drawer, she drew a pair of stockings and pulled them on. From the same drawer, she removed a flowered dress to change into, and a white shawl which she wrapped around her head and face. Finally, she took the black silk cloak reserved for afternoon walks and locked the cupboard.

"Going already?" asked Sophie.

"To get some fresh air," she said defensively, as she did every time she was asked such a question. "The pot's on the stove," she added, turning to Sarah.

Saul gave her a long, encouraging look. When she pulled the cloak over her head and stuck her arms through the openings, a dark shadow passed over his face and he murmured, "good for you."

5.

The heat was still in full force and a dry breeze blew across her face. Tomorrow is the first of the month, she recalled and automatically lifted her eyes to the scorched skies as if to locate the crescent moon. Tammuz is over and Ab is coming. *Ab the month of heat and gale, is hot enough to scorch a nail—and yet to winter points the trail; Elul comes after Ab is out, a time to travel all about.* The world behaves as its wont, and who can foresee time's upheavals. They will no longer be here. By month's end, they must return the house keys, and they are already looking for buyers for the new furniture they have not had a chance to enjoy. Saul would drift to some other place. It didn't look as if he would live with his brother. A big house and they are offering to set aside a room for him, but even in Shatra he preferred to live by himself. He has pride. He'll live like a gypsy rather than depend on his brother's table. And people respect him. Abu Aziz. He walks with head held high, and hides his sense of failure inside him. He's no longer what he once was, he tries to behave courteously and doesn't raise his voice. But a man is not cured of old habits. He hasn't given up the *arak* glass at night, though he drinks less, and the drink lifts his spirits instead of drawing him into quarrels. Zakiya, come sit with us! He hasn't been cured of that snuff tobacco either, which makes the handkerchiefs filthy, nor that disgusting chewing tobacco, which on the Sabbath he occasionally spits into the corners of the room. "You spat on the floor again," Sarah rebukes him. From now on, he will go back to living by himself and there will be no one to rebuke him. There will be no one to sit with him at night and keep him company. He'll be forsaken in his old age. What good will his brother's family be? What kind of comfort will he take in his brother's children when his own are in a foreign land? "And you won't come to see me?" Why not, indeed? Men are miserable alone. I'll wash his clothes if he wants. And for all that, maybe he will have a partner and manage. That way he'll preserve his honor, and what is more precious than honor?

She met no one on her way in the street. At some houses, the residents watered their front gardens; she greeted them and continued on her way. On her return she would find many of them sitting there to relax in the cool of the evening. Others would go up to the roof and the lights would remain lit until late. The street conserved its customs even as new tenants entered the vacated houses. Muslims and Christians were replacing the Jews, and by summer's end the street would change its face, like many of the other streets in the new quarters beyond the eastern gate.

The breeze fluttered her cloak, and she drew it in so it would not slip from her head, but she didn't bother to wrap herself in it as she would in strange places. Everyone knew her here, and among the Jews she was not scrupulous about her modesty. The leather sandals on her feet dragged slowly and continuously on the burning asphalt; it was an unmistakable sound. At the old house, the children would identify the sandals' drag while she was still at the end of the alley, and Farumi would hurry to pull the rope of the latch before she could touch the doorknocker. Iya. Two joyous syllables in Sophie's small mouth, which had just started to sprout teeth. Come to Iya, come. First daughter, a darling girl who found warmth and comfort in her bosom just as Hamida had done before her. There will be no one to call her Iya anymore, and Sarah would no longer have a sister to support her and be her confidante. "You are a sister to me," she said to Sarah, "take me into your house and I will be your maid."

She had been an innocent girl when she began visiting the Jewish neighbors. She was just past childhood, that same wretched childhood which had been arrested the day her mother dressed her in a bridal robe and told her: "Listen to your husband and do as he wishes, for the husband is master, and the master must be served faithfully." A young girl who played with rag dolls was handed over from her father's protection to that of a strange man. She had not known what was expected of her in married life, and her mother had not bothered to explain it to her. So she did not grasp what was happening to her when the pains came and something bloody fell from her body in the bathroom. But after time, when it became clear, she was relieved, and said to herself: "I'll bring no children to that no-good man!" A young girl, a violent man, and five years of suffering and miscarriages. And when she returned to her mother after her husband's departure for the war, her body was small and tough, the skin covered with bruises. Her father was no longer alive, and her brother Mahmoud, two years her senior, had fled the house after getting embroiled in a quarrel that led to the death of a butcher's assistant. He was a hotheaded boy, who in fear of vengeance hid with acquaintances and finally disappeared. Some said he escaped to Syria, and some said they had met him in a border town in northern Iran. She had no other brothers, and her mother had remained alone, going to live in the big house her sister lived in, where they found her a dark room near the gate. She stayed there with her mother and waited for the end of the war. The British entry to Baghdad, which was followed by the return of the surviving Turkish conscripts, brought terror with it, and she frequented the alleys to hear what she longed to know. In the evening, she would go into the wretched room with her mother and tell her about those who had had the luck to be taken prisoner by the British, and those who deserted and hid in the desert until they were saved. Her husband was not among them, and no one knew what might have happened to him. Morning and evening she would pray to the One Who Dwelled on High, that same prayer that had burst from the depths of her tormented soul in a mighty cry of despair from the roof. Only after she was informed of the religious decree accounting the missing as dead, did she hasten to make her pilgrimage to the tomb of the Imam Musa al-Kazim to light candles of thanksgiving.

Those were the days of her belated adolescence, her spirit full of youthful rashness, and her face radiant with life and alertness. Once more she was not under the care of a man, not father nor brother. Her sister's husband, an older, reticent man, neither asked nor demanded, nor did he see it as his obligation to marry her off and divest himself of responsibility. In the large, open courtyard of the tenement building, she found herself in the center of the women's activity during the day, when the stories flowed and quarrels broke out among the washbasins and cooking stoves, in the din of the infants and cluckings of the hens. She assisted her sister in caring for the little girl, offered her help to the tenants, she was liberated and energetic, a young woman who had come to life, full of curiosity and her ear attuned to every rumor and bit of gossip. Her day was spent outdoors, and she did not enter the room until evening, when her sister's husband returned from the market.

Her sister's husband was a gloomy man, sunken in a closed and silent world. All day he sat in his small vegetable stand and in the evening would go to bed early. He exchanged no words with the tenants and no one spoke to him. Were it not for his cough, which would burst out at night from the phlegm in his lungs, no one would know he existed. Unlike her husband, who had been many years younger, handsome and energetic, her sister's husband had not been graced with attractive features, and he was indifferent to the running of his household. He did not ask his wife what she had done during the day, was uninterested in his daughter and never touched her. His behavior made her think that men of his type were the most desirable for a woman, for in their company she could run her life independently and without fear. In her conversations with her sister, when she would repeatedly express this thought and say to her: "Thank God every day that your husband does not control you," Naima would rebuke her: "And be left with one daughter?" This fear was caused by her husband's indifference. At night, he pushed her away from him, and even when he felt desire, he was like one casting wasted seeds on fertile earth. Hamida was two and there was no pregnancy. They said to Naima: His back is feeble and his seed is sterile. They said to her: His lungs are damaged from too much smoking and his blood is contaminated. And Naima went to seek the advice of fortunetellers and magicians, added herbs and babies' foreskins to his meals without his knowledge, until she was saved and her belly swelled. "A boy child will be born to you," prophesied the Sheikh, and he did not err. "And you shall call him Muhyi, for the Lord has revived your soul, as it says in the verse: You shall take the living from the dead and the dead from the living!"

She was already considered a widow when Muhyi was born, and she did not feel obligated to cling to her mother and sister's company in the big house. Her curiosity was limitless and her trips outside the house grew more and more frequent, between doing errands for the tenants to walking about and meeting the neighborhood women. At night she would go into the narrow room with her mother and tell her what she had heard and seen during the day. The room had not been intended for habitation, but for hoarding coal and twigs for fuel. It became unusable when the kerosene cookers came out. The room was a dark and damp crypt, whose solid walls were covered with a thick layer of salt from the dampness. Daylight penetrated only through the door, which opened on an entryway shrouded in dusk. A mat was spread on the floor and two mattresses, one next to the other, were laid on top of it at night, then rolled up in the morning and placed in a wooden chest. The room was so small that there was no place for her tiny cupboard, and she put it in Naima's room, where it stayed for ten years until she moved.

The Jewish neighbors' house stood at the top of the alley, and on her daily outings she always found an excuse to visit them. Their way of living attracted her, and the mistress of the house welcomed her, gave her all kinds of small errands and invited her to eat of her food. Over time, when she had earned the good woman's trust, she visited daily, and the errands grew in number and size. She no longer came for a few hours, but stayed from morning until evening with her hands full of work. She swept and washed and laundered, and on Fridays and holiday eves accompanied the father of the family to carry baskets from the market, and to buy chickens and have them slaughtered at the Jewish butcher. In this way she learned the laws of *kashrut,* to separate dairy and meat dishes, to remove threads of blood from the meat and to salt it before cooking; she learned to boil the pots for Passover, to prepare the pot of *hamin* for the Sabbath and even to make *kiddush* wine from sweet raisins. She also learned to adapt her tongue to the Jewish dialect, to use the turns of phrase peculiar to them and to weave Hebrew words into her speech as they did, until it was impossible to discern her difference. That family became her adoptive family. Sarah, who was her age, enchanted her with her personality, her nobility of spirit, her sensitivity, her devotion to the members of her household. As the years passed, she worried to see her remain unmarried, helping support the large family and stuck between two handicapped sisters. Her father could not supply her with a large dowry, but he did not want to marry her to someone he did not like. The matchmakers came and went and nearly despaired until Saul's name came up in their conversation, and the father gave his approval after he had looked into his doings and found nothing wrong with him. A tobacco merchant who had recently taken up residence in Baghdad, a handsome, light-haired man whose desire to marry into a good family was greater than his desire for wealth. The day before her wedding she said to her: "Sarah my dear, we are like sisters and separation is hard between sisters." She did not say that she felt no love for Saul, despite his attempts to endear himself to her; she stored her doubts in her heart until time proved them just.

The children grew. Yes, and anxieties came, too. The demonstrations and the fear and the government resignations and the hanging of the Communist leaders and the cursed war in Palestine! All, all at once! Farumi, my soul's beloved, my boy. My darling boy, how? Why? Iya, I'm coming with you. Yes, my child, I'll take you to the dairy, I'll take you to the bakery, I'll take you to the Mother Superior, who loves you and gives you candy. Iya, what are you cooking for us? My boy, how did you become a Communist, how? And suddenly, like that: I'm going! There will be no more Iya for you all. Sarah will cook. God grant her health. And I will be with Hamida. Four children and pregnant already. I'll help her raise the children. Such is my fate. I'll raise children who aren't mine while the children I've raised are leaving me.

6.

The sight recurring daily: A policeman stands at the gate and blocks the entrance. The people gathered outside are excited and impatient, and some of them hang on the bars of the tall iron fence and shout to the crowd filling the courtyard in front of the synagogue. At the far end, people press about a youth reading names from papers tattered from too much handling, and those gathered about him pull on his arm and shake him: Why am I on one list and my husband on another? Why is Nissim's name before George's, George is the big one! Nuri, not Nuria, you've made a girl out of him! "It'll be all right," says the one with the lists, "it will be corrected. If you're not on this list, you'll be on another. A little quiet, a little quiet!" And he leafs and leafs, erases and emends. Suddenly, a shriek from the direction of the entrance to the prayer hall. Someone has thrown himself to the ground: "I won't move without a receipt! I won't move!" A circle closes around him and conceals him from the eyes of those gathered outside.

"What did I tell you?" A pot-bellied man, dressed in a summer suit with a tie about his neck, turns to the man standing by his side, who is smoking feverishly.

"But they promised him," said his conversation partner nervously.

"They promised? Who promised? How can they give him a receipt?"

"The one who took the money promised his son. Why did he promise if he couldn't do it? That's not right!"

"Are you naive? That's all that's not right?" the man smiled mockingly and looked about him importantly.

"We must have faith in the men of the movement," declared a third man, whose face was etched with pockmarks.

"True," murmured a woman who stood behind him, "when there is no choice one must have faith."

"Have faith in them?" the man in the suit turned to her with the same mocking laugh.

"You apparently have no need of them," the pockmarked one countered.

"So it would seem," the man with the nervous air supported him, and inhaled deeply from his cigarette.

"There's a policeman here," a second woman alerted them in a hushed voice.

"And the policeman doesn't hear the shouts? You think he doesn't understand?" responded the man in the suit.

"Still, why did they promise the son?" the nervous man continued to express his astonishment.

"Do you know what it is to give receipts for silver and gold?"

"True. It's dangerous," the pock-marked one confirmed.

"But if they promised, it's suspicious," the nervous one summed up, and crushed the cigarette with his shoe.

"Enough, enough. Stop it," the woman silenced them.

"Woe to us," wailed the woman standing behind the pock-marked man, and he turned to her: "Trust in the Lord."

"If it's not the government, the movement robs us," a young man, bare-chested and smiling arrogantly, tossed into the confusion.

He was met with blank looks, but no one responded.

She listened to the exchanges, leaning against the fence with her face to the courtyard, where she saw the teacher, Juliet, with her little brother. She had lost a little weight, but was still full-figured, and her dress fit too tightly about her hips. It had been a while since she had run into her, but she had heard that her two brothers had fled to Iran while she stayed behind with her mother and little brother. A wonderful girl, and how she had suffered in that first year! Sophie had loved her and would recount angrily how the little girls tormented her and how one day she had cried in class. And she had loved Sophie, too. All the teachers loved Sophie, a diligent girl and always first in the class. While she was still meditating on this, she discerned Salha the matchmaker. She's going, too? What would she do here when the Jews leave? She was still energetic and her eyes danced. You could not tell she was all of seventy. There would be no lack of work for her over there. To whom had she entrusted the silver and gold she had amassed? Such a wily woman would not hand over her treasure hoard to a stranger. Where would she find him there? And if he denied he had received it? And maybe he would flee to another place, to Turkey, to America? Is there any lack of countries to flee to? Who would find him for her? Such panic. As if their house had collapsed on them. Saul is right. Were it not for the bombs this would not have happened. The law for the cancellation of citizenship was to be in effect for a year, and only a few had registered when the bombs fell. Had the Jews themselves thrown them as people said? Who knows. A tangle of threads whose beginnings were lost. In another few days, all these people would no longer be here. Others would fill the courtyard and they, too, would go. By the end of the summer, perhaps there would not be a Jew left in the old Jewish neighborhoods. And in the meantime, the Palestinians came. What a world!

Farumi would not have deposited money with these men. If he had any! He is not naive and knows how to be wary. He worries about me. "Don't leave your jewelry in the house, because the police raid the houses of Jews ready to leave and confiscate gold." Where should I take them? Have I any place to hide them? Guard them for me in your safe. You work for a great man, a senator! Farumi my darling, whom shall I trust if not you?

The gate opened and before those who were leaving could get out, those standing outside pressed together to enter, so the policeman was thrust from his place. "I won't let anyone in if you push," the policeman threatened in rage.

"He swore on a Torah scroll," said one of the men coming out. Someone had apparently asked him and she could not hear.

"If he swore what more can you ask of him," noted the pockmarked one.

"Swore on a Torah scroll," jested the bare-chested youth. "He can go wipe himself with his oath!"

Once again, no one reacted to his words, and he shot a brazen and challenging look at the crowd, finally smiling at her as if she shared in his statement. She turned to face the courtyard. He likes to stand out. What can they answer him? He says what the others may think in their heart. But where has Juliet disappeared? Just now she was standing here with her brother. Maybe she's gone into the building. If her brothers took savings with them, she won't need the movement people. And maybe they've already left Iran. And if they were robbed on the way? There have been incidents like that already. Someone interrupted her thoughts, said something she did not catch. A brown-skinned woman, with curly hair tied in a flowered scarf at the back of her neck. Her gaze was demanding. "God save us from troubles," she resorted to the routine phrase instead of answering.

"Your sons are inside?" asked the woman.

She wondered what to answer and finally said: "Yes, they've gone in."

The woman continued to look at her with the same suspicious curiosity, and when she turned once more to the courtyard, she grabbed her arm: "Where are you from?"

She had expected a question of this sort, and even though she had no difficulty in inventing an answer, the woman's persistence was distressing. "We're from Shatra," she said.

A big smile spread over her companion's swollen face. "I knew it," she said, "you can always tell Baghdadis."

"We're all in the same situation," she responded mechanically.

"What can I tell you, here one meets Jews of all sorts."

"And you are from where?"

"From Qanbar 'Ali," she answered immediately, and tilted her head to the side. "The children have already . . ." she winked and waved her hand to hint they had fled. "Only my husband and I stayed behind. He's sitting there beside the tree." She nodded her head towards a man squatting at the end of the walk with his back against a eucalyptus tree. "He's diabetic and can't take the pushing," she added, a ring of whining resentment in her voice.

"God grant him strength."

"But there they have good doctors, the best in the world," she spoke now with authority. "And what do we want? Just to get him back on his feet!"

Once more she faced the courtyard, wishing to put an end to the conversation. She had no heart for idle conversations. Normally, she did not turn down such conversations. On the contrary, she always knew how to draw her partner out, and it was enough to show interest in her to gain her trust. But for now, and in this place, she preferred to watch from the side, especially as women of this sort were not desirable company. She had already been tested by the likes of her, women whose suspicious gazes pierced her despite her impeccable Jewish dialect. She did not look like them, and the shawl wrapped over her face aroused their wonder. Only in the rural towns did the Jewish women dress like Muslims. Once in Baghdad, they bared their faces and tried to hide their difference. She had never tried to look Jewish, and Sarah had not asked this of her. She just said to her: "Among us, black is worn for mourning," and she saw no deviation from tradition in exchanging the black dress and shawl for a colored dress and white shawl. The dresses Sarah sewed for her pleased her, and the white shawl, edged with green beads, made her handsome face younger.

The push to enter, which had renewed when the gate was opened, gave her an opportunity to leave her place and distance herself from the woman wearing the flowered scarf. She stood now at the edge of the crowd, and a hostile, accusatory voice echoed in her head: "*Wa-llah,* she's not a Jew, she's pretending!" The woman had been standing behind her in line at the butcher's, and she had not reacted. She swallowed the insult in silence. For some reason, she had been at a loss for words and did not retort scornfully. Pretending. Did she pretend? The wickedness of some people. All this grieved and vexed her. But she was at peace with herself and could not recall ever regretting her choice to live with Sarah. She lived among Jews and had already adjusted to their customs and borne their imprint. Everyone respected her, surrounded her with affection and could barely conceal their envy of Sarah for having such a companion. There were also those who tried to tempt her with high wages to come to work for them. She would relate this to Sarah and add soothingly: "Such a thing will not be. I don't sell myself for money." Sarah's home became her home, and her children were like her own. Yet sometimes, in moments of confusion and introspection, musings over her identity would attack her, and she would ask herself if her choice had not ultimately been one of a lack of alternatives. What kind of life would she have had if she had stayed with her sister? No, she had no regrets, not ever; nor did she torment herself much with unanswerable questions. And when, in conversations with Naima, she was caught using words and phrases in a Jewish accent, she would laugh contentedly. "You are more Jewish than Muslim," Muhyi would chide her jokingly. Yes, more Jewish than Muslim and a Muslim among Jews. This is what her life had been. This is how it had been and how it had ended. Would it be easier for her now? But the memories? And the sorrow that wracked her soul?

A car stopped near the sidewalk, and a young man carrying a leather briefcase got out and was immediately surrounded by the crowd. With vague murmurs and gestures he tried to calm them, and strode towards the gate. There he exchanged several words with the policeman, who turned his head away indifferently and moved away. Everyone now hastened to enter, even the man with diabetes stood up and joined his wife as she urged him on. She was among the last to enter, and began to pass through the crowd in the courtyard, trying to find Juliet. She thought of asking her if she had heard of any intention to stop the emigration. Juliet was an educated girl who read newspapers. But her search was fruitless, and she turned toward the synagogue hall.

The crowd formed into groups in the great hall. Since its transformation into an emigration center, the benches had been pushed to the walls and the crystal chandeliers burned day and night. She stood beside the doorway and looked about; suddenly she heard someone calling her name. Abraham the carpenter stepped toward her.

"How are you, Zakiya? And how are the children?"

"Thank God. And all of you?"

"You see," the man spread out his arms. "Waiting."

"So is everyone," she said, gazing into his wrinkled and smiling face.

"I sold the carpentry shop for a pittance. I liquidated everything, and for two months now I've been sitting at home."

She weighed whether to ask him the question boring through her head, and finally, casually, said: "One hears all kinds of rumors."

"What kind?" he asked in astonishment.

"They say that perhaps they will not allow any more to leave. You didn't hear?"

"Who told you such stories? On the contrary, now they're moving faster. Everything's moving quickly now."

"Just rumors, apparently," she retreated.

"And how's the family? Ready yet?"

"Abu 'Aziz isn't going," she emphasized.

"And the children?"

"His brother, too, is staying with all his family," she added as if she had not heard the question.

"What can I tell you," he answered musingly, "I didn't want to go, either, but what more can be done here?"

On leaving her, he requested that she convey greetings to the children's father. "And don't be sad, Zakiya. God is great!"

Disappointed somehow, she continued to search for Juliet, turning this way and that, gazing carefully at the people gathered about the three tables of the emigration organizers, which were arranged end to end in the middle of the hall. Where had she disappeared? She hadn't seen her leave, and yet she wasn't in the courtyard! Her disappearance disturbed her, and the more she tried to account for how she might not have noticed her leave, the stronger her desire became to see her. A good girl who always greeted her with joy, and who recalled her support and encouragement during those difficult days. It had been hard for her to listen calmly to how the little girls mistreated her, and she had decided to wait for her by the school gate and try to cheer her up. She had been so miserable, and so distraught, that she had invited her home, and there burst into bitter tears: "The principal threatens to fire me!" And the mother began wailing: "How will we live if they fire her? An orphan and her brothers still young, there is no mercy! There is no mercy!" God saw her in her distress and gave her strength and understanding. You must believe. God does not abandon one who has faith in his heart. The beginning is always hard, every beginning is hard, but if you are not caught in despair you succeed. That was what she wanted to tell her now. Just remember how it was then, you didn't despair and you succeeded in controlling the class and became one of the best-loved teachers in the school. Now, too, you'll succeed in your new life and find the man you deserve. She wanted to take her into her arms and kiss her farewell. But she had disappeared. As if she had flown into the air.

7.

She trudged far into the hall and sat herself on one of the benches that had been shunted aside. Her knees tormented her from standing, and now she began to bend them a bit while massaging them with both hands. Live and see, she said to herself as she cast her eyes over the hall, live and see the wonders of the Lord among men. These masses, this flight for which you could find no explanation, these glittering eyes and the hope pounding in the heart, what are all these if not signs of the Merciful One in His servants. What could make people abandon everything and depart for the unknown, if not faith? God plants faith in the heart and guides His servants whereso He will, and God has plans for His creatures. Yes, so it is written: God has plans for His creatures. A State of Jews, only Jews, even the *fellah* a Jew, whoever heard of such a thing in the past? Live and see, live and see!

She took a deep breath and leaned back in her seat. The air was dense and heavy, and the high ceiling fans dispersed a hot breeze saturated with cigarette smoke. Lethargy spread through her limbs, and the roar of the crowd was kneaded in her head like a thick and sticky dough. Wrapped in confusion, she raised her eyes to the lighted chandeliers, which seemed to her neglected and desolate in their glorious heights. The days of splendor were over and gone, when the hall would be filled with people in holiday dress come to pray, while the cantor stood at the ark trilling his sweet and melodious voice. When all this was over, how many would come to pray here on holidays and Sabbath eves? And how would they feel, praying in this great and empty hall? Do any of these people running from table to table think of that? Preoccupied with themselves, tossing cigarette butts and scraps of paper onto the marble floor, scolding their children, pleading with those in charge of the lists, grumbling, enraged. They are impatient and have no time to think about what they leave behind.

A thick layer of dust covers the benches stacked in the corners, and the blue velvet curtain that covered the ark was dusty, too, as if it had been untouched for years by human hands. Olive branches and flowers were embroidered on it in gold thread, and in the center the four letters whose glitter had faded. These letters were familiar to her and she knew their sanctity. Even in her distant youth she had been asked to light fires in Jewish homes on the Sabbath, but since her attachment to Sarah's family, curiosity had led her to visit the synagogue on Rosh Hashanah and Yom Kippur. There she saw the people praying dressed in white and would wait for the blast of the shofar which leapt in the chambers of her heart and sent hidden waves through her. Later she came to know the ancient synagogue near the tomb of Sheikh Ishaq, where she would take the children to receive the blessing of the Sage Ezekiel. His head wrapped in a turban and his hoary beard spread over his chest, the sage sat cross-legged on a divan with a thick book between his hands. He would close the book and open it, then set before her two pages covered with big letters in straight rows. She would put a finger on a letter, and he would thumb through the book and read her in a rich and quiet voice what the ancient pages revealed to him. It was all written there: what had frightened them and what had caused their hurt, and what remedy she needed to concoct for them, or gall-nuts to stitch to their clothes to protect them from Satan's wiles. And after he would bless them, she too would incline towards him to receive his green hand on her head. She did not desert this synagogue even after the children were grown, and at regular intervals she would pass by to light a candle in the open courtyard, on the holy man's tomb, just as she had gone to be blessed at the tomb of the Imam Musa al-Kazim.

Now Farumi laughs. The Sage Ezekiel? His hand green? And he does not refrain from calling him names. God forgive him and guard him from the Evil Eye. He doesn't believe. Just in what is written in books. And always impetuous. He knows no rest. How old was he when he decided to fast? Not even twelve. To be a man, that's what he wanted. I won't eat. The milk stood on the table and he wouldn't touch it. You're still little, my child; the fast will hurt you. But he persisted. Sophie and Aziz thought he was joking. But they didn't eat, either. And so the three of them, all at once. He is the youngest and draws the bigger ones after him. And, actually, he suffered more during the fast than they did. Like his mother, who would return from the synagogue with her last ounce of strength and lie down in bed unable to lift her head from the pillow. Then suddenly, just like the decision to fast, he decided to stop and even to mock and blaspheme those who did fast. Restless, and so aggressive, and his tongue so quick he might be reading from a script. Now he doesn't speak. Shut up in his room. And yesterday he sat and burned the papers! If he thought he could return he wouldn't have burned them. Muhyi with his foolishness. Saul, too. Return? How will they return? Who will return? In the end, he'll go, too. How long can he hold out by himself? At his age? And Sophie who wanted me to go with them. Naive. The mother goes with the children. True. That is how it should be. And what am I? Who worried about them and watched over them in the streets? Who talked to the teachers so they wouldn't harm them and wouldn't overlook them? Their hand in mine when they took their first steps, and their hand in mine on the way to school, and from school back home. If only I were a bird, to see them in their new lives, if only I were a bird!

Seated in her corner, removed from the noise of the crowd and immersed in her misty thoughts, a feeling of acceptance and fulfillment came over her. She said to herself: For what does someone complain to God? Lost riches, a fatal illness, a frustrated hope? What have you to complain about? Has God removed His grace from you? Surely, since that dreadful day, He has shown you abundant goodness and surrounded you with warmth and love, and look how your life has passed pleasantly and without worry. Thank Him for what He has granted you, and ask mercy for the children and for Sarah. For what is harder for a person than uprooting from the land that has nurtured him, than abandoning the place he grew up? And you are staying in your place, and you're not left childless, Hamida is also like your daughter and her children love you. And perhaps this is all for the best? No more uncertainty and fear. Suffering and repressing the insults, hearing words of contempt and not reacting. All our troubles come from the Jews, they tell you. They're the ones who have brought us this Communism and Zionism, they tell you. A cursed race, they tell you, and God has condemned them to wander among lands and be degraded among peoples. And you keep silent. And you keep silent.

For a long while she reproved herself, but the memories would not leave her. They came on together like a long continuous chain, or attacked her in a stampede, so that she could not fix them in time and place. The head is too small to hold them, and things get foggy and are forgotten. Here, she tries to seize the end of the thread and remember how Hamida was born—was it before her husband was taken to the war or afterwards, and the thread slips away from her and she cannot decide. She remembers well that Hamida was a baby when she moved to live with her mother in her sister's house, but before they found that wretched room, they lived in the Baab al-Sheikh quarter. How long had they stayed there? Not long, obviously, until they despaired of her brother Mahmoud's return, and Naima begged them to come to her. Hamida was still being nursed, and she remembers that she had her front teeth and would bloody Naima's nipples. Was she born before the general conscription? She wasn't there when she was born. Why? Had her husband forbidden her to go out? But how could she not remember? Something like this, she must remember. And if it was after the conscription, what prevented her from being at her sister's side when she gave birth? And furthermore, when Mahmoud escaped, Hamida was already there. So when was she born? It's all mixed up. Loose ends of memories with no connecting thread. I'm getting old. I'll be like my grandmother, she didn't know where she was and was always complaining that she was being starved. And we laughed at her. And when she was incontinent, we would go wild: "Grandma made in her pants!" And she would yell with her toothless mouth: "Where's the stick? Get me a stick to beat them!" Naughty children. Mother died an easy death, still full of strength. She closed her eyes and sent her soul to the Master of Souls. If only it could be that way for me, too, to die without suffering, without contempt. Oh, just so Hamida's children don't laugh at me! Lord, guard me from such an embarassment! Take my soul while I can still stand!—she whispered her petition with her eyes on the four letters in the curtain's heart.

When she roused herself, there were only a few straggling groups in the hall, and a servant with a broom began to sweep away the filth scattered about the floor. Abraham the carpenter was no longer there, and Juliet had disappeared. You see Jews of all sorts, the woman had said. You meet acquaintances, the ones you want to and the ones you don't. Sometimes many, sometimes none. She swayed on her seat. Perhaps in the meantime the washerwoman's son had arrived, she said to herself, and got up heavily.

The sun was already hidden, and a light breeze blew in the emptied courtyard. The guard was sprawled on a chair by the gate, smoking a cigarette. He glanced at her in wonder, but she ignored him, not even bothering to draw the cloak over her face. Sitting so long on the bench had worsened the pain in her knees, and she wanted to get home quickly, to sit on her low bench and stretch out her legs. She walked slowly, her face buried in the ground. She was preoccupied with her thoughts and too tired to be stopped by neighbors who by now would have settled themselves in their front gardens, or on the strip of dirt along the road, which had been sprinkled in advance.

8.

Sophie opened the door for her and she immediately noticed the absence of the tin suitcases.

"They told us to get ready," Sophie hastened to say when she saw the astonishment on her face. "They said the suitcases must go tomorrow."

She gazed at her, unbelieving, speechless. A tense, hesitant smile was on Sophie's face as she pulled her forward as if to embrace her, but she was frozen, submitting only to being pulled, drawn with her towards the parlor.

The sight revealed to her penetrated her awareness slowly and painfully. Sarah was sitting on the floor among the four gaping suitcases, Aziz standing beside her in short pants. Saul, sitting in his place, smiled at her expectantly. "Tomorrow already?" she said hoarsely, holding onto a chair.

"After you left, they came to notify us," Saul said, still gazing at her as if to gauge her reaction.

Piles of clothing stood on the sofa and all about on the floor, and Sarah folded and placed them in the suitcases. Her face was flushed and damp, and the fan disordered her hair. "That's the way it is, all in a hurry," she said with a trace of resentment and without looking at her.

"There's no hurry," Aziz tried to contradict her. "They said to get ready, that's all. It's not at all certain that we'll have to send them tomorrow."

She sank into the chair and the cloak slipped about her shoulders. The carpenter's words rang in her head. He had spoken the truth. They're speeding the departures now, not planning to stop the emigration.

"Some families canceled, so there was room," Saul explained to her, crossing his legs.

"What do you mean, canceled?" Aziz now contradicted his father's words. "Can they cancel? They've just been delayed for all sorts of reasons."

A melancholy, disconcerted smile came over Saul's face; he watched her as one who shared in his sentiments. He's seeking reinforcement in idle rumors, and she had been willing to listen. The two of them were the same, dispossessed and left behind. Hadn't he eaten yet? The question leapt into her brain.

"And where's Farumi?" she asked after a silence.

"He went to the office," answered Sophie.

She didn't ask why, just now, he had gone to the office and not to the senator's house. She was too tired to ask questions and receive clarifications. What a short while before had been inner turmoil now became a whirlpool dragging her with it, madly spinning. All the words had lost their meaning, with the gaping suitcases before her, and Sarah's quick hands folding and stowing things within them, back and forth. Their time had come. For more than a month now they had been standing in the vestibule, and every time her glance had fallen on them, the faint, illusory hope flickered that they would not be used. Tin suitcases painted orange. They tear the leather suitcases to rummage in their linings, they said. She had gone with Saul to buy them in Al-Shurja market. Mounds upon mounds of suitcases. The Jews are going, the Jews are going. It was a grand time for the tinsmiths and suitcase dealers. Liquidation sale. The seasons of sales to the Jews were over. Earthenware platters for Passover, palm fronds and pomegranates for Sukkot, noisemakers and masks for Purim. There would be no more Jews and their holidays would no longer be felt in the market. The tin suitcases close the season. To each one a suitcase, to each one the space they leave behind.

"Don't put in the coats. They steal them," Saul's voice came to her ears.

"I'm not going to wear a coat," Aziz said emphatically.

"They'll take it from you, a new coat!" his father rebuked him.

"Two pairs of pants, two shirts, a sweater and jacket, and then to wear a coat in this heat!"

"How will we look with all these clothes on our bodies?" Sophie laughed.

"It's simply absurd." Aziz smiled, too.

"It's all absurd," Saul hastened to give his opinion. "And leaving this way, like refugees, isn't that absurd?"

He gazed at her again, but the melancholy smile disappeared to reveal a severe expression. His words met her thoughts at that moment, and, taking heart from them, she stirred herself from her long bewilderment. "Abraham the carpenter sends his greetings," she said to him. "I saw your teacher, Juliet, too," she turned towards Sophie, "but she disappeared in the crowd and I couldn't speak to her."

Except for Saul's mumblings, her words fell into silence, followed by the immediate resumption of the debate over the coats. She thought of telling them about what she had heard about the immigration officials and the man who had been yelling, but she hesitated, seeing them preoccupied and unable to pay attention to her stories. Meanwhile, she realized that all she had to say was now meaningless to them. In one fell swoop, like a cloth ripped long and loud, the awareness of her new condition descended upon her. There's no going back. The time when they would have listened to her stories had irrevocably passed. She was entering a new time, and a curtain was already separating them. They were considering what to take and what to leave behind, calculating what could still be pressed into the suitcases and what might be possibly forfeited. They are preparing themselves for a new life, journeying far away from her, and she is only watching them from the side and no longer has a place in their world.

Once more she felt dazed, and it seemed to her that she was walking in winding alleys but getting nowhere, as it was sometimes in her dreams. At the same time, the feeling of acceptance and fulfillment came back to her, this time overflowing with self-pity. Yearning stirred within her and made her heart beat faster, an indefinable yearning which pressed and hastened. It was a kind of tortured desire, hopeless, like an ongoing song of grief, like a mysterious chime on an autumn day. For a long time she stood, dazed, not listening to the remarks or Sophie's nervous giggling, until she awakened to the creak of the key in the front door. "It's Farumi," she straightened up.

Ephraim entered with quick steps. "Everything's ready, I see," he said in surprise.

"We're not waiting for you," Aziz answered drily.

She looked at him expectantly, and he smiled: "You see, already packing."

The tone of exultation in his voice surprised her. "You're glad?"

"I want this nightmare to be over." He stood facing her and handed her the box of her jewelry. "I went to the office to bring it, because I didn't want to leave it until tomorrow."

Surprised and confused, she took the box without uttering a word. Her face remained tautly expectant.

"It had to happen. What difference does it make, today, tomorrow, next week?"

A sharp pain stabbed her heart and made her light-headed. Was he calming her? Was he trying to master his feelings?

"Come and help," Aziz pressed him.

"I have no time now. I have to run to the Old Man. He's waiting for me with the replacement."

"Leave him alone," said Sarah. "We're managing without him."

"I haven't finished packing the books yet, either," Ephraim said, and turned towards the stairs.

"He thinks only of himself," grumbled Aziz. "He doesn't even want to know what we're packing and what we'll wear."

"He'll wear what you do—a coat and hat as if we were going to Siberia," came Sophie's rolling laugh.

She stuck the jewelry box into her dress pocket. With a great effort, she rose from her chair and turned to the kitchen, leaving her cloak on the chair. The kitchen was dark and just a shaft of weak light entered from the parlor. She noticed the cooking pot in the sink. Saul must have eaten before they came with the news. The burners were extinguished. Put water on to boil? she asked herself, and immediately recalled the washerwoman who was supposed to come tomorrow. How would the laundry have time to dry if they send the suitcases tomorrow? Will they take dirty laundry with them? She caught herself musing again on things of another time, a time to which she belonged and was now banished. No more would she be asked to answer or advise. It had all slipped away from her, it all had nothing to do with her. A strange feeling of resignation and indifference came over her, and she sank onto her bench and stretched out her legs. To rest, to rest, to think about nothing—she said over and over to herself.

So she sat in the shadowy kitchen, emptied of thoughts, stupefied as if in a faint. After some minutes she heard Ephraim's steps on the stairs. Immediately after, she saw his shadow in the doorway.

"Why are you sitting in the dark?" He turned on the light and entered. "Alone like that in the dark!"

She blinked from the light and did not answer.

"I brought you something," he said, standing beside her. He handed her a book, bound in green and adorned with gold letters. "The Qur'an I give to you."

Rooted to the spot, she stared at him mutely, and his features blurred gradually before her eyes.

—*Translated from the Hebrew by Susan Einbinder.*

SAMIR NAQQASH

SAMIR NAQQASH is one of the last, and certainly the most important Jewish writer in Israel to continue writing in Arabic. Born in Baghdad, Naqqash has lived in Teheran and Bombay. Novelist, short-story writer, and playwright, he presently lives in Petah Tikva. A remarkably dense and innovative artist, Naqqash's life and oeuvre attest to a steadfast act of resistance towards the massive socialization process undergone in Israel by Jews from the Arab world. Naqqash's work is unique and stands out among the writers of his generation in its boldness to plumb the depths of the historical moment he is living through in a highly personal and uncompromising way. His prose, whether written in standard literary Arabic or the assortment of dialects he masters, expresses an enormous semantic range that is scathingly ironic as it cuts to the quick to touch the nerve of wounded dignity and human suffering. In another interview, Naqqash has stated that: "I feel discriminated against for a number of reasons: First, a Jew writing in Arabic is not read in Israel and gets no institutional support from the literary establishment. Second, the general attitude towards a writer like me is not positive. The question always looms in the background: why should a Jew write in Arabic? Third, I would like to emphasize an absurd fact: I am much more well-known in the Arab states and abroad than in Israel. Doctoral theses have been written on my books in Italy, the United States, England, and Arab countries including Iraq, Egypt, and the West Bank." The Egyptian novelist and Nobel Laureate Naguib Mahfouz has called Naqqash "one of the greatest living artists writing in Arabic today." While Naqqash is often categorized as someone obsessively concerned with the past, the selections included here show him to be very much a writer of the here and now. In "Prophesies of a Madman in a Cursed City," Naqqash takes two venerable tropes—that of the prophet chosen to prophesize against his will, and that of a topsy-turvy world, where everything is the opposite of

what it seems—to new imaginative heights. This text, perhaps more than anything else written in Israel, epitomizes for Arab Jews the experience of the total transformation of values, perceptions, and aspirations that accompanied exile from one homeland to exile into another homeland. The other text is an excerpt from Naqqash's novel, *The Angels' Genitalia;* the scene takes place in the consciousness of the narrator, in the space of a minute or two. As the narrator (a Jew from Baghdad traveling out of Tel Aviv), reaches in to present his ID card to an Israeli checkpoint guard who is convinced that this man might be an Arab, that is, a "terrorist," Naqqash relentlessly interrogates the arbitrary nature of power and offers a remarkably profound and and far-ranging meditation on the absurdity of racism. His books include five collections of short stories, *The Mistake* (1971), *The Story of Any Time and Place* (1978), *Me, Them and the Disassociation* (1978), *The Day the World Was Conceived and Miscarried* (1980), *Prophesies of a Madman in a Cursed City* (1995); three plays, *Caught On a Reef* (1980), *In His Absence* (1981) and *The Chilly People* (1990); as well as four novels, *Courtyard Dwellers and Cobwebs* (1986), *Perfect Blood for Sale* (1987), *The Abomination* (1987) and *The Angels' Genitalia* (1991). In addition, an essay, "When the Sides of the Triangle Have Fallen," came out in 1984. Only one of his books, *The Day the World Was Conceived and Miscarried,* has appeared in Hebrew, translated by the author's sister, Ruth Naqqash. In both 1981 and 1985, Naqqash received the Prime Minister's Award for Arabic Literature. The novel from which the excerpt below has been taken, *The Angels' Genitalia,* was brought out by al-Kamel Verlag, a publishing house run by Iraqi exiles in Cologne, Germany.

SIGNS IN THE GREAT DISORDER: AN INTERVIEW WITH SAMIR NAQQASH BY AMMIEL ALCALAY

You came to Israel at the age of thirteen yet you maintained your Arabic, something very few people of your generation were able to do. Can you explain some of the processes you went through?

To tell you about this, I have to start at a very early age. I don't know how this might sound, but I distinctly remember things that happened to me from the age of two. I remember them and I see them. My mother decided to send me and my sister to school early. My sister was just under three and I was just under four.

As a child I preferred to be alone, to think about things, what was beyond the stars—it made me sweat, it really scared me! I encountered the problem of death, believe it or not, then as well.

I was drawn to books, even before I could read. I devoured my father's library, I would see a book and tell him: Father, I want that book. He bought me books even before I knew how to read. But there, we were reading by the age of five. That was when I read Eve Curie's book about her mother Marie. Death was a great fear for me so after reading about Madame Curie, my first wish was not really to be a writer but a scientist, to study in the Sorbonne and find out how to overcome death. At the age of nine or ten I got a prize from school and we always got books in English because the program of study was in English. I remember a book called *The Bottle Imp* that I started translating. Even then, I used to edit a family magazine and at school I was very active in publications.

Those years, until the age of thirteen, are extremely strong in my memory. Because of my parents' professional and business life, and the atmosphere around the house when I grew up, with all the great political changes taking place that would effect us personally, I reached maturity at a young age. My mother worked before she was married and continued to do so afterward; she was the head of the maternity ward in the government hospital. My aunt also held a similar position in the Jewish Hospital. And my father always had Muslim partners so that our house was a place that everyone came to and I heard a lot as a kid, so that all of this influenced me. As I said, my sister and I entered school at the same time and there—it was a private school—we were exposed to all of world literature: French, Russian, English, in Arabic translation. So that when we came here, everything changed in an instant.

From a palace with three floors to, well, you know the rest of the story. We found ourselves in a tent; thus began the trauma that turned into a personal and family tragedy. My father really loved his children and our parents had plans as to what we would be in the future. He always thought about the future of his children. But to our misfortune, the weather in the year we came was extremely harsh. There were fourteen days of nonstop rain that winter and there were incidents in which the army came and took children away and tents went flying. All of this influenced my father enormously and within two years he had a stroke and passed away. I was fourteen at the time and it was a tremendous blow because my father was truly a model for me. But the trauma inflamed this desire to write and I started writing a lot.

I also started translating books, even *Hamlet* at one point, since there, in Iraq, we had real English teachers. I remember that I went in search of books in Arabic. I went to Jaffa. I managed to get newspapers too. Before he died, my father and some of his friends organized themselves to figure out how we could leave the country. Iraqi Jews came with nothing, nor did they have any options since their citizenship had been taken from them so anything could be done to them here because they had no status at all. There was an organization and attempts were made through the U.N. to get international citizenship. This was from 1951 to around 1953. My father died in 1954. I felt quite defeated.

We managed to bring a little money but there wasn't enough food. The allowances were a little meat for kids, powdered milk, powdered eggs, and one-quarter of a kilo of rice per child per month. We lived right here, our transit camp was right on this street, in Petah Tiqva. Because of the shortages and the profiteering on the black market, the money we could have bought a house with went in less than two years just on food. At one point, I became desperate and crossed the border into Lebanon with an older cousin; our intention was not to stay in Lebanon, but to try and make our way to London eventually. I was fifteen at the time. We soon found ourselves in the hands of an Israeli agent who took everything I had written: notebooks filled with stories and longings for Baghdad; also the translation of *Hamlet* I had done and taken with me. Needless to say, I never saw those things again. We were turned over to the authorities and stayed in Beirut for six months before being turned back to the Israelis.

What kind of a welcome did you get from the Israelis?

Nobody knew where I had been taken. Not even my mother. There were rumors that she heard but no one told her anything. No one knew where we were. I was in a cell, not in prison, but in the police station in Tiberias. I've written about this but I had mercy upon the reader and described it in a much better light than what actually happened. I remained in prison for about six months.

Were you tortured?

Don't ask. I sometimes ask myself how I was able to withstand all of that. Apparently, they really wanted to get rid of me. For no reason. When I finally got to court they just sentenced me for crossing the border and the six months I was already in served as my time. Meanwhile, the police had prepared files on everyone who had tried or requested in one way or another to leave the country. A lot of them were imprisoned, charged with treason, and all kinds of other things. I too was questioned about these people who, after all, simply wanted to leave the country, believe me. A number of my stories dealing with this also were censored. I don't believe anyone has ever really written anything about this whole phenomenon. When I finally got out of prison, I didn't follow any of this up because I simply wanted to leave. This was the end of 1956. And in 1958, me and my aunt left with the idea of trying to recover some of our wealth from Iraq. When we got to Turkey, we did get in touch with my father's ex-partners who said they would come but then we again hit a spot of bad luck. Turkey and Iraq had a pact then and the streets of Istanbul, where we were, were filled with flags in anticipation of a visit by the King but then the monarchy was overthrown and Abd al-Karim Qassem took over. So everything went down the drain. I wasn't in Turkey long because our intention was to go on to Iran which we did, settling in Teheran. I was also in India for about a year so I know Farsi and also some Hindi.

Do you know the work of Sadegh Hedayat?

Of course. But you know he was an anti-Semite. He killed himself in Paris. I think, though, that despite his leanings he was very influenced by Kafka. But I did get to know quite a bit of Persian classical literature in the original, Sa'adi for instance. I was in Teheran for four years. And I was also in Bombay for about a year. I was only in my twenties, so I really wasn't that much in touch with writers. By chance, my best friend there was a Communist; all the intellectuals—Jews and Muslims—were very much on the left. I worked in the American Embassy there, the very same one that has since become so famous. I ran the commissary there for around two years, after I got back from Bombay. Before that I worked in a company run by Iraqi Jews. I wrote constantly. For ten years I wrote novels, stories, and plays that I simply put away, with no intention of publishing them. I wrote a novel on India and one on Iran after I returned from there, but they never came out. In the 1970s I gathered some stories that I had written in the 1960s and put out my first collection. We were living in a project then and we had the money to either buy the place or bring out the book. Everyone in the family thought the book was more important so we didn't buy the apartment in the end. That was the beginning, in 1971.

Given everything, why did you come back, were you still trying to get to Iraq?

On the contrary, a good friend of ours offered to help us go back, he even offered us his house which was empty and in a very good location. But I didn't want my family to stay in Israel while I went back to Iraq. I did try to stay on in Iran even though I was quite against the regime there. Staying wasn't a problem because we had Iraqi friends there who were quite powerful and I could have gotten Iranian citizenship. What finally prevented me was the family situation. I had another brother who died here in a boarding school under extremely unclear circumstances. I was the only son left in the family and, ultimately, it was my mother's situation that made me return. I had wanted her to come, but I couldn't organize a way for the family to join me. That's the only reason. I just got up and told my aunt one day that it was simply too difficult for my mother and I had to go back. That was in 1962. I was in a deep depression for two years. Israel hadn't changed at all. The family had gotten out of the tent and into a little block house. In 1964, I was working in the *Histadrut* and I had an accident so I left. Then I worked in the Tax Bureau until 1966 but the job was phased out in 1967.

After that, I went over to the *Voice of Israel,* during the '67 war, where I was a news editor. I worked there until 1972 when I decided to go study in the University. In 1971, there wasn't a chance in the world that someone would publish my work so I did it myself and it cost me a lot. As I said, our last apartment, not far from here, cost as much as bringing out that book.

Getting back to the issue of language: In Arabic, despite everything, there has been continuity. But there are layers of Hebrew that have been cut off. Because of the exaggerated connections between language and ideology, there often seems to be something missing in a lot of contemporary Hebrew prose, something that makes it difficult for writers to express themselves in a fully personal way. Since writers cannot express themselves in a fully personal way, their work doesn't fully address the human condition but ends up being somewhat programmatic. I think here of things like pain, which don't come into a full personal expression within what can be considered the consensus. Can you comment on this?

I think a lot of Israeli writers were brought up, almost exclusively, on what I would call "Zionist" literature, that is, modern Hebrew literature in its early stages. In Iraq, I grew up on the whole breadth of world literature, we read everything. As far as pain is concerned, this is something general to all people. In the preface to my first book, I wrote that pain is the most genuine thing that exists in human life.

Among many writers, though, even pain becomes methodological, systematic; as if it were something general and not something felt in particular. You see within such writing a certain process of projection which, I believe, reflects both a personal and a national problem.

Because of this I wanted to speak of my writing as *opposed* to Israeli literature. I am against "committed" writing, partisan writing that takes as its goal a certain problem or a certain theme. Jews, in general, write about the "Jewish" problem. This also occurs in Palestinian writing, where many writers focus themselves only on the Palestinian "problem." I believe that literature must be universal or, more precisely, individual. Because it is irrelevent whether a person lives in Singapore or South America, a person is still a person who has the same existential problems. The human condition, this is what remains essential. Because this whole life of ours can only be thought of as some kind of a ridiculous or vulgar joke. I don't even know why man exists or what the purpose of man's existence is; it is because of this that I have written and said that suffering and pain are the most substantial things that exist, the most substantial things that can be felt in life. The rest is just like a dream, it comes and goes. And death, of course, arouses pain amongst the living. So that any problem connected to something historical or to a particular group of people, these are transient things. The essential thing is the human condition with its timeless problems, not something here today and gone tomorrow. I have criticized Palestinian writers, for example, for simply taking the Palestinian issue and writing only about that. When it is solved, there will be little value to everything they have written; it will simply be a historical document. I am also against politics or sociology in literature. Writing is writing: it has to deal with the great human issues and it cannot offer any solutions because there are none. I express the problems that any person anywhere faces. In one of my first novels, which remains unpublished and probably never will be published, I was very much under the influence of Marxist theory but I realized that people are people, made of genes and drives that cannot be changed so that theory is one thing and humanity another. From then on, I formulated my maxim: man has no chance of being saved or redeemed, and I still maintain this. People will always suffer, and there is no chance to save them. So one of my central themes is simply human misery. In general, I would say my writing tries to give people material to think through existential questions.

You have said you don't have a specific theme in your writing, you deal with humanity particularly and in general; at the same time, your language is extremely complex. I would like to connect these things: style, language, and the complexity of your characters.

First of all, I think language is of extreme importance. Words are already in the process of losing much of their power even as they are being used. Language, the sentence, must be measured with great exactitude. And there is no end to this. A writer must use great exertion, both in terms of technique and also in simply choosing words. Our lives have become more and more complex and complicated; writing has to reflect this reality. Reality is not something with a beginning and an end, with a fixed point of view. I would claim that what is called the absurd, symbolism, the fluidity of a style with no beginnings or endings—all of this disorder is our reality, this is our life. Our world is a great disorder; our thoughts are a great disorder; our lives and what we do are a great absurdity. We follow after signs and this is what we love—to give someone a flower, this is a symbol, everything is a sign. People are bound to signs; this is a person's reality. All realistic literature with its beginnings and endings and its descriptions of things does not represent anything—the term itself is absolutely illogical. On the contrary, all the disorder of writing is reality. We cannot even control our own thoughts, we can't even know what we will think about in the next moment. The past, the future, everything gets mixed up, that is reality.

Can you talk about how you translate this reality into writing?

I think that I can enter into the thoughts of specific characters. If I understand a character, then I also understand their way of thinking so that it is often said that I have this ability to create a specific character by grasping the idiosyncratic ways in which they think.

This disrupts the idea of a master narrative, where ideology controls character; when you say that you enter into a character this means that you partake of the human condition as an individual and this allows you to get out of the constraints imposed by ideology.

Researchers say, since I don't really have critics, that I can describe a character without saying a word about the character. The sense of the character is conveyed entirely through speech or thought processes.

This question of speech in writing is of great interest. We've often spoken of how there is hardly any difference in the speech patterns of characters in most Israeli prose; in your writing, as soon as a character opens their mouth, so to speak, a picture already emerges—who this is, what their thoughts are. Can you comment on this?

This, of course, is expressed much more in "popular" speech. Spoken dialogue is much more trustworthy and exact than dialogue written in literary language. And this is one of the difficulties that makes some of my work virtually unreadable. So that I find myself forced to add translations below the dialogues. I myself don't even know how I got to this point of being able to use the language of each character, regardless of their social standing. Apparently, I absorbed every word that I heard. As I said, our house was a kind of meeting place for may different kinds of women and men. My mother and my aunt in their respective professions knew many Muslim women of all classes and they were always our guests so I had the opportunity to hear and absorb all of these different dialects and styles and I would listen to them and it sunk in.

In deciding to continue using Arabic, did you feel that something was missing in Hebrew, particularly in terms of rendering speech since the ability to depict various classes or types of speech is quite weak?

A number of writers had the pretention to switch to Hebrew. There is a proverb that goes like this: A stork landed on the roof of a church to do her duties. The keeper of the church wanted to catch her so he put out some meat but she didn't eat it. He gave her wine but she didn't drink—Why? he asked her. You are using the roof of the church as a bathroom so you're not a Christian, you don't eat meat, so you're not a Jew; you don't drink wine, but you're not a Muslim—so what are you? I think that someone who professes to change from one language to another loses all direction. I don't think it's possible to write in a language that was taught to you at the age of twenty or twenty-five nor do I think it is a wise thing to attempt. Naturally, I prefer the language that I can express myself best in. Nor do I think I know Arabic well either. Colin Wilson spoke of the bankruptcy of language. There are simply senses that we don't have language for, taste, for instance. Odors. So why would I limit myself by writing in a language that I know less of? To get back to your question, the issue of speech was definitely something I was aware of. In Arabic, you can convey various levels of spoken language in a way that you cannot in Hebrew. There are also personal obstacles and reasons why I went into the Arabic language in such great depth and these are connected to the new reality here and the trauma we underwent. This resulted in a kind of roadblock between me and not only the language but everything that is Israeli which has lasted until the present.

Yet, you are a kind of privileged witness of this time here, with an outsider's perspective that sees somewhat further, beyond the borders of the state and its daily problems. Do you see this as a burden?

First of all, it is a choice, but also a necessity. The choice is very personal and connected to the whole story of my family and my father's attempts before he died—along with a group of other Arab Jews—to leave the country, to get international citizenship. But we weren't allowed to leave. After my father died, we tried to get passports but we simply weren't able to. So my idea of going to Lebanon wasn't simply to stay there but to try and go to London. That's the personal side. From the point of view of necessity, the truth is that I cannot bring myself to terms with this society. I am an honest man, and society here is not straight, it's as simple as that. Everyone is at war with each other. Even if you don't intend to offend anyone, you are marginalized in one way or other. Even in Egypt, which is not completely an Arab country because of its strong Western tendencies, I feel an enormous difference. When I am there I simply find myself. I can enter into society. I have better friends there than I do here, even though I only go on short visits. These are the two things, the necessity and the choice. As far as my writing goes, of course I've been here even though I don't feel within my spirit as if I live here. I live either with the hope to leave or to travel. But the fact remains that I have had experiences here and a person cannot simply slough off everything that is around oneself, reality always penetrates at some point. My two novels deal very much with Israeli reality. In every work of literature there are things that come from the experiences of the writer, that the writer takes advantage of. Even when you are writing a story that is symbolic, things get in. Often this is subconscious; a writer is like a reservoir in which things keep getting stored and it inevitably bursts forth in one form or another through the writing. To claim this, from a literary standpoint, is both correct and incorrect at the same time. It is correct in a personal way. I made a choice, there is an obstacle between me and Israeli society. From a literary standpoint, a writer has to write of things that he understands and knows more about. For me to come along and start writing a generalized narrative of Israeli society is not something I could do, for Israeli society is still composed of *a number* of societies. You see people that still speak many different languages; customs differ vastly amongst groups of people. The society hasn't crystallized completely. But the things that I did encounter and understand here are things that I have written about.

Every writer consumes their own previous work, how have you seen this happening to yourself?

This is a very difficult process to trace in one's own work because it involves your own assumptions. In my first book, I wrote stories that took place in Iraq. In the second book, I started to use the dialects of Iraqi Jews and Muslims, and this is something that no one had even attempted before. At that time, I wasn't even thinking that I was setting down dialects that were in the process of being forgotten, but it seems that I must have thought it would be more faithful, more representative of reality, to use the dialects. In the preface to that book I wrote all my thoughts regarding the absurd, the use of signs, and the boundless nature of reality. I also wrote that innovation is not every gimmick that a writer can come up with but a very arduous task, something that must be pursued consistently.

How would you define innovation in your own work?

Innovation is anything that hasn't yet been attempted. Everything that hasn't yet been written. Something that hasn't been read, hasn't yet been encountered.

Someone who writes fifty or sixty books cannot help but repeat themselves, whether intentionally or not. Of course, the essential philosophy keeps coming back again and again but every story that I write avoids repeating a technique I've already used. In my last novel, the narrative is based on parallelism in which several time frames are depicted simultaneously, jumping back and forth in time, from the present to the past and the future. All the events are fragmented and they must be put together by the reader like a puzzle.

Can you say something about influences?

Of course reading changes. Writers that I once devoured are no longer of interest to me, but this is a natural process. Every writer is influenced by other writers, but also by everything they have gone through. Every writer that is really a writer has an area of uniqueness that one cannot make light of. Every true writer has aspects that no one else has expressed. Lately, I've been reading a lot of North African writers in Mahmoud Darwish's journal *al-Karmel,* some of them not very well known, and I must say that I am quite impressed. As for the known ones, at one point I was captivated by Sartre in Arabic translation, but when I read him in English I wasn't as impressed. I don't know if the English was a bad translation or if the Arabic made it into something else. I'm not sure if I would read Sartre again now. Naguib Mahfouz is a writer who, it seems to me, is barely understood by the majority of his readers. Each one of his sentences can be penetrated to find many, many things beyond the apparent. Naguib Mahfouz is a major writer. When he got the Nobel, I said that this was a debt paid after a long, long time. But the prize was given to books that I don't even think are among his best. He has books that are much greater but that the committee couldn't even read; he himself said there were books of his that he would rather have been judged for. I don't think that the Nobel prize is such a great arbiter of literature.

As you know, often the factors are not literary at all—I think here of a number of Russians who got it simply because they rebelled against the system. I would say it's simply a case of discrimination, Europeans always think themselves above the East or Blacks or even Latin Americans, while these are the places and the people that are really producing literature. I think it's simply a question of superiority. If the Egyptians didn't translate those six books of Naguib Mahfouz for which he got the Nobel then nobody would have done it and he wouldn't have been recognized or come to the world's attention in the way that he certainly deserves. This is really a problem which must be dealt with. It is absurd, for instance, that such a committee choosing the Nobel only reads works written in or translated into the major European languages. In my case, the problem is even more complex. If the Egyptians saw to it that Mahfouz's work was translated, who will see to it that my work gets translated? A Jew who writes in Arabic presents all kinds of problems to everyone, yet I am simply continuing to write in my own language. Perhaps I need to deal with this, the way I did with the money for the apartment that went into publishing my first book!

To get back to writers, I followed the *nouveau roman* very closely, particularly Robbe-Grillet. At this point, everything that is remotely conventional or traditional is no longer of real interest to me. I'm looking for new, experimental works and I see a lot of this in Arabic writing, particularly amongst the exiles. Edwar el-Kharrat, for example, is someone I follow. I think that he must have read a lot of Sufi texts, I see him as being very influenced from that direction, even though he's a Christian. Another writer that I liked very much but who, unfortunately, died very young, was the Egyptian Yahya Taher Abdallah. I think he could really have become a major writer. As I mentioned, the things that I see from North Africa are of great interest. But, as others have pointed out, my writing is really mine. I try not to read before I start working on something; my thought takes a long time to ripen. Every time I try to write in a new style, on a subject that is different than what I have written before. Of course, subconsciously all kinds of things from other writers find their way in. So I try to distance myself from other writing when I'm working on something.

As far as things go in general, I am not very optimistic. In my opinion, literature is in a constant decline because there are all kinds of factors distancing the reader from a text, like television, for instance. When my sister and I were the age of my kids, we would read. There was no television. So we read all day. Naguib Mahfouz has also commented on this. I just don't think people read enough. Writers are not read. At this point, I am more interested in getting translated into English or French because it is only then that I will truly be able to evaluate myself. It is very difficult for a language to assess itself from within, it is only in the process of a response of readers and critics that this can happen. It's true that people are writing doctorates about me but I don't want to remain an "academic" writer or a curiosity. I want my books to be read so that I can get a response from readers in a universal sense, who are not familiar with me. But I never feel as if I have exhausted the possibilities, I always want to go further and further and further.

— *Translated from the Hebrew by Ammiel Alcalay*

PROPHESIES OF A MADMAN IN A CURSED CITY

"Here I am" is the utterance I had gotten into the habit of reciting axiomatically. It went with me as I was permeated by a kind of dizziness on the long road to the cursed city. Probably this "Here I am" made its way along the road to "my city" instead of me. And between the "Second Tower of Pisa" and my house there is a desolate stretch where the Lord's spirit first descended upon me to call out in refutation: "Son of Man." And for the first time I said to my maker: "Behold, here I am." And since then I have been saying it to Gomer and to my son and my daughter and the old man hidden in his den waiting for me and saying it to my dog and my doctor and my covetous friends and to everything.

The road isn't long anymore, and my clothes, my tattered work clothes I had changed for others, no longer dusty. And the plumb line is in my hand and without even a gesture I embody its cold inanimate form without sensing the swiftness of my steps and my imagination departs taking me back against my will to the site of the towering building. There I see myself like countless times before prostrating myself in front of my other ruler, the dwarf giant. And the echo of my recitation, impotent and defeated, reverberates mechanically: "Here I am." And his voice silenced me, the way the Lord's voice had silenced me the first time his spirit descended upon me and comanded me: "Go into the darkness of night to search for Gomer. Then marry her. She is expecting you at the crossroad."

Overcome by an awesome fear I seized onto my battered thoughts and words until I was able to speak: "How shall I take a wife when you have created me unfit to wed or to seed."

And my other master, the dwarf giant, glared at me with fire in his eyes and shrieked in my face: "You're unfit to work as a builder. Go shut yourself off in that ivory tower of yours to lecture and starve to death."

And God said to me the first time I prophesized: "As long as you follow my commandment and take Gomer for a wife, then Gomer will bear your offspring."

And I do not stumble to avoid thrusting my weary strides towards the cursed city. I no longer see my steps nor do I see the path I have traversed. Face to face at the site of the towering building with the "Other Lord," the dwarf giant, my brain struggles and like a fool I ask him: "What sin have I committed that you even deprive me of hard labor and drudgery?"

Here I am. Still walking. Stepping along the way leading to my house. My thoughts inundate my steps as they strike this straying desert of prophesies. And I know some of the crimes I have committed and I swear to the dwarf giant Lord using the most terrible oath of all that I am not a Freemason and that I never used the plumb line except to straighten the building so it would rise up to heaven bearing itself erect and not bend its back. Then my second Lord dwarf giant glared at me, another fiery stare that singed me, aiming the darts of his fiery tongue to consume my reason, before quickly turning into a heap of ashes and saying: "That is the folly, and this is the crime. How could we contend with the Tower of Pisa if the building were straight? And do you think it could become a new wonder that would attract millions of people to it if its crookedness does not outdo the crookedness of the Tower of Pisa?"

Just at the threshold of the mechanically reiterated reconsideration of the events, after I had already gone halfway by intuition and divination, without relying on certain knowledge (something unavailable except to someone in full possession of their faculties), precisely at that point in the wasteland where I had first prophesized, where the spirit of God had descended upon me, my ears wide open to hearing the Lord's spirit from within the feverish sea drenching my limbs, his voice came ringing from my depths and utterly pulled down my being, reverberating through the walls of my head in his call to me: "Son of Adam." It was then I uprooted every bit of "Here I am" I had within me, unfurling it in sacred awe before my Lord, and he asked me: "What do you see in that desolation stretching out all around you?"

I freed myself from Gomer's hold, from the hold of my children, from the hold of the sick old man, from the hold of my psychiatrist and, finally, from the hold of my Lord the dwarf giant and his building, that he wanted to set as a challenge to the Tower of Pisa or the Tower of Babel. I uprooted myself from the grip of things, of everything, and gazed at the surroundings as the sights before me clearly distinguished themselves. My eyes roamed the desolate expanse and I was horrified at what I saw as I whispered into the ears of my maker, barely hearing my failing voice: "I see a wasteland, my Lord, filled with bodies, and I see the bodies; they are the bodies of men and women. And they are naked as you created them, shamelessly exposed. And behold, the naked bodies are rising to their feet. The men, my Lord, are seeking the women, and the women, my Lord, are seeking the men. I see them all craving flesh and in this frenzied, delirious craving, the male is drawn to the female and the female drawn to the male. Some kind of unstoppable match is taking place in which the players make no distinctions between one another nor is anything loathsome to them. A father refrains not from coupling with his daughter nor does a sister recoil from mating with her brother. Each cleaves to the other. Then the wilderness returns heaped with naked, enmeshed bodies."

Silence. I try swallowing the spit in my mouth after it has gone dry from the horrors I had just been a witness to and that I could still see around me, permeating the world, and which I had described to my Lord like a game on TV. Whenever I stopped describing in order to swallow my spit, the Lord's indignant voice struck me like a whip and commanded me again: "Son of Adam, keep on describing what your eyes see. In this brief moment of quiet, you have surely missed things that would have made your Lord happy, and in this random sea of inattention other things may occur that would uplift your Maker's heart."

Indeed, by all means! And "Here I am." I look to see what is going on around me again. My initial madness evaporates in the melting pot of my other madness: "Yes, yes indeed. I look at the sky, your sky, raining gold down on them. Then they all pounce at once stained by the defilement of their contagion, without cleansing or purging themselves from impurity, and run toward the gold rain which blinds them as each tries to seize more than the others. And behold, someone who had just been coupled to his sister is digging his nails into her now to snatch whatever gold of yours she had managed to take, and the fingers of someone who had been coupled to her father recklessly sink into his neck until he again falls to the ground, unconscious, the gold tumbling from his loosened hands. And the daughter, aroused, bends over, this time not to see her father, the motionless lover, but to gather the blinding bits of gold."

The Lord's delightful laugh sent a shudder through me. Then the smile froze when he asked me again. "And now, Son of Adam, what do your eyes see now, Son of Adam?"

I refrained from swallowing my spit and fixed my gaze at the wasteland without delay. "My Lord! This is the greatest sin . . . the calf." Panting, I burned with zeal for my Lord and called out: "My Lord, this gold of yours is turning into a calf at the blink of an eye. They're all around the calf, making noise, rejoicing, dancing, and carousing."

And the Lord whose spirit had descended upon me said: "Do you know, Son of Adam, who these people are?" And without waiting for a response, he began explaining to me, as I penetrated and went into the fiery melting pot of my second madness: "These are the dry bones that I showed your friend the seer in Tel Abib, and I restored them to life."

I couldn't control myself and I cut the Lord short as I beseeched and requested: "By your mercy, my Lord, restore them to what they were before, the dust of bones. They deny you, acting licentiously and indulging in the vilest of sins and, as if this were not enough, they even worship the idol of the calf." The second this came out of my mouth, the heavens thundered and lightning flashed and fire flew from the raging Lord's nose, passing right by and almost singeing me, and then my limbs began to tremble at the reverberation of his rumbling voice: "Keep quiet, oh Son of Adam, and go back to Gomer."

But I did not stop imploring him: "I am bedazzled by you, Lord." The sparks flying from his nose pursued me as they became spits of fire. His voice made me quiver: "You are going against my will, Son of Adam." I kept beseeching him. "I don't understand anything. Explain it to me, my Lord, exalted and all powerful one." But the Lord called: "Go, Son of Adam. I have decreed that you eat your own waste until my wrath passes and I grant you favor."

My consciousness sank into my abdomen and choked in my stool and I am still in this emptiness leading to the cursed city, getting down on my knees and continuing to demean myself and beg before the Lord whose spirit descended upon me and whose ire poured down on my head: "Oh Lord . . . you were the one who commanded my friend who prophesized in Tel Abib to bake his own bread on fire fueled by human waste. But your compassion was quickly stirred and you changed it from human waste to dung. Would you not, as well, make my sustenance dung instead of excrement?"

"No, you must survive on your own filth. This will not cease until you're cured of your madness and you come back to stop acting against the will of your creator." I fell on my face and mingled the cursed earth with my tears until my fallen countenance was rolling in the mud.

★ ★ ★ ★ ★

Everything here is afflicted, and Gomer is my first malediction. Many tasks await me, but my only skill is in following the command and uttering "Here I am." And I have nothing in my dominion but this covert mission that fills my very being, measureless and without color, but whose weightlessness already makes it like lead. And if I dare to rebel against its voice, it will transgress and put me to death—if I do not say "Here I am." Yet, it is my most prized possession, even though people refer to it as a mental defect and even distance themselves and, utterly convinced, call it insanity. I wiped the mud from my face and dried the tears and got up. The Lord had already gone and the wilderness reverted to its silence and tranquillity, no longer disturbed by the raging voice of God ringing throughout my very being as he commanded me to do the kinds of things that, were they imposed upon the sea, the waters of the sea would dry up in fear; and were they imposed upon animals, they too would die of sorrow and revulsion. As for me, I have my tears, my flesh, and my suffering. I quickly learned that shedding tears and expressing grief are but the other face of revolution and rebellion. They are the resistance of an impotent madman from whom, in every syllable of the words flowing from his mouth, can be heard that here is his sole and only possession: "Here I am." So it is I feel nothing but the obedience permeating my being. But I found consolation in Gomer no longer finding any more blood in my veins to suck.

The minute I get home, she'll tell me: "Bare your soul . . ."

My faithful dog will howl and sadly lament, taking pity on me until he gets hoarse and his voice fades from weakness, seeking refuge in tears that he will shed like rain, his spittle drying up as his tongue cleaves to the tattered rug. While the bastard and the bitch still . . . No . . . no . . . even just thinking about it makes me shiver. I know that this is the unadorned truth, but I came up with the miracle in order to struggle with it using simple logic . . . The wonder of it is our world's disposition, despite denial of the cardinal principle. I am the Lord's prophet, his spirit descended upon me a few minutes ago, and he released me from my dependence on that arrogant dwarf giant and everyone else, from the moment he determined my fate. . . .

My Lord! Make this food that you have commanded me to eat taste like the manna you once sent to the Israelites. Make it sweet to my palate for, after all, you are the almighty.

★ ★ ★ ★ ★

Come lightly Gomer, my beloved, sorceress with bloodsucking fangs, you whom I sought in the darkness of night at the Lord's command and found in the pitch black and married in a moment of forgetfulness. I held my nose for fear that your hungry breath would kill me. You used to rummage through the garbage looking for food since no one gave their heart to you, just as no one paid any attention to the old man, lean as an ancient palm tree. I found him in the street, his head between his oarlike thighs, complaining of hunger and the pains of a rupture. I adopted him the way I took you for my wife. And "Here I am, Here I am," unburdening myself before you, as I thought of going to him. Now you are groping for my jugular vein, to stick a straw in and begin sipping "my wine," red as crimson, my aged, vintage wine.

No . . . no . . . don't you realize that everything comes to an end sooner or later? I'm left with nothing: my exquisite wine has turned to vinegar and my blood to excrement. And you blurt out: "Take your clothes off!"

"At your command, Here I am."

And the whips crack down over my body.

"What do you want?"

"Steal!. . . Steal!. . . Steal!. . .

And my four-year-old "son" comes toward me with a kitchen knife in his hand. He spits in my face repeating after his mother like an echo: "Steal!. . . Steal!. . . Steal!. . . Do as my mother commands."

He drops the knife on me but I block it with my hand. My palm is wounded. In the center of my palm a river whose waters are yellow blood flows . . . the color of waste.

I swear . . . this boy will soon become a bloodthirsty murderer, even before he grows up. And the girl, her mother's daughter. Five years old and she stands in front of the mirror putting on jewelry and makeup and swaying . . . impudently showing off her little body, paying no attention to the din about to ignite in this house.

"Aren't I pretty, Father?"

Father, what a slanderous word that has become in our city. I stare at the little tease and my senses become even duller. All the thoughts in my head are struck dumb, yet I see the signs of early revelry, just about ripe for the picking. I swear . . . this little girl, like her mother, will soon walk the streets, swallowing them up in the darkness of night, even before she comes of age. I call my dog. In my confusion and weakness, it is his help I summon. The dog steals an aggravated look at me and growls. He has my food in his mouth and, in his eyes, a look portending evil. I brought him here from a distant city, he was a stray. When I first encountered him I had some sardines and the dog stared at me with the imploring look of a beggar. His gaze rent my heart and tore the bag with the sardines in it. The fish scattered over the ground and the stray dog ate them until his loyalty could be judged. Then he stuck to me, nor did he leave until he came to this cursed city with me.

"Steal!. . . Steal!. . . Steal!. . ."

With the ringing lash of the whip, the baby wailing, the girl's insinuations, and the growling of the dog, tensed to leap . . . in a moment of absentmindedness, inattentive to common sense and reason, he surprised me. His bite savagely pierced my thighs . . . the signs of his fangs, and the holes through which a yellow liquid oozed. Oh Lord . . . my madness touches every creature and infects them.

"Here I am". . .

I surrender and obey. Despite the foolish burden brooding in the depths of my consciousness to warn me: "Thou shall not . . . shall not steal!"

I'm pulled from both sides, my conscience rent asunder. Disobedience repels me, and the idea of stealing destroys me. How was it that Gomer put it? How could I let her starve to death? How could I disobey my conscience? And how could I steal?

My soul was burning. I'm drawn toward "obedience" by an unvanquishable force and then, by another force, just as unconquerable, I'm drawn to the foolish burden borne in my limbs. Finally, I'm split in two. Half my conscience shrivels up and hides in the bosom of my conscience and the second half, the "Here I am," is immediately dispatched to the blood bank. Searching for the container bearing my blood type. I know that this is the type Gomer loves to sip, as if it were the choicest wine. Here I am coming Gomer, here I am coming with my blood, at least spare me the malice of your lashing tongue. But the voice as well as the whip resound.

"Get up . . . the police are at the door looking for you."

I woke up swimming in a sea of sweat and astonishment: "Police? Why the police?"

"Don't you know . . . didn't you just rob the blood bank?"

"Does the police know what goes on in dreams?"

Gomer laughed licentiously as she bragged: "How would the police have known, if Gomer hadn't reported it?"

How could I have forgotten that Gomer knows all my deepest secrets and that she even infiltrates my dreams? I don't have much time. There is a lot to do. The window leads to the street. And the street leads to the old man who is waiting for me. I climbed up the window and jumped. I fell right where that traitorous dog had bitten me. I again heard his barking along with the dirge of my betrayed leg. With my last remaining strength, I fled for my life.

The second he saw me, he gave me that piercing look and raised that awful, thundering voice: "May the depths carry you off . . . Because of you I missed the prayers. How come you're late?"

Choking, I swallowed my spit in order to overcome my rage and I said: "And what's so terrible about praying alone? You don't have the strength to go anymore and if you insist on praying with everyone else then there are others besides me who'll take you to the place of worship." He trembled again and his eyes became like red hot embers burning in their sockets.

"Without you?. . . Don't you know that cholera hasn't spared anyone?" And after a long silence he said: "And what did you bring me today, is your mother mourning your death after she's buried you?"

I got more aggravated. The hate I felt for myself doubled. For if Gomer had been the first curse heaven had imposed on me, this man was a curse I myself had chosen. This old man represents all the abominations of this city. Despite this, I took pity on him. I met him one day on the street as he trudged along, suffering from hunger spasms, while no one showed him any mercy. I was the mad stranger then and I sympathized with him and took him back to his shabby quarters. Since then, I've been like an obedient servant and he's been like a tyrannical master who never ceases to oppress and degrade me. I remembered his question and answered in a whisper: "Bananas and apples, in addition to your usual dinner."

Suddenly the surrounding darkness became even more dense and my eyes got misty, so I added: "Do you still live in this suffocating darkness?. . . Extinguish this smoky oil lamp and turn on the light . . . I'll cover your electric bill so you can enjoy the light and . . ."

He cut me off as his fury reached the firmament: "How dare you judge me, you son of a bitch! I'll do whatever I want with my money."

"Your money?"

I swallowed the rest of my words. Gall is one of the traits of this city's residents, not to mention hurting other people's feelings. Their tongues are well versed in curses and insults. As for me, "the Stutterer," as I was dubbed, I swallow some of my words, and chew on others a hundred times so I can be sure that I've blunted their edge and they'll be incapable of hurting anyone. However, there was a question that I had no answer for which kept bothering me. Where does this old man hide the money he gets, and what does he intend to do with his hidden treasure since he's already got one foot in the grave?

I was upset. A mighty hand came down and gripped my chest. A strong desire emerging from my very depths entreated me to finish this foolish deed quickly so that I would be free to go and see my friends . . . so I said: "I'll make some food and get your tea ready and do your bidding quickly because there are some people waiting for me on pins and needles."

He laughed contemptuously: "On pins and needles! You run with the speed of a gazelle to commit your sins. As for good deeds—you turn your backs on them. Damn you all!"

Suddenly his voice trailed off. He looked dejected but he kept complaining: "I've got a terrible pain in my thighs and I don't have the strength to get to my room. Carry me on your shoulders and go around the room with me for a while."

As if in step to a command that could not be disobeyed, all my limbs cried out "Here I am," and behold, I kneel down before him as he hastens to mount me. I expected to feel something like the weight of a feather on my back but, oh Lord . . . the mountain itself had set itself down on my shoulders. I tried to get up but immediately fell back again. I was collapsing under this, the heaviest of burdens, as he bucked at my ribs using his feet for whips, pressing his knees against my neck until I almost suffocated. He prodded me like a donkey, relentlessly cursing me. And after slipping three times, when I managed to stand up straight, he began giving me orders.

"Fast!. . . Don't stop!. . . Turn!. . . Go over to the oven and put on the tea. Fix my dinner while I'm still on you! Stop breathing and don't complain about it!. . . Don't breathe!. . . If you breathe again, I'll see that you leave this world and go straight to Hell! Woe unto you if you drop me and I get hurt because of your stumbling!. . ."

My thoughts weighed heavily upon me, to the point of stifling me. This dry, hollow palm tree had turned into a mighty, legendary power on my shoulders, trampling me. Strange and sombre thoughts stirred in my head, almost blotting out the little consciousness I had left. Was I undergoing the adventures of "Sinbad," terrorized on an island by the evil monster? The answer came as the strangling grip of his thighs fastened onto me, causing a pain whose source was the feeling that my neck had taken leave of my body. This must be the monster. And the massive evil concealed within routs this ancient codger, turning him into this force that beats me and unconditionally surrenders my youth. And he calls into my ears in a dreadful din: "Stand straight, you sourpuss. By the life of God, if you trip, I'll strangle you with my thighs and put an end to your meagre, shameful, deformed self."

I beg for mercy and hasten to point out the services I had provided for him. But in his contempt for me, he is proud to take up his "privilege" from this world by force, at the expense of madmen like myself. Amongst the gloomy thoughts going through my mind, I wondered what I would do tomorrow—if I managed to free myself from his iron grip and get away from this ogre safe and sound, would I not come back to bring him things that are sweet to his palate and continue serving him like an obedient slave? But this question came up before its time since the only thing on my mind was getting away from this old geezer. I got my throttled mind in gear and put my nose to the grindstone. A ghostly memory flashed through the walls of my brain. A thousand and one nights. Sinbad the sailor. The wine, yes, the wine. "Yesterday I brought you two bottles of the choicest wine. Open one and drink in honor of your mounting my shoulders . . . I know you'd rather save them for the Sabbath and the holidays, but this world is not empty of wine, that much I am here to promise you. . ."

"Yes, I promise . . . I'll bring you twice this and more. If you drink one bottle, I'll bring you two more. If you drink two, I'll bring you four in their place . . . tomorrow."

Yes . . . yes. Greed was also a trait of this man and this city . . . He was convinced and said right away: "They're on the shelf . . . Bring them over so I'll be able to get four tomorrow."

It's odd that, despite the greed and avarice, you swallowed the bait and thus, with your own two hands you put the evil that had been spreading its lashes like a blind, crazed force along the lengths of your legs to sleep.

"Now I'll put you down to sleep and be on my way . . ."

The intoxication already spread through the cells of his tongue. He was overcome by drowsiness. Chewing his words, he mumbled: "You tricked me, you filthy vermin."

"Did you want me to buy the wine while you were still riding me?"

On the verge of sleep and wakefulness he again said: "You tricked me, you dirty rat."

* * * * *

I said to my friends: "Tonight I'm melancholy and spent."

As one of my friends said: "Your mood doesn't matter to us—it's your money that matters."

Infirmity took the upper hand and sadness reigned over me. I mumbled: "I don't have a cent on me tonight."

Like a chorus who knew the words by heart they said: "We'll lend you the sum."

I asked my friends: "And would you lend it to me at the going rate?"

Ridiculing me, they laughed till they were about to drop and said: "No, because you have to divide the sum by three."

My unbridled folly presented itself to me, but I felt completely powerless and heaped scorn upon myself: "Should I borrow money from you in order to spend it on you and let you get it back threefold?. . . I know I'm not all there but have you no mercy in your hearts for your demented friend?"

The word "mercy" titillated the hidden stores of their derision and laughter burst from their throats like a mighty torrent sweeping them off in its current while I stood agape and mute, waiting for an answer, expecting at least a slight measure of justice from them. Finally, the extent of this justice emerged in the form of a damning and judgmental declaration: "This imbalance of yours is, in itself, merciful. Choose then: either your madness or your association with us. Or get lost, ostracized right into the bosom of absolute solitude."

I was at my wit's end, completely thwarted. I had no idea what to choose.

Everything in the world shattered before me as I writhed amongst the shards.

The psychiatrist exacted half my salary in order to tell me at every visit: "You're crazy!"

There was nothing new in this for me. The truth is that in my former city I was a "person" but in this cursed city I am "insane." The general deterioration of things lately, and the contempt people had for anything reasonable, led me to visit my doctor urgently. I wasn't expecting a bandage. Since a bandage is impossible in this case, the only thing to be done was to remake myself from scratch. But the signs visible on my body led me to believe that I was crazy despite myself, and that the absence of reason over everything that transpires is the prime factor in upping the ante on my responsibility. I hastened toward him and before he could open his mouth, I said: "Gomer flogs me with her whip until my blood is drained."

I saw that something was bothering my doctor. But he said: "Delusions."

He retreated a step. I took a step towards him and said: "And my baby stabs me with a knife—and my dog, I feed him, yet he bites my leg."

The doctor flinched, his expression filled with revulsion. He again took a step back as he said: "Hallucinations!"

I went after him and added: "And the man that I adopted and took upon myself to deliver his every need has turned into a monster, riding me and trying to strangle me with his long legs."

My doctor began huffing and puffing, progressively retreating as he said: "Delusions, illusions, hallucinations."

How I loathed him; a murderous rage clouded my eyes. Driven blindly I started taking my clothes off until I had bared my body: "Look! These are the lash marks from Gomer's whip. And here is the palm bearing the stab wound, and the bites in my thighs and my dislocated neck and . . ."

He cut me off, still sniffing in disgust. It seemed like he was trying to keep from vomiting, as the surge of nausea knocked against the doors of his throat.

"Listen! All this attests to the fact that things have deteriorated to a perilous point. As delusionary seizures take root they can have physical effects. Your persecution complex has gotten to a point of physical materialization that has left real signs on your body."

I was flabbergasted. And not because what he said was shocking but because throughout this whole thing he didn't stop grimacing as his gloomy countenance showed signs of repulsion and he reached into his pocket for a handkerchief to cover his nose.

"But tell me . . . what is that stench emanating from your body? Excuse me for asking, but did you soil yourself?"

I shrieked at my doctor as my honor bled before him: "This is an insult I cannot tolerate."

"So what is the smell coming from?"

Feebly I said: "I have taken upon myself the Lord's decree."

"The Lord's decree? What kind of decree?"

I stammered: "I have been ordered to eat . . ."

When it became too difficult for me to finish my answer, my hands began to make gestures that would do the job . . .

My doctor understood. He became very serious and looked quite decisive as he said: "Then I am left with no choice but to hospitalize you."

My heart sank. My Lord, this was not agreed upon between us. Wasn't your punishment and what had happened to me in the cursed city enough? And isn't it enough for the lunatic to be chastised in his home and in the company of his friends and in the squalid lair of a greedy, monstrous and avaricious man?

"Flee!. . . Flee!. . . Flee!. . ." The words rang deep within me. Leaping in my ears. I didn't strain after their source. I didn't know whether they had come from within me or whether they were inspired by God or the Devil. This is a city inundated with curses but the wasteland of my prophesies stretches before me, and behind me "The Leaning Tower," and the dwarf giant clinging to his theory that "perversion is a miracle." And here is the door, and my doctor is quite troubled at having to phrase his decision to "lock me up" nicely, but I take advantage of his distraction to stretch my feet and flee.

The wilderness again. I walk along looking behind me. Thinking to myself and gathering in my madness and innocent conscience. I walk despite myself. Despite myself I turn my back on the commitments I made, toward people who reward kindness with evil. People who, it seems, think good deeds are utter folly and craziness, deserving punishment. When I had gone well astray from this city's curse, I could see its malediction like an octopus, spreading its branching tentacles out to other cities and infecting them with the curse.

This is the plague. A scourge. Spreading like quivering pride. And "Here I am," here I am, punished for my very own crimes. And the Lord is punishing me with a punishment that the heart of the Creator could not serve upon a being that was created in his image . . . Was I really created in the image of God?

Obliviously, I found myself wretchedly castigated, the roaring of harsh winds deafening me. Grains of desert sand filled my mouth and blinded my eyes. Like the Lord in the eye of the raging storm. He had been looking on at my thoughts, and trailing after my abundant heart. The strength of the storm made me realize how angry the Lord was. But for a split second, so rare and wonderful, I overcame my weakness, I routed my defeat. For this awesome moment it became clear to me that I was at the height of my insanity and that I had never used reason to think for I was drawn to my surging heart and my own desolation without recourse to the citizens of the cursed city. And as for the Lord—what could my crimes have been for him to prevail upon me and saddle me with a wife like Gomer and my wayward children and the sinful people of this damned city? What crime did I commit for him to decree what he had decreed to no man before me? And for the first time, I said: "No!" As loud as I could I said: "No." The call thundered throughout the wilderness and got stronger as it reverberated ringing "No" a thousand times . . . a million times "No."

And behold, the spirit of the Lord descends upon me. And behold as our raging spirits meet. And the Lord precedes me by saying: "Who are you, that you say "No" to your Lord and Maker?"

My limbs quaked and shivered, and I retreated into improvisation: "Me? The one you demeaned and created from flesh and blood, and created with a good heart, and then you punished me and decreed that I eat my own waste . . ."

The echo brought back the Lord's irate voice, foaming in fury as he shrieks in my face: "You have brought shame upon your Lord. Flee, then. Get out of my sight at once."

Since I had already turned to nothing among other things, I asked him: "What was my sin?"

The Lord said: "I made you in my image but you disobeyed me and refused to remain in my image."

"What was my sin?"

He shrieked until his voice got hoarse: "Flee, before my anger gets the better of me and I turn you into fleeting dust."

I was perplexed and suffering . . . I was frightened and filled with dread. I remembered "al-Ma'ari" and "Cain" and I could no longer think at all.

"How shall I flee from you when you are to be found everywhere?"

Right then the desert flashed with a spark as sharp as a knife just whetted on a grindstone and the end of it, like the eye of a flame, struck me in the stomach. The sight of my stomach caused me to lose whatever balance I had left. My stomach was split open and my guts were pouring out in front of me, mingling with the dust of the wilderness. I sensed death at hand and began my plea: "Have mercy upon me, Lord. Pardon me. I took the hand of that licentious sorceress and I ate my own filth and did not transgress your orders, so why won't you let me loose?"

The Lord screeched like a madman: "Woe unto you. You even dare to argue with me? Flee immediately."

I struggled against the shudders running through my limbs, the chattering of my teeth, the pain within me, my confusion and insanity.

"How?"

I heard the racket of the Lord's uproar: "Flee!"

"Just tell me how and to where?"

Nothing but his thundering voice reached my fading, almost dimmed consciousness:

"Flee!. . . Flee!. . . Flee!. . ."

I was astonished. I gathered up my entrails and stuffed them back inside myself as I bent down on my gaping stomach, pressing my wound with one hand and keeping myself from falling and stumbling by supporting myself on the ground with the other. No, for if I was crawling it was on my stomach, going forward I know not where like a swaying drunkard, but I did flee. And the Lord still pursues me. And Gomer is pursuing me. And my son and my daughter, and my psychiatrist. And all the citizens of that city are after me, the city in which people are dead and God has a heart of stone, and the Devil does whatever finds favor in his eyes.

— Translated from the Arabic by Ammiel Alcalay, M. Joseph Halabi, and Ali Jimale Ahmed

from THE ANGELS' GENITALIA

7:47 A.M.

Ben Gurion Airport. The big sign welcomes me, wishing me a bon voyage. It just stands there, opposite the monument to the Unknown Soldier, coldly and monotonously saluting in reproach, arousing doubts as to its intentions, as if flattery or deceit were meant, creating a sense of transient pleasure with nothing to cover the debt. But this security barrier always divides us and shatters the calm, spreading incomprehensible shadows of fear. Here you just have to swallow your fears and keep going. Maybe you have to do this everywhere, but to a different extent. And so it has been, as well, throughout time in different ways until it seems as if this fear came down from heaven with Harouth and Marouth, the two sinful angels, to lodge itself within the human soul, as a decisive hereditary trait that you can't get rid of. This fear becomes internalized. And it's irrelevant if their blazing spirits scorch you like spooks expelled to materialize all of a sudden before your very eyes as immediate and plausible danger, or if their motives remain concealed in the very depths of your being in the form of a hidden crime that imposes itself unexpectedly before you, just as the danger of being caught in the act hovers by. You can find this fear in the air here, shrouding the invisible. And I breathe in, filling my lungs with it. Before I know it, the fear has doubled and I become a possible victim whose turn will come; at the same time, though, I have it in me to become one of the two hangmen, a decisive cause of this very monstrous intimidation. You are amazed, my dear fellow, in addition to being short of temper because your car has been stopped twice, and your astonishment grows as you see me get still all of a sudden as I take my identity card and passport out of my pocket, though they constitute one of my two fears. I draw it out fast, to finish with it. My appearance always arouses suspicion, and this happens to me "here," any time I happen to be in this place. Does my face look like that of a "terrorist?" I realize it's round and dark brown and above it there's a mane of wiry thin kinky filaments that curl and fork but I've got the nose of a vulture and, besides, I've straightened this all out before more than once. That day it was the very same guard, but his memory fails him. When they look at me, it's as if they're struck by amnesia, their faces cloud over, their eyes fill with suspicion. I can assure you that at this very moment his suspicions have gotten the better of him. He dons the role of a hawk to go after its prey. And he amuses himself with the hope that he won't come back empty-handed. In another second he'll ask for my ID, his head bent down to the window of your car, and he'll check its contents with his nose borne toward the sky; afterwards, despite all the facts recorded on my ID card, he'll refuse to believe me and order me to get out. I am not telling you a story from the collection of tales about angels that I have in such abundance, this is precisely what took place the morning of that sunny day, so awash it dispersed the very clouds of illusion.

Here comes the hawk's assault, just like I promised: "Your ID card!" He struck me with his fiery look. My countenance, for reasons whose nature is not completely clear to me, took on some metaphysical traits since I proclaimed my decision to carry out research on the angels, and it's entirely possible that I had been contaminated by some phenomenon that has no logical explanation, in a way, in fact, that counters the very principles of research. As if I had chosen what Melissa herself had chosen and was shattered along with Satan's demons. Be that as it may, I do come from the city of apparitions. And if one takes into account the influence of the environment on a person's formation, all this will seem less amazing. My face began to conceal this tremendous power that aroused a tendency towards such aggression, hidden in their chests like the germ of tuberculosis. "Your identity card!". . . No change yet. That splendid day of the discovery returns to be taught everything, down to the very last detail, at the crossroads. Better not interfere in my favor, if that's the case, it would just complicate matters even more. As if the facts written plainly in my documents weren't convincing enough by simply glancing at them; getting a good word in my favor from the cab driver won't make it any easier. You just have to wait and I feel sorrier for you than I do for myself or even them. I'll just get out before he commands me to. The morning of that day an argument flared up and turned into a fight. And this was the beginning. Which will still become the conclusion that comes before the beginning. Once again this complex problem chews its own cud as its jaws are stricken with paralysis and come to a halt before invigorating themselves again so my teeth can grind steel. This is that other complex problem which is not directly connected to the play of words and the hypocrisy of semantics and the multiplying face of meaning. It steals into the world of vague and different beings and hands over the imaginary borders drafted between the angels and the demons. And it brings me back to the question of scientific research, and compels me to whet my appetite and talents for exacting study in order to seize the evidence proving to them once and for all that the apple is not a quince and that there is a difference between a stork and a giraffe, and that conjecture alone is not truth, that holding onto illusions simply in the name of honor just in order not to humiliate yourself by having to say "my mistake," already signals a departure into pure self-degradation.

Luckily, I had gone through this experience more than once. I had already rehearsed the part that would be acted out here, in this place, until I had it down pat. And now I can appear on stage in a style befitting the part, and this should keep things short. Here I am, outside. I take two steps into the fresh air, hopping like a mountain quail, but no one notices my limp. I'm already adept at covering it up and my stocky build contributes to this deceit, to the point that all the women I knew who tried to force themselves on me, or whom I myself tried to force myself onto, never managed to discover it. Now it doesn't really matter. Preferences compete with each other. They're as selfish as people and recognize neither limps nor any other limitations. They don't submit themselves to your bodily compulsions but emerge as "they" please. And then they assail you with an eraser in their hand and immediately, with absolute impertinence, begin rubbing out the oppressive circumstances . . . much to your surprise.

Nonsense. Destiny knows no mercy. And its heart already hardened and turned to stone the moment this guard began examining my ID card and upon his face the flies of suspicion and doubt and misunderstanding began to invade in great groups. In the next five minutes we will have to stand face to face with this stone-hearted fate and shatter it. And you uproot your astonished gaze stretching out over the guard's look of astonishment, directing him to me. Of course shattering destiny's heart is impossible, but we shall at least force such an impossibility to kneel. Allow me to abandon my exaggerated sense of self-confidence and reserve my opinion. Nothing is for sure. That day the sun shone brilliantly in the morning and in the evening the light and the splendor disappeared in its absence. This occurrence was certain, being a standard existential phenomenon that lost any need to prove itself for millions of years, and it's liable to remain a natural phenomenon for millions more. But I am speaking of another sun, that rises and sets within, to no set order. And at this crucial moment it clouds over the guard's suspicious look. I swear to you now that his look is resting upon the name, seized by confusion like a bee who's missed the flower and come to rest on a thistle. His look reads "Akram al-Khayyat," as if he'd been stabbed with a dagger, and then he slides over below the name and is gripped by more pain, as if he's been led astray. And the two pains meet and give birth to rage. He made a mistake. And it won't be easy for him to go back on his word and apologize. For people think retreat loathsome and often find no path to it. I went after it for three whole unblemished years until I found it. And don't expect me to get stuck here at this checkpoint for another three years until this guard finds a way to retreat. Such a supposition cannot but arouse fear, laughable, ridiculous, and remote as it may sound in the face of more pressing and logical assumptions. This guard is not guided by the inclinations of his heart alone. He is subject to those whose charge he's under, nor is he in control of his own time. It's not in his power to be generous with years or even hours. And behind us a line of cars has formed, and with it an increase in the chances—no doubt cutting your instinctive equation regarding the speed and increase of the space in half—that will come to determine his immediate behavior, with one simple difference. He will still search rashly after something to hold onto and a second won't pass until he erupts, since an outburst remains the easiest, most familiar way for him to act. I am reconstructing the events that took place on the morning of that day, and I see them come back and repeat themselves. Those very events drawn, or rather, chiseled into my memory as if it were a marble slab. Between the rising of two suns and their miserable setting. They're crowded and painful. Like my name and the look on this man's face. They aren't shrouded by the fog of the ethereal creatures stretched out in their graves within foolish minds hovering over legendary skies. The demonic hand of an "angel" passed through the front lines of my wit at the end of that day and wiped the dust off, then a crystalline light sparkled and faded before this beginning that still stumbles and limps appeared like my wooden leg and, despite itself, came back to the beginning of endings to pull me along with it by the obduracy of shabby words, in vanity and significance cloaked in the garments of fraud and cunning. Here it starts "in the beginning," along with the name and the ID card.

Akram al-Khayyat. Their problem and mine. And he always creates these winds that blow into tempests out of nothing. And I cling to him in pride, and the guard clings to him in order find some justification for his position and deceive himself into thinking he didn't make a mistake. Can you imagine that he actually charged me with forgery that day? No. He wasn't referring to the name but the identity and since identity is of the essence that is what he made into his object of desire. Names are of no consequence. Didn't we already reach an agreement over this? Yes . . . yes. . . . In this case the name assumes a legal importance and I don't think there is any need to explain or clarify the reasons for such a thing. Why didn't I change it like everybody else? Don't make me laugh. Haven't you heard the one about the donkey who put on glasses, donned a cloak and called himself "Professor?" A whole stable of donkeys followed in his footsteps. They reaped their reward by taking in a lot of other donkeys, but they never quite figured out how not to remain donkeys.

Identity is an element as decisive as fear. And "Akram al-Khayyat," despite anything I might have said, is part of that identity. He's different than all the things that have been borrowed to pull the wool over our eyes. And as for me, I wasn't born with Melissa's demons and exiles so that changing my form won't do me any good. My identity was forged a long way from here. It was fixed before I knew of it since I was born and I exist. And some of my most distinguishing features include the fact that I am a man, my religion is Jewish, I live in Baghdad and my name is Akram al-Khayyat, something that simply can't be blotted out so easily, even though the guard over there, in an attempt to maintain his honor and in fear of betraying it, persists in charging me with forgery. And in just a second or two, after an expedition through the lines of my identity card and the evaluation of that journey telegraphed through the twists and turns of his head dedicated to finding a substitute for retreat—and when the first signs of the imminent storm already strike his face, covering it in dust, and wrinkles as delicate as a baby's begin to appear—we will conduct a dialogue I know by heart. My back is broken, afflicting me with pain. Here, at the beginning of my journey, dreaming in the cistern of light from my other sun. The morning of that same day, the end of the straw appeared and evolved from the guard spitting on my existence and my very identity to the spit alighting on me glob after glob until it became a river within leading to my retreat. Thus was I drawn in by its current and when I reached the end of it I found myself before this beginning. Excuse me! This is my fate, like my identity. And fates, like identities, cannot be obliterated. His thin, purplish lips quiver as he goes on asking: "Where did you find this identity card?" Making a long story short, I tell him straight off: "ID cards are issued, not found like garbage or stones left at the side of the road." Then he will say: "So where did you steal it?" No. I won't open this door for him, a door leading to an abundance of the imaginary that would make him wander between all the possibilities that have any connection whatsoever to his sole but rootless intention, so that he could create an imaginary root from one of these imaginary possibilities to grant him at least some achievement or gain some praise that might seem like the praise garnered by those considered a "success" in our time. An era fit for those who accompany others to get the interest, an era when simpletons are taken advantage of for the brilliant fulfillment of their achievements and stolen ideas. I'll still cut through his sandy, twisting cords and put us at the very end of the road by asking him: "Is something not in order?" And just as it happened that day, the eyes that had been seized by such confusion as they rested on the lines of my ID card, ferociously align themselves in wait for the expected rain of words to come down. They always need the pace to be gradual in order to find the arguments justifying their random assumptions along the way, just like in scientific research. Yet you still lead them, with an unexpected burst of energy, to the very bosom of an assumption that has no basis in reality, for in this case the axiom spares itself. The flash of logic pales, clarifies, and confounds. And in such a situation you force them to confront their error face to face. Since they've kept themselves from admitting anything, their thoughts become confused and reason fails. The last chance, as it were, hangs upon the measure of gain that can be found in failed excuses. And the question then is, how can such excuses be made to come to their senses? This guy lacks the experience; after all, he's not like the donkeys who pulled the wool over the eyes of the other donkeys, he didn't even acquire a black cloak or put glasses on the way they did, nor did he specialize in preying upon innocent fools. Thus, like on that very day itself, he diligently concealed the blood rising in his face between the lines of my little ID card, when the heavy skies in his head filled with barren clouds. The excuses dry up on his tongue together with the words, but there's no way out of it. He has no choice left but to invent things, so his tone tries to reign in the tempest: "Yes . . . yes . . . there's something here I don't understand."

The name, no doubt. "Akram al-Khayyat." An indivisible part of me. And I will not cease pronouncing it simply to avoid obstacles and problems such as these. Once upon a time Akram al-Khayyat shone forth, and many spoke of him, happy and jealous and proud of him, even abjuring him, but one thing was unanimous: Akram al-Khayyat was the most outstanding student in all the schools of Iraq. And Akram al-Khayyat was not simply an expression or a phrase that could be exchanged for another. In other words—the name signified a human being in itself. An identity that has its own overt and covert characteristics: origin, age, sex, place of residence, as well as many other traits. And all these characteristic traits together constitute the most outstanding amongst all the Iraqi students. That student was . . . me.

But all that is over and done with. Left behind, there, in the mist. Turned into the "heritage" of the past and plundered from me like that very past itself, and I have no right to it except in memory alone. Time circles round, despite words growing old and the deceptive turns of meaning. And here I find myself behind everyone, taking up the rear. And Melissa's words alone still ring in my ears, roaring and thundering within. These are the kind of words born by chance, but they cannot be crushed.

Of course I won't tell him this. What matters to me now is refuge from this moment, with my dissected past and identity trapped in his eyes and mind. Right now another past ripens in that head of his, another past of mine made up by prophetically inspired rumination given unto him from the text of my identity card. A new life, like my very future, drafted in their own hand; just by chance, since I announced my willingness, with such great celebration, to keep on the trail of bodies that evaporate in air, just because I was enchanted by the impression the word "angels" made. . . . Just imagine!. . . "The angels . . ." The emptying out of impossible abstract meanings into a form made of the tiniest speck. We invent the nonexistant in order to find in it something to inflate our superegos like a ball in bloom, or to strengthen the belief in our existence, reassure us, and calm our spirits. But this guard has already forced himself to take the obstacle course of invention. And he wants to invent, at the spur of the moment, a whole life, when his only point of reference is a faded word in my identity card. On that day the word was turned into dough kneaded in his hands and taken from the material out of which the bodies of Melissa's "friends" winked. And if you were looking at him that very moment, you would have thought you were looking at the Lord creating Satan in order to send him down to Hell. He was trapped by the magic of his own being just as I was trapped by the magic of my angels. And the sun's glint within my limbs in angelic glory. And he already turned nothing into a solid as he ordered me to get off the bus, and then: surprise, surprise! Isn't it odd that an illusion will battle another illusion and dispell it? I must confess. I am indebted, at least in part, to the guard for being here and putting the soles of my feet down on the threshold that I refer to as "the beginning" and you "the end." At the end of that day, a divergence from the paths of folly began and its beginning, the initial signs of the straw that broke the camel's back, struggled in the guard's eyes, appearing from his brazen wish to invent. Here the words branch off from his mute gaze yet to be forgotten or washed away before they are uttered. So I was already prepared for this well-rehearsed dialogue, imprinted upon the back of my mind with the letters of reality's own typewriter, nor did I invent this prophecy, I simply picked it up from a memory that knows no betrayal. While the guard still betrays my expectations, confoundedly and wearily asking me: "Are you traveling?". . . "Yes . . . yes . . . here is my passport." The data on both documents coincides. And I can't have pulled the wool over everybody's eyes. Now he's fallen into the trap. This poor, inexperienced fool cannot be counted, even in their elasticity, amongst "my geniuses" whose ability to manuever, whose talent to pull things off and produce profits drawn from defeat, like water from a well, is so well known. He's been wounded to the quick again and it hurts. Retreat surprised him, heading him off at the pass, but he is still trying to reach a compromise with himself so he doesn't have to apologize in front of me. His rosy cheeks turn the color of a pomegranate and his hands, stretching out to give me back my ID card and my passport, tremble. His resentful surprise bears both the echo of his rage and retreat. "Why didn't you give me your passport in the first place? You think I have time for this kind of nonsense?"

Nonsense?. . . That's how it always is. They try to loot your very being and after they're stricken by helplessness, they make you responsible and call it nonsense. . . . You, my dear fellow, this is probably unknown to you but I established a border in the middle of my life and left the tatters behind me since I intend to start from scratch. And all this because so much "nonsense" of precisely this type was piled onto my back until it broke that day. So be it. We subdued the impossible, we softened the flint of destiny, and we needed no more than two or three minutes to do it. I can see that you are lamenting these minutes in mournful silence. Perhaps, if you dare, or just to comfort yourself, you could ask for compensation. No, dear fellow! You're better off asking from heaven. I have long ceased covering the expenses incurred through the mistakes of others. And wouldn't it just be your luck to be the first one to bear the blame for acting justly towards myself. There's nothing wrong with that! The world won't rid itself of fools just because *I* abandoned the donkey stables; after all, the world is still full of stables and you will, no doubt, get paid back right after your car expels me that very moment that waits in ambush for me, at the entrance to the airport. And this moment has already come, in the blink of an eye. And both of us, me and that moment, quickly rush to overthrow ourselves in each other's embrace, and I don't know who was responsible for this. I had been yearning to look at this moment from the distance, but that's not what happened . . . it didn't happen! As if we all conjured together to make it not happen. The moment. And you, and me. The moment—miserable and wretched, pulled into the abyss of nothingness through a mighty, invisible power, and you, driven by your instinctual perseverance into an endless race in the arena of time; and me, pillaged without end in a world whose thoughts push me back to a before I had finished with, but that tells me not to let my face ever turn back towards it. Indeed, in my broken back there's an alarm warning me, emitting a cry of anguish every time I try to turn my face, except the tumult of coercive thoughts that recur again and again is even more painful, swallowing up the rattle of my broken back. My thoughts are stranded on an abstemious shoal and I have come down to "here" only to see them "there," at the checkpoint, stupified at their estrangement, almost mute but penetrating as the call of a cricket, "Why? Is this the face of a 'terrorist'? And what do you expect someone who hasn't stopped running for three years to look like, following the trail of pure, white angels, just because it wasn't in his power to sustain the complexion of a person bearing the perfection of all colors?"

★ ★ ★ ★ ★

When creating his magnificent and autonomous realm, the Lord did not forget to make soldiers who would defend him, and their numbers are so great they cannot be counted.

There are many brigades in the Lord's bulwarks, each with a different mission. There are brigades that penetrate the human heart with a piercing coldness. And there are brigades that invade their members in terror, and others that unfurl fire upon them, and brigades that abort their illegitimate offspring, and . . .

There are those who believe that this mighty bulwark of the Lord is made up of nothing but his dutiful angels. And the widely circulated name uniting the platoons of this army with its various units exists, a name whose very pronouncement inspires awe in the hearts of people. "Angels of Terror!" A name so well known the creatures and days have studied it repeatedly. . . . Except for three years, sweet and dreamlike, of all the years of your life . . . and your mind!

So rejoice, fools and makers of nonsense!

—Translated from the Arabic by Ammiel Alcalay and Ali Jimale Ahmed.

UZIEL HAZAN

UZIEL HAZAN was born in Casablanca in 1945 and emigrated to Israel in 1955. He attended Ben Gurion University and Hebrew University where he graduated with a degree in law. A member of the Israeli Bar, Hazan has a law practice in Jerusalem. His first book, a collection of stories called *Barking at the Waning Moon,* came out in 1976. This was followed by *Armand: A Moroccan Novel* (1981), and a children's book: *To the Snows of the Atlas* (1987). His latest and most ambitious novel,

The Mark of Berberia (1991), moves from the Atlas Mountains to Paris, New York, Mexico City, Hawaii, and Casablanca. As Hazan says, the protagonist John/Aziz "is a person who, precisely there, amongst the Berbers, finds culture. Classical music is not culture. The Nazis also listened to classical music. Neither is religion culture, there is too much killing in the name of religion. Culture without humanism and social justice is not culture. An intelligent person can see precisely what the situation is nowadays. This culture of ours hasn't rooted out the horrors one bit and this has led to a sense of disappointment that has become the legacy of the twentieth century The situation is bad in Israel as well. We have a culture of war here that already creeps into the house with childrens' toys." In a review of *The Mark of Berberia,* Ronny Someck wrote: "On the cover of the book there is a photograph by Avraham Edri of feet sculptured in sand. In the case of *The Mark of Berberia,* this is the window to a travelogue. 'Wanderings,' wrote Alterman, 'become your homeland,' and Uziel Hazan has turned this homeland into a philosophy. In *The Mark of Berberia* these are wanderings to God's portion of the land, where the words "In the beginning" have not yet lost their simplicity. From time to time this journey reads as though through a camera whose lens is focused on wild scenery. If you like, this is the human jungle book, only the jungle is not the preying teeth of animals, but the smooth skin of women who can still be excited by a waterfall, and from whose bodies the rays of the sun take pleasure. *The Mark of Berberia* should be stamped into the passport of all our dreams." So much more than exoticism, *The Mark*

of Berberia is a conscious effort to approach complex and hybrid cultural and historical circumstances through an analagous complexity of narrative. In this, Hazan's work is reminiscent of other North African writers such as Albert Memi, Edmond Amran El Maleh, and Assia Djebar.

from THE MARK OF BERBERIA

Section I: On Sin and the Refutation of Memory

No matter how Aziz, now called Juhan, wandered,
And took on forms, and cast off forms,
Took up ways of life, changed cultures and trilled languages,
Imitated customs and bowed to other "gods"—
The mark of Berberia ever clung to him,
Sometimes a lily-shaped birthmark,
And sometimes a mark of shame,
But always, to him, unblemished,
Primal, perfect . . .

—*U.H.*

1. Silence, pain and time pursue Caliph, but the day of liberation keeps them at bay.

He was impervious to the dull, stupefying cycle of his life because he lacked memory; neither had judgment been given him. That is to say: Is sensationless slumber behind a smooth, white screen preferable, or is beholding the picture of everyday life preferable, more blessed the excitation of being "engaged," though it bring exultation and pain?

Caliph peeked out of his lair—a stable adjacent to a dump—and, as was his habit every morning, greeted the first rays of the sun with a grunt. This was his prayer of thanksgiving to the light, to the sun god—a god he could not see, though he felt his caress and, sometimes, tasted the fruit of his blessings. Caliph's daily barely audible moan gradually grew to a roar; this was the only sound he made from the moment he rose until he lay himself down. For what had he the power to express, with mind eradicated and mouth sealed? . . .

The men of the village knew to tell—or so they had learned from one of those released from prison—that once upon a time, Caliph had spoken; indeed he had spoken until his fortieth year.

He was shocked into silence the day the prison warden told him that, from that moment hence, he was a free man. After twenty years of imprisonment, he would now be the master of his own time.

Often during his prison term he had been among those gathered in death's antechamber. He had envisioned a strange angel of death: no black cape, no long scythe, just a formless invertebrate of violet-magenta hue. Thus, at moments of hallucination, death was borne on puffs of contemplation, or in drops of time that slowly dripped from his veins, like blood collecting in an hourglass. When memory yet marked him, he had not conjured time as a liquid—though he knew it was surely not a solid—but rather as something elusive, like the olive oil made in the village of his birth. At such times—times of depression that came on the heels of oppression, times of writhing insomnia that sucked at his marrow, times of starvation that made passion languish and lust expire—he thought of suicide.

His lust for life depleted, he longed to cease to be, as if it was his awe of time that begged for his end, obliterating in him the sense of eternity—an illusion that lived in the soul of every living being, in whom the flow of life suppresses consciousness of the end. Once released, Caliph was again given power over light and darkness: a choice that was itself sometimes pitch darkness, sometimes luminescent.

An extended stay in solitary confinement—a dark, dank pit in the center of the prison courtyard—had severely damaged his eyesight. Now, only a few years after his release, a tremble still shook his nerves. Nausea was kindled in his bones whenever he recalled the isolated red clay fortress, that rose from the south-eastern flanks of the High Atlas Mountains, a day's ride from Mzawyat-Ahensal.

When first brought to that monastery, a youth clutching his grandfather's hand, he had met a Sufi monk who had talked of how human beings toyed with one another, building their graves while they yet lived—castles of stone and palaces of sand, fortress walls, cities of refuge, chambers of solitude—all as an expression of their powerlessness, of the fear that gives birth to evil or, under the best of circumstances, to flight.

★ ★ ★ ★ ★

One bright morning the prison warden called for him. A bony-faced guard, shriveled and scarred, was sent to fetch him.

The messenger amused himself with the keys to the cells, swinging them like a pendulum. Those twisted, rust-scored hunks of iron had seen little use: Only infrequently had the residents been subjected to light and wind, even though most had once been mountain-dwellers who had taken their freedom, like the wind, for granted. To them the keys looked like lively creatures whose clacking was the call of liberty, like the bells that galloped through the fields on the backs of noble Arabian steeds . . .

"Caliph Ibn Zaidan!"—the guard's cry echoed up the narrow corridor.

The echo was heard many seconds after the squeaking of the key in the abyss of the lock. Caliph's cell opened with a creak—a sign of life for the tormented heads that poked out between the cell bars, their eyes lifeless and wan, drained of hope.

Skeletal palms grasped the bars, too limp to shake the cold iron. A few, who looked like chickens, heads shaven and struck by apathy, gazed through the slats of their coop, staring at the blank world they never entered, much as the green pastures and adjacent snow-covered hills ignite no spark of recognition in the eyes of a grazing cow chewing its cud. The guard strode past the cells, an exalted king leading a soundless procession devoid of calls of triumph or cries of camaraderie. He clung to their enforced dependency and reveled in the hierarchy of rank and control, in the blessings of power. The prisoners slowly turned their heads toward his steps. After he had vanished, they were again swallowed up behind their bars in silence, or with a subtle, hushed murmur. Sometimes a voice barked out like the yelp of a tethered dog. The lone sign of life—the clanking of the chains on Caliph's legs—echoed. Once brought before the warden, the guard-escort labored long to free him from his rusty shackles. A heavy hammer was needed to break the decomposing chains. Now, the burden removed, the body which had for years been an affliction was relieved, as if delivered of an actual physical weight, of spiritless flesh and blood, of a ball and chain, of clipped wings. What was left of the body—was nothingness. How buoyant the life of a butterfly! . . .

★ ★ ★ ★ ★

He stood opposite authority's desk, his face sealed, his arms limp at his sides. The warden nodded at the guard. An ink pad was brought to the prisoner. He did not budge. When the body is paralyzed, events die. The guard seemed to be holding the wings of a tame and acquiescent dove, or of some guileless creature for which all seemed rosy. "Press your thumb on the ink pad and sign, you fool!" The flush of anger was invisible on the brown face of the fortress servant. Caliph remained in place, senseless. Should he, like an illiterate, sign with a thumbprint? He had known how to read and write since he was six; from earliest childhood he had been devoted to ancient Arabic poetry and Berber rhyme; he could quote verses from the Qur'an and recite tribal tales of heroism—on and on unto forgetting. Even at such a moment as this, his heart embraced the *kabyle* poem which ran, broken, through a hollow corner of his mind:

Love in our time—to bread will I compare it:
With toil and great sweat will I till, will I plant.
When it blossoms in spring—I will reap and so grind it.
In the *kanoon* will I bake it, when hunger strikes sore.
When the lion has sated—then will I forsake it.
Love in our time—a hard loaf on the water:
Reach out to grab it—it will crumble in your hands.

Love in our time—like a moonlit stroll
On a festooned balcony across from Samira's room,
The wick's light flickers on her face as she combs her tresses.
Seven steps will I falter; the eighth—an abyss.

The guard took Caliph's dumb thumb and led it to the ink pad. Caliph acquiesced without a word. The finger was pressed to the bottom of a faded, yellowing page: A release document. That moment, he had signed away a period of his life.

The guard lifted a slight bundle wrapped in woolly cloth and hung it on Caliph's arm—the personal effects that had been taken from him twenty years before. There was the box of snuff, silver-plated and embellished with arabesques, a rhyme of Khayyam engraved on its side: "Come, fill the glass . . . look at the rose blooming around us. . . ." A verse from the Qur'an was engraved on the convex lid: "There is no God but God;" the God who once had walked by his side, but with whom contact had been severed. Thus had the aroma of tobacco, the jubilation of wine, the beauty of the flower and the omniscience of God once been intertwined. There was more: pages of parchment, handwriting, faded pamphlets of poetry, a cloth turban. A copper scimitar was left him for defense against the beasts of the field, without fear that again the bloodthirsty Satan would enter him, causing him to take the life of a man. An amulet swathed in sheepskin was in the bundle—why had it been taken off his neck? . . . Caliph was led to the wooden gate, which opened with a creak. The palm of a hand pushed his back. The guard waved him away: "Go, flee, run for your life." His sign language added nothing to the hints of creation, of the free world that lay before him, for his soul was still prisoner.

★ ★ ★ ★ ★

He stood there a long while, rooted to the spot. His liberty weighed heavy on him. The gates were locked behind him. He wondered and stared at the horizon, greeting the new world—an awesome universe, threatening, unfathomable—with skepticism and fear. In it he was like the young cub of some wild beast which has just now been pushed out into the world, abandoned by its mother. The creaking of the impermeable gates still echoed in his ears. Suddenly they opened again. He did not turn to look. A sharp kick in the behind knocked him to the ground. He did not hear the turning of the lock. For a while he lay among bushes and brambles. He got up, his face streaming blood. From dust and blood came his punishment. He did not remember the deed. The pain gave him the strength to walk on. A backward glance showed curiosity mixed with a primal fear, fear that was both flight and warning, fear that felt like the forest, and the being lost in it.

He stood and studied the walls of what had been his compulsory home for twenty years, walls that had protected him from the sobriety granted by the revelations of the outside world. In this state of freedom and loss he tried to talk to himself, to rage or to yell, to express himself. Caliph coaxed from his vocal cords a growling that was strange to the human ear but not to the beasts of the field. Outcast from the tribe of bipeds, he crawled and slithered on his belly. He could not recall the directions of the four winds because he had lost his way, and his memory was extinguished. Twenty years of damp blows to the head had indeed chased away the memory of the sin, but had left nothing to pine over. The striped *tsamir* that he wore, which reached his ankles, fluttered in the breeze, revealing his nakedness to the immaculate sky. "And they were both naked, the man and his wife, and were not ashamed." The Garden of Eden was worthless to him, because he did not know he was in it. They had robbed him of his senses, obliterated his past. For what is liberty if not remembrance? And what is remembrance if not longing for the sites of desire, for the assembly of figures, of indelible faces, for homecoming, for joy and for sorrow? Memory is a river to be sailed down, an archive of the history of time, dispelling loneliness by enriching the imagination.

★ ★ ★ ★ ★

Caliph was like a being from another planet. He did not know his name, he did not remember from whence he had come or whence he should go. Absently, he groped forward with blow-swollen steps. He passed his hands over his shaven pate; moles sprang up there like mushrooms. When he had first been imprisoned, he had shielded his head with his elbows and large palms: Nevertheless, most of the blows had found their way there. He preferred the *falakah,* and the kicks to his ribs. Being put in solitary confinement was more pleasant than the meeting of club and head. How strange: Before, when liberty had yet lived in his consciousness, he had made many escapes. It was these that had brought upon him the punishment of the obliteration of memory, and with it, of the sense of liberty.

He wandered far afield, arriving at the banks of a perennial stream. His watery reflection stared back at him and asked: Who are you, Caliph Ibn Zaidan? He continued on his way, growling to the trees of the forest and the rocks of the hills like a wounded animal. The hands of memory stopped before fleeting experience, from which he could not have gotten the full measure of pleasure or sorrow. He strode back and forth within a radius of several miles, always returning to his point of departure, as he had done on the "circular marches" in the prison courtyard.

At nightfall he would again find himself facing the wooden gates, guided there by sound waves of hunger—that basic instinct that sharpened his senses and lifted for a moment the dull pall of indifference.

Although it spoke to his heart, liberty filled him with an insecure, hidden dread, with loss and fear of the unknown. Again and again a magnetic force pulled him to his prison, to the high walls that had closed in his fears. There they had suppressed in him the world of sensations that enervated and prevented rest. He stood before the wooden gates, his arms flailing at the great doors. Guards were startled from their watch. The gates were opened. Disturbance led to violence, to an outpouring of destruction, calling forth blood, which flowed over his eyes, coloring his sky red.

A merciful guard threw a rock-hard loaf of barley bread at his feet. He felt how evil and mercy descended from the heavens, entwined. Caliph drooped in a swoon. At dawn he found himself hungry, frozen, and in pain—sensations that brought back some of his senses. He grasped the loaf of brown bread and tore at it with beastly fervor, his eyes popping from their sockets. When he was a shepherd, he had often seen the hunger in the eyes of the leopard devouring its prey. The pain abated; the sun shone; his hunger stilled. Again, sensations faded. He quickly distanced himself from the walls of the fortress. Dimly, like a baby who has touched fire for the first time, he understood that they were a danger to him. He looked at the sun, thrilled by the rays of light he had so seldom basked in. Slowly his rebirth began. He blinked at the flood of light, and harkened to the singing of the village girls. Their voices echoed from afar as they walked to the river to draw water into bloat-bellied clay jugs, or to bathe and wash their clothes. The sweet, pleasing melody and hypnotic rhythm of the Berber mountains teased his ears, like drops of rain on a windowpane. The words of the parable danced around him without penetrating his mind:

Woman:
My beauty and youth—
In barren furrows of the field!
Whence the seed that will make them bloom?
Whence the cock that will consume?

Man:
If planted yet not implanted—
The seed is stolen, lost!
From the mountains of that caliph
Comes the call of the man!

Suddenly he ceased his plodding steps and began to leap like a young gazelle. Did he hear the sounds and understand the words of the song? Did his memory come back to him? He did not feel the open, bleeding sores on the soles of his feet until he sat in the shade of a tree to gather strength. A shiver passed through him. Pain elicited an incoherent mumble: "I hurt—I am alive!" A shepherd blessed him in greeting. Caliph looked at him with a calf's questioning eyes. The shepherd smirked, dismissing him with a wave of his hand. "Be careful of the water," he heard the shepherd say; the stranger did not know how his words had touched the heart of the lost one. Were these the waters that had drowned his lovely years? How strange: People are wont to call them "the waters of life."

—*Translated from the Hebrew by Marsha Weinstein*

DAN BANAYA-SERI

DAN BANAYA-SERI was born in Jerusalem where he still lives. His short stories, novellas, and novels depict life in the old Sephardic communities of Jerusalem; his rich and allusive prose style, as well as the sudden twists his narratives can take—at once fantastic and mundane—have often been compared to Agnon. Yet the nature of his allegience to language and what it has come to replace point to very different circumstances. In a recent interview, Seri commented: "I did not experience uprootedness, but the people in my Bukharian neighborhood are uprooted and perhaps I absorbed some of their frustrations, longings, disappointment, and nostalgia. I think that in my journey of writing I was helplessly uprooted from my neighborhood, even though I came to glorify it. Every word I write takes me another few steps away from the houses from where I came. Through this, I can feel the pain of being dislocated, even though I am Israeli." While Seri has been labeled a "folklorist," the dilemnas faced by his characters, and their unique reactions to them, embody an absolute awareness of the equivocal nature of culturally sanctioned norms and assumptions. His work is never static as the arrows of both tenderness and irony seek targets that are both close to and far from home. Seri is almost alone amongst Israeli prose writers in the extent to which his language and cultural references seem, in a doubly ironic sense, at "home" within the context of traditional Jewish textual culture. Even as his characters embody the certain knowledge of the intentions of Biblical incidents and personalities, Seri's narrative distance limns the very precarious nature and tragicomic circumstances of the lives peopling his creations. His books include *Grandma Sultana's Salty Biscuits* (1981), *Birds of the Shade* (1988), and *Mishael* (1992).

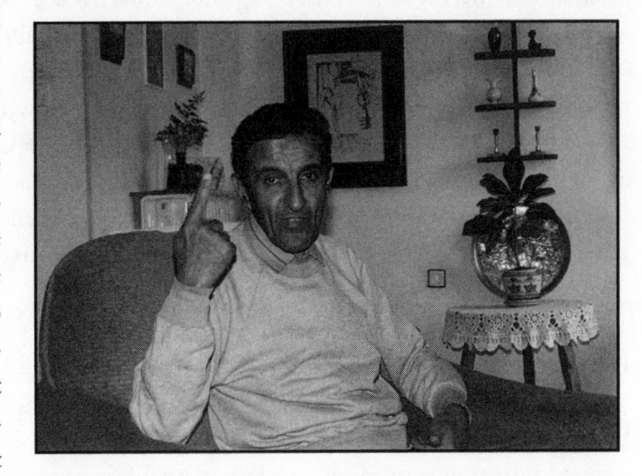

from BIRDS OF THE SHADE

Naftali gazed at the houses. At the broken windows. The weatherworn walls. The children's mattresses yielding their spirits like straw. Who was sage enough then to know how a spiny black spider would climb to the ceiling? And the kitchen crannies, where women lost their souls for a pot of lentils. Could any keep from sniffing the udders of the goats that jingle-jangled under their windowsills? Fortune's favorite who found a pair of chicken wings in her kitchen treaded on air. Feather by feather, a hymn of praise. Oh why had the great storm not spared these wretched houses, he was suddenly shaken out of his revery. What was he doing here? He had meant to go to *Hakham* Duek's. It was for his sake that he had put on Sabbath clothes. But as he turned to go, he found himself standing outside his mother's house, staring in through the rubble.

★ ★ ★ ★ ★

It was many years since his last visit to the house. It had been abandoned long ago. The entrance lay in ruins, the doorpost had collapsed, and the shutters on the window, like the last feather on a dead pigeon, were slowly rusting away. He stepped into the fusty room and leaned trembling against the shattered basin. The smell of cat droppings pervaded the air, and the wormy, dilapidated furniture, the rags and the housewares left behind gave off a putrid smell. He turned to the window and ran his hand over the wreck. This is where the bed stood. The table and the two chairs. And here, mutely reproachful, Mother would light the candles. And when darkness came, she would fold the Sabbath tablecloth with a look of chagrin and stare at the desolate pita from Nadra the Yemenite. He remembered, for many a year she had fed him from Nadra's oven. Pita and more pita. When they fared better, she would sometimes cook him gruel as well. Thus until the winter nights when an evil spirit took possession of her. Worst of all were the times when she cursed his dead father. She could not forgive him, not until her dying day. Her visage was seared with rancor. "It's lucky I have you to say 'Kaddish' over me instead of him." Even in the wrinkles that pitted her face she saw his crimes. "He is responsible for every last one of them." Sometimes he would ask her to tell him. Why was it so? Had not Father done his duty by them both? But all she could say was, "He was old." Still, Naftali never forgot him. A kindly old man on stunted legs.

★ ★ ★ ★ ★

It was Mrs. Duek who opened the door.

"Ah, Mr. Siman-Tov," she was surprised to see his fine clothes. "Please, come in."

Naftali nodded silently.

"Is *Hakham* Duek at home?" he asked.

"Where else would he be?" his sullen face affronted her.

Hakham Duek was just then sitting down to study his daily chapter of *Gemara*. Hearing the voice of his wife, he looked over her shoulder.

"Mr. Naftali," he greeted him, "welcome. With respect, please come in."

"Another time," Naftali declined in a feeble voice.

"By no means," he insisted genially.

Naftali continued to stand as before, with a look of perplexity on his face and a negligible smile.

"*Hakham* Duek," he began.

The *Hakham,* seeing that Naftali's face was not of a cast which favored the intrusion of women, touched his wife lightly on the arm and said, "Whenever Sarah our mother saw guests approaching, she would hasten out to the pen and find a young lamb for them."

"But we have none left," she was distraught.

"And coffee?" he asked with a twinkle.

"A little."

"Heaven be praised," he blessed the miracle.

When she left the room, he did not conceal his opinion of her. "A good but simple woman," he said, leading Naftali out to the courtyard. "Now today she cooked me lentils. And yesterday, this woman of valor, rice with raisins. And on Sunday, stew from the Sabbath fire. And tomorrow, God willing, cracked wheat with honey. And then it will be Friday and after that, bless my heart, Sabbath stew again. Ah, what can I tell you, Mr. Naftali, each day with her is better than its fellow. The gift of first fruits and the 'sheaf of the waving' rolled up in one. In faith, Mr. Naftali, if Jacob our father had given Isaac food as savoury as my wife prepares for me, he might have thrown in Mt. Seir. But Jacob was an innocent, and Rebecca was Laban's sister, and Essau who planned to kill his brother—did not do so in the end, and in this too, if you think of it, there is a great moral. Though you, Mr. Naftali, have not come, I daresay, to discuss the conquest of the land."

"True," he sighed profoundly.

"I could see at a glance," he replied. "Now then, let us sit there on the bench," he led the way unhurriedly, "Soon my wife will bring us coffee."

"I drank some before," he answered.

"You drank nothing," he scolded him to a mischievous tune. "Grain coffee, have you never heard of it?" he brightened, lifting his robe in back as he parked himself on the old bench. "With respect, sit down."

"I'm not tired," Naftali continued to stand.

"Is it your daily sustenance you wish to speak of?" he waxed serious.

"No," Naftali sighed again," That, thank God, is not worth discussing."

"What, then, is the problem?"

"I hinted already," he revealed.

"What?" he wondered.

"Flora."

"Has anything befallen her?" he was alarmed.

"That's just it, *Hakham* Duek, nothing has."

"Tell me more," he urged him.

"In faith, I know not what to say."

"Has she left off cooking, heaven forbid?" he inquired.

"On the contrary, she cooks more than ever."

"And the house?"

"Clean enough."

"What are we left with then?" he chaffed him.

"Everything, "*Hakham* Duek, everywhere you look."

"This, in faith, I do not understand."

"The tea, the coffee, even the sugar," he complained, "Everything comes out wrong."

"Why these riddles, Mr. Naftali?" he interrupted him, "Tell us plainly, pray."

"Yesterday, by way of example, she put cardamom in my coffee."

"Very good."

"Indeed, but can you guess what came out?"

"Coffee," he answered confidently.

"No, coriander!" cried Naftali.

"By your leave, Mr. Naftali, this matter requires some probing. Cardamom is only cardamom, nor does coriander sprout from a holy scroll, and if you put them both together in a pot, what comes out is soup."

"But that's the point," he cried, "Please, listen to her latest exploit. Last week she poured salt in a bowl. A spoonful and a half, perhaps. Can you guess what came out in the end?"

"Let's hear," he observed him with concern.

"Rice!"

"But what could be finer?" he answered suspiciously, "As I said before, lentils today, and yesterday, rice with raisins."

"But she had already put dough in the bowl to rise," he stopped him testily, "Sugar too. There were even figs in her hand."

"And what, pray tell, did she stir with?"

"A wooden spoon."

Hakham Duek folded his robe about his knees and reflected.

"How long has this been going on?" he probed.

"For some time now."

"If so, let us reckon the days," he urged him.

"Five weeks perhaps," Naftali considered.

"Is that all?" he suddenly smiled.

"Perhaps six. Or perhaps a month. In faith, I don't remember anymore."

"But that is the thing, Mr. Naftali," he reassured him with a deliberate hint.

"What is?" he was alarmed.

"What you just said," he laughed aloud.

"What did I say?" he mistrusted his words.

"Calm yourself, Mr. Naftali, where are you going?" He beckoned him closer, "One month. A fine reckoning. This is clearly the source of the matter."

"What matter?" he plummeted down on the bench as in a faint.

"Very well then," he clasped his hand," Let us make the matter plain." He smiled as he took a yellow snuff box from the lining of his robe," Here, until my wife comes out with the excellent coffee," he stood up and tapped the lid with his finger, "let us stroll over to the fence like a couple of ne'er-do-wells," he opened it and offered the box to Naftali. "Would you like a pinch?"

"No," he declined.

"This too must be for the best," he smiled as he sniffed. "And now, if you will look over there," he blinked in the direction of the two ancient pines that shaded the roof like an awning, "the birds. No doubt you too hear them singing."

"Where?"

"In the branches!" he reproached him for his pretended deafness.

"Those creatures."

"Those are birds," he instructed mirthfully," Do you not hear them? There is no finer song in all the world."

"What?" he was perplexed by the vagueness of his words.

"For thousands of years," he rehearsed the old, old tale, "we have learned about prayer from them, and sustenance, and now, rain. They clearly betoken the prayer for dew and rainfall."

"Those creatures!"

"They're birds," again he scolded him fondly. "See how they float, smooth as the curtain of the ark. And it is likewise with women."

"Which wise?"

"As with birds. When the rains are held in check, we do well to eschew them."

"But why?" he fell silent.

"They do not catch," he revealed their secret. "They are like eggs without a shell. Everything turns to glue. Only now, heaven be praised," he glanced at his wide trousers, "we have had ourselves a real first rain."

"But does it never befall them without the rain?" he protested despairingly.

"By no matter of means," he gently disclaimed. "Each and every one of them is slaked by the rain. Forsooth, Mr. Naftali, have you ever known a woman who does not pray thrice over rain?" He led him out to the fence, and took another pinch of tobacco. "That is their prayer by day, and even more by night." He stifled a laugh at the fence. "So it was with Sarah, and so with Rebecca, so with Rachel and even so with Hannah. They all dipped in the same tub. And even Moses, may he rest in peace, though he herded Jethro's sheep in the wilderness, his wife could not refrain from bearing two sons."

"By another man?!" he gasped.

"Perish the thought," he silenced him with a secret smile, "have you never heard that she found a lodging and circumcised her son?"

Naftali stood beside him, silently gazing at the pines. There were birds still perched on the branches. Sometimes they soared above him like mighty eagles, till he realized it was only the rustling of the wind. The other trees showed no less forbearance. This was their strength. Pollen and wasps and nasty blisters of sticky resin, and the sickening mildew smell of mud wherein Mother would burrow after the rains to hunt the forbidden mushrooms she put in her basket. Father's only food in winter they were, and though he begged her mercy, she stuffed him so full that his heart gave out one day and he crashed to the floor. By the time the doctor came to the house he was already shrouded in a sheet. "Dead," she calmly informed the company. She was courteous to the pall-bearers. She offered them coffee and dates. And when the funeral procession began, she dragged Naftali back into the house. "In Jerusalem it isn't the custom for the son to follow his father," she said.

She never remarried. "I've had my fill of them." She shunned the men who knocked at her door.

So she raised him alone. Through the years. He was careful always to stay within her reach. Wherever she went, he followed like a lamb. A shirt, a hat, and the little trousers she cut out of one of her dresses. Sometimes, when he strayed after a lovely thistle or blade of wheat, she would call out the neighborhood, believing he had been preyed upon by a jackal or a lion. "There are wild dogs, too," she sobbed when they brought him home. And when he was old enough to attend the "Talmud Torah," she led him there as though she were tearing out a rib from her own body.

And still the people tried to persuade her. "Have mercy on the child. Take a father for him." But she remained obdurate. "I've had my fill of them."

As he grew older, she taught him other things. About people. "Never trust them," she warned. He learned their telltale signs. Most sinister of all were those with pockmarked faces. These, she taught him, were bearers of disease. And she instructed him on the subject of women too. "They are all the same," she revealed to him, "they bleed." At length she opened a store for him. He would go out in the morning and return in the evening. Then they would sit together on the bench and sip their coffee. The air spread softly over their knees. He would doze. On and on till darkness fell. Then she would firmly rise to her feet, shutter the window and make his bed. "What more do you need?" she seemed to scold.

Sometimes, on winter nights Arojas the matchmaker would surprise them with a tap on the windowpane, "Mrs. Siman-Tov." He grudged her felicity. But she refused to be made a fool of. "So much the better, go to the Zirkaioff's house instead," she frightened him away.

On Sabbaths, dressed like a bridegroom, he would take her arm and lead her to the synagogue. He would hand her a prayer book under the awning and turn to the men's section inside. At home, they doffed their good clothes and stowed them in the closet. He in his old shirt and she wearing a flowered apron would dish out the Sabbath stew and garnish it with a strip of radish. "And for this you need a woman?" she rebuked him again.

Thus she taught him over the years. And the tell-tale signs of women too. Their walk. "Never peek at them behind," she scorned, "it's full of stink in there." There was nothing worse except mosquitoes, which like him, Mother would smash against the wall with the heel of her shoe. And thus did she contend with her other vexations. To each she gave the name of a prophet. Isaiah, Amos, Obadiah. Of these her ailing joints distressed her most. Ezra and Nechemia she called them with loathing.

In old age her rancor seemed to wane. She would draw back the faded curtain and stare mutely out at the path. "Why doesn't he come?" she asked one day.

"Who?" he peered astonished at her tearful eyes.

She fell silent. Slowly her body foundered. The last of her joints deteriorated. Something inside her was trying to escape, and one Monday when they came to take her away in a wheelchair to "Rachel's Tent," the Bukharian home for the aged, she opened her eyes for the very first time. "Why don't you shave?" she grumbled. He could not recall anymore what happened in the end. Except that when they wheeled her out of the house, one of her worn old shoes had fallen off and someone picked it up and threw it by the wayside.

"But I heard something different once," he awakened from his revery, and spoke in a changed voice.

"What did you hear then?" prompted *Hakham* Duek.

"That sometimes women can manage without the birds."

"What?"

"To bring children to the world," he stammered.

"Heaven forbid!" *Hakham* Duek exclaimed.

"But that is what I heard!" Naftali bellowed in despair.

"From whom?"

"From the *goyim.*"

"What did they say?" he asked mischievously.

"Something about a woman."

"Which woman?"

"I don't remember," he turned to look at the tree again, "they say a spirit entered her."

"The woman from Nazareth?" he inquired jestingly.

"That is what they said," he replied.

"Naturally, Mr. Naftali, what did you wish them to say?" he mocked.

"If so, then it is true," he waxed stronger.

"Not a word of it," laughed *Hakham* Duek, "And did you never hear that in the woman's house there was a carpenter?"

"A carpenter?" his face fell.

"And not only in the woman's house," he teased, "but in the town as well. Ten carpenters. A hundred carpenters. Master craftsmen every one. Each with his sword upon his thigh." He burst into laughter, "You see, the woman could not stop changing her furniture," the laughter continued as he grabbed a pinch of snuff, his nostrils flaring, "but this is what I have been telling you all along, Mr. Naftali: The birds, you see, the whole world conforms to their singing. Wherever woman rests her head, the songsters lay their eggs. Only I wonder, Mr. Naftali, how came you upon this idea from the teachings of the infidel?"

Naftali fell silent. He remembered, his visits to Mother at "Rachel's Tent" had been few and far between. He had stayed at home, dully sipping from the cup. Thus he waited for her to die. In the morning he opened the store and in the evening he closed it. Then he came home and sipped his coffee. What do they give her there to drink? He was occasionally moved to pity, only soon he became inured to this emotion too. He would go back to the kitchen and light the burner. The days were overcast. The room grew chilly. She had never permitted him to visit his father's grave before, but now that she had fallen ill, she wished him to. He found the gravestone on its side, gnawed by the weeds, the few surviving letters dark with moss. But then he noticed the little stone beside it, looking ever-new, "In Lasting Memory." Not even the gravedigger could explain this. It must be a baby's tomb, they guessed.

"Ah, here's the coffee," *Hakham* Duek hurried to take it from his wife, "we'll serve Mr. Naftali first and let him taste the grain." But when he turned around Naftali was already opening the gate.

"What's this?" he stopped him.

"It's time I went," he explained.

"But you haven't drunk your coffee yet."

"Some other time," he promised lamely.

Hakham Duek watched after him. his wife approached and stood petitely by his side.

"Where did he go?" she asked.

"That's what I was wondering," he nodded.

"Then what did he come for?"

"A good question." He slowly sipped his coffee. "A very good question."

— *Translated from the Hebrew by Betsy Rosenberg*

AVI SHMUELIAN

AVI SHMUELIAN was born in Rafsanjan, Iran and now lives in Jerusalem. Among many other occupations, he has been a porter, skin-diver, construction worker, hypnotist and restaurant owner. Also an artist, Shmuelian attended the Betsalel Art School in Jerusalem. Only at the age of forty-eight did he publish his first novel, *Moonstruck Sunflowers* (1992), which has been compared (by the Israeli novelist David Grossman) to the work of García Márquez. Shmuelian's novel, along with the work of Yoel Hoffman, has marked a definitive turning point in Israeli fiction. Like Hoffman, Shmuelian has been able to transform the myriad particulars of his chosen narrative space into a completely autonomous realm, overarching so many of the pitfalls that artists working with such materials are prone to. In *Moonstruck Sunflowers,* Shmuelian has created a work of abstract and radical imagination, at once composed of wide, bold strokes and fine, rich textures. He is presently at work on a long novel that draws its powers from texts as varied as *The Mahabharatha, The Hebrew Bible,* the Greek epics, and the Farsi classic, *The Shahnameh.*

MOONSTRUCK SUNFLOWERS

For years Mula Youssuf had harbored a desire to see the sea, ever since the time Haim Dalal had used incantations to bring rain to Rafsanjan. Those had been years of relentless drought. After three barren winters the wells and aqueducts—which flooded the fields and even the city, when all was right—were nearly dry. With the onset of summer the sun had shortened the distance between itself and the drought-stricken, had scorched the carcasses of beasts in the fields, had seared the parched trees. When it had dried even the tears in the eyes of the citizens, when a burning dust had gathered on everything, the Muslims turned to the Jews and asked that they use their powers to bring forth rain.

Haim Dalal, who had only just learned the secret of commanding ghosts and spirits, sat with the other founding fathers in his house amid the ruins. They scoured the old tomes, combing their crumbling leaves until they came upon something about a reservoir. Finding King David's lament for his beloveds, Saul and Jonathan, they read: "O mountains of Gilboa, no dew, nor rain be upon you, nor fields of offerings. . . ." One of those present asked: Where then, did the rains that did not fall on the Gilboa, fall? Haim Dalal sent his twin sons, Joshua-Two-Wives and Arai Diono, to the dried-out river, and they brought him a startled frog. He filled four clay bowls with water and placed them in each of the four corners of the yard, sprinkled salt on the frog's back, and then set the frog loose in the center of the yard. Instantly the frog leaped into the northernmost bowl of water. Thus he determined that the rains of the Gilboa had fallen for thousands of years in northern Persia, forming the Lake of the Kuzars.

That very day he gave the Muslims a parchment of eagle's skin on which were written explicit names and he told them to slaughter an ass in the fields, put the parchment between its teeth, immolate the decapitated head with the talisman in its mouth, and scatter the ashes over the waters of the northern lake.

That summer a party set out from Rafsanjan bearing the ashes of the ass's head, and at the end of autumn they scattered the ashes over the waters of the sea. At the onset of winter grey clouds gathered above the city, endless rains fell, and raging floodwaters threatened to obliterate the city, as in the first days. With no letup—the clay houses dissolving around their inhabitants, the city sinking like an island in a stormy sea until none came and none went—the Muslims turned again to Haim Dalal, this time asking that he call off the siege of the city.

Haim Dalal, who, with his family, had found refuge in the synagogue in the lower city, passed through the door of the house of prayer, burying his head in his long coat for protection against the rain and cold. He climbed the tower in the city wall. Alone, gazing at the turbid, turbulent waters, he stood shrouded in thought. To get to the heart of the matter he took up his childhood habit of sticking a finger in his mouth and sucking it for hours. When at last he climbed down, drenched and trembling, he confronted those who awaited his judgment with these enigmatic words: "The waters themselves are wise; their power is hidden within them." Right then and there he ordered the carpet weavers to weave a flying carpet, according to his design.

In the synagogue that Saturday he took aside the young Mula Youssuf, the only Jew with green eyes, and told him to prepare for the day when the flying carpet would be ready, as he was to fly to the lake and scatter above it a powder for the dispersal of clouds. When the weaving of the carpet was done, the winter ended and the clouds vanished, revealing the faces of the citizens, which were as grey as the clouds. In the days to come, the carpet would give Haim Dalal a place to sit cross-legged, but the longing to see the sea would stay with Mula Youssuf, and it was this longing that brought him from the crossroads at which he found himself, to the sea.

When at last he stood on a cliff overlooking the sea, it seemed to him that he was seeing a familiar sight. Even when he went down to the seaside fishing village, the sea could not teach him anything new—neither by its appearance nor by its properties. All was as he'd read in the Bible, even the mirage he saw at sunset: an enormous metallic bird landing on waves at the edge of the horizon. He compared what he saw to God's chariot, as described by Ezekiel in his prophecy. The next day, when the bird appeared again, he turned to the fishermen, whose language he did not know and, with gestures, asked what this could mean. The fishermen, who were busy salting fish and laying them out to dry on palm fronds, rose as one, leaned forward, spread their arms out to the sides, skipped around in a circle and, with gestures, explained to him that he had seen a *tayara*. Years later Mula Youssuf would be the only Jew in Rafsanjan to believe Arai Diono when he returned from serving in the army of the Reza Shah and spoke of having seen with his very own eyes metal flying machines that could rise as high as the clouds, even with all the Jews of Rafsanjan inside them. All the others just laughed and called him mad.

Mula Youssuf joined a caravan of camels bearing sea salt to Rafsanjan and this time he was determined not to stray from the path. Yet by the first day his mule was trailing behind the camels, unable to keep up. Only at midnight did he manage to catch up with the caravan. The next day Mula Youssuf lifted her long ears and whispered magic words into them, then stroked special places on her long face, as Sariav had taught him. Within a few days the beast had learned the ways of camels and was carrying Mula Youssuf on her back at the head of the caravan. When he was but two hours' ride from the village of Meherabad, near the city of Bam, the sky filled with thousands of humming bees, which landed at the outskirts of the village. When he had seen quite enough of the bees, Mula Youssuf tugged at the mule's reins, and turned toward Bam.

★ ★ ★ ★ ★

In the days when Mula Youssuf was journeying far from Rafsanjan, an eye-healer came to town—a Dr. Yakoubian. Hassan Choupori the town crier, who had the longest pipe and the biggest mouth and was the tallest of the Rafsanjanis, made his rounds down the main street and through the maze of alleys, spreading the news at the top of his lungs and drawing after him a crowd of the curious.

Without warning the many Muslims who were stricken with trachoma, the blind and the half-blind, gathered in the upper synagogue. The eye-healer and his assistant Raphael Kermoni sat themselves in the center of the courtyard and began to receive patients who were still on their feet, one by one. At first they treated the mild cases who came and stood between them, each in turn. Raphael Kermoni would press their backs to the bloated belly of Dr. Yakoubian, who would yank them by the scalp and drip red iodine into their eyes.

Among those who were treated with iodine was Ali Paloo, a face so familiar among the Jews that he often got confused at the mosque, praying "Sh'ma Yisrael" when entreating Allah to keep him from going blind, for since the trachoma epidemic his sight had deteriorated with each passing year. While the other patients saw the world as a sinking sun and whimpered as if salt had been thrown in their eyes, Ali Paloo endured the searing pain, straightened his back, and stood at the head of the line of severe cases, to request more treatment. In the meantime the eye-healer and his assistant ground copper sulphate with dried tortoise eggs and medicinal herbs. When all was made ready for the operations, they called to the blind to pass under their hands.

The first was Ali Paloo. He kneeled. Raphael Kermoni stood over him, legs spread, and yanked his head back. Doctor Yakoubian tested his new method on him: First he poured black powder into his eyes, then passed a long, heated needle between his eyelids until smoke rose from them. A quick, sharp pain pierced Ali Paloo's brain, passed to his heart and from his heart spread in needles of heat to each limb of his body and like an echo back to his head, until it was no longer possible to keep him from shaking. They bound his hands and legs like those of a terrified beast being brought to the slaughter.

Seized with fright, the other blind people fled for their lives, stumbling over one another. The eye-healer hid his disgrace in trembling hands as he lay cloth compresses smeared with vaseline on the seared eyes of Ali Paloo; then he and his assistant gathered up their bundles and the hat full of coins. That very day they vanished from Rafsanjan, leaving behind Ali Paloo shuddering on his back like a drugged cockroach.

The worshippers who arrived for afternoon prayers were overcome with dread, fearing what would happen should the matter become known to the Muslims of Rafsanjan. They passed a long pole between the bound hands and legs of Ali Paloo, hoisted him aloft, and carried him to the dim room of Rivka Katchali. They stood out on the balcony for afternoon prayer, then sat down to ponder their plight. Not finding a solution, they determined to delay their decision until the day of the solar eclipse. The next morning they placed a large and deep copper tray in the synagogue courtyard, filling it with water they had drawn from the Paayab. They stood around it, entranced, gazing at the pale countenance of the sun. Baba Bozorg, the elder among them, pointed at the quivering stain and stated gravely that this was the solar eclipse. The worshippers passed their hands over their faces in blessing, then spilled the sun on the garden. They then gathered in the synagogue to discuss how to remove the stain of disgrace left by Dr. Yakoubian.

When a week had passed, Ali Paloo was put on the back of an ass and, accompanied by Hassan Choupori the town crier, sent to the hospital of the "English" in the county seat of Kerman to get false eyes. By mistake, he arrived at the old hospital. There they opened Ali Paloo's eyelids, which had coagulated, dug out his sockets, and replaced his eyes with two painted dove eggs. When chicks burst from them, they tried painted wooden balls, but these were slowly gnawed by worms. After other unsuccessful attempts, his caretakers left him to the mercy of the "English." There, attended by the Jews of Kerman, he waited months for the arrival of two eyes, ordered from the land of the "English": one blue and one black, with metal weights for stabilizers. Later, when Ali Paloo would be asked how it was that his eyes were two different colors, he would answer that he was half-Muslim, half-Jew. When he had adjusted, Ali Paloo returned to Rafsanjan, where he made a living turning off lights on the Sabbath in the homes of the Jews, who passed him from hand to hand.

One Sunday, as he sat on a stool in the store of his friend the cobbler, cradling the end of his walking stick, his eyes were suddenly drawn out by a magnet in the shape of a horseshoe which, in his search for nails, the cobbler had unwittingly passed before Ali Paloo's eyes. Thereafter, the removal of Ali Paloo's eyes with the cobbler's magnet became a stunt that greatly amused his friends. Later it became a source of income. Enlisting Hassan Choupori, they bought from the old Muslim grave digger an ancient owl that could turn its head all the way round like a spirit, and a parrot, which Ali Paloo taught to speak, and grew a watermelon in a glass bottle. They went from village to village posing as a band of magicians, and made a fortune presenting the wonder of the removable eyes and the bottled watermelon with the owl on top. When the parrot would ask: "What's the time? What's the time?" the owl would turn its head like the hand of a clock. Ali Paloo walked about without eyes, aroused the pity of the onlookers, and collected money in a hat. He promised that if they gave generously, the cobbler would climb into the bottle and eat the watermelon. Meantime Hassan Choupori would strut around on stilts so tall he could pull fog from the sky and obscure the eyes of the skeptics. Thus it was that the cobbler could prove he had entered the bottle and got out again: he did it while the crowd was lost in a fog.

One day, when they arrived at the village of Meherabad, near Bam, they found a surprise waiting for them in the form of Dr. Yakoubian. As they entered the village, Hassan Choupori noticed a large crowd gathered in the square. Raising his head, he picked out Dr. Yakoubian in the center of the crowd. After a brief consultation the band decided to retrace their steps and wait in ambush at the edge of the village. The next day they caught Dr. Yakoubian and his assistant Raphael Kermoni. They bound them together, back to back, until they were as one. Then they smeared sugar water on their eyelids, left them there beside a bees' nest, and went on their way.

The next day, those who passed on the road from Meherabad found the bloated carcasses of the two healers. The bees' venom had left marks of advanced decay, and the two had been cleft in twain by the pressure of the ropes. The villagers dug a deep pit and poured into it the sticky mass of deadmen along with a few bees that were still sunk deep in the sockets of their eyes, and sealed the pit with clumps of earth. Spring water gushed from the bowels of the earth and the sides of the rocks at the base of the freshly-dug grave. Flowing downhill toward the valley, it watered the fields.

One day Hassan Khoury, an old, blind man who was born with his eyes closed, came upon the spring. The instant he doused his face with the spring water his eyelids opened, sprouted lashes, and stayed open two whole days and nights for fear of closing, never to open again. On the third night he succumbed to his body's weariness. He lay on his back beside the spring, asleep with his eyes open, and dreamed the first dream he had ever dreamt in his life: The eye-healer stood on a hill like a white, gleaming angel, and spread his wings over countless hovering bees. His assistant hovered nearby, drawing a trail of dizzy bees after him. When the eye-healer had reached the utmost height he stood, weightless, on the chest of Hassan Khoury; in the terrifyingly soft voice of the dead, he demanded a fistful of bees in exchange for granting him sight, lest his eyes refuse to close, forcing him to witness the deeds of men even if he turned his head away. When Hassan Khoury woke he sacrificed countless bees, mashing them on the grave, and began to see like any man. That very day he appropriated the site, erecting a marble monument and an impressive, high-domed structure, as befits a holy place.

The rumor of the wondrous healing powers of the waters of Ein Yakoubian spread through the county, bringing pilgrims from far and wide. The number of visitors and the mashing of bees were so great, that many supplicants fainted from inhaling the venomous fumes that rose off the grave. The situation became so dire that only Hassan Khoury, who was immune to all poisons, could enter the mausoleum. He stood at its doorway and, in exchange for a modest sum, took sealed jars of bees and sacrificed them gleefully on the grave. Within a short time the waters of the spring had became poisoned, and any careless enough to swallow water when washing their faces died on the spot.

At that time there was a great shortage of bees, and those in need of even one stinging bee had to pay bee hunters in gold ingots, on which was embossed the visage of the Reza Shah.

★ ★ ★ ★ ★

As he set out on his sojourn, he saw people in the fields. At first startled, he soon realized that they were merely moss-covered stones, and regained his composure: "They are busy, they will not burden me with wearisome farewells."

He turned his mind to other things and his efforts to prodding the beasts, to hurry them on their way up the mountain.

His extended stay in Bam and his idleness had done him no good. From time to time he was forced to stop to rest on a stone by the side of the road. During one such rest stop, in the afternoon, he looked toward Bam in surprise. The city and the valley had been completely obscured by clouds. He rose and continued on his way. Soon enough he found that the higher he climbed, the wider the area covered by clouds. Were he to linger, the rain would catch up to him and beat at his back.

At the end of the day he reached the plains near the summit of the mountain and sat down, his back to a rock. Exhausted and drunk with the altitude, he looked down on the clouds and immediately fell asleep. At dawn he woke surrounded by mist. He thought he was floating in a cloud. Before he knew it, the mule was floating beside him. As he got to his feet, he remembered where he was. The sound of a flute reached his ears.

He was enchanted. He harkened after the sound. On the crest of a hill at the far edge of the chain of mountains, he saw a pair of shepherds following a flock of sheep.

"Perhaps it is Baharouz? Perhaps it is Parvin?"

He listened to the shepherd's playing until the sun rose. Then he discovered that Shaheen had gotten stuck between two pillars of rock. The pillars framed a mold in the shape of Parvin's body, and formed a gate.

He released the horse and led it to the mule, then went back to see whether it was possible to remove the mold from its place.

From out of nowhere a bird appeared. It had a human form, with neither wings nor feathers. It sat by the gate, its talons gripping the outcroppings of rock.

Mula Youssuf wondered whether it was Hushang. The bird disappeared into the mold and sang a song of love. He remembered what Gizh and Gizhak had said.

"What can a wingless bird do?"

He heard himself answer: "Capture the heart of Parvin and build its nest there."

He brought the mask of Parvin's face and rested it against the gate, to give the mold a head.

He heard a song of thanksgiving.

He passed through the gate. A voice rose within him: "You have passed through the gate of illusion."

Mula Youssuf was glad, and said: "My friend has returned. Now I know that the roots of life are anchored in the heart of man; for nought have I wandered."

★★★★★

Though Mula Youssuf's heart grew heavy, he had the strength of beasts. He left behind plains and mountains, villages and towns. So anxious was he to return to Rafsanjan that he skirted towns and took shortcuts. In the end, he lost his way. He would point himself in the direction of one town, but find himself in another; turn down the path to Bapht—and be greeted by the gates of Sirjan. Yet he kept on. He would close his left hand around the ring, and keep on. When he entered a town, he would stay only to buy fodder for the animals and provisions for himself. One time he needed kerosene, to fix Shaheen's shoes. Another time he sought a harness-maker and a rope-maker. He would quickly acquire what he needed, then continue on his way.

One evening he came to an oasis, and stopped there for the night. In the morning, he found it difficult to rise.

He said to himself: "It is mere idleness getting the better of me."

He forced himself to sit up, but instantly his head became light and dizzy. He thought: "The sun is unusually hot today."

Stealthily, slowly, a chill came over his body, and he trembled. Pain pounded in his head and brought tears to his eyes. It spread to his neck and his armpits and his groin. By nightfall he was burning with fever, hallucinating. At midnight, when the moon rose, he saw tiny figures dancing among the date palms. He said: "If these are spirits, I must have reached Rafsanjan."

Later he was blessed with many visitors. Montazeri, sailing on the ocean, riding on a tree stump, extended his hand to him, then grew distant. He also saw Sariav, a cock chasing him. The figures and shadows flickered, disappearing into abysses and behind peaks, returning to his side, prating in his ear. The most bothersome was Mula Rahamim, who chided him in sign language, sitting on his chest and pressing his bones until, no longer able to breathe, he wheezed and fainted.

He was awakened in the afternoon by voices which he took to be imaginary. He was encircled by the blurry figures of soldiers. One said: "The man's burning with fever."

Another corrected him: "He's dying."

Mula Youssuf's eyes closed.

"He's dead."

Alarmed, he tried to open his eyes to show that he was alive. One of them rested a hand on his forehead and said: "Wake up, Mula Youssuf, wake up. I am the Messiah . . . I am the Messiah . . ."

Years later, when Arai Diono came to Mula Youssuf and confessed: "I'm crazy, I'm crazy," Mula Youssuf would answer by saying: "Once upon a time you told me that you were the Messiah, and I believed you, for I was ill."

Indeed, so grave was his illness that those who cared for him despaired, and at the end of two weeks grew doubtful whether he would ever awaken. But one evening he surprised them. He opened his eyes and, seeing a clean-shaven soldier with the face of a youth leaning over him, asked if he really was the Messiah—then promptly fell asleep again.

The next day he woke, his body bathed in sweat. He tried to find a comfortable position. His limbs were so stiff that he could not move his hands. He let his eyes wander, trying to fix his gaze on something. He saw smooth clay walls plastered with palm fronds. He realized he lay in a bare room, at an oasis. He slept fitfully, vaguely remembering voices and blurred figures, until at last they melded together and stood before him in the person of a farmer. In those days Mula Youssuf could rise from his mat and lean against the clay walls. The farmer would come and go tirelessly, tending him in silence. He would dissolve various powders in water, support his head and bring the balm to his lips. He would bring him fruits to eat and quench his thirst with camomile tea.

One morning he awoke to the sound of neighing and whinnying. He rose and found his belongings. They had been there beside him all along, resting against the wall. He walked out of the room, happy. Shaheen and the mule were drinking from the trough in the stable.

He went up to the mule and lovingly stroked her back. She trembled in response. Shaheen received him calmly, as if they had never been apart. He thought: "How sated and happy are the beasts. They have been lovingly tended."

He remembered the farmer. He said: "I must thank him for his deeds."

He did not find him in the granary or in the meadow. He went back to the clay hut. Not a soul was in its four rooms. He went out. He saw countless sunflowers in full bloom. They encircled the house on all sides to the horizon. Nothing but sunflowers and the farmer's hut.

He sat in the doorway of the room on a straw mat and waited. Hours passed. Besides him and the beasts, who waited nearby, not a soul was in sight. Nothing moved; nothing stirred. Even the sunflowers stood as if eternally bent in morning prayer. They did not turn their faces toward the sun, or follow its movements.

For hours Mula Youssuf sat sunk in thought, trying to recall what had happened to him. There were days missing since he had come to the oasis, and he didn't know who it was that he had seen. Had the spirits of Rafsanjan forgotten their custom of helping him in time of trouble? Who was the Messiah? Why did he appear in a soldier's uniform? Where had the farmer gone?

All that day the farmer did not appear; neither did he come that night. At midnight the moon rose, and the sunflowers followed its movements until dawn. In the morning they again stooped in prayer, unmoving.

"Moonstruck sunflowers," thought Mula Youssuf, and added: "The laws of nature must have lost their force, if sunflowers can turn toward the moon." He rubbed his hands together. He noticed that the ring was missing; it seemed curious to him that someone would have coveted the ring, but not the rest of his belongings. Later he found food and drink in abundance; he understood that he was not to leave the hut until the farmer returned. Nights and days he waited, never diverting his thoughts from the sunflowers. Those were moonless nights, and they, forsaken, went back to staring at the sun. The sun scorched their leaves, dried them and bent their stalks.

Mula Youssuf went to look at the heads of the sunflowers before they buried their faces in the earth. He lifted one and tore a handful of seeds from its face. He cracked open a few. They were tawny-hulled, and white inside. Eating a few seeds, he said: "If I continue to wait, signs of day and night will also appear before me. I will set out before waiting becomes my existence, as idleness is for the mule."

He went to the stable and fed the beasts sunflower seeds in anticipation of the journey. This time he piled all his sacks and bundles on Shaheen's back. Astride the mule, leading Shaheen by the reins, he sadly distanced himself from the withering sunflowers.

★ ★ ★ ★ ★

One night, after not a few days' journeying and without knowing whether he was getting closer to Rafsanjan or farther from it, the wind kicked up, obediently carrying the scents of opium sap and pistachio, reminding him of the forgotten events of days gone by. At dawn he rose and prodded the beasts. By afternoon he had crossed the opium fields. He neared the walls, then entered Rafsanjan by the southern gate. He hurried to the center of town, to see the statue of the ass. The marble slabs of the pool had cracked and the granite of the beast had faded, but the Shah was still in place, placid as ever (though his weight bowed the back of the beast somewhat). For a long while he stood and stared at the visage of the ass, to decipher the secret it held.

"She is glad I have returned," he determined.

He yanked the reins of the beasts and headed for the upper city, down the alley of the Jews to the Baha'i quarter, to the house of Baba Bozorg, which was by the tower.

That night there was a great commotion. Everyone gathered at the house of Baba Bozorg to see the long-forgotten one, the one who had vanished, the dead man who had come back alive.

While Baba Bozorg was glad that Mula Youssuf had returned, he was also not a little embarrassed. After all, Mula Youssuf had left his son Moshe in his care and he, Baba Bozorg, had not tended the boy as he should have. Within a week of his father's departure, Moshe had fled to his uncle's house; Baba Bozorg had not troubled himself to try and bring the boy back into his custody. When Mula Youssuf had sent him signs of life in the form of precious gems and medicinal stones, he had not told the boy of his father's existence, but rather had kept the secret to himself. Caravans would come to the city. A messenger would come to inform him. Baba Bozorg would go to the king's post office and pick up the packages himself. He would bring them straight to the bazaar, to the new silversmith, Joshua-Two-Wives, son of Haim Dalal. With the money he would get in exchange for Mula Youssuf's gems he would purchase lands and prepare dowries for his daughters.

Toward evening Mula Youssuf left the wing of the house that had been given him. He asked to see his son. Baba Bozorg said: "He is residing with his uncle. We have sent for him, but the boy is not quick to come. Mula Youssuf should not trouble his heart. He has not seen his son for years; surely he can wait one more night. He will be placated; he will come."

The night passed, but Moshe did not come. Mula Youssuf went down to the lower city, to the house of Haj Mukhtar, to see his son. He came away disappointed. Instead of a boy, he was shown an overgrown and antagonistic youth, who gazed at his father as at a stranger. Mula Youssuf's heart did not weaken. He said: "For years he has found refuge in the shade of his benefactor. The ways of father and son are foreign to him. I will come back and visit him every day. I will build a warm home, so he will have a place to go. My blood flows in his veins. He will be shown real love. He will yet open his heart to me."

He purchased a lot in the alley of the Jews. He set aside part of it for living quarters, and part of it for various other things: distilling *'arak,* collecting medicinal stones, raising pets. He left the construction to the deaf-mute Ali Gongi, a master home builder. Mula Youssuf stayed at the home of Baba Bozorg until the work was finished. He didn't meet with former friends and seldom went out; he pored over *The Book of Amghoshi.* He and Baba Bozorg made themselves a habit of sitting and chatting every evening until midnight, he with his smoking implements and Baba Bozorg beside the loom of loneliness.

One night Baba Bozorg said to him: "The pleasures of a man of middle age who sits alone idly are, perforce, idle. Mula Youssuf should choose himself a young woman, and establish a family."

He called his daughters to come fill the samovar with water from the well and heat it with coals from the fire. The girls did their work and departed, but Rokaiyeh, who was sixteen, lingered longer than necessary, staring brazenly into the eyes of Mula Youssuf.

The next day Mula Youssuf was favored with a visit from Tuti the widow, the mother of the twins-whose-time-was-past. She sat with Mula Youssuf and spilled out her heart's sorrows. Many cheap copper bracelets adorned her wrists, and she made artful use of them as she spoke. She would lift her hands to her face, jangling her bracelets noisily and fawning like a sycophant: It has been years since her husband died and she has been all alone. It has taken much effort to raise her daughters. They are skilled in housework, nimble and hard-working. He is invited to visit. He may choose one of them for a wife. Both would be servants at his feet.

Mula Youssuf said that he understood the heart of a mother who wished to protect her daughters. He revealed a secret to her: Last night he chose Rokaiyeh, the daughter of Bozorg, to be his wife.

Tuti rose from her place in a rage.

That's it! The end of all ends has come! The last hope is gone! The Jews are heartless! They pass over my daughters, sentence them to desolation because they have no dowry!

Baba Bozorg's daughters came running, fans of braided reeds in hand, to banish Tuti with curses: Ignorant-indecorous-slanderous-tongued-woman! Opening your big mouth and your evil eyes! Screaming shamelessly at a guest as if you had a hornet in your pants!

Wailing, scratching her face and tearing her hair, Tuti went out of the alley of the Jews and vanished into the rubble of her house.

— Translated from the Hebrew by Marsha Weinstein

YITZHAK GORMEZANO GOREN

YITZHAK GORMEZANO GOREN was born in Alexandria in 1941 and emigrated to Israel with his family in 1951. After studying English and French literature at Hebrew and Tel Aviv Universities, he worked as a scriptwriter and director for television, film and theater. Along with his wife, the prominent actress Shosha Goren, he founded *Bimat Kedem,* a theater company dedicated to producing plays on Middle Eastern themes. From 1974 to 1980 he lived and studied in New York. The critical establishment generally refers to his novels *An Alexandrian Summer* (1978) and *Blanche* (1986) as expressions of nostalgia. The theme of these works, however, is much more complex. To begin with, Goren's work is firmly rooted in a Mediterranean tradition that includes the pathos of Italian opera, the dramatic detail of Pirandello, and the ability to seamlessly weave the materials of popular culture into a complex fabric of history, politics, and social commentary. Through a dense narrative layering, Goren sheds light on the intricate web of relations between the colonizer and the colonized, whether through a depiction of class relations in Egypt or the dilemnas of new immigrants facing an alien culture in Israel. His latest novel, *Shelter in Bavli,* is a major work that charts new territory in narrating the underlying tensions of Israel's social, political and cultural life. Presently, he is working on a new novel based on the life of his father and set in Istanbul at the turn of the century.

TEL AVIV AND ALEXANDRIA: AN INTERVIEW WITH YITZHAK GORMEZANO GOREN BY AMMIEL ALCALAY

How did you come to the subject of your new novel, Shelter in Bavli?

To begin with, it's partly based on an actual incident, the case of Shimon Yehoshua; he was killed in 1982 by the police while resisting a court order given by the Tel Aviv Municipality for the demolition of an addition he built on his house without a permit. I had come back at the end of July 1980, after being in New York for six years. I immediately became active in various *mizrahi* groups; my wife Shosha, who is an actress, and I began *Bimat Kedem,* a theater dedicated to representing *mizrahi* culture and confronting the social issues of Israeli society. Then, in December 1982, right in the middle of the war in Lebanon, this incident took place. It clearly showed the balance of power between the institutional establishment and people like Shimon Yehoshua; it showed precisely how cheap the life of someone like him, from a poor neighborhood, is here. The incident gripped me for a number of reasons; to begin with, it verified all the social, class, and ethnic issues involved. But there were also dramatic elements that drew me: Shimon Yehoshua's father had gone to court to get an order delaying the destruction but by the time he arrived he already found his son dead. This made it clear they had no intention of waiting to begin with. And then, as he was wallowing in his own blood, they just took him away and destroyed the house. Even though he was dead, they demolished the house. Then the policeman who shot him disappeared, only to be found a few years later. Also, rumors were going around that he was Moroccan. He was actually Romanian, by the way, which is irrelevant. What was interesting was the fact that this rumor about him being Moroccan started at all, as if that somehow justified it. This too is irrelevant; a Moroccan within the system will act like anyone else. Disturbances followed. And then everything quieted down. So the whole thing seemed quite dramatic to me.

I can't tell you exactly from where Heli, the heroine, is derived. First of all, she comes from me since her character is a lot like mine; on the surface, she is very much like my wife Shosha. Maybe I also wanted to write about the feminine side of myself. I very much like writing about women. In addition to *Blanche,* I wrote a play, *Masques in Venice,* based on the life of Doña Gracia Nasi. I also just wrote a play that we are doing a movie of called *Angel Fingers,* about a woman—a mother and her daughter. More precisely, a woman and her daughter since if I say a mother and daughter then it appears as if the woman is only a mother. So my intentions combine an instinctual preference with an ideological agenda.

Take Israeli film, for example. For a long time, all we had was war films so all the roles were for young guys. I wanted my protaganist to be a woman, and an older woman, because that's also part of the problem. What happens, again in film, is that most of the filmmakers here are my age. But there are almost no films about either men or women my age. Most of the films are about young people. So the movies are either about foolish kids or the army. So an actress like Shosha is automatically thought of for roles as a mother. The play we're doing approaches it as a woman who has a daughter rather than a daughter who has a mother. I've often wondered why these forty and fifty year old directors make such movies and the only conclusion I can come up with is that they want to screw around with young girls! So they make movies with young actresses. Why else? Why wouldn't they tell their own stories? Why do they keep telling stories from the point of view of twenty years ago? These are all factors that led me into creating the character of Heli, a woman of fifty.

A few things were clear to me as I began to put all these elements together into a narrative. I wanted to write a novel in which there would be a wide variety of *mizrahi* characters representing a wide range of options, in order to create a microcosm. I didn't want to create "curios" because most of the *mizrahi* characters in Israeli literature are just that, "curios." Or everything takes place in the diaspora, like the two novels I wrote about Alexandria. That's legitimite. Why do you think it was so easy for me to get *Alexandrian Summer* and *Blanche* published? Because it's legitimate for us to be in the diaspora, the transit camps, or some magic realist neighborhood in Jerusalem, like in the work of Dan Banaya Seri or even Albert Swissa. There's nothing wrong with this, I have nothing against it. But everything is fine, as long as you stay in your ghetto. The second you start writing about the *mizrahi* middle class, the tune changes. It's no coincidence that I portray two kids from the other side of the tracks, as it were. Both are students, one is even outstanding, like many that I know, like I myself was. While there are also real underdogs in the novel, it was important to me to portray this middle class. Heli's uncle the lawyer comes right out of Shosha's family: Shalom Darwish and Yitzhaq Bar Moshe, for example, are her uncles; Darwish is a lawyer, Bar Moshe is a journalist and both are well known as writers in Arabic.

The setting of the novel at the university also gave me a chance to vent some of my spleen against academia and present the dilemnas faced by *mizrahim* aspiring to join the middle class through education, like the character Moshe / Morris who realizes that, although he says he is building the addition to his house for his parents, he may actually be building it as a shelter or escape from his family. People have this image of academics, particularly in Israel, as the enlightened elite. But the universities are actually strongholds of conservatism and racism, particularly towards *mizrahim*. I was also conscious that I was writing the first book of its kind, the first book to deal with this range of contemporary *mizrahi* characters. People who read the book confirmed this, proving I wasn't the only one conscious of this lack. Part of consciousness is simply awareness, not to automatically accept a panel of five white Ashkenazi males on TV as being normal, things that are simply taken for granted here without asking where everyone else is. That's why Nafi says to Heli at one point that awareness is a prism: Once you look through it, you can never go back to seeing things the way you did before. It's impossible.

In reading the first version of Keys to the Garden, *how did you feel encountering writers and texts in English that you hadn't known in Hebrew?*

Embarrassed, like when I went to Egypt and had to face up to just how bad my Arabic is. But another reason I didn't know some of these writers well enough is the fact that *no one* knows them well enough. There are even texts you translated that have never been published in Hebrew. I know there are certain writers who might have felt uncomfortable in this grouping, but for me it was the opposite. I was very happy to be in their company and very happy to see that there were so many writers producing such good work.

What I'm interested in is the problematic of getting this stuff so circuitously.

It's a bit odd but since I already come from such a linguistic and cultural cocktail to begin with, I don't find it disturbing. In fact, I read *Keys to the Garden* in Turkey where I went to get some kind of feel for the setting of my new novel.

This touches on things that are very hard to pin down. A writer like Shimon Ballas, for instance, is not trying to identify with the Hebrew language. He works in the space of difference between what can be done with the language and his own sense of exile. In general, mainstream writers here have not yet seen themselves as others, as the "other;" they haven't looked themselves in the mirror and said "I am the other." It also seems to me that since the whole pool of literary possibilities has not been open, as it were, to the free market here, the writers that are taken to be representative of Israel in the world have reached that position in a very artifical way and not, as critics like to claim, simply because of the "inherent quality" of their work. How do you see your own place in this context?

I often consider myself lucky to have been born outside of Israel because it allowed me to soak up other cultures before I got to Israeli culture. On the other hand, I got here at a young enough age so that I didn't have the problem of people who came when they were older, like Sami Michael or Shimon Ballas, and who had to face much deeper splits within themselves. I've been able to integrate my worlds more fully and this has allowed me to make choices. There was a certain period when, if I wanted to, I could easily have become part of the mainstream here. I can appear to be a sabra, I know what it means to be a sabra. On the other hand, I have the experience of another world and this gives me a certain privilege. And it is all within, so that I could *choose* to be other. Also, since I'm Sephardi which is not as bad as being *mizrahi* in Israel, I can pass for white. This too allowed me to choose. And having decided the matter for myself gave me great power and satisfaction, precisely because I chose to throw my lot in with those who've been screwed by the system. But being born here doesn't guarantee that you won't be thought of as other either, as you can see from the work of younger writers.

While I have no problem, for instance, defining myself as an Arab Jew, my Balkan ancestry betrays me. Of course it is less pronounced, in the first place, than when someone like Shimon Ballas says "I am an Arab Jew," since he is a full participant in that culture. But sometimes I say this just so it can be said. Even when I first saw *After Jews and Arabs,* I had to think for a split second. We are so unaccustomed to contextualizing things like this—people say, oh, in Spain, that was fine, but beyond that our context is not considered Arabic.

But I don't even think the issue of Jews or Arabs here is important; the Israeli approach to identity dictates that it is impossible to be two or three or twenty one things at once.

There is always something that takes precedence.

When I read your work or that of Shimon Ballas there is a certain complexity that is simply part of the circumstances. In the case of Ballas and his novel, And He is Other, *you first have to take into account the fact that here you have a writer from Iraq who writes in Hebrew but the work is actually being written in Paris; the character is a Jew who converted to Islam and, naturally, as a reader you are asked to accept the fictionality of a text that is in Arabic since it is "written" from the point of view of this convert, as a memoir, yet the actual text is in Hebrew. So you already have a very dense prism at work here, before you've even begun.*

What you are saying really adds another dimension to this whole issue of what has conventionally come to be called displacement or alienation but can more accurately be looked at in terms of the richness of complexity that the writers themselves bring to the text.

The innovations in a lot of the work here, it seems to me, are not necessarily formal in the conventional sense of that term but have to do with the struggle to come to consciousness and express that through a use of language and set of assumptions trying to deny that very consciousness. Given this, it has been very difficult for mizrahi *artists to contextualize themselves in a wider sense. I think that the appearance of* After Jews and Arabs *helped do this in some way and had an effect on people I wrote about; how do you see this?*

I can speak only for myself here. It definitely had an impact. Before even getting into politics, my problem—and not just mine—but that of most *mizrahi* artists here is that we work in a vacuum. If you take a triangle made up of the artist, the audience and someone we could call the critical or professional reader, this last side is missing for us here. So you begin to develop an attitude—who the hell needs them, the critics and researchers, in the first place? And those few who manage to write something go on and on about, for instance, how folkloric *Blanche* is, or how anti-Zionist. I'm not particularly offended by this but what's the connection to literature? You're talking apples and oranges. When people asked me what *Blanche* was I said it was a telenovela, a soap opera, a romance for maids. That's how I defined it from the start and that's what I had in mind when I was writing it. But you say this in the hope that someone will come along and say, of course you are using all the conventions of this particular genre but something else also seems to be happening. You hope that someone will come along and say, you know, your use of time is very interesting. Until I read what you wrote in *After Jews and Arabs* I only knew that I was doing *something* with time—not because I intended to do something in order for it to be interesting but because that's simply the way I think. I knew I was playing around with different strata of reality, various points of view, and the relationship between the writer and the reader. But you also want someone to notice, for better or worse! There was an interest in our work, for instance, from people like Semadar Lavi and Ella Shohat, but they weren't coming to it from literature as you are. Suddenly here was a book I could hardly understand so I knew it had to be serious!

On the Way to the Stadium, the novel I am working on now, begins: "On the 23rd of November 1963, my father died." The day after Kennedy's assassination, my father came to me and said: "You know they killed Kennedy." Then he went to bed and died that morning. So I don't see any other way *except* to begin with the date. Now if I want to write a novel about my father who himself had wanted to write a novel, which is what I am now doing, how can I not involve myself in all these issues of point of view and who wrote what and why and so on and so forth? Take my grandmother. She existed in life but she is also a character in my novels. As a real woman she no longer exists, but she will live on as a character. So where does that leave "reality" and "fiction"? We even know historical characters through a certain imaginary construct. So how is it possible for artists to cut themselves off from the question of how characters are created? All of these issues interest me on the literary level and your work gave me support. Because of this my dialogue with you is extremely important, not simply because the value you put on my work is far greater than anything I seem to be getting around here, but because I decided to follow a less compromising path than many others, so every bit of support counts.

from AN ALEXANDRIAN SUMMER

From a distance of twenty years

Sporting Club, the race-track neighborhood, on the other side of the tram tracks. At the intersection of Delta Street and the Corniche stands number 24, all seven stories of it (we used to go up to the roof and shoot paper arrows at the ants busily rushing back and forth—as if there were some purpose to all that movement—down on the sidewalk). The Arab doorman, his name was Badri, his face dark brown and parched, squints before the sun. His youngest son Abdu crouches next to him, helping him watch the shadows stretching over the sidewalk, and the cars passing on their way to the beach. Badri and his son would warm-up anyone coming into the building up with an *"Ahlan, Ya Sidi,"* vigilant and filled with expectation: will they give *bakshish* or not? If so—they would get a bowing escort right to the very door of the elevator. If not—a hand pointing indifferently towards the musty darkness. The elevator is ancient, girded by black cast-iron bars with faded gold engravings eaten away by reddish rust. The door shuts with a metallic clatter, and . . . miraculous! The elevator starts going up, whispering, buzzing, laboriously dragging the loop-tail that gets longer and longer as it rises. Hair raising stories are told about power blackouts between the fourth and the fifth. Quarrels between neighbors that start in the hall intensify in the dimness of the elevator before completely dissipating outside, in the subtropical sun that scorns human endeavors.

The second floor, no farther. If you weren't lazy, you could just walk up. A brass plate, and the name engraved on it is that of a Jewish family, descendents of exiles from Spain (whose family name is the name of their city of origin, with the "ano" suffix). The bell rings. A dark, thin servant answers, immediately addressing you in French with a Mediterranean lilt: "Oui, monsieur, qu'est-ce que voulez?" And you stutter and ask: "The boy Robert, Robby, does he live here?" The servant is surprised that a thirty-year-old man is looking for a ten-year-old boy, but doesn't give his opinion as long as he's not asked. "Robby? Over there!" And he points toward the balcony, at the far end of the apartment. "Should I call him?" "No, no. There's no need." The young Arab looks at him with a hint of suspicion. "Who are you, monsieur?" And you tell him your name, Hebraized in Israel during the fifties, when "foreign" sounding names were met with revulsion. The servant, naturally, sees no closeness between the names. This foreign name could be Greek or Turkish or Italian or Maltese or Armenian or French or English or even American. Alexandria, after all, is the center of the world, a cosmopolitan city. You want to add: Yes, I used to be Robby. Twenty years ago. I have come from a distance of twenty years. I won't interfere. I just want to see what's going on here. I won't butt in, God forbid. No one will even notice me. I only want to tell the story of one summer, a Mediterranean summer, an Alexandrian summer.

A Family from Cairo

Wave upon wave rises and falls carrying memories of the city. Alexandria. The story of an Alexandrian summer is not easily written. See, it is wrapped in layers of nostalgia, of forgetfulness, of generalities. And I am trying to put my finger on the objective, the distinctive. Should I tell it in the first or the third person? Should I call people by their names, or perhaps just give them fictitious ones and write that "Any resemblance etc. is purely coincidental"? Trivial details, yet they hold you back.

But it is of the Hamdi-Ali family that I wish to speak. What is it, in essence? Look, the Hamdi-Ali family is the joy of life, the unvanquishable Mediterranean edge. Yes, Mediterranean. Really. Maybe it's by right of that same Mediterranean that I sit here unravelling this tale. Here, in the land of Israel, bordering the shores of the Baltic Sea. Sometimes you find yourself utterly perplexed—is Vilna the Jerusalem of Lithuania or is Jerusalem actually the Vilna of Eretz Israel? It's because of this I wanted so much to tell the story of the Hamdi-Ali family, and the story of the city of Alexandria. A Jewish family from Cairo, *al-Kahira,* that is, comes to Alexandria to spend a summer of leisure. Alexandria from the time of King Farouk, with his handlebar mustache and dark glasses, that same Alexandria that I knew in my childhood, that Alexandria which has nourished my imagination over twenty years, from the time I left on the 21st of December, 1951, when I was ten years old.

When we sailed out of the harbor towards the lighthouse, a squall raged that didn't let up until we reached the shores of Italy. There, we were welcomed by a Christmas snow. The middle of winter. But I, I'm talking about summer in Alexandria: vacation, horse-races, sailing, fishing for sea-urchins, devouring crawfish, Platonic affairs (and not so Platonic), traffic jams, traffic jams, traffic jams, and the horns, horns, horns of cars and cars and more cars. All converging on the Corniche, the boulevard overlooking the sea, where vacationers would rent huts so they wouldn't be forced to undress in the public lockers "with all the Arabs."

Servants

Surrounded by water. Water, water, water. From the north, her ample breasts are splashed by the waters of the Mediterranean. From the south, the waves of Lake Mariotes cool down her backside with overpowering carresses. From the east, her fingers are immersed by the streaming Nile, wearily and sluggishly carrying its bustling waters. To the west, the sea of Libyan desert dispatches wave upon wave of hot air onto her blazing neck, with the fever of desire. Alexandria. Alex. Sea. Delta. Desert.

"I hhhaaaaaate the desert!"

"It's suffocating. And it's so provincial. Ahh, for a picnic in the snowy Alps, in the cloudy forests of Europe. Ahh, Christmas in Paris!"

"When were you in France, Annette?"

"I wasn't, but I went to the Lycée Française."

Urbanites. The wilderness? Only in Hollywood movies. The Nile—too filthy, and teeming with Arabs. Sunrise in the desert? That's fine for Lawrence of Arabia—if that's what he gets off on! The pyramids? Sure, they're not bad. At least they're not too far from Cairo. You can visit them in the morning and still get a game of rummy together by the afternoon at friends' in Heliopolis. Not to mention that all the American tourists are crazy about them so that must prove something, no? But to go to Luxor? To look at stones? The Temples at Karnak have surely earned an honorable place in posterity, but to stay there overnight, down there at the end of the world, in a place filled with Arabs, completely removed from civilization? That's how they are, the city folk, to the very marrow of their bones. They speak to each other in French, English, Spanish, Italian, Greek. They only know the absolute minimal amount of Arabic needed to get by. Most of the servants speak French and anyways, it is they who communicate between their masters and the locals.

You who were spoon-fed on progressive Socialism, comradeship between nations, and racial equality—so to speak, at least, and for external consumption—surely you must be grinning with a patronizing and contemptuous leer; it's difficult for you to understand how refined people could reconcile themselves to such a debilitating form of colonialist feudalism. In truth, Alexandria was rotten, but its decay possessed a tradition, saturated in history. Dig deep into the layers of rot, and you find tattered papyrus fragments or a lock of hair from a mummy's shrivelled head. There is something really and truly rotten in the kingdom of Alexandria. That's why I love her so much, Alexandria. A city that let you live the carefree life of a lord without even being rich. It was enough for you to be a Jew or a European of minimal intelligence, and even that wasn't always a requirement. Money? Money was to be spent on pleasure and mischief. Only the old folks saved for a rainy day. Dancing, trips, sailing, races and cards. You earn between thirty and a hundred pounds a month. You pay four and a half pounds in rent and you live in a castle, surrounded by servants who each make two pounds a month. What a wonderful gap! And even so, when it all adds up, you're just a miserable petit bourgeois. In Europe, you would have had to tighten your belt nicely to get out of the month in the black, and your wife would be scrubbing the floors all day in the wretched little garret you'd be lucky to find within your means in Paris the bejewelled or London the magical. But here, in Alex, Monsieur Nobody easily retains two slaves that work for him and are his subjects. You can't be a nobody if you have two servants, male and female, who live in your house and work twenty-four hours a day, six and a half days a week (half their day off is spent getting to their miserable village to see their sick parents and their hapless younger siblings)—and all of this for just four Egyptian lira, two and-a-half for the male and one and a half for the female.

"They don't deserve more!"

"They're so lazy!"

"The worst thing is when you've got a pair of doves at home. God help you!"

"He harrasses her all day, and who does she come to complain to? To you, of course. Worse than children."

"They don't exactly sit by idly either."

"And when they get trapped in a delicate situation—what a scene!"

"I had a Beduin maid once with big, green eyes. Then we hired a Sudanese servant, as black as asphalt. Once they cleaned the bathroom together. Don't ask! Suddenly I heard screaming that sounded like someone giving birth. I ran over—the door was locked, so I called my husband Isidor. He summoned the concierge and we broke down the door. What did we find? Don't ask! The two of them . . . I'm even ashamed to hint at what state they were in. She, poor thing, her clothes were all torn up, she had practically fainted in the bathtub, and he, naked and black, stood there beating her senseless. Apparently, she wouldn't give in to him . . ."

"Awful!"

"That's nothing. You know my aunt Fortunée, right? Mother's sister. Once she was home alone and she asked her servant, I think his name was Ahmed . . ."

"All of them are called Ahmed."

"Anyway, the point is that she asked him to go down and pick up her husband's suit from the dry cleaner. He came to her and said: I'm not going to budge from here until you go to bed with me!"

"Nnnnnaaaaah!"

"What do you mean, Nnnnaaaah? She told me herself. But, Fortunée, you know how she is, she doesn't scare very easily . . ."

"I would have died on the spot!"

"Cool as a cucumber, she said to him: 'Fine, why not? A hunk like you! Wait for me here while I go get ready.' A Don Juan like that, he was so sure of his dizzying conquest, that he didn't think twice. She ran down to the concierge. Meanwhile, he got himself ready . . ." The first hesitant gurgles of laughter broke out amongst the group— "and when she and the concierge came back, they found him all ready!" The first isolated giggles blended into a light and steady bleating, though still somewhat bewildered. Little by little, the perplexity gave way to conspiratorial guffaws, nourished by their imagination. One more step and the laughter would be overpowering, wild, even somewhat crazed. Alexandrian society suffocated itself with an entangled web of conventions, so that even the slightest hint at something lewd released passions and powers deeply suppressed under the cloak of appearances. It's hard for me to imagine that one of them drifted so far as to fashion visions revolving around the insolent black servant's proud member, but it's quite possible. And if you will allow me to depart from the narrow and severe perspective of the facts in order to toy with conjecture, it would be Madame Livia that I would tend to suspect; the elegant, stuck-up, almost aristocratic (for there is no real aristocracy in Alexandria) Madame Livia. But how do we know what went on there in the heads of forty-year-old women upon whose characters no aspersions could be cast? At any rate, she calls her friends to order, militantly reminding them that they didn't get together for idle gossip, but something much more serious and venerable: a game of rummy. Gina, please, your deal!

Rain

The tiny Topolino slowly rolled along the sidewalk. The regal family stood next to it. How their stature had diminished. Four came and three return. No longer would the tiny car overflow with gaiety as it tooled along the Cairo-Alexandria road. No longer would there be that expectation, that waiting on tenterhooks, the suspense that comes with the beginning of summer. The cloudy sky rested heavily on the flat roofs of the taller buildings. As if the city had gotten old before its time, overtaken by a turbid greyness that settled over its surface. Emily Hamdi-Ali, once a queen, was draped over her son's arm like a black sack, old and bent over, her life emptied of substance. Few are the women in Egypt who have their own lives. Most of them live the desires and hopes of their husbands. From a young age, they are taught to be faithful companions, like this shadow.

In the accumulation of greyness, the sun looked like a pallid, feeble spot, lacking even the strength to cast shadows over the sidewalk. Objects seemed scattered without rhyme or reason, without any relationship between them, like a collage in a comic book.

The preparations continued without any plan, in an extraordinary silence. Salem took the suitcases and packages at his customary and distinguished pace; even Badri the concierge and his son did't really exert much of an effort: after all, *Hawaga* Hamdi-Ali was not known to be amongst the most generous of people.

It came as quite a surprise to everyone when, after the bags had all been loaded, David gave each of the three a full *real*. Salem said to himself: The grief must have made *Hawaga* David lose his reason. The concierge's son was beside himself. He had never, in his whole life, had such a sum in his hands: twenty *piastres!* But his joy did not last long. His father seized the booty from his son and when the boy protested, Badri dealt him a stinging blow on the neck. The boy was vaulted onto the sidewalk where he broke out sobbing. Salem had mercy on the poor kid and reached into the pocket of his *galabiya* for a one-*mil* piece that he gave to the boy. He was proud that it was within his means to give, like a real *hawaga*. Salem . . . he was really quite something in his own way; alert, intelligent, neither too diligent nor too lazy, with an incredible knack for picking up languages by ear (French, some English, and even Ladino). But more than anything—he had a world of his own, a world into which no stranger could intrude. If he was born into another class, in different times, maybe he would have gotten far. And what if he did, even as things were? Maybe Salem was one of those for whom the Free Officer's Revolt had opened new horizons. For years and years Robby wondered what happened to the kid who had grown up in the same house with him.

Robby stood by the railing on the balcony just as the tiny car made its way off and got swallowed up in the street skirting the Corniche. He looked into the dense, sad sky for a moment, and felt his throat contract. Why was it that today, in particular, with an almost feverish desperation, he insisted on jotting down license plate numbers? Quickly dipping the nib of his pen into the inkwell that rested against the railing, he wrote and wrote and wrote. He only missed one car. Not bad!

Suddenly a drop of water landed on his head. He raised his eyes again, and a drop went into his eye. Another on the tip of his nose. The first rain. Robby ran in and announced, "It's raining, it's raining!" throughout the whole house.

The notebook remained on the railing and the rain came down on the numbers; the water washed the ink off, distorting the lines, erasing everything.

In a gust of wind, the notebook flew off the railing, and the water resentfully poured down over the ground.

Summer was rinsed off the city's streets. Winter was coming to Alexandria.

That same winter, on the 21st of December, Robby and his family left Alexandria and Egypt.

From then until today, the 10th of April, 1977, he saw the city of his childhood only in memory and dreams.

from BLANCHE

Child of the Happy Islands

Her recollections of Corfu were hazy. Impressions. Strong colors. Long narrow courtyards filled with flowerpots and climbing vegetation. Deformed, shrivelled-up peppers hanging up to dry. Loud, half-naked kids. Pink-bottomed cupids whispering in the bosom of a burning red geranium, or a thicket of yellow dandelion. And when peals of laughter rang forth from between jasmine shrubs crowned in white flowers whose aroma inundated your whole body with a pleasure close to fainting, petals hung from their hair and wreaths adorned their heads. Little Bianca also ran bare-assed among the children of the happy islands.

No, she didn't long for Corfu. Her memories of it were sparse and its sights faded. There were too many faces: strong, dark men setting out to sea every day to earn their living and, perhaps, even meet their death; women dressed in black looking after them through a sea of cares. And in this mass of countenances, the portrait of a woman distinguishes itself. Mother? She didn't know for sure. Even the photograph she found amongst *Nonna* Sandra's things was not enough to prove that the face staring out at her from the mist of childhood really was her mother's. She was three when she was brought to Alexandria, her grandmother's prisoner. Now this grandmother herself is waiting for her in their modest apartment in Little Sporting, poor stepsister to the adjacent neighborhood of Sporting Club.

A small house with a courtyard. Peppers and garlic out to dry and a few tins of climbing vines. Her grandmother sits, pedaling at the sewing machine; for fifteen years already, she tirelessly casts miles of thread upon miles of fabric. The machine is an old Singer, with bronze engravings. The belt connecting the upper wheel to the lower wheel before latching onto the pedal often came undone and *Nonna* assigned little Bianca the job of crawling under to hook it up in its place again. Sometimes the old woman would rub her eyes and, with an apologetic smile, say: "I'm seeing double," and ask her to thread a needle.

The old woman remained under lock and key, from the fear of thieves and vandals. Even at the height of summer, the windows remained locked overnight, for it was a ground-floor apartment, a house that you would want to get out of . . . to leave . . . to go. . . . Blanche was sent to a Catholic school. Her grandmother kept to tradition, but she didn't have the means to enroll her grand-daughter in a Jewish private school. Blanche learned everything she needed to know with the nuns, except, perhaps, what the nuns themselves didn't know, the things that one learns later on in life. She even learned shorthand there, something that opened up the gates of clerical work for her. But the nuns at school were hateful to her. She despised them for having turned their back to life, and for trying, not infrequently, to find some salvation in caressing the students.

Meanwhile, war raged on in the world and it suddenly became apparent to the Alexandrians that there was a huge desert to the west of them, with bitter fighting taking place in it. Suddenly they saw columns of dust in the newspapers sown with fuzzy, dark spots, a visual echo of the battles raging somewhere down there—armored vehicle by armored vehicle—in a barbaric world of sand dunes and Eastern windstorms. It was then that Sandra found out all her relatives from Corfu had perished. She sat *shiva'* and told everyone who would listen that a bomb had fallen on their house. The awesome horrors of the Holocaust were beyond the powers of her imagination.

A number of Jewish families chose to flee to Cairo. It seemed to them that the battle for Alexandria was near. And when the situation got worse, neighbors offered to take her fourteen year-old-granddaughter with them to Cairo, but *Nonna* Sandra said that God would watch out for both her and the child; her heart surely confirmed that the bombs would pass over her house. The neighbors told her that even if the bombs had mercy on her, the Germans wouldn't. She said: "The Germans can't be worse than the Greeks, and if we got along with them, then we'll manage now."

As opposed to the lackadaisical attitude of Sandra Aguiyos the Jew, her Christian neighbor Pelagia Pappadopoulos harbored a mortal fear of the imminent German invasion. "They even rape lonely women!" she told everyone within earshot as she packed her meager possessions; meanwhile her neighbors smirked nastily at the sight of her huge, imposing body, telling her that she could sleep soundly.

The evening of her escape, *Tia* Pappadopoulos tried to persuade Blanche to leave her grandmother and come with her. "After killing your mother, she's trying to kill you!" Madame Pelagia said, her eyes filled with hatred. "Come with me and be my daughter." And again she tried to force that same sweaty embrace upon the girl. Blanche was already fourteen and it was no longer possible to bribe her with a glass of cherry syrup. In no uncertain terms, she told Madame Pappadopoulos that she could go to hell. Madame Pappadopoulos felt wounded to the depths of her soul; she left with a dim hope in her heart that the Germans would take their revenge for her upon the ungrateful old woman and her granddaughter. When she returned from Cairo, *Nonna* Sandra welcomed her with a smile and asked after the well-being of "the refugee." Blanche didn't so much as look at her.

One morning Blanche opened the door on her way out to school when she saw that the door lintel and the *mezuzoth* were smeared with excrement. From the window opposite, the wicked face of *Tia* Pappadopoulos stared out.

Not many months after this, Pelagia Pappadopoulos passed away. After the neighbors noticed that she hadn't left the house for several days, they began asking whether anything had happened to the childless old Greek. Somebody said: "Maybe she died?" But no one dared approach the house and check.

Blanche raised her eyes from *Vingt-ans après* by Alexandre Dumas-Pére; she put the man of the iron treatise gained through suffering torments in cellars down to rest, quietly folded the corner of the page and closed the book. She got up, passed through the courtyard, skipped over and beyond the stone wall, then stood for a moment before approaching the door and knocking on it.

No answer. She pushed the door open and a hot wave of putrefaction assaulted her. Before letting out a choking shriek, she tried to ward off the swarms of teeming flies. She got her strength right back and went in again, to protect the face with a veil.

The bloated body of Pelagia Pappadopoulos almost filled the whole room. Mount Edom. Blanche felt her whole body tremble, she bit her lips and ground her teeth. She stayed in the room for a long moment before she started throwing up. She stood like that, as if nailed to the floor, with the bitter taste of vomit still in her mouth. Then her eyes found the familiar crystal pitcher on the shelf. The pitcher was almost full, and dead flies floated along the surface of the cherry syrup.

Almost choking with tears and measuring her steps to overcome their haste, she left, pale as the border of a shroud, but with a slight smile on her face.

Pelagia Pappadopoulos's house remained empty for several months, until an Arab family came and settled in the abandoned house, to the sorrow of *Nonna* Sandra. They stayed for a few years before uprooting themselves to Port Said. When Sandra heard the sound of hammers setting the place for the *mezuzoth,* her soul was greatly relieved. The Vital family was moving in—Tovula Vital, whose husband Moise Vital had already been settled in Palestine for a number of years, her unmarried daughter Flor, and her dear son Raphael Vital.

Romansa

The whole time, Blanche Aguiyos couldn't take her eyes off Raphael. She rushed about to help him take care of Maurice Rosenberg, before someone else had the chance, like that Josette, for instance, who kept staring at him. And as they were helping Rosenberg, Blanche gave Raphael a heavenly smile that would have melted anyone's heart.

"Sing for us, Raphael," she said in her coarse, smoky voice when they returned to the party after helping Maurice Rosenberg to his apartment. Raphael was taken aback. How did she know he could sing? There was a tango on and many couples were dancing to it, but Raphael overcame his natural shyness and, disregarding everyone, broke out into song with his powerful voice. The tango went down in the background before fading out altogether. The couples on the dance floor just stood. Everyone looked at Raphael in amazement, but he only saw Blanche.

With a crystal-clear tenor that had the timbre of a baritone, Raphael sang *Morenica* in Spanish, to someone who wasn't dark at all, to Blanche Aguiyos, with her snow-white skin and golden mane. But she knew that the song was just for her, as if it had been written that way.

Dark and burnished they call me
my skin was pure
and it is only from summer's blazing
sun that my darkness comes . . .

And all the young people that had been swaying to the dance music and the vocalists on before, now recalled the songs of their childhood and their grandmothers and they began to sing along with Raphael:

My dark beauty,
so, so beautiful!

Your eyes blaze fire,
My heart is yours alone.

And now they all sang to Blanche:

They call me dark and burnished,
all the sailors sailing off to sea,
If they call me but once again,
Just watch how fast I'll go with them.

And then suddenly, from the corner of the hall, the crackling, deceptive voice of Robby's grandmother could be heard, exultant at the apparent success of the romance between Blanche and Raphael:

Morenica,
MAVRA MATIA MU
Sus ojos graciosikos son
MAVRA MATIA MU.

We cannot but recall the beauty of Raphael Vital's throbbing voice without a thrill. Almost forty years have passed since then. Before the unfurling of the sixth decade of our century, Raphael finally went up to Palestine, which had, in the meantime, become the state of Israel. When it was our turn to leave the fleshpots of Alexandria behind in exchange for the booklet of food coupons awaiting us in the Israel of the 1950's, we made our way down south to Beersheba one day, to visit Raphael in the miserable, scorched concrete blocks sticking out of the desert. It wasn't the scarcity and desolation that shocked us so much—after all, even Little Sporting wasn't a luxury neighborhood—and even in Alexandria, Raphael was not unfamiliar with economic straits. And even us, we ourselves lived in a transit camp at the time. The shock came when we asked Raphael to sing something for us and he apologized and bashfully mumbled something about losing his voice.

"*Ayde,* he wants us to beg him," said grandmother, in rebuke. But that was the truth. In the wasteland between Alexandria and Beersheba, Raphael Vital's voice had dried up.

In Beersheba

The temperature in Beersheba got up to 110 degrees. The boy Moshe, named after his grandfather Moshe Vital, killed in Jerusalem by a bomb in the Anglo-Palestine Bank, loved to roll around in the sand. His mother, a housewife about to give birth again, went out looking for him. Levana, ex-Blanche, Vital cursed the imprisonment of her pregnancy.

Three years had passed since they came to the capital of the Negev. With Vita Shimon's small inheritance, they managed to buy an apartment in one of the two-family house blocks with small courtyards. Vita Shimon rescued them from the burning tin huts of the transit camp. Close to the time of their arrival, Raphael was supposed to be drafted into the army. Blanche was already carrying little Maurice in her womb, Moshe that is, and she threatened to cut her veins if Raphael went into the army. The IDF wasn't very impressed by the hysterical woman, but Raphael knew his wife was quite capable of going through with it. A compromise was finally found and Raphael enlisted in the police force and was stationed in Beersheba, which is how they happened to end up in the desert city. In Egypt we fled from the desert to the openness of the coastal cities, and in Israel the desert blows its arid heat over our faces and the backs of our necks in this Beersheba of theirs, which is just a small-scale Cairo, without even the Nile for relief.

Blanche-Levana and her husband Raphael's years in the capital of the Negev were hard, hot, and dry. It is difficult to write about them. The eastern winds seemed to dry up the ink in the pen, and nostalgia for hopeful youth smuggles the narrator back to the cool sea breeze of Alexandria.

Blanche and Raphael, a good-looking, romantic couple. I see them sitting at the L'Auberge Bleu of memory, but I know there is no avoiding the

Beersheba story. It isn't just that the Land of Israel served as an incline for them to roll down. Everything already started there, in Alex, but the affliction was covered up, certainly from the sight of a boy like our Robby, from whom everything unpleasant was hidden. But beneath the sun of the Negev it was difficult to hide anything, even from the eyes of a child.

Blanche was twenty-six. She had put on a few pounds. In Egypt she occasionally filled out a bit under the influence of the drugs prescribed to her by the clinic, but here she really put on some weight. We've already spoken of how Robby's grandmother discovered that Blanche was short. Now even those who didn't have her eagle-eye vision could see for themselves, particularly since she spent most of the day in slippers. Her golden hair had also begun to lose its sheen and even become sparse in parts, worn down from anxiety, to the point where she thought some treatment might be needed. Only her hoarse, whispering voice retained the magic of the old days, particularly when she smoothly negotiated the difficulties of Hebrew.

When she felt good, dressed well, and made herself up, she just about managed to reach her former splendor. But when she started making herself up and dressing well, it was also a sign that it wouldn't be long before she would go out on one of her mysterious sorties, disappearing for a week or ten days, leaving her husband and child to fend for themselves. Raphael found himself obliged to miss work at the police force more than once, and even when he reported for duty, his mind wasn't on his work.

Little Moshe became the charge of three neighbors, a Moroccan, a Romanian and an Iraqi. The neighbors, who had kids and worries of their own, organized themselves to take turns of duty helping out with little Moshe. When Blanche returned from her escapades, she would cross-examine the boy and ask about the neighbors and whether or not they had said anything bad about her.

What does a man do as he sees himself sinking? What does he do when he realizes that he has lost his voice because no one says to him: "Come on, sing something for us"? There are some who cannot help themselves out of the quicksand, some just keep on sinking.

Playing cards, for instance. It starts with an innocent enough game, to break the monotony, and develops into a marathon of days and nights, especially during his wife's absent spells. And then, after a night of cards, there's hardly any strength left to get up for the first watch. The route from here to getting fired is not long.

In 1956, Raphael is the father of two children and out of work. His wife has deteriorated even further. He already is thinking of divorce, but every time he intends to go through with it, she winds up on her back. Into the hospital again. A baby and a toddler without a mother.

When Raphael arrived in Israel five years prior to this, he searched for the country he had known and fallen in love with on his visits before the establishment of the state. For all intents and purposes, it was the same country; in many ways, it was even better. Nevertheless, it was like another world. Raphael knew that the changes could be found nowhere else but in him. Something in him had died.

He sits on a bench by the entrance to the block, at dusk. He wears shorts and a tattered undershirt, draped over him like a rag. Unshaven. Out of work. He looks at Moshico and little David. Both of them play in the sand. Distress in his heart. Poor kids, growing up with no mother. Their mother is in the hospital now. It seems that Blanche, who had always had her wits about her, was the first to crack under the pressure. Maybe it was heriditary. *Nonna* Sandra finally ended up crazy too. And who knows about her father or mother. Maybe if Gaston was alive things would have ended up differently. Raphael looked around. What kind of a chance would these kids have, growing up like this? And with this hereditary time-bomb, to boot. If they can get out of it all unscathed, maybe only then will this struggle to bear the yoke of life be worthwhile.

Suddenly he heard Moshico crying. Little David, only a year old, threw sand at him. Moshico didn't retaliate but explained, between tearful spasms: "Because he's a baby. No fair. I'm bigger—that's no fair. No fair, Daddy, it's no fair!"

Raphael gave him a big hug.

Georgette, the Moroccan neighbor, came by. She lives on the other side of the block, with her husband Armand Cohen. Armand was Egyptian, like Raphael, but from Cairo, not Alexandria.

"How are you making out with the kids, Rafi?" Georgette asked, stroking Moshico's hair, her fingers accidentally brushing against his.

"Comme çi comme ça, thanks."

"They eat?"

"I'll take care of it in a bit."

"Let me make something, then we'll put them down to sleep."

"Where's that Armand of yours?"

"What do you mean, where? Three days he's already in the reserves, didn't you notice?"

"Sorry, you know, everything with Levana . . ."

"I know, it's alright."

Raphael watched the screen door snap back behind her. Georgette was his age, thin, with short hair. Her nose was kind of big but her lively, slanting eyes, joyous and enticing, drew your attention away from it. She didn't have any children, so she had a little more time than the other neighbors to help out in taking care of the two neglected kids.

"Where do you keep the oil? I can see you haven't got any margarine in the icebox," she called from inside. Raphael got up despondantly. In blue shorts and a white sleeveless shirt, she stood in the kitchen lighting the wick; for a second, the flaring match illuminated her profile, brightening her eyes. Raphael stood by the entrance. For a moment he imagined that this quiet woman was his wife. On the marble countertop in the kitchen, she had already cracked the eggs for an omelette.

"What are you looking at me like that for?" She smiled: "Something wrong with what I'm wearing?"

"The oil is in the cabinet under the sink," he said quietly. As if moving towards her, his hand went to the light switch but stopped in mid-air. He went closer to her. She turned the light on herself. The heat in the kitchen was almost too heavy to bear. Without warning, he broke out in sobs and sought her shoulder; not hesitating, she drew in his afflicted face, and her neck became drenched with his tears. Suddenly he showered her face with kisses, until he found his way to her mouth and her tongue.

That was the first time Raphael had sought solace in the bosom of another woman since he had taken Blanche as his wife. The next day he got up and went out to look for work.

Epilogue

More than twenty years went by. Robby grew up to become a man. In the summer of 1976 or 1977, he was invited to Moshe Vital's wedding. He hadn't seen Raphael's son since he was a kid. His mother asked him to go— "Your cousin will be very happy"—and he surprised her by saying: "With pleasure!"

The wedding was held at a hall in the Haifa Technion. Moshe had finished his studies at the Technion the year before and was making a good living as an electrical engineer for Elbit, located at the foot of Mount Carmel. His younger brother, David Vital, about to be released from the standing Army at the rank of captain, wavered as to whether he should go to the Technion like his brother or open a small business with the money he had managed to save during his military service.

The hall was packed. The guests sat at round tables and, after the feeding, couples got up to dance. A wedding band played some things in Hebrew, a little in English and a lot in Greek. A somewhat sweaty Mediterranean atmosphere. Robby overcame his bashfulness through a push from Zorba the Greek, and even he got up to dance. His mother was happy.

An hour, then several more hours passed, and the tables started to empty a bit. A plump, older woman sat at one of the tables, contentedly smiling. Robby looked at her for a second. If she hadn't taken off her glasses just then so he could get a look at her eyes, he never would have recognized her. When he was a boy, her eyes looked to him like those of a lynx, that wild cat he had seen in the *Larousse Encyclopedia.* Their splendor had dimmed somewhat but they were, nevertheless, the eyes of Blanche Vital. From time to time Moshe and David went over to bring her something to drink, sitting by her and talking for a while, since she was sitting all by herself. Most of those summoned were friends or members of her ex-husband's family. From her side, there was no one except these two tall, handsome young men.

Raphael finished dancing with Robby's sister and took a seat by an empty table.

Here they are sitting at separate tables and looking at their two children with great pride.

That look of theirs is what prompted me, I who was also among those called, to set my heart upon the idea of writing within a book the story of Blanche and Raphael Vital.

No, there cannot be any connection whatsoever between the two people sitting there like solitary islands, and the characters who will be created from a reflection of their sorrow.

If they themselves read these things one day, maybe they won't even recognize themselves.

It's enough that I recognize myself in them.

Today is the 10th of August, 1985.

— Translated from the Hebrew by Ammiel Alcalay

from SHELTER IN BAVLI

The novel takes place in Israel at the end of 1982, during the Lebanon war. Excerpts from articles written by Dr. Naphtali Mimran at the beginning of the 1990s are woven in throughout the book. During the period the book is set, in 1982, Naphtali Mimran is still a law student.

Heli (Rachel) Da Silva, a lecturer in law in her mid forties, arrived with her parents from Iraq in the 1950s and made every effort to become an Israeli in every respect, to the point of turning her back on the world of her parents. Her slogan: "If you're good, you'll succeed!" According to her, she herself served as proof to this claim. In fact, she is about to get her doctorate. But just as she approaches what would seem to be a peak in her life, Heli feels an emptiness, and the yearning for something truly wild to happen to her grows. Morris Rahamim, a student of hers from Kfar Shalem (a working-class neighborhood in Tel Aviv), arouses in her the very same feelings of anger and resentment that usually serve to cover up a secret love. As Heli's feelings for the enigmatic Morris ripen, she undergoes a process of growing self-awareness on the way to finding her own identity. In an effort to flee from the illicit love she harbors towards one of her students, she joins her husband, Mano Da Silva, owner of the Mano Tours travel agency, on a trip to Egypt. After a visit to Alexandria, the city that Mano spent his childhood and adolescence in, the couple travels to Luxor in Upper Egypt. At first, Heli acts like any tourist, but just before boarding the night train to Cairo, she suddenly decides to send her husband back to Israel alone and remain in Luxor.

★ ★ ★ ★ ★

"It is crucial for the establishment to understand that the struggle for Easternness is a national objective, for the good of Israel as a whole, and not some ethnic episode led by frustrated, unsatisfied agitators. If we take this approach, there can be no doubt that the Arabs—today our neighbors and enemies but also our potential friends, will see in this a genuine act on Israel's part to integrate itself within the region, instead of simply relying on its ability to secure itself militarily. Even beyond this, there can be little doubt as well that—in global terms, and particularly in terms of the West—we will no longer be portrayed as imitators but as bearers of bold tidings and perhaps even as a watershed in their own development. And there also exists the remote possibility that they too will reach the conclusion that an Eastern spice can enrich their western culture, caught up as it is presently in such a dire state of stagnation and confusion."

(From "Are We Crusaders?" by Dr. Naphtali Mimran, Ben-Gurion University; an article published in Arabic and appearing in the journal *al-Ard* [The Land]; September 1992.)

★ ★ ★ ★ ★

The hour of dusk tints the hem stitched onto the banks of the Nile. The heavy sun is like the golden circular sail in the vessel of the God Ra, turning astray toward the scalded western mountains. Everything belongs to there, everything belongs to then, everything belongs to once.

Perhaps only Heli, walking barefoot along the seam between the present, the past, and eternity, still belongs to a present that can somehow be grasped. Eternity bears no relation to conceptions of time like "always, till the end, forever and ever." Eternity is actually the negation of time, bringing it within everyone's reach. Eternity is that part of time without borders that can occur in a split second and then vanish. You are saturated by the eternal so long as you don't set boundaries on time. This is the secret Heli understood and repeated to herself again and again. She didn't concern herself as to how long she would stay within this bubble beyond time; thus, she felt herself splash within eternity's very heart.

Barefoot, wearing one of the *galabiyas* she had bought and armed with bundles of beads and bracelets and anklets, Heli strayed within the blessed anonymity of this utopia, as her trappings jangled—copper on glass and amber—expelling all the bad spirits from her path, as they tried to trap her in their sticky fingers. Many anniversaries ago she had loved a certain Morris and been jealous of a certain Niva and separated from a certain Mano who was swallowed up in the darkness, mouth agape and thunderstruck.

Luxor—a provincial town where colossal temples overflow the brim, like the body of a camel adorned with the skeleton of a dinosaur. It is difficult for the Egypt of today to sustain its past. Is she trying to compete with it, Heli asked herself, or are the past and the present one within eternity? And what does all this have to do with me? Heli struggled to make the analogy, but it was as if the questions evaporated in the hot, dry air. It's cold and rainy everywhere else in the world, it's hot and dry and sunny only here, and you can walk along in your barefeet treading through the sand, you can see and stay unseen. Do I even exist at all? asked Heli, but this question, like the others before, also dissipated.

How can it be that no one is attending to her, offering their services or their wares? Could it be possible that they, with their keen eagle-eye vision, wouldn't have spotted her for a tourist, despite her Arab dress that shook off western affects? That just couldn't be. Even Heli was aware of the limitations of her attempt to adorn herself in a garb of Arabness. When does clothing cease to be a ridiculous form of disguise and start to be an essence? Heli knew that, at most, she had a chance to come closer, shed a layer, maybe even touch with a hesitant finger—and that would be it.

She sat at the bank. A mighty river, upright palms and desert heat; the setting sun cast its last shadows among the peaks. Another river, no less mighty, began to flow along the horizon of her consciousness; it too sprouted palms right where it gave in to the desert. A little girl is sitting on the banks of that river, her eyes are big. She doesn't yet know rage, nor is she aware of bitterness. She looks at the river with clean eyes that know nothing about the past or the future. It is a powerful and stormy river—but the mighty rivers of the Garden of Eden turned into a disappointing stream as they arrived along with the little girl to the gates of the Land of Israel, dragged along like the train of her white party dress that was ruined in the hardships endured in the flight. Suddenly Heli had a craving to speak to that little girl or, at the very least, to write her a note. To ask her forgiveness. For what? Perhaps for seeking sanctuary in anger and bitterness. Perhaps over feelings of estrangement and arrogance that coursed within the older woman regarding the child within, and what she represented.

Thus, along the banks of those waters, both so foreign and familiar, a new kind of Tigris was born, and when the guttural voices of the kids from Luxor reached her from behind, she began to form within her a delicate embroidery of reconciliation towards the distant and estranged city of her childhood. The generation of the desert was born in Baghdad, her parents were born there—she hastened to shake herself free of them when they brought her to the borders of the promised land. In Zion, the very existence of their lives was emptied of content and only she and her siblings were deemed fit to bite into life itself and dare resemble the upright, smiling giants of Canaan. Maybe Elik knew he was born of the sea, while Rachel-Heli didn't know, or didn't want to know that she was born of the desert river or the river desert. The Heli of today no longer knows what came first, the reservations she held about her parents and what they represented—she who devised an almost sexual desire to prostrate herself before the Land of Israel and its idols, to roll in their dust—or, rather, whether the power of their attraction is what shaped her relationship to her parents, to their patrimony, to the trail of tradition they dragged with them from their ancient exile, without, perhaps, even being aware of that tradition or understanding its significance.

And her father and mother, drained in the exhaustion of their frustration, bereft of either the desire or the ability to reach her, only supported—without knowing it—her wish to please, to declare herself an orphan from the ghetto, offering herself up to adoption to whoever would take her.

★ ★ ★ ★ ★

"Some Reflections on the Gulf War," from a series of articles by Dr. Naphtali Mimran from Ben Gurion University, published in the Israeli press between January and March 1991:

"What a dismal fix! Again we find ourselves on the side of a cynical colonialism regarding the third world. This time, the victim is the Iraqi people, and whatever people it might be, they will always win my support. Not the leaders. If those perverts decided to drop missiles on my head, they left me (as someone who sees himself as an Arab Jew) no choice but to give up—at least temporarily—on my feelings of comradeship for my Muslim brothers on the banks of the Tigris. All that's left us is to hope together for a future where a union will be possible between third world peoples, without differences in religion or nationality coming between them."

—*Translated from the Hebrew by Ammiel Alcalay*

ALBERT SWISSA

ALBERT SWISSA was born in Casablanca in 1959 and emigrated to Israel with his family in 1963. He has been involved in theater and spent a number of years in Paris as an actor and student; he presently lives in Paris. His first

book, *Bound,* is an interconnected series of episodes that constitute a novel, set in a Jerusalem neighborhood inhabited primarily by North African immigrants. Quite unlike anything that has come before it, Swissa's remarkably bold and dense language has opened a completely new space for exploration within Hebrew prose. In one of the only readings of Swissa's work that takes into account not only the literary but also the historical and social circumstances of his work, Yerach Gover (in *Zionism: The Limits of Moral Discourse in Israeli Hebrew Fiction*) writes of the physical setting of the text: "Initially placed in transition camps, the immigrants were moved during the early 1970s from asbestos huts to a newly built neighborhood. By all accounts, this resembled a penitentiary, or area of containment. The constraints of this setting constitute a first principle of unity in the novel. A second is found in the life of the three main protagonists, Yohai, Beber, and Ayiush. They are children, not yet thirteen years old, and they provide the perspective and voice of the victims and heroes of *Aliyah* (immigration). Growing up in the newly built slum neighborhoods, they witness the sacrifice of their community to an ideal and, at the same time, are exemplary figures of its survival. The sacrifice and the struggle, the third principle of unity, are configured as a condition of bondage *(aqud)* and an obligation to wait. The protagonists define a zone of conflict, hence freedom, in the prison in which they find themselves, without preparation and for reasons they cannot understand. This struggle for emancipation can only be challenged ironically. The only available weapon for their struggle is a carefully contrived and disguised defiance—defiance of authority, and through that the development of a sense, often vague and inchoate, of both the oppressiveness of authority and how their knowledge of it constitutes their own power." In a discussion of *Last Winter* by Shimon Ballas and *Bound* by Albert Swissa that concludes his book, Gover writes that "both Ballas and Swissa have produced authentic extranational, one is tempted to say postnational, novels. To that extent, they speak within and of a history that subsumes rather than merely opposes that of the Jews, and it is that history that Israeli culture ultimately must recognize if it is to produce works that are genuinely self-critical in their moral reflection, if it is to permit the rediscovery of the self as other that is essential to recognizing the other and therefore to any nonsectarian morality."

ESCAPING THE CAULDRON UNSCATHED

"It was on a particularly lovely day," my parents recall, still surprised at themselves, "that we found ourselves on the bow of a ship that took us away from Morocco, where our forefathers had lived some thousand years. Despite all the planning and the many preparations—selling all of our property and exchanging our money for silver and gold—which were carried out in the strictest secrecy—we were as surprised at ourselves then as if we had seen the Messiah himself riding toward us on a white ass." In the picture I am a boy of three, swathed in a white silk caftan and seated proudly on my mother's lap, a crystal fish in my arms. But even then, in the heart of the child whom I've never abandoned and against the background of the lullaby with which she would serenade me in French, I knew that my mother's face was turned toward "Paris." The ship that sailed for the Land of Israel docked for three weeks in Marseille; but before my mother could see even the corner of a boulevard in that city my father had yanked her away to the Land of Israel. Ever since, her thoughts, her ways, and her dreams have been turned toward Paris. My father's face has always been turned toward "Zion." Yet despite having lived for thirty years in a far-flung neighborhood of Jerusalem, he, too, still longs for Paris, longs for the longing for Paris, and wonders at the "Zionism" that had so turned his head. . .

Indeed, decades before the great drama of the ingathering of the exiles had begun, a different drama was unfolding for the Jews of Morocco, a result of the French rule of that land. Like prehistoric eggs hatching after hundreds of years of gestation, the Jews began to flock from the villages to the great metropolises by the thousands, astir with the passion for modernity. My father, the first-born son of renowned jewelers, bookbinders, and circulators of liturgical hymns on my grandfather's side, and a long line of dentists on my grandmother's side, left his ancestral village of Tiznit—nestled in the Draa Valley between the base of the Atlas Mountains and the southern edge of the Sahara—for Casablanca—the city of his dreams in those days—taking with him his tiny family and his seven orphaned nephews. One fine day—after years of struggle and hard work—my father found himself strolling in a leisurely fashion down the Boulevard de France from his dental clinic to his home, there to dine with his young family and take his afternoon siesta before returning to work.

For years I pestered my parents about that picture of the departure for the Land of Israel in which was hidden the key to all that would come after; it was too romantic. The word "Zion" that my father knew had little in common and often much that was at odds with Zionism. Ideology, revolution, and policy, as the secular government of Israel then understood them, were essentially foreign to my parents.

However, since memory—shaken by shock-waves in the intervening years—deceives us, let us open the photo album at the following picture: My immediate family and other relatives, sprightly as Tu B'Shvat saplings in old tin cans, stands on a dusty dirt road in the heart of Ir Ganim, the "city of gardens" (though there wasn't a single garden in sight!), one of the many abysmal concrete enclaves hastily built during the 1960s. The men sport hats and white wool suits, their black eyes steady, and the women wear sleeveless, floral summer dresses. Because of the sun, the smiles on their faces are wan; yet they seem to be floating, as if intoxicated by the exhilarating scent of a new world about to begin.

It wasn't long before that rarified time crumbled in a devastating collapse of all that had been dear to them in life. All too soon my parents discovered that they and all their kind were pariahs, ostracized from the economic, social, cultural and—worst of all—spiritual life of the nascent State of Israel. "The *shekhinah* has abandoned them [the Oriental Jews]" was only one of David Ben Gurion's unfortunate utterances regarding this ethnic group, and not unlike those of many other leaders of that time. Culture shock—not to mention the objective difficulties of being stirred into an hermetically sealed "smelting pot" bubbling with renewed life yet struggling to survive—threw out of joint, in truth, smashed to smithereens—what had been most sacred to this group of immigrants: the family. The crisis of language and new patterns of behavior and education caused a serious rift between the generation of the fathers and that of the sons, as well as between the entire Oriental Jewish population and 'Israeli' society, particularly during the following two decades. My own father was totally consumed with the travails of making a living, which included being embroiled in a long, drawn-out legal battle with the state over his right to ply his dental trade (for my father, akin to profaning the sacred); though he was vindicated after years in court, the trial left its scars on all the members of the family.

At the same time, our world was full of words that enfolded and protected us, like a womb its embryo: In our eleven-member family's two-room apartment there was space enough for the thousands of letters that floated in the air and joined to form word-objects, word-experiences. Words created a world we could relate to and live in, as in a separate country: the words of my mother's songs; the words of my father's Talmud; fragments of verses and rhymes we dragged in from the synagogue and from the street. Yet this does not mean there were personal, heart-to-heart talks deep into the night—neither among siblings, nor, certainly, between children and parents. I sense that a clear memory is the sign of clear, defined emotions. Yet it seems that—for some unfathomable reason that I labor to comprehend—in my emotional education, personal feelings were fated to be forgotten. In fact, despite the cradle of words where we found repose, we were taught according to a long tradition of silence. Despite being anathema to the modern age of communication, silence was still the most important element of an education that was based traditionally on what went unsaid and what should not be spoken of, more than on what could be given voice. Later I understood that in the world of my parents, the psychological aspects of the human soul were best left unmentioned. Not because they weren't familiar with psychologists or psychology, but because their attitude toward these bordered on revulsion: Exposing the secrets of the human heart was no less wanton and untoward than speaking the secrets of the Divine Presence with a layman was heretical and defamatory, in principle. That, precisely, was their world view.

Therefore our childhood—albeit, absurdly, a happy one for having been lived in the "no-man's land" of barren hilltops, abandoned groves, and nooks in boulders at the edge of Jerusalem created for us by the collapse of the communal, economic, and social systems—in its linguistic, spiritual, cultural, and socio-economic aspects became, in effect, the most worn of battlefields. There, the heart-wrenching struggle to salvage the remnants of idiom was waged. Though my mother's native tongue was Judaeo-Berber, she loved and made festive use of French; my father spoke archaic, biblical Hebrew; and my own language was a motley mix of all these languages poured into modern Hebrew. As children we experienced the childhood of the rejuvenated State of Israel. Out of ignorance, religion was identified then with the traditional, old-fashioned world that stood in opposition to the new world order. The generation of our fathers could not confront the generation of its sons on the field of clever rhetoric that was the Israeli street. Oriental culture was identified then as now with the culture of the 'enemy'; it was therefore necessary to play it down as much as possible—if not to ignore it completely. And as a result of sudden changes in their social and economic behavior patterns, those who were arbitrarily thought of as "backward" were suddenly thrown into the very heart of a class struggle, where they were "naturally" placed at the bottom of the ladder. Overall, it fell to the Oriental Jews to fight on all fronts of Israeli society, to fight against the society itself, and to fight against the image Israeli society ascribed them—and I am not sure that this was such a bad thing.

Bitterly disappointed with the Western-secular Israeli reality and fearful of the growing chasm in communication between himself and his children, my father tried to bring his ship back to the calmer waters of the good old ways. One by one he took my brothers out of state schools and transferred them to yeshivas or ultraorthodox Sephardic *heders.* "During a time of wantonness, we must turn inward," he would quote the Talmud, calling the situation one of "exile within the Holy Land itself!" But it was too late: The seeds of freedom and rebellion had already been sown in all of his children, and it was not long before they had flowered into a difficult, painful, and long-standing disagreement between parent and offspring, almost without exception.

After mild deliberation during my youth, and before I was to exchange "creed" for "creativity," I chose to continue my studies at those simple yeshivas which are to my mind still, in their traditional format, the wellspring of all Jewish wisdom. The process of confrontation between "acceptance" and "denial" between a wounded cultural "past" and the modern, overbearing "present" into which the Oriental Jews of my generation were thrust, transformed us from a silent and subjugated majority that had inherited the remnants of fundamentalist social behavior into a democratic and dynamic majority that has developed a special sensitivity to the problems of the unnatural cultural minority in a democratic society. This new majority is gradually formulating a political, social, and cultural alternative to the old collective Israeli stance; this process was most clearly exemplified by the political upset of 1977 (the Likud victory that unseated the Labour party after nearly thirty years in power), as a result of which the face of Israeli society is changing practically beyond recognition.

But in the final analysis, for good or ill, there is one very damaging fact: In the cauldron of the generation that founded the state, whole cultures melted into oblivion, were eroded, vanished—life experiences, gestures, customs, sights, smells, sounds, languages, people—all, among them the creatures of my childhood, sank slowly into the sea of modernity before my eyes, nothing remaining of them but scant archival shards of folklore. Though this is supposedly the way of the world, I balk at taking comfort in it, and rebuke myself as God rebuked the ministering angels after He had drowned Pharaoh's army in the Red Sea: "My creatures are drowning and you sing songs of praise?!" I am driven almost obsessively to write because it is writing alone, "magic words" alone, that can restore us at once to the lost realm of childhood; in writing alone is there the comfort of reconstructing the illusion—so very necessary to our sanity—that our past is not doomed to be lost and forgotten, that it may come back to us with renewed meaning.

It would seem that it is my childhood, passed in the shadow of that same, terrible "silence" that hung between Abraham, who went forth to sacrifice, and Isaac, who went forth to be sacrificed, that has pushed me toward creativity—whose essential purpose is to shatter silences—and particularly toward the literary creativity that gave birth to *Bound*. This book is an attempt to recall memory even as it is being forgotten. I will keep working the alchemy of emotions and memories, calling up the spirits of the past until the faces of all the dead of that desert are rewoven before my eyes.

—*Translated from the Hebrew by Marsha Weinstein*

from BOUND

A. IN THE CONCRETE COLONY

But before then there were heights of ecstasy and fields of sewage that flowed wildly down the black gorges, past giant tractor tires and thistles and lush hawthorn shrubs and many more trees not known by name, and the flowers of the fall and spring that stood there too; and past phantasmagoric Arabs and fowl and wild animals, and wild, black children who rode donkeys and picked almonds and figs, or dragged the hulls of cars or rolled tires down the *wadi*. Until it came to pass that what those here are wont to call "fortune" turned its wheel their way, though it seemed to Mr. Sultan that they meant to say—with fervent national pride and a kind of viciousness that one professor from the university, who was half Moroccan and half Ashkenazi but very radical, called "Bolshevik"—that they meant to say: "Here we will build a royal roost for hens," more than they wanted to sing, "We have come up to the land to build and be built by it," chanting out innocently toward the hoary virgin valleys; except that only yesterday, on the twenty-fifth anniversary of the State of Israel, when Mr. Sultan had heard the tune of "we have come up" from the radio of a rickety, stinking—but very jubilant—public bus that had charged through the streets of the capital, he had been seized by a strange and powerful tremor of both sorrow and joy, which in fact he regretted—since it didn't befit a man as tough as he was, whose toughness helped him keep his distance from men of religion and houses of prayer. But then the heights had been dug up; and into the wide, deep pits they had poured row after row of concrete bomb shelters, on top of which (day and night a strange wind beat like the silent, rusty derrick in the grey and dusty frames) the huge cranes had hoisted wall-door, wall-window, narrow-bridged hallway and stair upon stair; and huge tenements the pale yellow color of beer had grown skyward and bored into the eyes of the firmament; then they were peopled with young men and old, children and women—nearly a host in a day—family by family, each to its source of salvation from exile: Persians and Moroccans, Tunisians and Algerians, Iraqis and Cochins—even a few Ashkenazi families, who were called "our brothers"—each having to suffer the lives of the others (if patiently and with great, odious hope, without excessive success) under the blazing, sparkling sun that shone false against the pale periwinkle, pardoning the anemones and wild carnations with a bolt, and daily hurling the fiery pallor of the sky onto the tenements, spent with containing.

Yamna his wife shouted something to him about the relatives from France who would be coming again that evening, but Mr. Sultan no longer listened to his wife's rantings. He turned on the ancient yellow light on the narrow balcony elevated eleven storeys above the boulders of the *wadi,* took a pack of nonfilter Dubek cigarettes out of the drawer of the old buffet—the last remnant of the furniture from Marrakech—and with his thumb sprung one, which did a double flip straight into his hand. Under the fleshy cloak of his broad body, bent silently forward in an expression that bode ill, his thoughts swirled banal and murky, like motes of dirt in a glass of turbid water.

From the balcony on this side of the tenement only bloody remains of the sun were visible; but over the unseen horizon hung an incandescent bluish mist, which implored the pale pinks and dark purples to portend the coming of night. Three days and three nights his little son Beber had been missing, ever since he had fled the battered hands of his mother, after foolishly letting her shave his head—with scorn only a woman could muster—the way they shaved the heads of thieves and traitors. What had the poor kid done, thought Mr. Sultan idly. He didn't worry too much about his children. "Ineeway they weel manige beatter by themshelf," he would tell the teachers at the amusing parents' nights in his heavily accented, broken Hebrew. "That's more polite," he thought, "than to tell 'em: 'none a your business.'" For him, concern for his children was a pointless need, a mild form of indentured servitude, a mechanical slip of the tongue whose necessity calls to mind an unpleasant yet unavoidable sensation in the anus, portending ill. Nevertheless, the apathy with which he was accustomed to treat his children could not help him banish the child's image which, having been unconjurable in a familiar place for three days, was now oddly stalled between heaven and earth as if hovering; nor could it banish the sense of dismay aroused especially by the sight of his weakling arms, which had not been weaned of the stigma of childhood and which would need developing if he were to become a real boxer. Mr. Sultan esteemed the boxer's build, and so always wished that this wonderchild, his small heir, might one day cloak his body in the full, healthy, and beautiful limbs of a man of the Mafia in his prime. Mr. Sultan organized his thoughts one by one in a prearranged order, and contemplated the "reward" he'd give the boys and the "beasts" for having tormented little Beber (who cleaved covertly and with incendiary fervor to his clandestine daughter at the Jerusalem girls' orphanage).

The clanking of dishes that came from the kitchen roused him to say aloud angrily: "No verbena, no mint—*Vishotchky!* Vishotchky tea!" Mrs. Sultan hastened to come with the tea tray. Positioning the cigarette in his mouth and flipping a burning match between his fingers, Mr. Sultan made an effort to focus his eyes under his brows; without lifting his head he turned to his wife and said, singsong, "How many children have I got?" The match still burned in his upraised hand as if he meant to illuminate her face. She stopped and leaned forward, stunned, the tray suspended inches above the table. A mischievous and coy smile scrunched her face into many wrinkles, but she knew that first she must answer the question she'd been asked: "Ten, *ya azizi*," she said flirtatiously. "Great!" he cut her off with a nod of his head. "And where are they?" At once the wrinkles vanished, and her face took on a benevolent, apologetic expression. She let the tray fall onto the table, and as she disappeared into the yellow steaminess of the kitchen she shouted back at him, "I threw them to the street, life is stinks, got to clean the whole house, don't I? And your kids is no kids, they barbarians."

Thickened air rested like a lukewarm, damp blanket on the waves of heat exhaled by the earth, and in the distance halfway between the balcony and the edge of the *wadi,* scattered clouds of darkness swirled in a circular whirr, flowing together until the world was enshrouded by a black veil punctured by a few tiny lights light years apart. Mr. Sultan furrowed his brow and twisted his lips into a puckered and silent kind of "moo;" with that expression he scoured the shaven valley as if struggling to comprehend something. There was no rustle of bushes, nothing to evidence an anticipated wind, or some possibility of a cooling.

Nary the flicker of a thought about his children. His bitter ruminations turned to ordinary concerns; he mused over the things, people and events forced upon him against his will, which he listed as if from some responsibility he had taken upon himself. Then he turned to matters in which something always remained beyond his grasp. He recalled how he had shamed himself in public that day at the internal revenue office, when he'd hurled at them, "whorsh," blunt and sharp, in a Moroccan accent so thick as to make his mildest words sound like epithets. And how (this he would emphasize over and over, even without being asked) he was ashamed mostly because he had always wanted to earn only untainted money in his life—without taxes and without any "collaborators"—but hadn't succeeded. And then, passing the *shtibels* on his way to Mahane Yehuda market (before that he'd let a whole portion of felafel drop from his slackened hand into the garbage. "Felafel!" he'd said with false and undangerous fury. "That's not felafel!") he'd conspicuously and scornfully refused to complete the quorum for afternoon prayers and, finally, had been forced to smash the scale that belonged to Eini's Arab with two boxing punches because it had lied by at least 50 grams. As a result, he'd had to stop by the greengrocers' stalls to settle things, as he called it, with a few of Eini's brothers and his Arabs, on account of which he'd missed the important, frightening, and unexpected appointment that had been made for him with the doctor on—of all days—the day after the Independence Day of the State of Israel.

And at the edge of the neighborhood, where the earth continues down from the mountain at a moderate slope poor in scrub and ruts, the boys of the neighborhood were playing soccer, now dispersing to the brink of the thickening darkness, now returning to gather on the cement railings and lighted sidewalks with gleeful cries of communion—except for three blurry figures that were waving a smallish but stocky boy by his legs and wiping his head again and again in the dusty earth as if he were the sacrificial chicken being whirled aloft in atonement on Yom Kippur. Mr. Sultan's bovine face was probably drawn to the spot by the wan and indirect light of the party clubhouse lamp; the boys moved wildly toward and away from the child until he disappeared completely behind their legs kicking high in the air and their arms waving in clenched fists, with the dust rising in columns around them until they seemed a vague apparition. And when the dust finally settled and the shouting ceased, Mr. Sultan could make out one big, round boy who, with a coarse and evil laugh stayed seated astride the stomach of the child pinned under him, who writhed like the severed tail of a lizard. Then Mr. Sultan said between clenched teeth, "Devils, devils bedeviled," exhaling a sigh but not lifting even a finger. The child had already been forgotten when he shouted into the house: "Barbarians or not barbarians—home! You hear? HOME!" feeling himself a fool. But meanwhile night had fallen completely, and down through the eleven storeys, long, white, fluorescent lights, which save electricity, and dark yellow 60-watt bulbs had been turned on, and all the voices of the street—loud cries, kicked cans, screams, keening wails of lament, curses and howls, guffaws and sobs, rolled-down garbage cans—seemed to collect, wafting up from the box-houses and mingling to a senseless roar with the newscasters in various languages, and the shrieks of the television in Arabic, and the clatter of pots and pans and tools, and the shatter of breaking dishes—a roar that surged like a thick and steamy waterfall down the eleven storeys to the denuded garden that lay there exposed to the black expanse of the world, languishing under the burden of garbage and junk that had been hurled on it from the balconies; where only as if by some marvel, some incomprehensible stubbornness, a few humble and sickly buds of ancient Jewish Agency oleander still poked through here and there.

The door to the house burst open wide onto the bare stairwell between the inner slabs of the prefabricated structures, and the relatives surged inside with the victory roar of a covey of boxers who have heard the gong that releases them into the fray. The house—suddenly overrun by the gay abandon that only a stranger can bring—was invaded by the glass-walled cafes, brightly lit and full of people, and the amber boulevards teeming with life, hinted at in the ties glowing with tiny stars that were displayed magnanimously on the small paunches like national flags; and by the studied gait of the merchants who moved gingerly and cautiously under their suits of midnight-blue gabardine or deep grey English wool, intoxicating the members of the household with light gusts of cologne, aftershave, and deodorant. Even though they came to "La Terre" every year for a visit, they still made a point of talking mostly about a life that was meant to sound to Mr. Sultan as if it happened "elsewhere," And as they talked they slapped him on the back, or wound their fingers around the back of his neck and butted their foreheads lightly against his, like partners in a relay race who have accepted their decisive victory sportingly and with a healthy attitude; and Mr. Sultan, his head hollow and soft from a spot of aperitif, ruminated on "life is stinks," feeling as if he'd been smeared all over with grease. Like that fixture of the neighborhood, ancient and covered with construction dust, who has been graced with a few charitable words from a seventh-rank canvasser stumping for votes, he listened to their words with that rare and baleful cognizance that usually overwhelmed him—as if by the grace of God—after several shots of *arak*. He would have liked to have said to them, with pain and with a generosity full of goodwill: "So, you've made it;" but instead he stared past the balcony and said nothing, then looked at them, silent, as if in confession.

Then the child's head was pressed dangerously back against his neck, one hand clasped at an unfathomable angle in the pudgy and indifferent arms of the fat kid who rode on his back, the other shielding his face from breathing in or biting dust; only his head and one of his legs could move from side to side in relative freedom in an expression of pain, or in a daring and hopeless attempt to get loose; when they did, the spot where two scars crossed on his shaven scalp shone like the glint of a distant lighthouse; and these reflections of the light from the party clubhouse lamp were like hidden signals in Morse code to the fat kid above, who every few minutes would alter the twist of the hand or change his hold on another limb with such surprising and promising ease that it would force free another groan of suffering from the child's vale of torment;

now the child was suffused with a totally new pain, a heart-wrenching pain, which stung his belly and brought forth tears: the pain of shame, which he could not endure, and of the betrayal which had felled him to the dust on sharp stones that wounded his whole body, and which had brought him into contact with that stupid, flaccid flesh above him. For an instant, when the glow of the stars and the wide, endless sky were revealed to him, and he noticed, too, with a kind of inner relief, the significant improvement that had taken place unexpectedly in the weather, and the tranquillity of the unhurried rustlings of the night, he felt that he could no longer stand it all; deep inside he was paralyzed by the fear of breaking down, the earth deep and impervious beneath him; and even if he was able to stop the hot tears choking his throat at the ledge of his damp eyes, he could not refrain from freeing his pained rage by moving his leg to and fro and swinging his head from side to side in defiance, to which his torturer responded with groans of undisguised and unrestrained pleasure.

Then Mrs. Sultan moved with great and exaggerated intent, pushing her children away from the table with short stabs of her elbows that were well hidden from the eyes of the guests. The table was set with the best food she could prepare—which never satisfied her—and the children lay siege to it with obsessive voracity. With their widened, hypnotized eyes they studied their relatives' jaws, skilled in eating and speaking, as if they were dwarf scientists from another planet—despite the flesh-bluing pinches they suffered from their mother under the colorful tablecloth embroidered with animals from the Book of Genesis, which they deflected with mechanical slaps on the back of her hand like the switch of a horse's tail on blood flies. The relatives sat down to eat with obvious and keen appetite, which gave great pleasure to Mrs. Sultan who, tasting at intervals, suddenly embarked on a loud price comparison in Moroccan-inflected, French-accented Hebrew. She got up to serve them and her husband and her eldest son, and in her falsely humble voice—she had the strange habit of waving a large, sharp kitchen knife in her hand when she spoke—detailed the delicacies she would have prepared for them if only she had been able to get a few more dried prunes, and good wine, or a few lamb chops. She spoke with a kind of bitter apology that was not directed at them at all, but rather at herself, at her own misfortune, as if she had failed irreparably at something. They diverted her from her complaints by abandoning their Moroccan-inflected Hebrew and exaggerating their praise of her delicacies, which sounded even more well-seasoned and delicious in the North African French they spoke.

Then the party clubhouse lamp went out; in the darkness the child had long since lost his energy. The fat kid was busily giving a dry and indifferent explanation of his decisive position to the new boys who had gathered meanwhile, and who were gazing with interest at the bodies entwined with such shameful inequality. Occasionally, after he'd long been thought a corpse, the child's free leg would jerk suddenly, kicking like a whip cracking against the back of the fat kid, and the gang would come to life. The fat kid would intensify the bend of the little child's hand—in retaliation and to cool the excitement of the onlookers—until the child's face became like a blackened, shriveled fig. In the meantime the two boys who were with the fat kid came back and held a brief pow-wow with him. They suggested he change the direction of the hand, since it might have gone to sleep already and might not be feeling any pain. The fat kid waved them away in disdain, but not before instructing them to hold "the little worm" tight until he himself could finish taking a crap behind a nearby hill. At once the child's face was in the dirt, his mouth gurgling and his tongue lapping dust. The boys around him began trying to reason with him. Taking advantage of the fat kid's having gone to take a crap, they said to him: "C'mon already, give in, just say ya' mutha's a whore." The child was silent. A little, inconsequential pipsqueak with weepy eyes said he should say just "yes." They silenced him and said that he would have to at least say "she's a whore" —except that the boys probably wouldn't be satisfied with that. A couple of the stronger boys promised they'd get even with the fat kid if he'd agree to say his sister, at least. That c'mon, he should take advantage of the fact that the fat kid had gone and say it now, 'cuz that way he'd be less ashamed. But the child said nothing. He didn't even hear them, but rather shut his eyes tight against the dust that blinded him from without, and against the exhaustion of having wandered about for three days, which sapped the strength he needed to keep from breaking down. Echoes of the voices of the boys in the gang, who talked at him with mounting ire, mingled with other, dulled voices, which had echoed from the rooms of the dying in the big hospital, inside the ward that was closed for renovation (dark and rank with the smell of construction and the stench of cold, clammy disinfectants); and from the high hallways of the school inside the basement workroom and bomb shelter-storage room; and from a door slammed in the clinic inside the pharmacy, by the waiting room bench (shaking the woman in the picture who held a sharp finger to her silence-sealed lips as if to say: "Shhh!"). Or the distant voices at the base of the *wadi,* which at first had urged him to hasten his steps, to break into disguised flight, long after he had listened through the undergrowth to the "clak clak" of the shepherd and his goats, which had filled him with incomprehensible worry and unease, but also with a shudder of delight like the one that seized him even now, in spite of everything, as he felt the pleasing coolness of the earth against his pained body and knew, with a kind of solace, that his wanderings had come to an end for that day; and that after he got free of the foolish flesh he'd return to his mother; and the ecstasy of that return would be so strong and real it would be more carnal than what the dogs and bitches do, since you are then so safe and sheltered somewhere in the world, far from the voices, far from even the echoes of the voices . . .

B. THE ENCOUNTER

When Beber left the cemetery and came to the neighborhood of the girls' orphanage his heart was beating wildly, as if he had crossed the border to a place where they speak another language and the people are called by strange names. The ball of the sun pounded on his shaven head and against his stiff neck, which shone with the sweat that ran from his scalp. At the entrance to the neighborhood he stopped as if calculating, looking alternately behind him and at the sun, then hurried on with the gait of an apprentice criminal. His head hung forward, sunk deep between his shoulders; with leery eyes he studied the buildings around him, without swiveling his head to either side. Most of the buildings here were low and made of stone or marble. Each building had a garden in front of it, well-tended and enclosed by a double fence: a pinkish stone wall, and behind, all along it and higher than it, evergreen shrubs, thick-branched and shaven straight. The huge pines that grew between the houses cast wide shadows and stirred the air with soft sweeps of their warm scent. It was they that emphasized the stillness at this late hour of the morning. It's too quiet here, he thought; half a minute after you've cast your black shadow in one of the entryways, somebody'll suddenly be there pulling you by the ear and asking you what you're doing here. And indeed, he didn't have anything to do in this place. He was to go directly to the girls' orphanage and take his cousin out of there.

An echo of "Yes, child," reached him even before he had crossed half of the main hall. The rooms on the second floor opened onto a wide corridor ringed by a wooden banister from which it was possible to overlook the main hall. Mrs. Druckman stood there, stock still.

Beber looked up at her, his body strained and hard as a rock. "Beber Sultan, I came t'see my cousin-yvonne," he said in one breath, poised to evaluate her response.

"Ah," she laughed, descending the stairs. She never caught their strange names the first time around. As she approached him she bent toward him slightly to examine him from up close. Beber retreated two steps.

"Sweet child," she tried a friendly tone, "Let's see. What is this week's Torah portion, do you know?" With its vaulted ceiling and supporting pillars, the entry hall was like the prayer hall of a mosque, and the voices resounded within it as if in a giant conch.

"Balak the son of Zippor the wicked," he shrieked at her.

"Yes. . . good," she said with somewhat confused revulsion. Nevertheless, she gathered her courage and asked: "And what does Yvonne do during her visits with you on the Sabbath? Do you sing Sabbath *zmiros?"*

"Tops."

"What?"

"Yvonne plays pop-the-top."

The child's answers were shot impatiently even before she could finish her questions, as if they were their natural continuation. A look of discontent spread over Mrs. Druckman's face. She thought it might be better to ask the child about his father.

"And what does your father do?"

"Dad's in the neighborhood association, and he plucks chickens, too."

The words left his mouth with increasing volume, the last of them sounding like a curse. Mrs. Druckman shivered under the blue shawl that hung off her shoulders; crossing her hands diagonally, she tightened it around her as against a chill wind. With a kind of threat she instructed him to wait in the entry hall, at the end of which she made a very sharp turn toward the stairs. Beber listened to her insistent steps fading into the depths of the upper hallway. His eyelids dropped, unfettered as a curtain in a breeze; he raised his head a little; and with his fists clenched by his thighs he tried to silence an unquiet rumbling that had awakened in his stomach. In his mind's eye he could picture Mrs. Druckman's two bespectacled children, symbols of an ambitious and honest day's work, tempered as steel. He opened his eyes all at once and began moving them slowly over the hall, until he noticed a white enamel garbage pail with a lid that you opened by a pedal, like the ones at the clinic. He was seized by an intense urge to hurl the pail with a resounding kick across the portico. But the clean floor shone in the cold stillness with a forcefulness that deterred Beber from breaking the silence, and his fists slackened.

Yvonne was not long in coming. She stood close to the banister with her legs spread carelessly, thrusting her belly forward and looking at him from above with a mixture of absentness and investigation, watching him daydream: kick, wiggle his shoulders, twist his face and expel meaningless syllables. It was only when she began descending toward him with a licentiousness that didn't suit the clean, ascetic stairs, that Beber came to and looked at her, trembling with pleasure and shame. Yvonne descended with hypnotic slowness; as soon as one sole had landed on a stair the other would hover with a kind of careless commencement, lingering a bit in mid-air before dropping as if without the help of gravity and landing gently on the stone.

Beber jerked this way and that, and what he saw, blurred, was the black hair strewn across her face like thin iron latticework; the strange eyes that stared at him from under her brows; the ankles that stuck out in a brownish curve; and, just at her knees—he stared at them, stunned—the countless scars. Again he trembled with shame, flustered: scars were for him like intimate parts of the body.

Nevertheless he continued to stand there as though possessed, wavering nervously and restlessly, as if he were trying to avoid her gaze, which strained vainly to see where he was going. Yvonne looked at him from inside her impetuous profile, which accentuated her girlishly rounded belly; from under the eyes that bored into him the slack jaw stiffened, its banks overflowing with a trembling, pink tongue; and Beber said to himself as he dragged his eyes over the scars and the belly and the breasts, that the way she was standing was what the girls in the neighborhood called "asking for it." This designation, which usually aroused mixed feelings in him or, at the very most, brought a flaccid smile to his lips, aroused in him now a fury that made him want to run toward her and kick her in rage.

Yvonne stopped opposite him and he melted at once, flopped like a fish on dry land, his movements suddenly ridiculous and incomprehensible, like those of a baby. Because of his height—shorter than was natural for his age—when he looked straight ahead he was forced to look directly at her navel, a wild animal hidden beneath the cloth that rose and fell. His hand moved by itself and clasped her wrist with such force that it caused her to lean her whole body toward the clasped hand, as if she could thereby loosen the grip; towering over him, she could smell the scents of brush and fire on his body and discern the slender rivulets of sweat that glistened on his furrowed brow.

"This is not a good place for me. I need to get out of here, fast!" he spoke with authority, in a whisper, as if there were others standing there besides themselves, and without taking his eyes off her navel. After she had thought for a moment, and after she had given up trying to release her hand from his grasp, Yvonne began to walk, half "before him" and half "behind him."

When they left the orphanage hand in hand, making themselves as small as possible, they turned through the devout neighborhood toward the cemetery; both of them—she with her coal-black hair shining in the sun, he with his shaven skull—took on the unreal appearance of worthless things, like crumpled newsprint lifted in a passing wind. The sun shot its vertical, leaden rays at the earth without leaving even the shadow of a shadow; and the west wind, too—which usually comes from the plain humid and roiling, cooling a little as it climbs toward the crests of the hills—waded burning through the scorched fields of thistle, and shook their dry, shriveled skeletons.

They descended through the scrubland that extended from the edge of the cemetery toward the tusk stone and, feeling like small wild animals that have stumbled on a place where men live, cleared themselves long, winding corridors—new and totally their own—between silvery, withered weeds and brush. "The shortest way is through the sky!" he shouted at her with prophetic pathos, striding ahead of her and pointing to where the mountain met the sky: "Until we can see the kites." He suddenly turned halfway around toward her, and as if with a decisive change of mood stretched his spine skyward, thrust his head forward, and awaited her thus at the center of a vast field of earthworks, where several bulldozers and cranes reminiscent of prehistoric animals sat exposed to the sun, until she came and stood at the edge of a mound of dirt opposite him, distracted but also with a faint expression of wonder at the sudden standstill. "If she makes things tough for you, I'll make her life miserable, if you want," he told her with a tenseness that made his throat go dry. But she jerked her head like a chicken, her face coming fast into focus as one clear, black dot, and waited a moment before saying: "She's a martyr of the Holocaust." She said it so venomously that he was taken aback and daunted, as if she had spoken the words of an evil Spirit; he jumped toward her, sending a swift simian hand to clasp her wrist again, then began charging with her across the field of earthworks toward the adjacent pine forest, and from there down a pathless path, past branches on the verge of collapse which scored them with dusty scratches, to a giant boulder—the tusk stone—which was as tall as a house. There, when they had stopped opposite one other, looking at each other like two wounded and panting wild animals, Beber extended his finger toward her like the seething head of a snake—warily, but with a determination that made her suck in her breath; when the finger reached her arid lips it rammed and pushed into her mouth; and Beber began to talk in a prattling whisper that sounded like a zealous vow, dangerous and uncompromising and containing a hint of desire and a hint of fear and pity. Yvonne, her ire growing, was about to dig her teeth deep into the flesh of the impudent finger; but then the blistering idea was swallowed with her saliva down the back of her throat, as an expression of acquiescence spread across her sun-battered face; little-by-little her tongue responded to the infantile insistence in her mouth, and her saliva swelled thick, coating his palm like ice cream melting in a child's fist. They swore on all sorts of objects that they owned, and Beber made an effort to call to his uneducated lips all the broken oaths, half-verses, and judgements from his class on the concise version of the*The Prepared Table* by the Rebbe of Lyadi, in the hope that they would have the power to deter her from the foolish things that women must do but needn't do, and that they might urge him, too, to refrain from deeds and crimes that could stamp a man's life for all eternity, branding him with the mark of Cain and marring his children's faces with red stains.

The sky had retreated utterly; the sun burned unbrilliantly and its dull light hung in the air; the inanimate objects, and the animate, too, seemed to answer it in kind and sat unstirring, with nary a spark of the will to glimmer even once before the coming of night; and as they crossed the valley that divided the vacant Yad Vashem Museum from the military cemetery, tranquil with its pastoral flora, Beber looked worriedly deep into the cleft in the crest of the mountains and thought sadly that maybe she wouldn't be able to see the kites flying while it was still daylight. But when he saw Yvonne skipping skillfully, nonchalantly hopping over the spiny shrubs far down the slope of the mountain that slid to Ein Karem, he took up the challenge hinted at in her step—as if she were provoking him intentionally. He immediately came to and stomped ahead, pushing aside the air and brushing up against all sorts of beings who were known and familiar only to him; and as he ran he ignored—amazingly—two mad dogs trying vainly to trot straight ahead and make him stray off the path; they would never have succeeded in making him stray had they not met up with him in the no-man's land by the abandoned sandbox that Beber was always fastidious about passing on the right—which he especially preferred—never crossing it in the middle for a reason that only he knew; but as it happened, he forgot that necessary debt he owed to caution because of the gangs when crossing Ein Karem via the main road to the territory of the tenements of the various neighborhoods, and from there to the slope of the *wadi* on the border of Costa Rica and the asbestos shacks; and as he crossed the burning asphalt of the road to Hadassah Hospital he straightened his spine, spitting from between his two front teeth two showers of spittle, one after the other, with measured sprays that sounded "tzitz" "tzitz," toward a gang of street cats that happened past. From the adjacent fence flapped an annoying cloud of birds that had lost its beauty from too much dust and heat; then he lifted his feet in a light canter, which made him say to himself: "I'm someone else; I'm not just anybody—whatever you think . . ." and other such things, with sharp turns of the head and horselike neighs—which weren't exactly like those of horses and which he couldn't use to ease the tempting pain-mixed-with-fear that gripped his body when, for an instant, he had the idea that, here, he could lead her into the *wadi*—but, thought Beber, the whinnies *were* loud and sharp enough to be thought a possible or even definite cause of Yvonne's having lost her balance and fallen off the green slippery rocks into the bay of sewage that was three spits away from him. When she got up from her fall, indifferently shaking off her embarrassment and with renewed courage, Beber stood and stared, thrilled at what looked like a tree stump dripping with strands of moss, moving and panting unevenly like the scapegoat, which only accentuated her whorishness in his eyes.

Not far away, on the crest of the shaven hill that had been gouged out all around by terraces of stone-cement-and-asphalt, between giant prefabricated cement configurations which sat in the deep gashes in the earth that were the vivid colors of internal organs, above the antennas and solar-heated water tanks, in the endless expanse between the electric cables, near the murky ball of the sun, wended a wounded, orange kite, which was attached by a string to a fat and magnificent boy, sweating and with a baleful expression, who was surrounded in a semicircle by all types of kids who stared like silent astronomers at the cosmos, where the kite fluttered its last.

And on one of the terraces Beber raised his head to watch, excited because he could feel one of those alien winds that are not good for kites coming suddenly over the roofs. It swung the kite in violent ripples, frightening the gang, which swayed together like a *lulav,* and making the face of the fat "king" go pale. But when Beber raised his head a bit more, he saw far inside the expanse of sky between tenements #404 and #202 the colorful kitish blossoming, and the many-splendored tails that almost tangled in one another, and the big, painted and colored faces that dipped and rose as if genuflecting, turning this way and that and bowing to each other politely, like cherubs; then Beber shouted a real shout at the heart of the sky, and swung himself through the ragged Jewish Agency bushes and in behind the balconies of the houses, swinging both arms in front of him and to his sides like a monkey; and he knew he was making a fool of himself because of this meaningless happiness; and as if to remove any shadow of a doubt about this, he began braying like an ass, and flung himself on the garden of a garbage heap that stood behind the naked balconies, throwing his head back and spreading his arms out to the sides with the fury of those unclean birds of prey pictured in the children's bible. He could already smell the dank, dark caves with their sweetish taste of campfire ash dampened with urine and smeared with crap as dry as clay. That's where—heedless—he must push her—the scarred "brown one" —his cousin! Still aiming his running at the space between the cement buildings that always closed in on him from both sides as if in siege, he weaves between tin cans riddled with holes and charcoaled tree stumps until—his skull rolls away from him and he rides on his steed, headless, in showers of blood: a slaughtered chicken jerking around the slaughterfield. Since in his mad race he's run into an iron wire which had been pulled across, unnoticed, to hang laundry from, and which had caught him right between his chin and his adam's apple. Shocked, lying on the ground immobile, he noticed as if by some gift of vision a limping sparrow waddling toward him red-ochrey with dust, and paused and looked at it with such concentration that he forgot the blood oozing from his throat, and only groped absently, again and again, at his neck, where a sharp pain was spreading.

From the cement terrace a dark figure called to him with a cry that was not meant to warn of danger or to wail over tragedy, but rather was like that of those who cry at being overcome, as from a stadium where a toreador has been condemned, gored on the horns of the bull. Yvonne, repressed and shrunken, sent a long, tense leg with guillotine-like fervor over the iron railing, closing it between her thighs for just an inkling, then quickly moving the other leg, too, which for a moment opened to the sky like a ballet dancer's before immediately swirling with spiral momentum and pressing itself to its predecessor like the two halves of a clothespin. And as she jumped from the terrace with that feline flexibility of hers, Beber threw his whip-like glance at her and, still recovering, asked himself how it was that he desired one so ugly and so wanton.

But Yvonne was already striding toward him down a winding but safe path—tainted red flowers, old newspapers, plastic bags, packing crates, and egg cartons occasionally blocking her way. She progressed steadily, attuned only to the agitation that spread like a rash through her whole body, calling her to stride ahead not "in his footsteps," but rather according to her own signs, special verses that she would dedicate to herself from her holy of holies; and so she cleared herself a path, which got ever shorter until she reached him and stood opposite him, making sure to look at his crown the whole time, not forgetting what her aunt from that God-forsaken village had told her: that all she need do was press those children to her firmly by their soft bellies, and squeeze them tightly between her deadly thighs.

But Beber went up to her and extended his hand toward her slowly, like the whispery head of a snake. His hand lifted the edge of her moss-stained shirt and stopped there. Intense dampness drizzled from the depths of her neck down her chest and flooded his hand, which touched only the nether-reaches of her belly. Hesitant and trembling with pleasure, his hand crawled by itself up the soft, warm dampness until it stopped again above the rise in the flesh that was especially soft and breathy, like a tiny, trembling infant; and as he raised his eyes to look at her his hand shook and lost all life-force until it would have fallen by itself, since her face, attuned to a hidden pain, and her eyes, shut in tense anticipation, cast a paralyzing fear over him. Suddenly her leg jerked and lunged like a flaming baton between his legs. The child crumpled, folded in two, his mouth gawping soundlessly. Then she thrust her leg twice more into his ribs and twice more into his testicles and turned away from him, sniffing out her surroundings vacantly, thoughtlessly, not far from where he lay. She heard his crying like an overgrown baby, his heart-wrenching moans, and so went back and stood over him. Despite the choking sobs and the huge tears that masked his eyes, the child did not miss the violent pounding of the muscles and sinews at the root of the girl's scarred thighs, deep, deep in the folds of the checkered skirt.

—*Translated from the Hebrew by Marsha Weinstein*

RONIT MATALON

RONIT MATALON was born in Ganei Tikva in 1959; she studied literature and philosophy at Tel Aviv University. She began publishing short stories in the early 1980s in the journal *Siman Kri'a* while working as a journalist for the Israeli daily *HaAretz*. Presently she lives in Tel Aviv, where she teaches literature and writing at Camera Obscura, a school of photography and film. Her first collection, *Strangers at Home,* appeared in 1991; prior to that, in 1989, *Story Beginning with the Funeral of a Snake*

came out; this book, originally written for young readers, has since been adapted as a film. Her latest work, *The One Facing Us,* was published in Hebrew in 1995, and is forthcoming in English. Met by widespread critical acclaim, this text weaves the fragmentary remnants of a family history whose sites include Egypt, Cameroon, Israel, and New York. These locations allow Matalon to weigh and interrogate some of the assumptions and classifications of worlds that have come to be called colonial and postcolonial. As in all her work, Matalon brings a unique amalgam of thought, emotion, and critical acuity to her writing in a tone that is both eliptical and uncompromising but never overwhelms or intrudes upon the very precise ambiguities of language itself. The text below, "Little Brother," alludes to the same circumstances regarding the death of Shimon Yehoshua as described by Yitzhak Gormezano Goren.

LITTLE BROTHER

For Uzi

"Look, look at the birds," said Niso, "the more you give 'em, the more of 'em come." He and Davidiko sat on one of the ornate concrete benches in Magen David Square and watched the pigeons diligently cleaning the cracks between the tiles. Legs splayed out, Niso crumbled the remains of the pita with his fingers, watching how the crumbs fell into the thick fold of his jeans. He watched the banal movement of the passersby, their vacant eyes resting for an instant on what was happening in the square and beyond. By the time they got to the edge of the sidewalk they could no longer see the pigeons, and that made him sad. He had become even more listless since the tragedy had befallen his family, and he wondered about this thing that gripped him with its massive hands for the first time in his life. Like the annoying buzz of a radio waking him in the middle of the night—not suddenly but automatically—it made him turn his thoughts to his mother or his sister-in-law Rachel, but especially to his mother, who held her sorrow as one holds up an infant, for all to see.

In that 9x9 room—two couches against the wall and an iron cot where the blind grandfather who'd tapped his cane at night had slept until he died—that was where he'd start, with the back that he saw every morning as she sat on the balcony barely moving, drinking coffee: a fleshy back with rounded shoulders, bra straps that cut into the skin, hair gathered in a bun. Opposite her, he knew, arranged as if for a play, was the scaffolding of the right wing; the left was in ruins. During the week of mourning he'd gone to see the destruction. He'd seen the bloodstains, touched the stones; he had wanted to see. "It ought to be finished," she'd said once, a month after the tragedy; he didn't know how to deal with how she lived the suffering, setting it in the innermost circle of her life not as a guest but as a member of the family who was instantly tarnished with the rust of her daily tasks, as if everything had picked up just where it had left off; like she said, "The dead are dead and the living, live;" she brought in a high school girl to help Avner's oldest daughter in arithmetic.

Davidiko stretched his legs in front of him: "If I sell five sweatsuits," he said, "the owner'll give me the price of one, and the food and everything I need's on him. Only thing's I need English, see, since there's a lot of tourists and they ask questions." Niso was silent, wiping his hands on the concrete. "Kids or grownups?" he asked at last. "Whad'ya mean kids or grownups?" said Davidiko, nervously passing his cigarette from hand to hand. "Sweatsuits," Niso said getting up, "are they for kids or grownups, it makes a difference in the money." Davidiko thought a moment: "Dunno, he didn't say. But you're right. Tomorrow first thing I'll ask him." He picked his teeth with a match stick he'd found on the ground: "Tomorrow first thing I'll ask him."

Niso stretched. "Boo!" he called, then ran, scattering the pigeons, his arms outstretched. "Why? Why did you do that?" the old man sitting beside them said testily. "Why?" Niso sat down again, leaning his neck on the back of the bench, "Because I felt like it. Let 'em go back to where they live." He half-closed his eyes, watching the blonde who'd been standing by the escalator for an hour and who was now discussing something with Davidiko and licking her fingers, filthy with ice cream, one by one. She was wearing a black and white miniskirt and her yellow hair had been done up in curls; no, on top it was straight and the ends were curled, that was the style now. Davidiko stood in front of her waving his arms and shifting his weight restlessly from one foot to the other. "He's not good enough for her," Niso thought when he caught sight of her protruding red knees between Davidiko's spread legs, and again when Davidiko moved, revealing her wide mouth, whose crooked position on her face made him uneasy.

"She agreed," Davidiko said, plopping onto the bench and smoothing the part in his hair. "We made a date, tonight at nine. She'll bring some friend of hers so we'll be two couples." He gathered up the plastic bags on the bench: "Let's go. I gotta get us a car," he said.

When they got up to go it was almost dark. Without thinking, both stuffed their hands into their pants' pockets, their heads sunk between their shoulders. Niso's new jeans made a rubbing sound. At fifteen and a half his round face, padded with full, smooth cheeks, still left an impression of diffuseness, of blur. His full lower lip extended toward his chin in the dreamy, revealing way of one who often contemplates himself. A soft down covered the sides of his cheeks and thick, close eyebrows masked his sunken eyes, which were shaded by long and lustrous lashes that he would bat now and then, absently, like Minnie Mouse. The two halves of his body, upper and lower, were disproportionate, as if they did not communicate: long, thin legs carried a wide, thick chest that was coiled between his shoulders like the edges of a roll of paper. Davidiko was a year older than he was; his bony body seemed to be wrapped around an invisible axis of cartilage that passed from his hawk nose through the center of his ribs and out his heels. His large nostrils twitched nervously; in general, there was a sense of scurrying under the taut and transparent skin of his face, like an insect trapped under glass.

Davidiko intently studied the "Gali" poster pasted on the bus shelter: A willowy, yellow-haired girl dressed in a pink-and-blue sweatsuit was in a green park, throwing one leg up in the air, her arms extended. On the bench, leaning his chin on his upraised knee, sat a boy who was looking at her and smiling. "Those are the good kind," said Davidiko, smacking his lips, "except for they're double the price of ours." Niso looked contemptuously at the girl with the upraised thumb, its nail painted red, and at the boy who seemed as pinkish as the sweatsuit, and pleased with himself and the park. The longer he looked the more these seemed false and unreal, the athletic pose implausible, mendacious: "Forget it," he said to Davidiko, "it's nothing, nothing."

They parted at the street corner and Niso, who had three hours to kill, decided to stop by Rachel's. The cinder-block story that Avner had added stood there drearily, as did the complicated tile roof that he hadn't known how to finish: agape, absurd, it looked like an odd turban from which a giraffe had taken a bite; its other half had been demolished. The house was very close to that of his parents; Avner had planned how they'd all live together when it was done. Again Niso looked at the scaffolding, the one on the right, where Avner had stood; he could see the tip of his shoe, a sneaker, from below: The radio in Haim's garage had blared "Just Me and My Surfboard" until one of the cops had shouted, "Let's get some quiet here," and someone had turned it off and rushed out to see what was happening.

A year ago, when demolition orders had begun trickling in from the municipality, his mother had thought the construction would be finished in six months at the most, and then everything would work out. She'd run from contractor to paint store to building supply store with their smells of dust and various metals, the screws and nails arranged each type in its own drawer like candies. She'd picked through them, haggling expertly, not like a petty merchant but like one of the guys, while he, Niso, stood behind her getting bored, staring at the tins of paint and the catalogs taped to the counter, smudged with the black fingerprints of customers wearing blue work clothes with small rulers and packs of cigarettes crammed into their shirt pockets. On Saturdays when she didn't work she'd slip away from grandfather and hand Avner the cinder blocks from below. Rachel would watch from a distance how she and Avner talked, and how they fought; they had the solidarity of partners, or comrades in a political struggle.

More than once his mother had abandoned the construction and kicked Avner out of her house. But later they'd make up. She would come to their house at night, businesslike but apprehensive, with prices written in her heavy, awkward hand. Instantly they'd sink into an endless squabble.

Once, after one of their fights, Niso found Rachel throwing up in the bathroom. She was leaning on the sink, her head between her arms. "Nothing good's going to come of that house," she told him, "good there will not be." Later she pleaded with Avner, who sat without taking his eyes off the television, to leave it all behind and move to a kibbutz or to Carmiel where her brother-in-law could find him work, they could live there in the Galilee where everything is clean and children play outside and know the names of flowers; she begged him to leave a house that wasn't and never would be finished. "We'll take Mother with us," she told him, "we'll take Mother and Niso, so he can go to school like a person, so he can be a real person."

Now when he came in he found her sitting in the kitchen shelling peas. The three-year-old twins were by her feet, playing with bits of wood and a pom-pom torn from a house slipper. He noticed at once that her stomach had deflated; really, he thought when she got up to make coffee, there's practically nothing left of her but that immense, wobbly belly. She walked very slowly, dragging her feet, and when she took out the coffee tin and the bag of sugar her hands moved slowly, deliberately, enveloped in an almost childish seriousness.

She placed the coffee in front of him and sat with her hands on her belly: "What's up, Nissimiko," she said. "Aces," he stretched his legs out in front of him, pulling a cigarette out of the pack. "Gimme one, too," she said. He lit a cigarette and held it out to her. "They were here from the municipality again this morning," she said, blowing out the smoke. "It's no good for you to smoke now," he said. "How much time have you got left?" "Another week or two, I've lost count." "What'd they want from the municipality?" he asked. "I don't know anymore, there're always these strangers coming and going, I don't even remember what my house looks like anymore." She was silent a while. "The kids are the only ones who are happy, they bring them chocolate and take their picture. They want us to move to a project like in the beginning, like nothing happened."

One of the children hung off her leg, swinging: "I didn't put on the new dress for a long time," he said. She plucked crumbs off his sweater. "It's because of his sister he talks like a girl," she explained to Niso, slapping the child on the backside and sending him away. "What's up with you, Niso?" she asked. "Everything's great. I started to work in the sweatsuit business," he lied, "and it's going great. I get the price of one for every three I sell. The owner is pleased with me. Maybe he'll make me his partner in another month or two. You need anything," he cocked his head toward her, "we've got stuff for kids, too. Just say the word and I'll bring it tomorrow." Rachel picked up the girl, who was sleepier and more listless than usual, and rubbed her back: "She gets stomachaches," she said. "Yesterday she didn't sleep all night." Niso got up: "OK, I've gotta be going." Rachel raised her big, moist eyes: "Do you have to go so soon? Stay with us a while." Then she added: "After all those strangers who get under your skin. Are you hungry?" she asked. Niso sat back down. "A little. I've got something on with Davidiko at nine. Really, I ate today." His gaze followed her, watching her stir what was cooking on the stove. "This owner guy is real 'large'—restaurants, and other stuff, all on him." Rachel smiled: "It's good you've found something, Niso," she said. "It's no good for you to be doing nothing."

When she and Avner were married she was only seventeen, a clerk at Tadiran; Avner would wait for her every day by the gate, watching her from his car. When they first started dating it got around the neighborhood that she was mute: For hours she would sit cross-legged, not saying a word.

She had lovely legs with girlish calves as slim as her wrists and her long, clean profile with the large, sunken temples that were like eggshells. Her small stature, the economy of her limbs, especially the measured voice which never stressed a syllable, spoke thrift and forfeiture of all that was not essential.

Niso smiled to himself: "You remember how they used to call you mute?" Rachel carefully set down cup, plate, and silverware, straightening them and smoothing her palm over the tablecloth. "I've decided not to move to the projects," she said.

The day it happened she wasn't home. She had risen early to take the boy for tests and then had gone to the market. At eleven, when she'd returned, the police and ambulance were already there: She stood at the end of the street, squinting; she was short-sighted and didn't want to wear glasses. The basket must have fallen out of her hand because when she got there, everyone was picking up tomatoes and squash. I was waiting for this, she said; was waiting for this.

She sat down on the curb just where the basket had dropped and gathered her dress around her knees and thighs; she sat that way until evening. Who hadn't gone to her, he thought; who hadn't gone: his mother and his sister and the sisters-in-law and the kids who hadn't understood what had happened, who played in the street beside her. Finally they brought the blind grandfather, each son taking an arm, he did her the honor of coming all the way out to her; they all knew how much she'd suffered since Avner had gotten the idea of the house into his head. "Come, daughter," the grandfather said to her in Arabic though she understood nothing. "We'll keep our laundry at home." He stretched out his hand and David, the eldest son, placed it on her head.

Two weeks later the grandfather died, and the ceremony they held with him every morning at four—he asked that they all drink tea with him; they would sit there quietly, sleepily, then go back to bed—the ceremony ceased. But he, Niso, who was used to it, still got up at four A.M. He'd wander among the furniture, the nylon-covered sofas, looking for the jacket that belonged to his older brother David, maybe there'd be cigarettes in it, and he'd sit on a chair in the dining alcove, smoking and watching the street lights reflected in the panes of the china closet. He'd note the slamming of a car door, wondering for hours what had come first and what after; if any detail slipped his mind he would shake his head impatiently and start over from the beginning. After a while he could anticipate the pitfalls—especially one stubborn one, that of Avner's sneaker seen from below—and he'd choose a circuitous route to circumvent and ignore them; he felt they shed no light on anything and he hated their opaqueness and how, because of them, he could feel his own heaviness, like when Avner's lithe, beautiful body had lain there, the woman beside him squalling "A tragedy, a tragedy;" he'd repeat to himself: "a tragedy." He would sit like that, digging his bare feet into the floor, until his mother's hoarse voice would call out: "Nissim, why don't you sleep?"

That same night, after he'd wandered through the citrus groves at the edge of the neighborhood trying to exorcise the terror he felt spraying his back like a cold shower, he'd found his mother in the kitchen. "Where were you?" She'd lifted dry, very open eyes toward him, "Where do you wander for whole days?" She'd said it in a threatening, broken voice that was like a car being dragged across gravel, a voice that had severed him, Niso, from her life, despite her efforts to put him back again. And though he couldn't stand the cold of the formica table that stood between them, he'd turned his back to her and thrust his arm at the shelf that held the glasses, sliding it over the wood from right to left, watching each glass make its shattering sound, like a xylophone. He thought of Avner and how she used to drag him by his ears from the midget's kiosk, where they played cards. "You make a fool out of me," he'd say to her, "a fool you make out of me." She used to iron his shirt cuffs, he remembered clearly. She would push the iron over the cuffs several times, then over the collar. The vein in her neck would tremble. She wouldn't say a word. Avner was twenry-three then, with his own car and garage. Later he'd beg her forgiveness, kiss her hands; twenty-three years old with a car, and girls to spend money on.

When he finished eating he pushed the plate away, lighting a cigarette. Rachel said again: "I've decided not to leave the house but I don't know if I'm doing the right thing. I know Mother wants me to stay, and the kids, too. She's very attached to the kids." Niso nodded, but what she said washed over him without leaving a trace. He tapped his foot nervously: "Do what's best for you. If the project suits you, move; if it doesn't, stay." The hollowness of his voice when he said it startled him. He stood up. "I'm going to wash up," he said.

★ ★ ★ ★ ★

"They're new, your pants, eh Niso?" Rachel said when he came out, studying the way he wore the flight jacket. Then she smiled, and something of the light and sweetness in her face in the photo on her ID card, her hair falling onto one shoulder, softened the little wrinkles at the edges of her eyes: "Have you got a girlfriend, Niso?" she asked. "Lots of 'em," he answered. "I've got lots of 'em." "No," said Rachel, curling up like a cat, "one. Have you got one?" He nodded his head, staring at the counter. "What does she look like?" asked Rachel. "What does she look like? What do I know what she looks like?" he scratched his neck. "Kind of blonde-like. Pretty." Rachel walked him to the door: "Bring her around sometime, Niso," she rubbed the top of his arm, "bring her over so we can meet her."

It was chilly outside, and he raised the collar of his flight jacket. Through the thin, silky lining of the pockets he rubbed his stomach as if it hurt. He walked in the middle of the street, happy to be walking alone and wearing something warm, smelling his own soap and aftershave as if they were someone else's. The houses of the neighborhood, half of them lighted and half of them dark, reminded him of the projects kids do in kindergarten: using cardboard boxes to make a house, drawing windows and cutting out a door and adding a roll of toilet paper and a cottage cheese container and last of all pasting on lima beans to make a path. He looked into the windows of the lighted houses; they aroused his curiosity and affection for the people sitting inside, protected and far from all the places they'd abandoned themselves during the day. Suddenly, coming around a trash can, he spied a small shadow by his feet: a cat that had been following him, he guessed. Niso and the cat stood and stared at each other. "Psst, psst," Niso said, holding his hand out to the cat. The cat arched its back and whined. Niso looked around to see if anyone was watching him, then said in a voice that was louder and higher than usual: "C'mere pussycat, c'mere." He continued on his way, speeding up his pace, but the cat kept following him. "Scat!" Niso called, hurling a stone at it. He broke into a run, opening the zipper of his flight jacket, paralyzed with fear. "What is it, anyhow?" he said to himself. "A cat." As soon as he'd said it he sensed the unreality of his words, of the word cat, of the cat itself. Like back then, when there had been all these signs around that he understood separately, like individual syllables, though he couldn't understand what they meant together.

Davidiko's house was dark. He ran his fingers through his hair and tucked his shirt into his pants. "Niso," a voice called suddenly. He looked around: Beside the house stood a pickup truck with its lights on. When he got closer he saw Davidiko leaning on the steering wheel with what seemed like two girls beside him, since something glimmered in the darkness, a jewel or a scarf. "Hey, Niso," Davidiko said. Niso looked at the girls. He remembered the blonde from the square. The other one was small and dark; her hair was parted in the middle and she was staring straight ahead. The blonde stuck her hand out the window without his asking: "Nice to meet you, Hani," she said. "This is Hani and Rivka," Davidiko said. Niso shifted uncomfortably from one foot to the other, not knowing what to do with his hands, one of which now gave off the oily scent of body lotion. He wiped it on his backside, grateful for the darkness. "This," said Davidiko pointing at the small one, "is a relative of my cousin." "And I'm a friend of hers," Hani said. Even though he couldn't see her face he sensed something warm and vital in her voice. He was especially surprised at her "r," which reminded him of the immigrants from France. "You going somewhere?" he asked. "We're going somewhere," said Davidiko. "My brother gave me the car." Niso was silent. He knew Davidiko was lying; his brother didn't have a car. Davidiko didn't have a license but, as he'd said often, he could drive by the fumes; he was crazy about cars. "There's no room up front,"

Davidiko said, starting the car, "hop in back." "What do you mean no room," said Hani, "there's room, we'll squeeze a little and there'll be room." The little one squeezed in, annoyed, and Hani crossed one leg over the other and opened the door for him. "It's lucky I'm fat and she's thin," she said, "otherwise how'd you fit?" His face burned. His hand brushed against her nylon stocking—a slippery, unpleasant sensation. He wanted to say something nice to her: "You're not fat at all," he said. He wanted her to say other words with "r": "Where are you from?" he asked. "I'm from Bat Yam, I live with my sister." Davidiko drove onto the coastal highway. "Want some music?" he asked and turned on his tape. "D'you have to drive like a maniac?" said the little one. Davidiko floored the gas: "Is this like a maniac?" he yelled, unable to hear himself, "is this like a maniac? I'll show you what fast is." Niso, who'd balled his hands into fists and stuck them between his knees, freed one of them and rested it on the back of the seat, behind Hani's shoulder. The road was almost empty and it seemed to Niso that all of them were boring their eyes through the windshield to the road, as if obeying the driver's imperative to look straight ahead, like Davidiko. He studied her full profile and the painted cheek that glowed in an odd, unnatural way. "I love going for a drive," Hani said. "My brother-in-law's got a car, and we always go for a drive on Saturday. But I sit with the kids in the back."

"What kinda car's he got?" Davidiko said, lighting another cigarette. She thought a moment: "A Volkswagen, I think. Some kind of pickup." "Why, what does he do?" Davidiko opened the window, leaning his elbow on the glass. "He's got a vegetable stand," she said. "In Bat Yam. Once I sat on a tomato." Her laughter pealed. "What's so funny about that?" said the little one, grabbing the cigarette out of Davidiko's hand. "I dunno," she said. "Really, it ruined my dress that day." They rode on in silence; Davidiko even turned off the tape. Niso was pressed against the door. If he made the effort to turn his head toward her he could see her pudgy hand with its babylike dimples and three silver rings, the kind they used to sell at the Central Bus Station, and which Avner used to buy Rachel by weight. He used to bring her colorful plastic earrings, too. Niso remembered one pair in particular: two orange flowers decked with feathers. Rachel had laughed and given them to the children. "You know I don't wear those things," she'd told him. Avner had gone and locked himself in the toilet for a long time. His mother was sitting with her in the kitchen. Later she said: "You didn't have to say that to him. He takes it hard." Back then he was already keeping the pistol in the drawer. "Every hour, every hour he'd run to check if it was still there," Rachel said later. He turned grey; even the palms of his hands. He stopped working on the house. After he died they poured the roof over the kitchen and the inspectors didn't say a word. A week later his mother came by with the workmen. She had that thing with her lips that had frightened him: Her mouth twisted involuntarily. Silent and full of hate, both women took his belongings out of the house. They gave the clothes to the Arab workmen: "Someone should get some use out of them," his mother said. He heard her talking to them from the kitchen: "How many kids have you got, Ahmed?" Rachel, who stood washing dishes, whispered, "I can't take it anymore, get her out of here." "What?" he asked like a fool, the words sticking in his throat like a glob of dough. "What'd you say?" She slowly closed the tap and wiped her forehead on her sleeve, then turned to him and said, "You're still young, Niso; you're still very young."

He stared at Hani, his eyes riveted to the bulbous, reddish earlobe illuminated in the headlights of an oncoming truck. As if troubled by something he asked, "What dress was that?" "What dress?" she looked at him, pulling her hair back around her ears. "Red with white flowers. And here," she placed her hand on her chest, "a kind of crochet design, like, embroidered." "Lace," the little one corrected. "And besides it wasn't red with white flowers, it was orange with green and white flowers, you washed it at my place." She had the memory of the malevolent, that little one; objects caught by her sharp eyes immediately lost their innocence. "Yeah, lace," Hani agreed. The thoughtful way she said it touched him; the vowels drawn just a little higher than necessary spoke eternal trust and gentleness.

"Where'd you get that "r" of yours?" he asked. She laughed. There was a tooth missing on the right side. "I used to work at a beauty shop and my boss was real good to me and she had an "r" like that, she's from Tunisia. I liked her so much I started to talk like that, too." "And now?" he asked. "Now I work in a beauty shop too," she bent over and pulled her stocking up on her calf. "All my money goes to hair color," she sighed. "Only last week I was a redhead." They laughed. "Boy, oh boy, can you talk," Davidiko said, stopping the pickup beside one of the darkened houses in the neighborhood where they'd been driving. "Where are we?" the little one asked. "Nof Yam," said Davidiko, jumping out of the pickup. Niso got out after him while the girls got organized inside. He stretched his arms and pulled his pants out of the crease in his ass. The sky was smooth and cloudless, and as he looked up at it he marveled how he had been there but now was here, in the yard of a house with cypress trees. He marveled at Hani, thinking of the girl in the poster, even though Hani didn't look athletic to him. Quite the contrary: a little lethargic and sluggish. Again he looked at her blond hair, recalling what he had felt in the square that afternoon when he had seen her for the first time, the banality of her being there along with all the other things he'd seen and not forgotten, as if he must remember everything, and with the same intensity as Avner's death, seeing he was his brother.

They entered a narrow, darkened room with just one lamp on one side giving off a yellowish light. Three guys were sitting on a couch, three profiles, one after the other, three drooping chins that fairly touched the tops of their chests, three pair of outstretched legs. The one on the edge, the fat one, greeted them with a listless nod of the head: "Hey, Davidiko," he said. "This's Itzik," Davidiko said, taking off his flight jacket. He rubbed his hands together: "What're we drinking?" he asked. "Everything," said the fat guy, his eyes riveted straight ahead and his lips barely moving. "We're drinkin' everything. Sit down, we'll have a nice evening." He looked Hani up and down from her hair to her black-shoed feet: "Very nice," he added. His stomach, Niso noticed, rose and fell under his hand, and the fingers of his right hand—short, fat fingers—squeezed the glass, the fat pad of each one tightening around it. "The blood went to my head just from his fingers," he told Hani later in the pickup, his head on her knees and his legs dangling out of the window. She ran her fingers through his hair, scratching the skin of his scalp as if she were washing it: "You've got dry skin," she said, then added, "it was nice, how you fought for me."

He'd gone up to the fat guy, his hands in the back pockets of his pants: "You, talk polite," he'd said. The fat guy had clicked his tongue and, shading his eyes with his hand, looked at him: "What's this you've brought us, Davidiko," he'd said. "What's his problem?" Davidiko had pushed Niso toward the door, slapping him on the back: "Go on, go on," he'd said, "get some air. Him, his brother got killed a couple months ago," he explained to the fat guy. The fat guy had crossed his arms over his chest: "He should apologize nicely," he said, "Ringo forgives and forgets."

Niso had felt his legs rooted to the earth like heavy rods of steel. Rooted like a tree, he'd thought, like then. Then too he'd thought, "Like a tree," rooted to the spot. Avner had said something to him from the scaffolding but he couldn't hear, it was as if he was speaking the language of mutes, waving his arms, and one of the policemen had shouted: "Watch it, he's hot." Then the tractor had started forward and Avner had shouted, "Moshe, don't wreck it!" He knew the tractor-driver by name. And David, his older brother, who was standing ten feet away from Avner on the scaffolding, had yelled: "Stop them, there's going to be a tragedy here." He hadn't yelled. They'd sent for him that morning to keep watch, they knew they were coming from the municipality that day. Something scratched his neck so he moved his head from side to side. Then he checked: He'd forgotten to take the label out of his shirt. Avner shot three times in the air, to the left, a few meters above the crowd that had gathered. The neighbor's two daughters were standing next to him, and when a strange silence fell, one of them had said to the other: "Which of your clothes are new and which have been washed?" Then their mother came, and a policeman took out a gun and shot him right in the head. His body crumpled like that of a child, as if all the air had gone out of it, one hand clutching his face. When he turned his back, reeling, they'd fired another shot. He didn't see the body; the sneakers with the mud on the soles had stood out.

Now he stood very close to the fat guy. The two others stood and stared. The girls leaned on the door frame. "Whadda I need with this Ringo," he heard himself, "who's this Ringo? *That* fat zero?" He stomped on the fat guy's foot, pressing with all his might: "So we're strong, eh? Strong and fat, we've got the world by the balls. So we can look at anything," he yelled, "anything. Why, everything's his, he just looks at it and it's his!" The fat guy didn't move. His face was red with fury: "Get him outta here," he said to Davidiko, "get him out, or I'll finish him." Davidiko and one of the other guys grabbed his arms and the third guy grabbed his waist. Like a cat, like a girl he bit their hands, scratched their faces; like a cat he slid down and lunged at the fat guy who still sat there; he pounced on his lap and grabbed his hair and his nose. The fat guy pummeled his stomach and sides with blind fists: "I can't see," he wailed, "I can't see!" The fat guy shook him off but he didn't quit. He and the fat guy stood face to face, the fat guy's cheek still in his hand, squishy and slippery like margarine. The fat guy landed a punch to his stomach and he yowled and let go, dropping to the floor holding his stomach as if he were holding oranges. Curled there, feeling the dusty smell of the rug and the tufts of wool scratching his nose, he waited for the blows. "Wait," he heard the fat guy's voice; then there was silence. He lifted his head slowly and saw the shoes and cuffs of Davidiko's pants as he stood there, waiting for him to get his. Niso brought his cheek close to the rug, feeling with stillness and certainty that now, right at this very moment, they were going to tear him apart; that Davidiko was weak and cowardly, and he was glad of it.

The first kick was to the lower back, almost the ass; then came a few more, one after the other, to the legs, the back, the neck. "Enough," Davidiko said as if from behind a door. "I don't want any trouble." Someone splashed water on his face, then arms hoisted him and laid him on the couch. "Get him out of here," said the fat guy. He closed his eyes. Rachel turned from the sink: "You're still young, you're still very young, Niso," she said. He wondered what she had meant when she said that, what her reasons were for saying, "You're still young, Niso," and for adding, "You're still very young," as if she'd gone over something in her head. On Saturdays when they'd go to soccer games in the motorcycle with the sidecar—he would sit in the sidecar and they'd lower the white cover with the dirty little window—she'd wave good-bye from the door of the house, holding the little one between her legs so he wouldn't run after the motorcycle and yelling to Avner, who had a quick temper, "Don't get into any fights."

Later they moved him to the pickup and Hani walked after them, holding the damp towel with which she'd wiped his face earlier, and the fat guy shouted after her, "Hey you! What's your name, anyway?" And she'd gotten flustered and said, "Nice to meet you, Hani," and he'd smiled to himself, the fact that she'd said "nice to meet you, Hani" didn't arouse his hostility, on the contrary, it reinforced his feeling that she would cause no harm.

And when he lay his head on her lap he lay it down decisively, like he deserved it, and his cheek brushed against her nylon stocking, and she rambled on with her aimless chatter, picking up right where she'd left off when they'd gotten there, smoothing his hair and ears; and looking ahead at the black square of the pickup window he thought—maybe because of the fatigue and the pain—he thought that now, for the first time, everything was alright.

1984

—Translated from the Hebrew by Marsha Weinstein

PHOTOGRAPH

First they put the black hood over my head—a hood, not something else, a kind of veil-hood—then they prodded me gently with a long, ribbed pole toward the breach in the hedge.

"*Ahlan,* ya Nurit, ya Ronit, ya madame," said Khaled, young escort.

His eyes were white, he was wearing other clothes.

"I'm interested in *On Photography: A Mirror of the Times,* I said as we took out our papers—mine yellow, his pink; mine red, his blue; mine white, his white—everything just so, precise. Khaled was pleased: "What strange symmetry; I could stare for hours," he said softly. "Is anybody with you?"

I spread my fingers for him and he counted to himself. One by one like roller-coaster cars the children crawled through the breach in the hedge, giving their clothes a fine dusting, then presented their fingernails to Khaled for inspection. "*Habibai,* my friends," Khaled marveled, "red gummy bears!"

"Khaled," I said. "Yes," Khaled said. "I have a personal favor to ask, is that all right?" "Everything's personal," Khaled said. "No, really," I said. "Seriously. A friend of mine and his wife have disappeared. I call and I am told strange things. Every time I get close, tiny animals start nibbling at my toes. Is that all right with you, do you think"?

"Don't insult me with such questions," Khaled said. "I've got my own cross to bear."

So we drove in a blue Mercedes to the home of my dead friend's family; we found the place, no problem. The light was faint, slanted; begonia plants burned in the windows—not many, a few. Khaled explained: "In this sad desert I suddenly come upon a certain photograph. It breathes life into me, and I into it. The photograph itself is not at all 'alive' (I don't believe in 'live' photographs), but there's something about it that breathes into me that bit of life which every adventure excites."

"I believe it," I said; I really do believe it. Meantime the children fell asleep, and we were glad they were spared the worst part; Khaled, too, admitted it if not directly; he, too, trembled a little when he wrote the words, "the worst part." So on we went. "What has any of this got to do with me?" I asked. "All I see is a house that is all interior, no exterior—the vine leaves twining, the pomegranate, the battered iron gate."

"This is the house," Khaled said. I looked at it to remove all doubt: It was whole, its face blank as a slate. I left everything behind and went into the house alone, loathing it, feeling obligated. Khaled came later, after he had peed. He bowed to two black ravens, sisters of my dead friend. I kissed the palms of their hands; I hated the ground they walked upon: I love Gaza more than a second skin, hell-hole offering of the world. "I know my friend was murdered at night, maybe his wife, too," I said.

Clasping a long candlestick, one of them illuminated the rough brown wall. "That's not enough," she said. I tried again: "I need a picture of him, even one from his identity card, so that I won't go on living my life with the image of a severed head, that's all."

They showed their napes, the bare territory of neck under the hair, not in denial, not in assent.

It's a lucky thing I had my marvelous job, a lucky thing I had importance to hide behind when faced with suffering, lucky I had the sudden transparence of Khaled, the nobody go-between, lucky I bowed my head only a little when they hurled the death at me, lucky that we all searched for the photographs in the crannies that emerged out of the darkness in the room, lucky, lucky, lucky.

We didn't find anything. Increasingly, we noted the unnatural darkness. Ultimately we fulfilled the wishes of the dead man's sisters, we said the darkness was unnatural, the wall silent, the stone screaming, the dead man alive in his death and dead in his life: objects, objects, and yet—when it's of a person and not an object, the power of testimony in a photograph has an altogether different fate. Looking at photographs of a bottle, the stem of an iris, chickens, involves only the corporeal; but a body, a face, more than that; and what of the body and face of a beloved soul?

We were close to giving up. Heavy, we sank onto low stools and waited, only out of courtesy. Suddenly we saw something on the rough walls of the crypt-like room: a flicker of brown and white which, when straining the eyes, seemed a giant close-up of a face that appeared and disappeared by turns. Had everyone seen what I had seen? Had I perceived something that someone else's memory had signaled to me?

One of the sisters, the bony one, tugged at the lapel of my jacket. "Look,"she said. She was clutching a pair of men's trousers, stiff as if someone were standing in them, stiff with congealed blood and mud: "These are his," she said. "No one knew what he was thinking when he wasn't with everyone else. Everyone was wrong about him—you, too." They grasped nothing. They thought he was one thing, when all along he was something else. Then the fool went and married an American woman who kissed the wounds of the wretched. No matter; she's dead, too.

I fell at her feet: "Have pity on me, I said." "Don't kick me when I'm down."

Khaled turned aside; with his finger he traced the path to the house of the parents of the young, foreign wife. Five months ago they were married at the home of an acquaintance, a doctor, her thin hair yellowed from summer, one arm crushing an orange flower on her skirt and the other cupping her ear, the better to hear. My friend is standing to her right, beaming—from the danger, it seems—his mouth very wide, his eyes like slits. But the expression on his face cannot be dismantled.

Khaled and I stood at the entrance to the young wife's parents' house, next to a strange winter garden. "An exaggerated strangeness, like in dreams I do not like," Khaled said. This time our paths diverged. The blueberry bushes, the neat bricks, and the lace curtains told us we could not breach this private realm. Khaled promised to try for me anyway, he said, then went silent a moment. He said: "Anyway. Though I don't have much faith in all these young photographers running around the world today, bent on capturing the present; they don't know they're the agents of death." I said my intention was different. Khaled gripped the iron chain around the gate. For the first time he pitied me: "The intention is always different; it's always different. But death must always have some place in society: if not in religion (or not mainly in religion), then someplace else. Maybe in the image that creates death even as it tries to capture life."

I climbed up on the iron gate to watch his image vanish. Go in peace dark escort, momentary ally. *Your worldliness allowed us to see the mundane in a place that is beyond simple sorrow. Go in peace, attentive ears with your sometimes selective attention. Go in peace, fraying Reebok sneakers. When all has been cloaked by the great, opaque chronicle, your memory will stand as a sign of humanity.*

The whole time the parents of the dead wife were watching us from the living room window. They stood side by side, alike, strands of hair from the mother's bun falling on her nose. She worried over something in her hands: a handkerchief? A scarf? The hem of the curtain?

The father's head leaned on the window frame. His fingers, holding a cigarette, supported his forehead. He is not from here; he is from Cleveland.

"You could have come or not come, it's all the same; the Hebron glass vase is always in its place on the handwoven oval doily in the center of the table, the red, straight-backed chairs are always turned to face one another," the mother said.

I was sorry from the depths of my heart. I knew the young wife well; only fear kept me from asking about the circumstances of her death. The mother stood before me, her arms supporting her belly and her head, especially the chin, bent toward her chest. She whispered in a flat monotone and I leaned forward to hear her: "When my daughter made this hole, this sorry city, her home, we had to believe, and we came; we brought what was ours, we adapted ourselves, we adapted everything to everything. The pictures you see here, she's in all of them."

"Where?" I asked.

"In order to really see a photograph you must look beyond it, or else close your eyes. The picture must be inanimate; this is not a question of perception, but of music. We achieve absolute subjectivity only in the state, and in the effort, of silence. Say nothing, close your eyes, let the person or thing surface, take form," the mother said.

Then I saw: There were dozens of photographs there, stuck to one another, they were everywhere, on the wallpapered walls, in small labels on the backs of objects, framed on the heavy sideboard. I took my shoes off, I began to sweat, I shook with fear. In every one of them I saw *madonna e bambino, madonna e bambino, madonna e bambino.* "That's her,"the mother's voice broke behind me: She is in them both.

"Forgive me," the father wept, "forgive me, is this a photograph or a painting?" He shook my elbow, wiping his face with a crushed hat.

"Shhh . . ." I said to him, "shhh. . . ." I had to understand; the pang of realization rent me. I knew that whether I looked at the virgin or the child, the young wife would live again, whole, unmaimed, by virtue of my gaze alone. Carefully she gathered up the hem of her skirt, tucked a few strands of hair behind her ear, and walked out of the photograph toward us, into the large, foreign room. I could see her, with her pale, birdlike profile and secretive smile, she came out of the virgin or the child, I knew her well. I had to keep quiet about what I had seen; I had nothing but my gaze.

Gaza, 1990

— Translated from the Hebrew by Marsha Weinstein

ILANA SUGBAKER MESSIKA

ILANA SUGBAKER MESSIKA was born in Israel in 1955 and grew up on Moshav Masliah, an agricultural settlement composed primarily of immigrants from Morocco, Egypt, and India. She went to a vocational high school and got her diploma while serving in the army. She studied at both Hebrew University and Haifa University and has been involved in alternative education for a number of years. In addition, both during her studies and after, she has been very active in Jewish/Arab issues, whether as an activist or educator. She is presently working on a novel that takes place in 1979 and portrays a group of *mizrahi* students originally from development towns who are attending Hebrew University in Jerusalem.

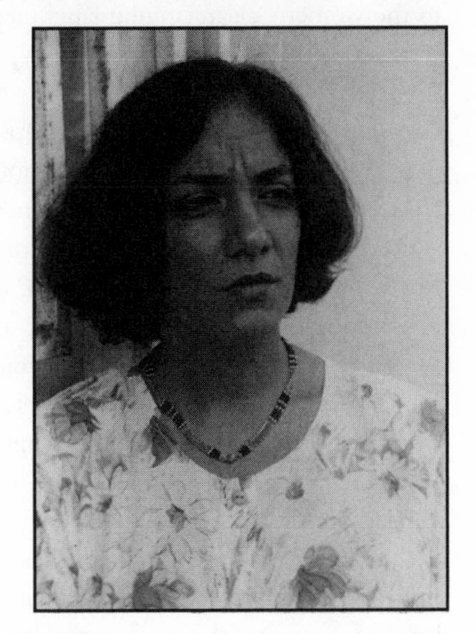

MEMORIES OF AN INDIAN UPBRINGING

So it turns out I'm an Israeli from India, that is, I was born in Israel but my parents came from India. In the eyes of many, I'm a "Yemenite," because of the color. Once, years ago, when women soldiers used to hitchhike, this conversation repeated itself again and again:

"Yemenite?"

"No."

"Persian, right? Moroccan??"

"Indian."

"Indian? It doesn't show."

Or: "How come I didn't think of that?" My mother does invitations for an "Indian" evening in Jerusalem. Years after I had left, yearning for an Israeliness that could be taken for granted. Like every year, thousands of the *Bene Yisrael* from India gather in Jerusalem, to see and be seen, to experience the shards of a culture still existing in them, the civilization of India. It's very *in* to talk about immigration, Ethiopians, tradition, Russians, Israeliness, Bukharians and whether or not the news about a community of six million Jews in Kashmir is true or not. Would it be good if a couple of million Indians come to the country? Under the condition that they're Jews, of course, why not? It's interesting to see what the leaders will put together for the community's annual evening, an evening of color, Indian clothing, great food, art, music, and Indian dance. Other people, all eyes upon them, with *"good manners,"* are not jostled in, to the women's clear, ringing laughter.

★ ★ ★ ★ ★

Crossing walls on the Tel Aviv–Moshav Masliah road. Preparing "Punjabidaras." Tel Aviv summer, get your mount ready for winter. At the last minute, I prefer pants and a white shirt, something casual. At parties with friends, I'll arrive Indian, Oriental, or Arabic with a *gallabiya* or something else. That's fine. But for there, for an Indian evening, I hesitate. The deference, the scrupulous observation of Indian aesthetics, the agreement down the length of the skirt, the pitch of the hips holding the wrap in place . . . but with me, the train of the sari falls right down, helplessly plodding along my shoulder. I'm awkward, I don't have the right moves to grapple with clothes like that. But I love them so much, they're so beautiful to me. But not *on* me. It's better not to even get tangled up in all that.

We're on our way, my mother Abigail, my father Menahem, my sister Sarale in a festive top embroidered in gold, my brother-in-law Asher and me. Just before we get on the bus coming from Ramallah, my mother warns: "We'll probably have to wait two hours because they won't start on time."

I know, but nobody cares, everything's cool. In the back of the bus, a group of kids, boys and girls, start singing Indian songs from the movies. I'm compelled to look: kids with shaved heads and a lock of wild hair dipped in gel, curling down to the neck. Young girls with waves in the style of Shuki Zikri or some other famous Indian star (is that her name? I don't even follow Indian movies anymore). The finest fashions for the young, those whose parents were probably already born in Israel and work for the Aircraft Industry or at El Al. Amongst them, second-generation immigrants sing songs in Hindustani.

The mid-fifties, my parents after the Gate of Ascent and before Moshav Masliah, at kibbutz Yagur. I'm a chocolate baby. Often, on walks through the paths of the kibbutz, in the area designated for immigrants from India, a comrade from the kibbutz would stop to express astonishment at the dark baby. I was a *sabra,* the pride of the family. These days, an unplanted *sabra* doesn't sound like much. The third of five children, but with the sole and special right to be a *sabra,* a real Israeli.

Binyanei Ha-Uma, in Jerusalem. In the parking lot, two women in white and violet saris rush towards the entrance. I'm struck by the colors. My mother says: "No taste." How come? Because you don't wear a sari that distance from the ankles, you cover them. And the wrap is too short for the shoulder. And the folds of the fan are vulgar. Got it? A different aesthetic, unfamiliar. She's right, my mother Abigail—and the sari takes on a different meaning.

August 91, *Binyanei Ha-Uma* in Jerusalem. Huge signs greet us: *"WELCOME TO THE ANNUAL GATHERING OF DESCENDANTS FROM INDIA IN ISRAEL."*

"The *Benei Yisrael* aren't even mentioned."

"What?"

"Didn't you notice that they don't even mention the *Benei Yisrael?*"

"I wonder why."

"They want us to forget."

One assumption takes the place of another and it is no longer *Benei Yisrael* but "Jews of Indian descent." And why should that really be important? We're all Israeli. Whether by chance or not, today marks India's day of Independance.

★ ★ ★ ★ ★

Indians came to Israel from a number of regions for, after all, India is half a continent, gigantic; to get from one city to another you can spend three days on a train, easily. Not like here. The Cochinis came from the south, darker than us, pattering another Indian, clanging along like silverware, quickly, quickly, quickly. Funny. Avi the Cochini from the preparatory course in Jerusalem, now a succesful lawyer, says the Cochinis integrated into the country well. The *Benei Yisrael,* those who came from around Bombay (like me), were not absorbed as they should have been, and many went downhill. I'm surprised, I always thought differently; after all, there, in India, the Cochinis were mostly peasants while we had the businesses, the education, the respected professions, the posts in the government and the railroad. How did that happen? Different services during immigration? The nature of the ethnic group itself? Maybe he's not even right? There are also Baghdadi Indians, Jews from Iraq who lived in Bombay for several generations. We, the *Benei Yisrael,* helped them out at times to fulfill the commandments of the ransom of the firstborn or the *bar mitsva.* There are no "kohens" in our community. We are Marathi speaking *Benei Yisrael* from the region of Bombay. The *Benei Yisrael* of the Bible are not the kind of *Benei Yisrael* that we are. We don't exist in any of the history books on the state of Israel. And there are even Indian Jews in Persia.

I almost forgot the degradation of the sixties. Then we were denounced as illegitimate, bastards, perhaps not even Jews. There was something suspicious there but nobody knew exactly what, before '67, before the Panthers, way before. Right around the time of Kennedy's assasination. Maybe after. Suddenly they told us we weren't Jews! Not Jews? Just like that, a discovery! And we're already here ten years, settling down the place and settling in our heads, on some "succesful" combine, Moshav Masliah, with our Egyptian neighbors (who think they're better educated than we are!), and Moroccans who also think a lot of themselves. Can you imagine? Why should we be less Jewish than anyone else? And why don't we have an alternative?

In those repressive years of the sixties, the competition between the three ethnic groups on the Moshav concerning the debate over who is "more modern," finally changed into who is "more Israeli." No one wanted to be primitive. It was agreed-upon that the Indians are reserved, the Egyptians diligent and the Moroccans . . . well, you know about the Moroccans. With the Egyptians, there were strong family ties; on the Sabbath, echoes of their joy even reached us, and we witnessed the sight of their two ringing kisses, one on each cheek, for "Sitti," or "Umti," and the trilling ululations at every festivity. When the children finished high school and the army, they went to work, permanently. Welders, careers in the military, mechanics, factory workers. R. Darwish was the first Egyptian girl from the Moshav to go into the army. A notch above me. At the end, she married out of the community. At first, the kids used to bring their salaries back home to their fathers, but that stopped later and they began to save for their own dowries; they bought a refrigerator, a stove, pots and pans. The sons even built houses for themselves. And with no warning, they made us Indians not Jewish. So degrading, so insulting.

We were seized by a kind of modesty that went right along with our reticence and patience from the absorption years in the homeland. How did the story end? We got what we wanted. We demonstrated. Quietly, in exemplary order, precisely following the commands of the police. Time after time we waved huge slogans opposite the Parliament: *"We Are All Benei Yisrael!"* Both men and women. At the rabbinate or amongst the politicians, they all said: "Things will be fine." But they continued checking our family trees. Comparing notes in black and white. Since then, the immigrants from Russia have undergone these tribulations. With them, though, problems are solved behind closed doors. And the Ethiopians. Only it doesn't look like things are going that easy for them. If at all.

It's better not to even go into it. A delicate matter, even these days, when an Indian wants to marry someone from another community.

The first *sabra* in the family. I was given a Hebrew name to cleave unto the land. I had the privilege of being their first Israeli. What would I have been there, in India, had my parents stayed in Bombay, like my two uncles? A teacher, perhaps, or maybe a diligent clerk. Maybe even there I would have had to struggle to get to the university, fighting my way forward, tooth and nail. Father would have been able to arrange a good, stable job for me. Mother would have worried if I was twenty-two and not married, the age she married my father. A tough age. No one ever came to ask for my hand. Were they afraid of me? Had I, in their eyes, become a heretic? Maybe even in India I would still be the same person. Yet, the hope to be part of a dream was implanted in me. I grew up with a great love of the Land, the earth was enclosed within me, the olive and the lemon trees, the Valley of Ayalon.

My sister Sarale, the oldest, was born there, in India. In the kibbutz, the "le" was appended to her name. She and her friends aroused jealousy when they wore fluttering skirts and bright scarves. In protest, I stuck to boy's shirts and jeans. A protective wall between me and the world. To be "modern" meant to look like someone from the kibbutz. I didn't want to look trashy, like a cheap slut, giving her body away to everyone with a thin blouse, a miniskirt and high-heels. But Nissim Sarussi was a heartbreaker:

I can't bear to see them go
hand in hand anymore
while she left me here alone,
Oh, why did she leave me so?

And Aris San and Aliza Azriki and the Oud Ensemble. . . . Wrapped up in a man's shirt. Cheap imitation of a *kibbutznik,* it seemed like I had turned into an "Israeli" everyone could recognize, even my parents, maybe even out on the street.

The annual gathering. Tables spread out with all kinds of artwork made by the community's sons and daughters. Drawings, tiny dolls dressed in the choicest Indian apparel. Different kinds of saris, styles from different regions of India, and the colors! Deep, warm, impeccable combinations of violet and red, dark green and bright pink. They weren't satisfied with the six basic colors there! All the colors were respected, even those unfamiliar to the West. In the middle of the display area there was a small table with a reduced model of a map of India on it, done up in the colors, so familiar to me, of the Indian flag. To the side of the flag, two dolls dressed in saris woven of the same colored cloth grip flagpoles with tiny flags. Between the two dolls, *"Blessings Upon the Indian Nation on Their Day of Independence,"* is written. I bump into Hilda, my cousin from Dimona. She's wearing a violet sari with red embroidery, pure silk. Spectacular. Hilda had been an excellent dancer, she'd even danced in the movies. How jealous all the girls in the Moshav were of me. Hilda, my cousin. She got to the country at the beginning of the sixties, ten years after us. Silently laughing, she and her sister Edna, may her memory be blessed, adorned with incredibly styled, golden ornaments, exuded magical scents, beauty and brightness. Her weight had gone up since then. She stopped dancing on her wedding day, and she was already a grandmother.

A girl in a sparkling pink sari was on stage, happy to be dancing about the love of nature. Members of Parliament are there too. Women wrapped in saris or Punjabi-daras embroidered in gold, men in Punjabi shirts, custom made, brought in directly from the finest shops in Bombay and London. There are also more than a few long braids, "ambra" and, here and there, smooth black hair as well, proudly flowing down to the hips. And some are dressed in the elegant, sporty style of Zahava or Ophra Haza. Not Margalit Sa'anani, though, or hardly at all.

And there are members of Parliament. My mother says again and again that, for an evening like this, the little girls are really superfluous. The kids should get their time on Hanukkah or Sukkoth. But not at a gathering of grown-ups. Asher, my brother-in-law, gets fed up looking at five year olds. The little ones arouse the amazement of the minister for religious affairs who had come to make a blessing. Avner Shaki, a member of Parliament, says that it's fine to continue being Indian as long as you remember that you are a Jew. Ah, I say, Judaism, again it comes down to whatever suits them. Let me be, it's not my problem, I'm Israeli through my Indian culture. The five-year-olds haven't been forewarned: all over the country they've got classes in Indian dance: in Or Yehuda, Ashdod, Dimona, Lod, and even Petah Tiqva.

Parliament member Eli Ben Menahem unfurls a speech, shooting from the hip. He calls upon the Indian audience to stop "withdrawing," to become Israeli. Hold it, hold it, hold it, hold it just a second. If Eli Ben Menahem is saying something like this, what is he doing here? He didn't even want to accept the flowers of honor, according to the Indian custom (because his shirt would have gotten damp and left spots on it); so let him take it out of the "bonus" they "organized" for themselves. Members of Parliament, corrupt as usual. Or better yet, he shouldn't have even come or done us any favors. The audience is silent, not reacting, waiting. Member of parliament Eli Ben Menahem finds it necessary to point out the community's mute docility: "They never came complaining and they built synagogues for themselves from money contributed by members of the community and not through aid from the government." Then, as if by chance, he finds it necessary to mention that of course he was born in India but his parents came up to Israel when he was a year old. The hall is silent: automatically those sitting in couples begin looking at those not sitting in couples.

"He's not *Benei Yisrael* at all."

"His parents came to India from Baghdad."

"From Bukhara."

"He's just cashing in on it."

"Just like Abie Nathan, the Persian born in India."

"The one who spoke well is the guy from Yavne, he was here last year, Meir Chetrit; he said he loves to pray in an Indian congregation."

"I heard that."

"You did? When?"

"At the gathering last year."

"You mean he always says that?"

"Sure, whenever he appears before Indians."

"What a crock."

The audience suffers the torment patiently until the flowery speeches are over. The young people in back clap from a lack of interest, they want to sing and dance, groupies of the Indian band from Lod. Why don't they show that group on TV? They already showed Kiryat Malakhi, so why not Indian dances by ten-year-old Israelis?

The evening is conducted around a competition of singing and dancing, held now for five years in a row at *Binyanei Ha-Uma* in Jerusalem, always with an audience of thousands. The young men and women reach the competition after qualifying in a first round; five representatives, four men and a woman. Out of the five, four chose sad songs. One of the songs is at least forty years old. And the songs are untarnished—boistrous and full of longing, interlaced with the beauty of childhood. As for hidden regions, it's doubtful there were any. Shlomo Bar says that Indian music is composed for different times of the day. There is music meant for the morning that depicts awakening from sleep to the aroma of flowers in the gentle, sunny air; for early afternoon, when nature is mercilessly laid bare with brazen clarity for all to see, there is different music. And so on for evening and for night. Interesting.

The orchestra comes on stage. Four kinds of drums. A set of tablas, a set of pop drums, two sets of African congas. String instruments: a sitar or bulbul tarang, a bass guitar, an accordion, and an organ. The crowd reacts with a cheer. Way in the back, like up in the balcony to the left of the stage, young men enthusiastically sing Indian songs. This year the liveliest crew came from Dimona. The ones from Ashdod were quieter. All boys except for a few girls here and there, but they aren't rabble-rousers. They just chuckle with excitement. The emcee is charming, polished Hebrew, no sign of an Indian accent: "r," "r," a French "r," pampered. The host is colossal. He participated in the singing competition last year and took second place. Hebrew is foreign to him so he conducts the evening in Marathi, the language of Bombay.

Almost the third singer, the host says: "The next song is from a movie that is familiar to all of us, *Bajai Baura!*" Cries of surprise and contentment are heard from all sides. The movie, as everyone knows, is sad, really sad. A philosophical movie. The hall is silent. A young singer, maybe twenty-five or thirty, gets up and bursts into a scintillating *mawwal,* with incredible embellishment—this is no fake. He is good. A first-rate *mawwal,* definitely in the league of Muhammad Rafi, the famous Indian singer. Bajai Baura is a small, poor town that suffers from constant pillaging by thieves. A pair of lovers whose song is like the song of the gods. Questions of existence, power over fate, the value of honor. Tough world, a war for change. Classically Indian. The song is musically complex and the words are in the form of a supplication to mortal beings:

> There were mortals, guests in our world,
> there were decent people. And those
> who think they have the world in their
> hand, grasping the movement of a cloud,
> the passage of water. Oh, bitter fate:
> when lightning strikes, there is no saviour.
>
> Time forever enduring, my time, our time
> is but a drop upon a cocoa shell borne
> in the heart of the spacious ocean.

The opening is riveting. An awesome silence reigns throughout the audience, the accompanying group blends in just when they should, leaving room for the quiet sitar. No one moves, the song replenishes hollow hearts.

Now, it should be pointed out that the Indians (or the so-called Indian immigrants), are not really still Indian. They're Israeli. More Israeli than Indian? They prefer the automated electronic beat of a drum machine going along to "Boogie, oh boogie, boogie," or "Love to love you, kudi, shugi, bugi." So Shlomo Bar's words light up my somber thoughts.

Applause from all sides. Indian songs, just like Indian dances, have a very complex structure but they remain alarmingly flexible. Through improvisation, the depth of the inner structure is maintained, intuitively. There is space to breathe and you can get lost. Exhilarating. The little guy on stage is improvising, really stretching out, breaking through the barriers put up between long years of disconnection. A society that knows what it wants imparts a rich existence back over to the other side. A society with narrow horizons, in eclipse. Now that we've gotten acclimated and learned how to get along, to be maniacs like everyone else, we can spare some time for music, to improvise, to ease the pressure.

The crowd keeps a record of what's good and what isn't. Wild applause. No matter what you think, it's a tough song that not everyone is up to singing.

To sing like Zohar Argov, or Arik Einstein. So here comes this little guy, he takes the risks, and sings. Flawless execution. The audience is transfixed. It touches that nerve, of once upon, of times obscured, stinging the neck. Now, the long, sad days come back to us . . . Now they are the long, sad days. In the end, he only picks up third place. Everything's fixed.

People mill around at the intermission: a friend from Yavne, another from Kiryat Gat, a chance to greet a relative who came this month from India—father went to school with her there.

On her second cassette, Zahava sings an Indian song. An Indian song in Hebrew. Zahava singing an Indian song. So what? But I still feel a little weird about it. Zahava takes something that is "mine" and interprets it the way she wants. After all, Zahava is Moroccan with a heavy Turkish influence, right? So Zahava sings an Indian song, what's the big deal? Neverthless, deep within me that same chord strikes, to sing, to dance. Just like in the movies, like in the songs, to be beautiful and have long hair, to be a great dancer. But, really, what do I have to do with Indian songs? Zahava sings an Indian song. Actually, that's nice. I would even say, really nice. Great, Zahava. Ten and a half.

The dancers have pure skin, their clothes are bright. With tiny bells on their ankles, they perform classical and modern pieces, to the pleasure of everyone. Long, fake braids. Sequins. Flowers. Movies. The winner is declared. A dancer in violet; a charismatic dance, but lacking spirit. They're well trained, these dancers from Kiryat Shmone, Beersheba, Dimona, Ramla, Lod, Ashdod, Kiryat Ata and Or Yehuda. Twenty year olds, at most. Salt of the earth. Israelis, like me. Like you.

★★★★★

At the grocery, everyone wishes each other a good New Year. The days flow on again, streaming off in hidden torrents. A magical spring, stories about life, stories from life. Once tales gathered the spirit in. Now a heat wave does it.

Allenby, the summer is full of sounds from the banks of the Volga, accordion tunes from Broadway, and I struggle not to dole out a cent. At the Carmel Market, Russian immigrants grunt as they inspect the loads of meat displayed at the butchers. Pork is at a premium. I see their eyes pop out at the huge, tender pieces. Craving for a taste. They're hungry, starved to the soul. For them, the Carmel Market isn't the crowds and the awful stench, the misery and oppression, not even the vulgarity. On the contrary, they don't even look at the people. Their gaze is transfixed. They can't get enough of the abundance of food displayed. Lusting vision. I take a look: Damn straight, there is a hell of a lot of food in the market. That the prices are high, that's another story.

What fascinated my parents when they came to the country? What surprised them in their first years? I don't know. My, my, am I sinking into all the miserable baggage that goes along with those days again? The dark fifties? My mother claims that if the water here is tainted the way it was there, that is, in India, then what was the point of coming at all. We were infected. Father, still an innocent boy, loves the country—he discovers innovative methods to raise chickens in the Moshav. The conveyer belt produces like a wood-chip factory in Taiwan. Taken hostage by technology. Something or other simply blinded them, one of the enchanted country's miracles. Maybe the army, maybe proximity to the revered West, maybe the myths of peoplehood.

Each generation and its immigrants, new immigrants and their distress.

It came to blows between Russians and Ethiopians at some hotel. It happens. So what? How touching. Maybe they were flabbergasted because they were black and had a different culture. They see strangers and strangeness in them and they're pushed aside according to some hidden, racist criteria under which society operates. So they'll become a social problem, so they'll live as if they're spiritually impaired (to say black is beautiful is another story altogether). The Ethiopians aren't interested in my sympathy. But I still feel for them, despite that. I'm no fanatic, not at all. They too will spend years passing through the obstacle course of the alien homeland. Some will fit in, some will never find their place and draw the line. And the blacks will continue to be likened to the ape, particularly by the Moroccans and the Poles and the Persians and the Iraqis and the Russians and the Kurds. And even the Indians. Of course. So?

The boardwalk. The end of August, one of "those" Tel Aviv nights. I love this city. Me, the farmer from Moshav Masliah, finally loves the city, fifteen years after I got here. At least for now. Or maybe altogether. By the circular plaza, a crowd takes up positions to watch some dancers. On stage, there is a disc-jockey and a dance troupe. Kids happily leaping. The beat of a samba freely flows into the lambada. Lam-ba-da. Two boys and two girls wave their hands and shake their legs, their heads rocking. The crowd is happy. So are we. A three-year-old jumps to the beat, a captive fan of the ten-year-old in the super-short fluttering skirt. And they are most becoming, and so cute, their eyes filled with joy.

I look over to the side, as usual, but my eyes continue to the left, a few people down from me, to a tall man with clear glasses and a stylish shirt. Good-looking. I quickly shift my eyes back, so as not to transgress the limits of politeness in staring at a stranger. A second later, I look again. Quiet, a concentrated look, soft eyes, no tension in his body. The same calm, the same look. Next to him is a very pretty woman. Her fingers are long and thin, adorned by rings of gold set with delicate, exquisite rubies. Her beauty is enhanced with strong colors. Her hair is black and short. She, too, has a calm look. Positive identification: Indians. He looks at me, she looks, our eyes converge: "Indian? *Benei Yisrael?*" And I think to myself: "New immigrants, from Kashmir." As one, our eyes shift back to the stage, back to the audience of elderly folk sitting comfortably on the municipality benches, watching the South American deejay, watching the children of Tel Aviv from the Yemenite Quarter, Ramat Israel, and Yad Eliyahu jump to the beat of the lambada. Children from Persia, Iraq, Morocco, Greece, Libya and Romania. The salt of the earth.

Bear well, my brothers and my sisters, bear yourselves well for another sad year that is about to come upon us. At the Moshav, they are wishing for rain. Rain also fell there in the summer, in India, steaming tropical rain. Maybe this year it will come on time, maybe this year it won't tarry in alluding to the signs.

— Translated from the Hebrew by Ammiel Alcalay

MOSHE SARTEL

MOSHE SARTEL was born in Istanbul in 1942 and came to Israel in 1949. After studying Hebrew literature, Jewish philosophy and the Kabbalah at Hebrew University, he went on to get a degree in Library Science; presently he

serves as director of the municipal libraries in Petah Tikva. The scope of Sartel's poetry is vast, striving toward epic proportions. The narrators of his dense, book-length poetic sequences speak like prophets or visionaries. Although the worlds they depict and inhabit might seem fantastic, as Sartel says: "I define myself as a poet-historian; as a historical poet, I am also a documentary poet." Few Israeli poets of the past several decades come to mind whose work is as ambitious, focused, and uncompromising as that of Moshe Sartel. His project—intellectually and emotionally—makes more sense when placed within the formal, visual and intellectual texture of other Mediterranean poets like Cavafy, Sikelianos, Seferis, Lorca, Hikmet, and Montale, not to mention Homer or Heraclitus. This, along with his extremely subtle, highly sensual and deeply allusive internalization of classical Hebrew texts, makes his work doubly difficult. While generally admired, critics accustomed to the assumptions regarding the use of a certain Anglo-American poetics in an Israeli context have not begun to fathom the magnitude or resonance of Sartel's intentions. His books include *He Who Bore* (1967), *The Way and the Flesh* (1970), *Flesh Upon the Coals and Other Poems* (1973), *For the Sun Shall Not Darken* (1979), *On the Road to Beith El* (1982), *The Book of the Great Victory* (1986), and *Behold the Fire* (1994).

THE LANGUAGE OF THE WORLD: AN INTERVIEW WITH MOSHE SARTEL BY AMMIEL ALCALAY

You came to Israel from Istanbul when you were very young. Tell me something about your education, in the wider sense of the word; how did you get to the materials that characterize your work?

When we first arrived I went to a religious school, through the fifth or sixth grade, but there was nothing significant in this. I got to things on my own, at the age of ten I went in search of Kabbalistic texts, all by myself, unrelated to anything I learned in school. I had some kind of desire to get to the things themselves and once intimations that such things actually did exist were revealed to me, I immediately went to search them out.

What language did you speak at home?

Ladino, and then Hebrew.

What happened after you encountered the texts you were searching for?

I devoured them! First, there were texts from the *Mishna* since the *Talmud* still presented some difficulties for me. After I overcame the linguistic difficulties, I started the *Talmud* and then moved on immediately to the *Zohar* which became central to me. I remember looking for it, in every place imaginable, until I finally found an old, beat-up set at a used book dealer. Such books were practically unavailable. The *Zohar* in particular was hard to come by and I only got to it on my own initiative. By then I was fifteen. After that I already started reading world literature. In school I just did my duty, everything else was a continuation of my own interests. Soon I got to the poet-teacher who influenced me enormously, T. S. Eliot. In him I found a union of poetry with the kinds of texts that interested me, the ability to integrate massive cultural elements within a poetry through which the poet could also find personal expression.

In what language did you read him?

In English. That's the reason I learned English! Actually I ordered the books from a relative of mine outside of Israel. *The Waste Land,* of course, was central.

As I'm sure you know, The Waste Land *is also a central text in modern Arabic poetry.*

Of course, it has had enormous influence. Particularly, I think, in terms of his religious position, the stance of a religious person who is actually not a believer. The ability to take a cultural icon, to take a text and mold it in the most personal ways, these were my first real lessons in poetry and captivated me completely. I was writing long before I encountered Eliot but the moment I began reading him I saw that I had a direction. The example, I think, that many took from him are in those passages where he attempts to put up some kind of a blockade against falling into the abyss of the texts themselves, whether this comes through the distancing of satire, through the concretization of things or the banality of mundane objects, like the cigarettes in the ashtray. Some poets only saw the banality but I saw the intertwining of the texts behind the mundane figures, the personal mark of the poet.

This process is very similar in the poetry of Adonis; like him, you've taken this approach as a tool and not a doctrine, in order to apply it to the enormous abundance of cultural materials that you have at hand.

Precisely; this integration of materials into a new reality involved all the material that came with me, the Midrash, the Kabbalah, and so on. You can't follow a recipe and go on to write poetry, yet when I read Eliot's "Tradition and the Individual Talent," I felt like he had taken the words out of my mouth because that was precisely the direction I was going in. After that, there was a short period when I read Uri Zvi Greenberg. I was very much taken with the length of his breath, the ability to say things and keep on saying them, with the kind of prophetic pathos that is so much a part of his work. I also saw that I was able to contend with such things, that I could express myself that way as well; also because he dealt with many of the same themes, primarily that he made himself into a prophet—to prophesize myself, in cultural terms, in local terms, without flying off into various forms of surrealism that are neither here nor there. To be able to say: here is a person, I am this person. I always reiterate that I do not actually write about myself—I sing myself, but only as a paradigm, the particularities of my particular self opened up to everyone but not as myself, as any one. This idea of being paradigmatic is very important to me. Although this "performance" of the existential I represents something universal, it is, in the final analysis, my pain, my reality, my torment, my celebration.

I also use all kinds of myths, Babylonian, Assyrian, Akkadian, very explicitly. I read these things unprogrammatically because I consider myself a professional and one has to ply one's trade with the right tools. Even though my vantage point remains Jewish, I use these materials insofar as they can be integrated without feeling artificially implanted. The language, Hebrew in my case, not only dictates that you write in a certain way, it also dictates that you write a certain thing. I believe that the language draws you in, it compels you to write according to its history and logic. The content of what you write in English and what you write in Hebrew cannot be identical, and vice versa.

To go on in terms of my reading, if Eliot was the teacher, then St. John Perse was the professor. If somebody ever makes such a study, I think they will find my work completely intertwined with his, to the point of utter perplexity. I read him over and over and he opened up a world of wonders for me. The colors—since I am already from the East, I felt like some primitive who has been given glistening rocks! I immediately learned French in order to read him. It was a real discovery for me, and besides revealing this magical world, he also imbued a greater dignity to the role of writing itself. Suddenly you realize you are engaged in an endeavor that is not mundane, that your scope is global, that you can conquer the cosmos. I am using his terms now. The feeling of the universal existential significance of the sun, for instance, or the moon. This finally gave me confidence in myself, and enabled me to make the transition from the prophetic stance of someone expressing themselves to the position of someone involved in the cosmos, someone for whom poetry is the language of the world.

When did you go on to to discover other poets we have spoken of, "locals" like Seferis or Sikelianos?

The Mediterraneans, the greatest in the world, but all "locals"! This was after St. John Perse, primarily Seferis, Elytis, and Cavafy. None of them signified a turning point for me, they came, rather, as a completion. It was already clear to me that what I was doing was acceptable, at least in the larger scheme of things that someone like St. John Perse defined. I wasn't out of my mind! But Seferis still managed to influence me a lot. I think this closeness to the Mediterranean poets simply comes from our access to the sea! We love the sea, we make its blue symbolic and the sky symbolic, this is the Mediterranean world. Even St. John Perse, though his roots are in the Far East, his spiritual, not his autobiographical roots, can still be found here—as in his use of Xenophon for *Anabasis,* for instance.

The general consensus when one looks at criticism on modern Hebrew poetry is that influences are almost exclusively English, German and Russian. You've spoken of Eliot and St. John Perse, but also Seferis, Cavafy, classical Greece, the Kabbalah, Babylonian mythology and so on. Your work makes a lot of sense in relation to other poets in the region, contending with a very similar problematic of conflict, identity and the legacy of an ancient tradition. It seems to me that critics here either don't have the tools, don't want to acquire them or, in some cases, don't even believe such tools exist in order to contend with poetry like yours.

Of course. Without entering into debates with critics, I think that the critics here lack access to materials that, for me, are simply an everyday matter. I am constantly astounded that people think it is possible to read poetry without having read other books before. Where is the context? For every line of mine, I've read ten books! These are simply the materials that I need for my work and this is a fact. It is not by accident that I try to speak about poetry as an occupation, a labor, because I take it very seriously, it's not some kind of a hobby. You have to work at it and invest in it and I am not sure whether critics are willing to invest as much as they would need to since they all see poetry only from their particular point of view. I hope that as the years pass, things will change.

Also I think you take yourself whole, your language is part of you. You actually feel good being here, part of this place, part of this region, and you aren't compelled to want to be somewhere else. This is a new phase in Israeli culture, one that may be difficult to swallow for some.

I don't think that I represent any kind of an average Israeli. On the other hand, I very much represent an Israeli reality. I am often refered to as a surrealist because, at least on the surface, my work might seem distant, not of this time or this place. But I sometimes feel like screaming: look, my work is *only* of the here and now, this is reality, and it is taking place before your very eyes. None of it is from my wild imagination, I simply looked around and wrote what I saw. How can this be called surrealism, it's pure reality. I even define myself as a poet-historian. I would almost venture to say that I am a hyper-realist, because I write about the real. If I mentioned the teacher and the professor, I would have to add that the textbook is Homer. I simply believe that in order to write an epic, to depict historical reality, you have to address the enormous historical conflicts that exist. I am now actually going back to school to get a degree in military history because I think it's important for my work. I am absorbing new materials, different relationships between things, and I think this will give me a basis to depict the reality we are living in which is nothing but one great big conflict. What remains, after all? The wars remain. Troy remains, the horse remains. This is reality. Within this, Homer circulated, to record. This is how I see myself. So I am not at all detached from reality. The opposite. I am writing today, but not *for* today. If not for eternity then for some other time. As a historical poet, I am also a documentary poet; as a documentary poet I am writing for the archives. If someone opens the archive at some point, they will find a documentary text.

How did you feel about seeing your work in translation?

It is a very interesting experience. Once I was sent to Turkey under the auspices of PEN and it was quite something to be there; they translated a number of my things into Turkish and I looked at the audience and I would be lying if I didn't say that there was a little leap in my heart at the recognition I felt, something that I haven't felt here. I sensed a lot of respect, an acknowledgment of the poet's role. Although it is a truism to say that something is lost in translation, it also gives the work another dimension. I was surprised, for instance, that the dramatic sense of my poems were retained in translation. I think the first time you read a poem it should be like a parable; though you might not understand the moral, you at least implicitly understand there is a story there. This is only one level but it should be available and open to everyone. Some connection has to be created between the reader and the creator; the creator has to make it clear that there is an existence there, that this thing is worth holding in your hand, that it's worth reading. After this, of course, there are many other levels. Translation allows you to enter, at least in the case of my work, into a few of the levels. I'm not quite sure that you can get all the way to the bottom of my work in translation since it is built on so many layers, archaeologically I would even say, and you have to go on some very precise and elaborate digs to get to those areas. Amongst other things, there is the linguistic level and you cannot get to all the Biblical connotations, for example, in translation since these work strictly on a linguistic level. Through imagery, for those familiar with the Biblical text, certain connections can be made. But there are linguistic charges that, in the original, send you straight to the Biblical text, and those are impossible to translate. But translation is important because it opens several doors, even though the last door still remains shut. But the last door is always shut, for the most part and for most readers, even in the original.

Can you say more about your relationship to language?

I think that the materials, language itself, has to be part and parcel of the content of writing. In Hebrew writing, there used to be a different, special relationship to the language since it wasn't spoken nor was it used in mundane texts but primarily in religious works. So there was a greater emphasis on the importance of language itself, to the point where you could encompass fixed linguistic elements in the form of citations and use them in other contexts. My own relationship to the language of writing is akin to those who wrote in a language that was not their mother tongue. I am writing in the sacred tongue and I do not forget this for an instant. By right, as an obligation, however you look at it, I am writing in the sacred tongue.

Because Hebrew is a sacred tongue or because every language should be written as if it were sacred?

Maybe poets in other languages generally have this same feeling of approaching something sacred, but I have receipts! So my feeling has this history, it's genuine and immanent within the very act itself, there is something to base it on. And maybe this forms the basis of another important element in poetry, celebration. Prayers are said in synagogue on holidays, on the Sabbath, those are occaisons when this special language is used. There can be no writing of poetry without celebration. It's a spiritual celebration, and a linguistic celebration, it's carnivalesque and colorful, such texts cannot be part of the regular week, the everyday. If you occupy yourself in such a way with language, if you speak with this sense of the sacred, then you sing when you pray and you have to listen to the sounds of poetry in its musical aspects. This, I think is the connection between language and its transformation into content; the immanence of language within the content. You cannot relate to language the way I do without internalizing these senses. With all the celebratory aspects of poetry that I spoke of, I am always conscious of the problematic that exists between the language and its uniqueness, the complexity of this relationship. As you said before, I am comfortable in the language, sometimes I even use the language of the Sages, for instance.

There is a tremendous difference between someone using the language—as you said—as an integral part in which the content is part of the language and someone who uses language as a means to say something, as a tool. In medieval poetry, as in the Bible, there are all kinds of examples in which language is a question of life and death. You can fall into a trap if you don't understand something. And one gets the sense that your language partakes of this life and death aspect of things, not simply to prove something or say something but as existence itself. Not existence in the ideological sense, to use Hebrew as a means of proving that it can be used, but as the fabric and texture of existence itself.

Of course, and these are things that will come back to haunt the language itself, that is clear. There is an obsessive relationship to language in my work, something that even people who don't fully understand what I'm up to are still aware of. There is an ability to reach into the historical layers of the language in the most natural way, so that it doesn't seem artificial, simply as part of experience itself. I could never write in a spare language, because my reality is "fat," colorful, and in order to depict such a reality I need all the historical layers of the language. If I can see any personal accomplishment it would be in the ability to express modern experience through all the layers of this language, in order to realize and emphasize those same elements that I introduce in the historical realm, the conflicts and experiences this ancient language was so adept in. If the Prophets wrote in such a language, it was to console their hearts and I also write for such consolation.

LAMENTING OF THE BIRDS

By every woman—a well, and by every well—a flock of sheep. Our blood is
clean, distilled of all fear
and our heart beats conducting blood. Like a river
of rose water.

And you look from your right and see recollections and you look from your left and see memory and you don't believe,
like someone aghast, you don't believe.
That they came to you and unto you, all those days, all of them. All those days, all of them, fearlessly.
Our head is like some beautiful vessel, flourishing on our body and our body is filled with a kind of sorrow, like a date palm,
softly swaying in the wind.
And what more is there to be in the world, what else is it up to us to be in the world, that your body be as fruitful as a vineyard,
that your tongue be as fertile as fire.
For close to every woman—a well. And by every well—the road. At the end of the road—a border stone.
At the stone's crown—the golden sign of a victorious kingdom.
Upon this stone, engraved in steel, is a narrative of the King's deeds.
And you raise your head from pain—the dust of the earth glitters like stars in the sky
and all the stones are of gold and of silver. And the land is embroidered in silken thread and the sky stretches over us,
like a mantle of purity.
And what more is there to be for us, what more is there to be of us and unto us, for by every woman—a well.
And by every well—a flock of sheep, and by the flock of sheep—the road.
As you arose aching from a tree, and as you lit out from pain up to the tree's crown, like leaves from the tree,
falling on our heads, one by one -
the birds.
And I, who bear upon my body the heavy burden of my limbs, unfurl my limbs one by one.
And lean on the body of birds wailing like a ploughman
bent over a furrowing ploughshare.
For my love is heavy and burning like the sands of the sea, within the sun's oven
and my love is burning upon the waves of the sea and my love is burning -
upon the sea and wailing birds.
And I say, here is one wailing bird, oh, here's one a bird. Here's a bird one
big and heavy and wailing and I flutter my wings and turn over and over in your bed like in the bed of a woman,
intoxicated by the scent of your skin, with the aroma of lillies of the valley.
And could trees witness this without uttering words of song out of sorrow?

And could plants remember this
without blooming green upon the world in recollection? Flowers see and shed spicy fragrance
like a shower from the sky.
For your cry rends my ears and your white flesh a bird -
dazzlingly strikes me.

Upon her body minted in fire, a sign from the King's signs, upon her leg a ring like a bird, upon his forehead,
it too is marked, like the sign emblazoned upon the border stone. Azure lines upon her breasts
and a black mole upon her belly.

And I am like a blind man, bearing my wings over her body and my wings flow above her, like sand.
And the man he is alone, the man is so alone. And the man he is alone sinking
into a single great silence,
like into the last sea.
And she said, bird, bird, I shall put myself to death upon your limbs, she said. And she said, I shall strike my head
upon every stone of the stones of your silence, she said. Unto death, she said.
Stone has four mouths, to scream out of the wall but he, he has not a single mouth with which to speak,
he has not one mouth to wail like a bird and to speak.
And he said to her, Behold, you are comely, most pretty, doves establish their nests within your eyes
and wolves in your womb . . .
And she raised her hand against him and opened his heart and from his heart, like vapors from the earth,
there emanated the scent of citrus groves in the month of Nissan.
And she unfurled her leg and opened her belly wide from pain and from it there arose the gushing sounds of the river that leads
to the final sea.

Then the man alone he is sinking, within a single great silence. Then the man alone he is soaring
within that same sorrow that is flowing
into the last sea.
And my voice hisses parched within my throat, oh final sea, last last sea upon the final border.

And I spread my wings, like one great bird wailing from pain, to cover the sun so light will not fall
upon the world, gliding over ocean and desert, over cities and land, these and those,
such and such a place I passed not, or these or those, this or any other place
I shall never pass.
And my blood stirred, a stillness within my limbs, like the wind's movement over my wings.
And my blood stirred, the blood coming out of my heart, like the last sea whipering at evening time.
And by every woman—a well. And by every well—a flock of sheep and birds wailing like the wind.

A poet man on shore. Upon his forehead, a heavy golden crown of words.
His eyes are full like the sea, wandering to the final shore.
Boats will not come from the sea, nor will a small cloud the size of the palm of a person's hand arise there.
Wasted and desolate man bird upon the water—forever and ever.
Only the sun beats down like a drunkard and the smell of the sea is like wine.
And you rested your two hands upon his temples and drew, like a knife,
the seagull out of his brain.
And you covered his eyes and let the seagull fly towards the last sea, into the final border, to tell of it,
for this is a blind man, having seen your flesh quiver between his hands,
shattering his body upon your body, like upon a rock,
he will never see darkness.

Here are our women, in white skirts, stained with patches of their blood, going to the sea each day,
standing at the shore, looking at the sea, learning the dance of love from its
waves.
And we, we whose bodies are as famished as the bodies of wolves in winter, lean and thin and grey,
follow in their heels every day to the sea, to bite and prey upon this flesh.
That our bodies were created from clay, our hearts from stone and rock and our eyes from sorrow, our eyes from the sorrow of birds.
And the young women's faces are bleached as limestone—and our faces are burnished like basalt stone
and all the wild birds of our youth arise howling from our mouths like dogs.

And a voice a shout comes from the East, like flight screeching, it comes.
And a voice a shout comes from the West, it comes.
And a voice a shout arises from the South, arises. And a voice a shout from the North, from the North. And they gather
and come into my mouth like birds
all the cries in the world
and they go out of my mouth, the roar of a lion from a forest, like out of a fiery kiln.
And you said, it is you holding firm in my body, with your two hands, lest I fall apart from love.
And I exclaimed, you hold my body firm, lest the sea swallow it up.
And a man cleaves unto a woman like someone holding, a flock of chirping birds.
And a woman cleaves unto a man like someone holding, a thousand wailing birds
and this boiling flesh -
did not come from dust nor will it ever return to dust . . .
because we are two and two, two and two, once and twice, four times.
For by every woman—a woman. And by every well—a well. And by every flock of sheep—a woman on the water.

Behold, you are comely as a bird, I said, for what else would I say when I have no mouth to speak. Behold, you are lovely, most pretty of all,
and doves nest in your eyes.

And you contended with me, three times, like Elijah. And I, like an old, sick dog,
vomit dreams from books and scrolls into your heart.
And I said, surely you are three sisters given one name by their father,
in the bitterness of his soul. And they came to me tonight, three sisters, offering themselves
to my bed and giving their breasts to my mouth . . .
Even were I to go from word to word, going along a road of dust and ash, within an awful mass
of kneaded words and letters, to hoist border stones upon my back, their breasts in my mouth -
unto dust and ash.
And you contended with me three times and you said, May the man bird live, may death never come to him.

And the taste of loam and bitumen came into my mouth and my lips, from
the book of Genesis,
their taste as intoxicating as wine.

On the border of our dreams, at the bank of the river, the queen mother
placed two bowls of silver,
in her womb and upon her head he wandered with birds, far from another
place.
For blood flows like a stream between her legs and the sound of her call is
like a bursting cloud,
from all the windows of the house.
And our world is as empty as a sea whose wives have left him upon the
shore, and our hearts are as empty as a desert
that night has descended upon and our eyes burn like the eyes of a poet who
has seen the desert
within his heart.
A dream, a dream, dreaming a dream. A man dreamt a dream. And in the
morning the taste of the clay
from which he was made is in his mouth, but the taste is of milk and honey.
And this is something you will never forget. Nor will you ever flee from this.
For you have no one else to whom you can go.
Even if we go there and never return, we have no one else to whom to go.
The taste of clay in his mouth and the taste of pain in his eyes. The taste of
summer and the taste of winter,
the taste of years that have no beginning and the taste of days that have no end.
And the queen mother placed two more bowls of silver in her womb and her
workers see
and amuse themselves with their members.
The meat seller, the fish merchant, the fruit and vegetable peddler.
A great crowd of people stand in the city square and listen in silence,
to the sound of her cries.
Dream, dream, dreaming a dream. A man dreamt a dream. In his mouth, the
taste of thorns and in his ears,
the sound of her cries
and an old poet man, who had lost his Lord in fire, comes back again to find
idols of wood and stone,
in the fire of her cries.

Murmuring lips, oh the rustle of lips under the bird's wings. Let go,
let go, this is where the pain comes from. Free from the barefeet walking and
passing through our dreams,

leaving their footprints in the sand, in our dreams without measure.
Oh sun, oh rain upon this world, oh idols of wood and stone looking upon our beds
from the walls of our houses . . . oh woman . . . oh bird lamenting woman. . .
. . .and my wings flutter and tremble, like a bird digging itself into the sand,
before her enemies.
Oh wind, oh oh river, we loved beyond all proportion upon its shore, and even if the river rose over its banks,
there is no power to raise a stone from the stones of the place and cover its waters.
Kings from distant lands sent their women to it, one every nine months,
to be impregnated by its seed, once every nine months.
And my dream of this hounds me every night, casting me routed upon its banks.
And I crawl and flee to its border, on all fours, like a man
who has had too much wine.
And they return to distant lands, to islands and countries. Their wombs full of seed, their hearts full of love,
their eyes blank and hollow.

Oh sun, oh rain, oh wind wind and a lamenting bird, like a dream, soaring with the wind.

And I, an old man, a poet, gatherer of words, like a widow, gathering twigs.
My body, once the color of honey, changed its countenance yesterday,
to the color of wine.
And pulling my limbs out of bed this morning, they bore the heaviness of the clay they were created from.
Put your hand upon my face, upon my eyes, upon my heart, lest they go astray. Put your hand upon my downy fingers,
the touch of your fingers upon my skin, like lips exhaling
upon the feathers of a bird.
And you touched my face, that dogs touched. And you touched my face, that wolves and jackals touched.
And you touched my face, that snakes and scorpions touched. And our face still glows from the touch of your hand,
like the face of the singer of songs, who ate from the plant of delusion. . .
But he would be unable to include even one of your fingers, even one he would be unable to include.

Then you carressed my face, with your eyelashes. And you bathed my two eyes, in light, in the light of your eyes.
And my blood rushes through my veins, like a wine of choice vintage from the vineyards of Hebron and Jerusalem.
Dream, dream, dream a dream, a man dreamt a dream -
a king from the south sent an urgent letter to the northern king with whom he'd exchanged wives,
and their laments rose to the heavens.
Behold, you are comely as a bird, behold you are comely, most beautiful, and doves nest in your eyes.

My head is heavy between your two hands, because of the crown of words and letters. My head is heavy within your hands,
like the stones of Jerusalem. And you bear my head just like the ten stonecutters at the quarry in Jerusalem
that fell into
the dream,
holding stones to their chests like infants . . .
My head is heavy in your two hands, kind of a crown of words and letters, and my heart weighs so heavily upon me.

Your two breasts quiver in my hands, like two birds who have seen an eagle.
And you said, Rest. And you said, Rest and I shall tend to your wounds and quell the flame that courses throughout your flesh.
I shall kindle all your hopes and give you life, more than those who gave you life itself.
Then the scent of your flesh came into my nostrils
and I called, life, life, and I came to you, unto death.
Only eyes that have seen your skin will not see death, ever. They will not see, ever.
And my two hands, dried and gnarled like two black carobs.
And my two feet, one steel, the other lead,
and my heart burnished brass . . .
For I am poor, an aching beggar am I. I shall not know life. Poor am I a beggar and my whole body aches.
And I came in you upon the banks of the river. And I came in you upon the border of a dream
and I ache in you, unto death. I ache in you unto death.
Only my eyes which have seen your flesh will never see death. Won't see, ever.

Behold, you are comely as a bird. Behold, you are comely, most beautiful, the doves nest in your eyes and in our eyes
the dream glows, all night.

And the kings sent unto us, to the banks of the river, that their wives burn and give birth,
one every seven months. One every seven months.
And a mother and her daughter gave birth on the same day, at the same hour, two girls to one father . . .
A voice rises from your throat—a myriad of doves coo in your mouth and I am your beloved
and a voice rises from your body like the sound of clusters of grapes being crushed. For your wine is the dawn,
splashing over our faces, your wine is the dawn on the walls of our room,
and the dim, heavy stains of our memory, upon white walls, in all the houses of the city.
You said, you are not a man, bird, not a man from the living lands. And you stepped on my heart with your hands
and my body cries out, incited, like a mute who sees the sea for the first time
in his life.
And our veins are open, flowing with love, like torrents into the sea. And our hearts are opened wide as a chasm,
that a thousand loves enter, to compose a thousand poems.
And we, who disembarked from our ships and went forth to the lands of the sea, who in the desert, at dusk,
saw the shadows extending without end, and we saw forests and snow on the mountains
and the wind with her thousand mouths blowing on our faces and making love to us, and the sun, with her myriad knives,
slaughtering our necks and loving our bodies,
we did not taste this pain upon our very flesh, unto death. The taste of pain
upon our bodies -
unto death
only eyes that have seen your flesh will never see death, ever. Never see, ever.

Lying by your side, like a coast and its sea. Wasted, like someone whose body has been passed over by a thousand whores.
Lying at your side wasted.
And just as the disk of sun begins to rise, it ascends upon our bodies to shatter.

And just as the wind begins to blow, it blows and scatters.
For your white flesh comes into me and cries out of my hands and your scent comes into me like a wave hitting my face.
Lying by your side like the sea and its shore. Wasted.
And our imaginations arose against us, floating like clouds in the wind. And our dreams fall from our eyes,
like torrential rain.
Lying by your side like a sea and its shore. Nailed down.
And I said, love, there is not the strength in a man to dream this dream to its end.
There is no force to starve this hunger too, like a wave seething in the sea and breaking upon our hearts.
And my voice is parched, like the sound of the sea. And my body is spilt, like the sand in the sea. And my heart is broken,
like the sea.
As to these and those and another myriad of such things, a poet man fell upon the sword of his dream,
for the battle had indeed become quite hard for him.
And the locks of my hair are long and hard, like the hair of a horse. Laid on your belly
and the hairs of my beard on your face -
like the hairs of nakedness.

Then you lifted your hand and extricated, one by one, all the stones of Jerusalem from me.
And you took up the light of a candle and drew it to my eyes and lit my eyes with your eyes.
And you swung my head in,to the palm of your hand and my mouth shed poem words upon your hands.
Only my thin silence, strikes you and dreams. My thin silence, strikes you and dreams.
At morning you'll see, light shining upon the world and upon your face
and the sun's disk did not rise in the sky today. . .
Lying by your side like the sea and its shore. Lying at your side like on sand, hot and wasted.

Our beds are dishevelled, our dreams cast upon them, naked and trembling.
See our body, woman, upon whose face remain the signs of unhardened clay.
For the traces of fingernails still scar our face and our body is cracked and spent,

like the sand of the sea on your body.
Our body is heavy and aching like a bird made of marble a bird made of marble lamenting and borne by the wind,
letting its soul go where it will, not to return.

In the woman's eyes—a man. In the bird's eyes—a dream. Her eyes are as green as the woods,
his eyes are red, having seen no sleep from the immensity of his dreams. His wings flutter to fly from the window
and his feet get tangled up in her hair.
Look at our body, woman, a thousand women all street-walkers come to it nightly,
to learn love's secrets from it.
And from the young women's bodies I strip a dress that hasn't come off their bodies from the day they fled
their father's houses and I bathe their skin in sea water and salt and I dry their bodies off with sand and wind,
before scalding each and every drop dried upon their bodies
with the hellish pleasure that is a human dream.
For their bodies are a beast's body, their eyes the eyes of forest animals and their hearts
are full of love.
And after all this and after all kinds of things like this or like that, the smell of the sea,
like the smell of our beds, after nights of love.
Oh victory over my limbs, victory over my limbs and there is no death!
Standing at the platform of my bed, my hands over my head, one clenching the other, victory over my body, no death!
And three old women who saw me at birth, left urgently tonight for Mount Ararat,
to cover the hole that had been prepared for me, at my going out into the air of the world.
Victory over my body, and no death!

A night of love descended upon us and in the firmament, one after another, seven beautiful and majestic moons ascend.

Listen, the sound of his steps in the rooms. Here is a poet man, going from one room to another,

for the tide of his dream has risen unto his very neck. And his shameful silence cloaks his body like the plague.
And he gathered the bodies of his dreams into a hole. And covered the hole.
And sat on the hole.
Then shadows converge on his house at evening time, like animals to water, gathering at evening
and leaning upon his body and drinking from his seed, in a hushed wail, until morning.
At morning a man floats upon all the city's beds, spreading out like a bird upon the water.
His tongue is as fertile as a forest and his lips are as fecund as a lake.

Oh, give me the power of your hips, to steal over the border every night.
Oh, give me the power of your legs, to walk the road, there and back, there and back every night.
And the poet man, master of rejoicing, moved the border stones away again, 500 parasangs
into the kingdom of the last border.

Oh, give me the power of your hands, to hoist border stones upon my head.
Oh, give me one of your shoulders, to rest my shoulder on. And like a rock at a crossroad,
you drew my body to yours and let my body rest in your hands and you opened your palms
and behold—a bird . . .
and the poet man, father of this song of the sea, tonight, as well, he moved the border stones 500 parasangs
into the kingdom of the final border.
Oh, woman, oh blind one, oh give me the power of your soft eyes, to dream the dust of the earth
that it sparkle like stars. Oh, give me the power of your body, to steal border stones of heavy marble.
To bear them upon my back like a dream, into mountains so very high up,
into mountains so very far off.
Oh, give me give, because the power of my breath is short within my lungs and my guts heave and rise
like snakes in my mouth. Oh, give me, even if the two palms of my hands are clenched like fists
and give nothing.
Oh, give me the power of your belly, to conceive. . .

And woman woman. Oh, woman woman. You will lie by his side the whole night when all his shadows will attack,
upon the last border and a kind of sea.
And woman, oh woman. Take his heart into your two hands once more, when a thousand and more horses
gallop over his face, bringing the border stones back to their place.
And the poet, like some embattled man bearing up his son, messianic sun, upon his horse
to show him his kingdom and his whole kingdom, passes again, very slowly, over his visage.

We'll still come back. At evening we'll come back. At the last rays of the sinking sun, we'll return.
Even if a drawn sword hinders me or afflictions equal to seven poets deter me, we'll still come back.
We'll return at evening, my torments in tow behind me, tied to a horse by rope. On our heads,
leaves from the valley, booty in our hands, emblazoned in the kingdom's gold.
And woman, oh woman, it is at the limit's of a man's power to think, beyond all his power and imagination,
that in a warm and dark place, like in your womb, one single word beginning as a kind of embryo
will don skin and bones and flesh.

And a man, mortal, on the shore of all shores, the last sea,
puts her flesh in his hand like warm sand, to rest his face upon it, having come to the last shore.
And his face is like a man's face smitten by wine, and his eyes are like the eyes of a dog, green eyes.
And his face dribbles spit, calling out, love, love!
And the wings of his dream strike against her head, death blows, striking her head death blows,
but they are unable.
And her hand renders his heart asunder, like an egg breaking in her hand and birds ascend from his heart,
tens, hundreds, thousands, a myriad,
myriads upon myriads!
And she puts her flesh in his hands like warm sand, upon his wings to soar high.
And he binds her body to his, by hand, by foot, by eye, by heart, by sex

and glides over the city in final ascending circle
to the last
sea shore.

A STONE I LAY FROM MARBLE OF MARMARA

Marmara, the Sea of Marmara rises over its shores within my heart washing down over my face, blue blue as star thistles.
And within my heart a man arose and said, We shall eat and drink and be happy and go. And I said to him,
We shall eat and drink and be happy and go to the Sea of Marmara. We shall eat and drink and be happy and go.
And I gave him my hand in support, and I let my hand rest upon his shoulder in support and from within my heart they all emerged and came
to instill excessive fear in me and express astonishment that I could not stand up to them.
And I pass amongst them, looking into their faces and calling their names -
Samuel Taragano, Isaac Benveniste, Avraham Almosnino, Joseph Alfandari,
they all converged and came, unto my visage and into my heart, like nine black birds, flying
in search of a white bird, the tenth for a quorum.
The Sea of Marmara is on my heart, the Sea of Marmara on my face and upon my beard, blue blue as star thistles.
I went on the road with them, and I went the whole way with them, into the fields, the cities and the villages,
and there is not a man other than myself who could say that it had been so real for him.
Cities and villages of shadow. Cities and villages in shadow.

Beautiful Eskudar, beautiful Ortakoy, beautiful Chorlu, beautiful Edirne.
Beautiful Gallipoli. Beautiful Chanakale . . .
A person sees and is afflicted, until his teeth turn black. A person hears and is afflicted, until his ears start ringing.
The sea of Marmara rises and falls within shade, upon my face, upon the face of my cities, upon the face of my villages,
blue blue as star thistles.
And people see this great miracle and beat their heads against a rock. . .
Our city's beautiful women, their scent more pungent than oil, their voices as sweet as birds.

And I get up to bathe with them in the Marmara, these thirty or more years the taste of that water hasn't come to my
skin and all this light, cast everywhere around us, to throw shadows like light from the Light of Life,
like light from the Light of Life.
Bekhora the daughter of beautiful Rivka Asseo, Rina the daughter of beautiful Sarah Botton,
Bulisa Abravaya beautiful, Estrella Matalon beautiful, Merkada the daughter of beautiful Rosa Galante
and I walk along with them on the sand and in the sea, my heart as red as pomegranates
and my face as yellow as an unblemished ethrog.
And they call out to each other, from window to window, and she says to her, and she says, Nissim Amira's younger
son is coming, the grandson of Moses Alkabetz is coming!
And I put a stone in my mouth, lest the words from my mouth come out as a cry, for I hear
the reading of the book and I do not understand, I see the names upon their faces and I cannot read.
And I take a piece of paper with letters and I fashion a likeness of people from the letters,
the letters call and speak and I remain silent from the pain –

David Morfugo sixth for the quorum, Israel Kapon seventh for the quorum, Yudah Kabillio eighth for the quorum,
Matityahu Rosanes ninth for the quorum and Moshoniko from the Land of Israel, may he rise and come forth,
tenth for the quorum.
And people see this great miracle and beat their heads against a rock, because ten people
have been laid to rest in the earth of the land of Tugar and covered in her dust. . .
The sea of Marmara, Marmara the sky blue sea, upon my face and upon my beard and this
pain is heavy from crying and from supplications, ten men will not endure the suffering.
And a man wanders about in those places, like ten men. And his shadow casts a shadow on the wall
as if it were alive, in light from the Light of Life. And the shades of cities' spirits rise up and cast a shadow

over my face and over my beard, like light from the Light of Life.
Haskoy shade of shades, Balat shade of shades, Balikasir shade of shades,
Izmir shade of a shade within a shade
and Istanbul my city, a shade upon every shade, like a thousand turrets.
And even were my tongue as long as a sword to tell, and my heart hard as steel to see,
whoever has seen all that, need see no further.
And whoever heard all this, has no need to ever hear more.
And I get up and put on my white clothes and take leave of that place, like someone retreating to the grave.

ONE DAY WE'LL BE OTHER

Since I'm here longer than I could have hoped. Since I'm here.
And I saw the stones and the knives the plowshares and the sticks and the fear.
Since I still see the light beating down upon the city and and the stone walls and the streets
and since I'm here, I came back to cross the scenery of words, the horizon and failure.
And I came and stood again at the ramparts of a distant city, to go off to the last war.
All because I'm here. Because I'm still here.
The fortifications of fear burst asunder. The cunning flanks of an enemy
sounding the call of attack behind the very lines of affliction.
Voices of the wounded like dreamers calling out the names of women the night through.
The standing of valor, of a whole life going out to yet another final battle, taking up the rear.
The vengeance of the solitary at the verge of defeat, in all this suffering and torment, all this beauty.
And the enormous emptiness surrounding, the silence and nothingness, with all the women and the children and the flocks
and the time wary of coming and the words.
One day we'll be other. We won't leave a thing carrying out hasty retreats.
At the borders of the desert and pools of turbid waters, we won't abandon yet another last fighter
trampled in the blood of his own dream.
One day it'll be otherwise—at the frontiers of infirmity and fear.

—*Translated from the Hebrew by Ammiel Alcalay*

SHLOMO AVAYOU

SHLOMO AVAYOU was born in Izmir, Turkey, in 1939; he came to Israel with his family in 1949 and now lives on Kibbutz Ga'ash near Tel Aviv. A native Judeo-Spanish speaker and student of Arabic and Turkish, Avayou brought new depth and sophistication to what had pejoratively come to be seen as the merely "ethnic" or "folkloric" works forming part of the virtual explosion of expression that came in the wake of *mizrahi* social and cultural movements in the 1970s. By stating (in "Fleeting Thrill") that "Origin is unimportant," Avayou refused the terms of categorization that both divided Israeli society and created a diverse set of limitations with myriad internal and external boundaries. At the same time, Avayou not only refused to negate his past, but mined the rich and variegated texture of personal and historical memory to recreate, if not home, then at least the conditions of home within a permanent state of exile. But even more importantly, Avayou has maintained a sense of autonomy by refusing simplistic nostalgia and insisting upon the complexities of a past read through the particular conditions of the present. His work spans a great formal and thematic range: By experimenting with traditional Hebrew verse forms and materials, he has created a dense and allusive body of work that constantly limns the borders between public and private concerns. An active member of Israeli PEN, he has also translated Catalan, Spanish, and Latin American poetry and prose into Hebrew. He is presently working on an opera in Judeo-Spanish called *La boda de los huercos* ("The wedding of the spirits") with the Uruguayan composer Leon Birioti. His books of poetry include: *Grass on the Threshhold* (1973), *Celestial Mirror* (1976), *Roots of the Sea* (1979), *Interior Shadow* (1984), and his latest work, *Compressed Strata.* He has also published two prose collections, *The Groaning Stairs* (1986) which appeared as *El ultimo niño de la Judería* in Buenos Aires in 1995, and *Stalagmites of Love* (1991). His most recent book *Cavallos en Jerusalen* ("Horses in Jerusalem"), came out in 1994. Two new collections, *Mahzor Sefarad* and *Silhouettes of Fire,* a series of twenty poems on the Holocaust of Balkan and Aegean Jewry, are in publication.

FLEETING THRILL

Origin is unimportant, even the
sources guiding me, the generations,
take them, just so a wooden gate
leading into a garden can be seen,
illuminating, inviting you in.

A fleeting thrill beneath some windows,
I was brought there by chance, abducted,
but like someone returning the streets
and the crowd swallowed me up

enforced by distance. The road's
strangeness, its whole length known,
gauges the pain. But in this there is
not even a spark from the fire in
the candle of a heart still yearning.

If they open up for me next time,
they'll recognize me and take me
in, right inside the rooms, and
for just a second I'll be home.

WILDWEED

Mother was still sixteen when
God's blaze laid the city waste.
A girl scurrying through the streets
among putrifying remains lying in wait.
West out of Izmir Greek refugees
vie for the sewers of Piraeus.
Smoke imprisons, heat flushes
the Armenians out of their crypts.
The blood of the innocent and the blood of whores
trickles out of her alleys down to the harbor.
Fire chastises her flesh, purifying
the city of all the nations' sailors.

After the Holocaust years of rain,
the run-off recklessly spilling down the mountain.
Noxious weeds and thorns of insolence
sprout from the altar within the church -
and wither under an indifferent summer sun.

Winter of '39: the scourge of
war, my mother delivers.

ODALISQUE OF THE LEVANT / AN ODE

The lore of rain is indeed ancient, the covenant of birds and roofs.
Vestal matrons administer bread, revered by everyone, wise hands,
daughters of all the tongues and nations. The sun dictates their daily
labor upon the stone-paved courtyards. Unto the very day that came to

deny such a city ever was: thickly bearded sages in long cloaks, mariners
navigating vessels of exile and deliverance through celestial jetties,
binding flesh to flesh with cords of fire. And in a frenzied climb to the
Lighthouse, armed with charged incantations and ethereal ladders,
    they storm the stronghold.

But she was really Neptune's widow, in whose sanctuary the marble torsoes
of naked men murmur Homeric hymns, a burial ground deep in bedrock,
    crypts
of moss. (After a squall marble shades spring abruptly out of the dust.)
    Now slim minarets, belltowers adorn her brow.

Or was she really the mistress of dreams attired in Oriental veils, gazing
out her window at the horizon, yearning to set sail, and be borne straight
through the High Gate to the Sultan's Palace (sometimes referred to as
Topkapi), to reign, from the Capital, in the House of Bliss, to the
    Golden Horn, over the high seas.

Here buccaneers from the Barbary Coast, facing the Frankish side, enlisted
    hands.
Straight off the deck, without so much as a gangplank, these guests leapt
into her waiting arms. How these mates, off Northern, Western and
Levantine fleets flew in hunger. Faithful, loaded with bounty,
    she welcomed them ashore.

Many a day they desired the embrace of her arms, the warmth of her thighs,
the softness of her white belly. And they tickle her mad all night long
with their wine-soaked beards and whiskers. The memory of her breasts
departs with them to the limitless depth of the sea, her mere name
anchors their very longing.

This abundance was decreed to perish, the harlot's flame to be extinguished
in her very chambers. Lashes of fire castigated this princess of love
and with a haughty laugh she descends to the sea from balconies
that were nothing less than flourishing gardens suspended in
space, intoxicated by spices, spirit, and flags.

An episode from the chronicles of a port, a city of oars. The wake left
after the daily sinking of a blazing horizon, a recurring miracle.
The cannon of the Citadel thundering noon from the mountaintop,
the city's sentinel, is mute today, held in check.

For the very day has come to claim such a city never was.

WASHERWOMAN UNDER A SHADY TREE

Your obedient forearms raise trunks
springing from the white swelling suds.
Like a cloud you bend over the water
in the washtub, heavy as steel.
Kneading with all your might
the seed and the sweat
the vain sighs soaked into the fabric
(the breath of solitude and intimacy).

And thus, still wringing out the wash
by the shade of the tree, you would
hear singing from the past, a song
of the ancient women's kind, opening
from the heart, a woman, your very soul
caged and shackled, ring by ring.
The song trickles away hopelessly
but its longing flows on spilling
out from a breast that holds
the source of both fire and milk.

This is the maidservant of my patriarchs, the men,
shifters of amber beads, tack upon tick and
tock upon tack. Wrapped in darkly woven gowns,
they would pass right by without seeing her.
Upon their mouths, their drooping mustaches,
and upon their heads, turbans the color of the sea.

MOTHERS WHISPERING INCANTATIONS

I intend to sing of mothers
backbreakingly bent over
perpetually reviving
our afflicted cribs.

Milk flows to us from between
their breasts unto the birthing
killing ground, nipples damp,
distended by fire.

Our mothers' eyes wait in the smoke.

FROM THE DESERT TO THE CITY VIA HOME

I was happy about the jasmine in my parent's garden,
about the potted hyacinth on their balcony.
Right by the huge Persian lilac that I planted
when I was a kid, I can see both of them, growing old.
Within the garden, right by the cypresses,
a fig tree offers them its unripe fruit.
My mother's heavy limbs ache and my father's
eyes have grown even dimmer than before.
The doctor tells him: "It's old age, Señor Avram,
there's nothing you can do about it."
And we the children say, let's get him
to a better doctor, to "Haddasah."
Here, in their courtyard, at my parents'
place, three medlar trees are blooming -
each at its own pace, each with its own taste.
A stingy, frustrated lemon tree

bears forth lemons with no juice.
November 73 is the time and the local line
covers Sinai to Kiryat Yovel Jerusalem. Rushing
to their comfort it occurs to me that,
when the time comes, it would truly be an act
of divine grace were my eyes to slowly
grow dim in a garden under the shade
of a woman and a Persian lilac.

YOU HAVE TO ABANDON JERUSALEM

Beneath the walls of Jerusalem
they excavate and expose—walls.
And what do they expect to find -
the shadow of the *shekhinah*
and an angel's wing?
For what do they burrow like mad?
Structures of walls upon walls
always close in to entrap.
If a man decides to finish himself off
and requires a vaulted ceiling
above him as if it were a marble sky
to link ancient steel rings
to the latest chains -
why, then, let him come
to Jerusalem, let him come!
A man craving to fall in love
at the very end of his withering years
in one last desperate attempt
to bear forth aching beauty -
let him come to Jerusalem, let him come.
But I remain a sceptic and
could not vanquish such a man
through extravagant demonstration.
I do believe it might just be wiser to go
down to the dwellings of the coastal plain,
upon the scattered shifting sands,
upright, unarmed before the sun.
Without seven city stratas

bitterness settles in under my bed
cursing and bewailing the night.

— Translated from the Hebrew by Ammiel Alcalay

EREZ BITTON

EREZ BITTON was born in Algeria and lives in Tel Aviv where he edits *Aperion,* a literary journal dedicated to Mediterranean and Middle Eastern culture. He has been extremely active for many years in cultivating relationships between and among intellectuals and artists in the region, and has traveled extensively to participate in meetings and conferences in both Europe and North Africa. One of the first poets to incorporate native Middle Eastern thematic, linguistic, and formal elements in his poetry, Bitton also performed dramatic recitals of his work to musical accompaniment. These poetic and musical performances, filled with joy, mourning, and intense human drama, released emotions that had long been held in check, and their public resonance marked the start of a new era in the open expression of the *mizrahi* experience. At the same time, while consistently categorized by the critical establishment as an "authentic" and "genuine" expression of Middle Eastern Jewry, much of Bitton's work explicitly and implicitly calls into question these very categories. His poem "Summary of a conversation" succinctly presents a dilemna that has faced not only *mizrahi* writers but anyone classified as "other" by a dominant culture. The question of authenticity, as posed in the text, can never be resolved within the binary possibilities "offered" within a skewed relationship, where there is a clear imbalance of power. Here, as in so many other poems by Bitton, resolution is found within the self, within the physical body, within sensation itself. This sense of resolve, "I fall between the circles / lost in the medley of voices," might seem more like loss and confusion to a reader unfamiliar with the sources of Bitton's sustenance. But here, the central theme has much more to do with the bitterly ironic circumstances following a childhood accident in which he was blinded. Playing in an abandoned orchard in Lod, he discovered an old grenade. Picking it up cost him his eyes and the partial use of an arm, but it also brought him to one of the better institutions for the blind, where he received the kind of education that those he left behind could never even have dreamed of. Thus, while being "lost in a medley of voices" alludes to the complexities of identity, it also rep-

resents familiarity and assurance. In addition to being read reductively as a representative of his race, many readers have also missed the acute pain and bitterness that Bitton has continued to nurture in his poetry. These feelings are used as an oppositional tool, an ironic weapon in which the tongue can be unsheathed to speak "another Hebrew." As an aside to one of the poems included below, it is worthwhile noting that a popular anthology, *The Modern Hebrew Poem Itself,* refers to Zohra al-Fasiya, the legendary Moroccan singer that Bitton writes of in one of his most well-known poems, as a "fictive" character. In addition to the continuing popularity of Zohra al-Fasiya's old recordings, she was also the subject of a one-woman show by the actress Shosha Goren. Bitton's most recent book, *A Bird Between Continents* (1990), is a selection from his two previous collections, *The Book of Mint Tea* and *Moroccan Offering.*

FAMILIES AT A SCHOOL FOR THE BLIND IN JERUSALEM

And us kids at the school for the blind in Jerusalem,
seven kids would grab another kid
and tell him
you be our father
and tell her
you be our mother,
the body of one kid stumbling upon the body of another,
an apparent encounter
to gather warmth,
at least as far as meets the eye.
And making families, families,
and calling one kid: Father Shalom
and another, Mother Shoshannah,
and the girl I used to call my sister my sister Rachel
and the boy my brother my brother Yossi
that's how we'd make make-believe families
us kids at the school for the blind in Jerusalem.

AT A SCHOOL FOR THE BLIND IN JERUSALEM

And us kids at the school for the blind in Jerusalem
hid on tiptoe, cheeks glued to the glass door
to hear the melody of your harp,
Ephraim Manopla.

Beyond the alien hallways
like noisy nightingales,
blindfoldedly singing.
You, who promised great romantic symphonies,
what do you say now
as you wring out a pittance
with your broken, three-stringed mandolin
at the Central Bus Station in Tel Aviv.

HOARSE *RABABA*

What are you searching me for, the palate of another time,
juice of a big watermelon
sparkling date pits
what are you searching me for, hands to play the "five" game with?
I went out with a harp to coax fertility,
I came back singed.
In vain now do
the little *tam-tam* drums summon lovers' fingers to me
in vain does summer's desire drive thirst from the apple of my eyes
two ruptured troughs
now
my heart is dead to white veils.
To the juice of a great watermelon.
Now
I am a hoarse *rababa* in the bosom of darkness.

EMENDATION OF THE AROMAS

What do want from me already,
the taste of *'arak* and the scent of burnt saffron,
I'm no longer the same kid,
lost amongst the legs of pool players
at Marco's Cafe
in Lod.
Now, my friends,
I am learning to eat ice cream from a crystal bowl,
from a car that emanates the chirping of birds
at evening,

I learn how to open doors
in ancient musical measure.

Now
strawberry flavored women
teach me to inhale volumes of Shakespeare,
from the seventeenth century,
teach me to play Siamese cat,
in a green living room,
my friends.

SUMMARY OF A CONVERSATION

What does it mean to be authentic,
to run through the middle of Dizengoff and shout in Moroccan Jewish
dialect:
"Ana min el-Maghreb, Ana min el-Maghreb"
(I'm from the Atlas Mountains, I'm from the Atlas Mountains).

What does it mean to be authentic,
to sit in the Cafe Roval in brightly flowing robes,
or to proclaim out loud: My name isn't Zohar, I'm Zayish, I'm Zayish.

Neither this nor that,
but despite everything another language moistens the tongue to the point of
renting the gums asunder,
and despite everything the repressed and beloved aromas are overpowering
and I fall between the circles
lost in the medley of voices.

SHOPPING SONG ON DIZENGOFF

I bought a shop on Dizengoff
to strike some roots
to buy some roots
to find a spot at the Roval
but
the crowd at the Roval
I ask myself

who are these folks at the Roval,
what's with these people at the Roval,
what's going on with the people at the Roval,
I don't face the people at the Roval
but when the people at the Roval turn to me
I unsheathe my tongue
with clean words,
Yes, sir,
please, sir,
very up-to-date Hebrew,
and the buildings looming over me here
tower over me here,
and the openings open here
are impenetrable for me here.
At dusk
I pack my things
in the shop on Dizengoff
to head back to the outskirts
and another Hebrew.

MOROCCAN WEDDING

1.

Who never saw a Moroccan wedding in their day -
We heard we heard
your blessed hands arched over the *tam-tam* drums,
Sarah, Dodo's daughter,
from one end of the village to the other end of the village
Arabs and Jews arrive.
We saw we saw
the kegs of *'arak,* the spits of roasted pigeon,
the layers of dates amongst the seven kinds
at the entrance to the house,
the proud jugs of olives,
your blessed hands arched over the *tam-tam* drums,
Sarah, Dodo's daughter,
Arabs and Jews, Come in!
Slowly our hearts expand and our souls rejoice.

2.

Ayima
ten birds want to sever themselves from my torso,
dear, as dear to my soul
as a Buskri date
which is the sweetest date of all
your lips are two dates
Buskri dates which are the sweetest of all
Ayima
I bear the light of that evening like the unsung burden of happiness.
Ayima
I feel like the land is two cubits lower than I am
my dear, dearest to my soul
your neck is like a fine handprint,
like the finger of fingers
adorning the fetters of my heart.
And they will still claim: Since your wedding there has been no wedding like
    your wedding.

3.

I also want salad of baked peppers, skinned at the start,
and seasoned with ten spices,
mother,
I also want bread and a hard boiled egg with *lebzar* and cummin beaten into it.

TE TE TE TE TE TE

TE TE TE TE TE TE TE TE TE

on the *tanbul.*
Naq-te'ish, that you may live, Sheikh Hassan.
Drink a glass of *'arak* with me, Sheikh Hassan.
You didn't have to bring all these gifts, my dear Abu Muhammad.
And you, playing the *tanbul,*
why are you off all alone in the corner while we rejoice in your music.

4.

Whoever hasn't been to a Moroccan wedding,
whoever hasn't seen Grandmother Freha
climb the scales of desire in the ears of the bride and groom,
whoever hasn't sat on the ground on bright featherbed cushions and Atlas
pillows,
whoever hasn't ripped the bread with their own two hands,
whoever hasn't dipped into a flowing salad and washed it down with wine
from Marrakesh,
whoever hasn't breathed in the fresh yearning of our fledglings,
whoever hasn't been to a Moroccan wedding,
here is a ticket,
come on in
to the disturbances
of the heart
that you couldn't ever kill.

ZOHRA AL-FASIYA'S SONG

singer at Muhammad the Fifth's court in Rabat, Morocco
they say when she sang
soldiers fought with knives
to clear a path through the crowd
to reach the hem of her skirt
to kiss the tips of her toes
to leave her a piece of silver as a sign of thanks

Zohra al-Fasiya

now you can find her in Ashkelon
Antiquities 3
by the welfare office the smell
of leftover sardine cans on a wobbly three-legged table
the stunning royal carpets stained on the Jewish Agency cot
spending hours in a bathrobe
in front of the mirror
with cheap make-up

when she says

Muhammad Cinque

apple of our eyes

you don't really get it at first

Zohra al-Fasiya's voice is hoarse
her heart is clear
her eyes are full of love

Zohra al-Fasiya

ON THE EARTHQUAKE IN AGADIR

That evening
the sky was blue to its gilded depth,
the earth silent, in the stillness of an ambush,
and those who remember say
the air was sweet to your breast,
on a Tuesday evening it was.
How does it happen,
oh mother, mother,
that respectable people, their minds at ease,
had to get up at once and grope around screaming in the dark.
And afterward,
oh mother, mother,
what does someone think sitting
before the remains of their house,
before the loss of their loved ones.
What's the first thing they do
that very morning.
Oh mother, mother,
would that the morning never come
and those who remember say
that on that evening
there was a sweet desire for sleep,
on a Tuesday evening it was,
oh mother.

SULIKA'S QASIDA

1.

Sulika, well known in Moroccan Jewish folklore.
A young woman whose beauty was notorious throughout the land;
the story goes that when rumor of her got to the King's son,
Ben Idris the Prince,
he took her straight to his palace in Rabat.

After some time had passed, she was found dead.
Laden under a canopy, adorned in all her jewels,
they say she looked more beautiful dead than alive.

2.

I come back again and again to turn your pages and mine,
here on the sidewalks of Ramat Gan I imagine myself calm
even though I know and hear the great clamor
like the blow your name then struck in my ears
at a party with Moroccan friends
ma'aquda in a plate and roasted peppers in a plate
and Kolomber wine in glasses
and a clean napkin across my knees.

3.

Your name struck like a blow then
around the glasses
and I felt your name
like a screen of tenderness and delicate beauty among those people
like the scent of sweets in the midst of conversation
around the table.
It was only me who felt like that
the blood rushed to my head
and the wine spilled on the clean napkin
spread out over my knees.
And I continue thumbing through and turning the pages in me
touching and not touching memory of you digested across generations.
From the thirteenth century to the fourteenth,
a cloud of tender remembrance

seized no longer than can be grasped
for better or worse all at once
I looked like a madman at that party
with spittle on my chin, spots on my shirt
so unpleasant to talk to
for me you weren't just the scent of sweets
at an evening spent with Moroccan friends.

4.

Departure's blow strikes me at the break of dawn
and all my limbs hide in the walls
but from those very walls I have snared the echo of their shadows.
Oh mother mother how could a whole life have passed one morning
how could my life have passed one morning?

5.

You old women of the house gossipmongers
you who anointed my feet with oil of Marrakesh
give me a blessing on my way to Rabat
for there is no other road but the road to Rabat.

You young women of the *mellah*
sisters to the creation of the bread in the clay oven,
give me a blessing on my way to Rabat
because there is no other road but the road to Rabat.

Your way to Rabat will be sweetened
our night sister in the revelry of date palms.
Your way to Rabat will be sweetened
you who sweetened our aging eyes.
Bear greetings upon the road to Rabat.

6.

Give me a hand good people before drowning
give me brightly colored cushions
and pillows of silk
to warm up before this cold in my heart.

7.

They robbed me of the blackness of your eyes in the middle of the day
Sulika
in the middle of the day they took the purity of your face away from me
the grace of your profile at the threshold Sulika
they snatched my life, my very life from me Sulika

SOMETHING ON MADNESS

And you ask that we not get dizzy like an angry squall.
And you ask that we sigh over allusions
through cigar smoke
or at most a rhymed whistle,
but our sighs are like a tempest.
We were loathsome to you,
our impact was hard and strange
yet why did you cast us out upon our birthplace
why did you banish us to all the ruins,
you stand at the brink of laughter, perplexed, lawless,
you stand bewildered before the lamenting,
but what was the revolt about,
for surely how can it be possible that in a place where vented
anger arouses lamentation even in the heart of dogs
in a place where great rage condemns us upon all the crucifixes
that our laments will not be foreign,
our mourning not superfluous,
and you keep on giving flimsy excuses
claiming not to really cry
except at the mere suggestion -
through cigar smoke or at most a rhymed proclamation of despair -
you claim to be indifferent
in a place where people are brought up
with sterilized tweezers
in a place where even the earth is redolent of spikenard bound by nocturnal sea,
you who scattered us to all the ruins
you who transferred us to all the shanties
do at least this much for us,
leave us to our laments
we shattered pearls of verse.

PARABLE FOR THE LAYING OF THE FOUNDATION OF THE HOUSE

to the victims of war in the Middle East

And we what are we, the stuff of wandering,
straying and straying,
a parable for the laying of the foundation of the house.
And I asked that you be
one of the olive saplings
storing up within you the fruit's promise,
the code of ripe old age.
And I asked that you be
like the foot of a date-palm inundated by mighty waters.
And I know they will come now
to appease and to glorify
and I asked that you just be,
that you be present.

—*Translated from the Hebrew by Ammiel Alcalay*

AMIRA HESS

AMIRA HESS was born in Baghdad and now lives in Jersualem. Though she began publishing late, she counts the renowned sixteenth-century woman poet and teacher Osnat Bat Barazani among her direct ancestors. Hess's poetry is often written in the almost hallucinatory language of the Prophets, but the demons that have come to inhabit their figures of speech reflect and refract other realities, like in a hall of mirrors. Sudden shifts in tone cut across thousands of years as the cedars of Lebanon or Judah weeping are confronted by "poetry of the rock and the roll savagery encircled by "uncles," dances / from the jungle calling TAM TAM TAM." Almost in code, Hess's poetry is fueled by a rage of love that refuses to give up claims on any part of her pain, any part of her ambivalence. Her work has been essential in reclaiming for Hebrew poetry, and particularly for women, the variegated uses of a native semitic diction and elevated rhetoric whose ties manage to remain closer to traditional culture than to texts mediated through the framework of conventional literary history. Her knowledge of Hebrew linguistic context and usage is deep, highly sensitive to untapped semantic possibilities, and constantly informed by the need to safeguard the bastion of her texts by allowing words to embody their own internal critique. At the same time, her radical questioning of personae, sexual identity and desire, historical continuity, and language itself puts her poetry at the forefront of that combination of formal innovation and emotional intensity that has come to characterize a certain kind of "postcolonial" writing. Her books to date are *And the Moon Drips Madness* (1984), *Two Horses on the Line of Light* (1987), and *The Information Eater* (1993).

THERE WAS A TIME: AN INTERVIEW WITH AMIRA HESS BY AMMIEL ALCALAY

In 1986 I saw you with Sami Michael on Yaron London's show and he expressed amazement about a poem where you wrote of Baghdad and Trafalgar Square, like it was some mystical or impossible connection. After an awkward silence, Sami Michael said; "After all, Iraq was under British rule and there are parts of Baghdad that look a lot like Trafalgar Square. " I use this as an example of the kind of non-understanding or lack of consciousness about that world, and how people from it are always categorized as representatives of it. Can you talk about your own ways out of these kinds of assumptions that are supposed to describe you and your work?

I would begin with the question of how one gets out of this. Or, rather, what is it I am supposed to be getting out of. I begin from the initial fact that I am myself. I was brought into this world in order to reach perfection, in every sphere, and I have to be strong enough to perfect my own inner world and my self in order to develop to my utmost capabilities. Until not very long ago, I was under the influence of all the various stigmas, each miserly and mean-spirited in its own way, that prevailed in this country. But I came from a wonderful family, extremely well-educated, wealthy, people who really did have "British manners." It was as if I was a blue-blood starting to turn a bit yellow, first in the eyes of others and then in my own eyes. I felt as if my blood was being drained and I was being turned into something I had never been, something not nice. Yet I had come from a very loving family, a family that respected others even more than themselves, with very high spiritual values, giving and caring and involved in public and communal affairs. I relied on the strongest side of myself here, so that my personality wasn't completely broken even though, in some sense, it was shattered into fragments. The only thing that pulled me through was the illusion I had that I hadn't been fully shattered. But there remains this feeling of nothingness, a human feeling of being null and void, of being a carpet under the feet of others who don't even have the vaguest idea what living culture means, people who only understand their own troubles. When I am critical though, I have to start with myself for only then do I have the right to speak. Despite the anger that exists, I first have to comb out all the curls in that anger so that love and grace emerge. If they put scorpion's blood in me, I would do everything I could to make it blue again. Even if I was sentenced to the hell of distancing myself from the home of my parents and reliving the death of all those who were burned in every ghetto there ever was, I would still come through to tell of it.

Your first book had enormous power, the amount of subconscious material was highly condensed through the complexity of language and structure; what kind of processes did you go through in your later work?

With that book, my damaged humanity, my damaged ego, had been embraced in some way; that helped stitch the flesh but it did not stitch my spirit. Think of flesh that has been stitched but there is a broken wing, teeming fear, falling into black holes—all of this is within my body. The poetry slowly gave me self-confidence, the feeling that with the passage of time there was suddenly this moment of embrace. But I was sceptical about this too because I thought that even with that touch, only a drop from the typhoon within me had come out. What would happen were I to let it all go? I don't know if I would even love myself. My cousin is serving in Gaza now, for instance, and he was telling me about the things he sees there, about people killing each other. I told him that if they're killing each other they're actually killing themselves because that's the point we've brought them to; it's we who've brought them to this inner suicide. For me there are no nationalities or religions, I am someone who exists within creation. In the second book, there was a thrust toward obliterating myself, going into the abyss, from fear of myself and everything else. When I read my poems, it was only then that I begin to consciously understand them but conscious understanding can also make you stop. I have thousands of pages that I don't know will ever see the light of day or whether I even want them to. Sometimes I just want to burn them, because I have guilt feelings, towards myself, toward my brothers—and they love me dearly. I feel as if I am uncovering their very souls, because I speak their feelings. I clash between the modest and innocent East within me and consciousness, which is not an innocent thing. I have turned into a person who is not innocent by any means and that makes me very sad. It is said that as a person matures, they lose their innocence. I have torn through many curtains beyond those that go with the orderly passing of time, and that makes it very difficult, for you become transparent and you see through things. I feel like I am a person of great compassion, I am even compassionate with those who hate me, simply because we are human, in spite of ourselves. This lets me out of that meager little thing we call self-respect. My self-respect can play a role in a variety of places, but not in these wider spheres, for we are truly nothing under heaven's dome.

—*Translated from the Hebrew by Ammiel Alcalay*

from AND THE MOON DRIPS MADNESS

There was a time
when I'd have said:
I won't defile myself
with this contemptible Orient,
I'll relegate my ancestral
home to oblivion,
my mother's owlish visage
weeping over the ruins,

my father's face like a cherub -
the Lord—graced him not.
And I also said:
the West, for instance,
has no caress to its spirit,
well-done within, singed to the shrouds.
East and West I'll set out in a strong beat
for there is no ark
to bestir myself, if daughter
departs more spirit
to make eagles soar.

—*Translated from the Hebrew by Ammiel Alcalay*

AND AS FAR AS WHAT I WANTED

And as far as what I wanted to further explain to you
what every sign says.
After all, surely you understand the way of colors,
the gilded light, the chlorophyll light,
the light of pain and the light of need and vigilant light
and the light of an arc in the sky
splitting through again to seed with drops of sun suddenly bursting
the essence of yearning.
The light of the eyes of dogs
shine loyalty in the dark to their masters.
The growing shadow of darkness placed late
in fading time.
How the radiant blackness disseminates its night
and how the arrows' whiteness smothers its light
how everything is lucid from so much pain.

—*Translated from the Hebrew by Yonina Borvick*

THEN SLAKE HIM FROM

Then slake him from
A wineskin flowing and a wineskin of milk and a wineskin of loveliness
Kiss and weep, for the time of loving has come.
Woman-dust-earth seeped into the lust in his touch
Keen after him
Kiss his footprints
Do not bind his freedom.
Place him as a cock
Rising early, at sun's fire,
As a madman, his body screaming desire.

—*Translated from the Hebrew by Marsha Weinstein*

WE'RE CHILDREN OF ATLANTIS

remnants alighting from the
sea
immigrant
busts.
And there are brigades of cavalry
stumbling as they gallop.
The golden horse pulls down the priestly vestment
his face resplendent.
Month of May moon
I didn't see moons
months I didn't count days
I just saw blood and took my pulse.
The Lebanon cries out to the cedars of Goshen.
Judah cry not Judah
rotting further in the dust
your eyes veiled
in terror. Dread heaven
sent deloused
municipal decree—cry not Judah.
Don't weep chosen
over the babble in paradise no-land
the poetry of mint stirs

onion poetry of the rock and the roll
savagery encircled by "uncles," dances
from the jungle calling TAM TAM TAM.

Restore me Oh Lord to my sister's bosom
set me upon the *gopher* wood
Oh Lord bring me back to the ark of Jeshurun
directly.
Turn my visage on a festive day to a vow of radiant
light good souls holding on to the world's foundation.

★ ★ ★ ★ ★

Inasmuch as the day breaks
I had been hoping night would fall
to continue sleeping as deeply as possible,
to gird up greater forgetting power to be forgotten
before you, inasmuch as the day breaks to get up
I wasn't oblivious already
because I wanted to go on to utter ruin
more and more,
but didn't have the strength
to ask myself
for a little more sleep without getting up in bed.

Wandering from world to world
surely even my father would
speak at some point and say -
"All in all dwarf you
haf face covered up in specs
wear minimal hat
go on
wear hat to the max."

Between tone and slumber
now seems like a passage
from letter to letter
from a high octave *do*
to *sol* on another octave's scale,
coming down many thresholds
face to face within my very being which, after all,
only asked to be born naked and simply.

Hebrew's a nice language for revolvers one generation to the next
looking for a source out of their slumber
as they tarry upon the hook of retention.
Lest it not find favor in my eyes
the realm of my garments overthrown
in the womb of holy scribes from Barazan,
I'm having a hard time finding a way out in origins
sometimes discovering my face by surprise
settling for tricks by the side of the road
crossing over another layer.

Yesterday I dreamt how the Nile rolled over its banks
and I saw the Delta inscribed upon the waters.
As I was still looking for other estuaries I suddenly
beheld interpretations on my palms
and between furrow and furrow
a white line of snow stood out
and the Delta was trampled by the running.
Afterwards the Nile made the water blue
as if a cycle of time had been shifted
and Mount Ararat was dislodged from its place
barren wastelands stood out covered with lavender
their peaks slightly green.

An armored car behind me
an ancient carriage before me
veering to the right, and the color of mud the color of mire.

I still stumble to catch up with the steps taken before me
the niche has been breached
and sparkling water bathes my face.
And we were kind of an assembly of people
from the first generation
unto the great-grandchildren.
My father was absent from his place
since he died while still alive,
and I didn't know if we gave birth,
if only my face was bathed,
if I'm the great-granddaughter,
if I'm a member of the tribe,

if my language is literal
if my lips speak the language of fresh twigs.
(That's how I remembered my anger
at their shutting their intent
to see the Aswan Dam
and the pyramids
from my eyes.)

And I still thought I governed myself that I had come for a little rest
without having to make much effort, except eating and drinking
bundles of lemons growing, pepper trees on the ceiling
I wanted to pick
so mother wouldn't get scared,
but she already took the initiative to go
to the other room, leading to the open field,
causing the sorrow in our hearts to arise anew.
She departs aware that she's going
and I'm aware of her departure.

I'm still disturbed by the form of the lemon that grew on the ceiling
like a yellow candelabra
and behold, a light is lit in my window.
I didn't reign in the switches
presuming someone always kindles a light in my dreams.
Something turns topsy-turvy,
something runs amok,
the world is poised to change its face,
whether Persian lilac or sprouts of
orchid, whether an abundance of
rolling sandalwood beats
against my window and wakes me to tell
of the Nile's blueness even
more splendid than that other blue.

— *Translated from the Hebrew by Ammiel Alcalay*

from THE INFORMATION EATER

The time of the singing birds will become the depths of poverty

1.

and beyond the unknown
I will yet know we don't know everything
and the thing of totality
that's the black holes
that I burn after you
cloaked face ablaze

and reason for this suffering

2.

I banished the forsaken from myself
and tonight amongst horses neighing like jackals -
how come

3.

if it was possible to give
to the soul via the body
for me to burn unto you without this suffering
spirits in flight perishing to block
the totality of the holes
until we know not

4.

the cycles the cycles their surface like hornets
the cycles why symbiotic
to tell me not to leave the house
not to run about to and fro and to tell me
not knowing whither without where to go no
place -

5.

I'm afraid of the library
and what's between its shelves to search in the letters
little birds pain the wings within me

6.

seems to me I'll have a saint's face
and find it had been used sometimes
and there were times I was a memorial flame
and flowers on someone's balcony
needing neither dung nor water
my face from which only a sunflower will emerge
without wasteland -

7.

and under this sun
normalcy will be bred if it can
without the grief of parental doctrine hit home lying in wait
from my two eyes and my mother's voice as it sings so like an infant pecking
away
and just think my breasts playthings sucked out from sucking
and what milk's left me to give the kids
within a spirit closed
quite hollowed out to nourish
where both our voices stop
in do re mi -

8.

and all this from that windowsill
I saw the dove brooding over time
and her rounded eyes embroiled lashes
the pulleys entangled within
pyres of melancholy
and longing for the openings out -

9.

and my mother asks: have you got flowers
in the garden
people want to see flowers
and when there's a garden in the wastelands of sustenance
in the wilds of that jungle of yours
echoing
I want to see your hair
like a field
in that man's room
so I know you're my daughter -

10.

I am Amira
going in my own captivity
and I have a papa buried on the Mount of Olives

the silence of the hush within me we have in common
and the hair brushing on my neck
if I was his secret
if his silent reigns bound me
without release -

11.

And there is a revolution on my face
as if I had been suddenly formed
and from a shorn lamb I had come to the raiments of favor and grace
and clemency and great reverence before the grief of my existence
in the stratosphere,
bottleneck of my soul.

12.

There are waters there are mighty waters
at salt's threshold.

13.

There are tremendous waters
my face is an ocean.

14.

And beneath your beauty if anything happens to me
I will see this night
and we shall gaze
ourselves above like a torch
and the eyes will shed tears in a blaze of fire.

For that's how we are the wind –

And I took upon myself the yoke of your love
to reckon ourselves within the midst of the cry

until I'd not be able to have left that night
the depths of my shriek's range
that day my mother gave birth to me
instructing my soul that it be thus with me
flying between the dreams
and kindred contentions
given birth into nature's lap
for I was born astern
and the sudden brilliance of the cord seemed real to me –

15.

and how can one migrate to the inner
depths as over the surface of flesh and blood?
Go in and go out and scandal bangs me –

16.

I'll know and summon you
gather spirit to bind me to the altar
and place your eyes upon me to brand me and hunger for me
to ride

and make it if you want I'll spread
and if not I'll want it open
to come
time diving into buoyancy

—*Translated from the Hebrew by Ammiel Alcalay*

LEV HAKAK

LEV HAKAK was born in Baghdad in 1944 and came to Israel with his family during the mass immigration from Iraq. He now lives in Los Angeles where he is a professor in the Department of Near Eastern Languages at UCLA. Hakak was one of the first *mizrahi* writers of the generation that grew up in Israel to confront the social issues facing *mizrahi* Jews through his academic and literary activities. His *Inferiors and Superiors: Oriental Jews in the Hebrew Short Story* (1981) was a groundbreaking study of the representation of *mizrahi* Jews in mainstream Israeli fiction. A poet and prose writer, Hakak has depicted the dilemnas facing an emigre Jewish Israeli writer with particular emotional depth and literary art. His poetry refers directly to the tradition of classical medieval Hebrew poetry, while his prose attempts to interrogate and dissect stereotypes and assumptions from within the narrative structure itself. His first book of poetry, *Still Bound in Spring,* appeared in 1962. This was followed by *My Lord, You Are Good* (1963) and *If I Forget Thee* (1981); his latest collection is *To Bequeath Hebrew Poetry in Los Angeles* (1988). Other books by Lev Hakak include two novels, *The Ingathered* (1977) and *Stranger Among Brothers* (1984), as well as the critical works *With Four Poets: Avraham Ben Yitzhak, Amir Gilboa, Natan Zakh and Shlomo Zamir* (1977), *Episodes in Oriental Jewish Literature* (1985), and *Equivocal Dreams* (1991). His lastest book, *A House on the Hill,* appeared in 1994.

THE HISTORY OF LITERATURE. POETS

The few different and innocent
sing of the deeds of their heart
rejoicing in verbal acrobatics
sing us one of the songs of your heart

They dispatch a silent tune over the night waves
to redeem the world with poetry and song only to pay wholeheartedly for
the conflagration
for the poem to be borne to understanding and stature
a single song for a thousand violins

Their plague is subsidized in books
as they call crumbs delicacies
gazing in awe over the tidbits of winking politicians
sifting words through thousands of facets

maybe their echo will reach a handful of the pure
in downy-bearded awe at verbal acrobatics
before they're worn out by the burden of kids and taxes

— *Translated from the Hebrew by Yonina Borvick and Ammiel Alcalay*

POEM CONTEMPLATING POETS

And Saul spear in hand
as David's hand is playing

a good fellow
and the Kingdom will be his:
he brought down the house
with his heartbreaking tunes.

And Saul heard. And Saul saw.
And an evil spirit entered him
and struck him and the wall -
and these are the generations of the masters of song
every day and every hour

behold the
corner of your cloak in my hand
and Saul saw
and David his hand playing
for I have slain you
when I cut off the corner of your cloak and did not slay you.
Is this the voice of David my son

answered Saul his voice trembling and breaking
David playing by hand
and Saul spear in hand

— Translated from the Hebrew by Yonina Borvick and Ammiel Alcalay

LETTER TO IBN GABIROL

Los Angeles, April 1987
parted from my brother my house my coffin
I scorn those around me unsuited even to be dogs to my flock

This spring again I won't go over
I hear you Ibn Gabirol
I am coming to you Ibn Gabirol
you have been cast out from the pores of my skin
you are the one who understands, because you're my age
and the spring is bewitched and you're a wizard
of anger refined by feet and vowels

Your heart called out from the wilderness
what will be is what was
your throat was parched in calling out then
come on, let's have a Coke
I stole—but did not deny—your words:
did you take them with you to the grave
covered with clumps of your wrath?

Did the one who uncovers the depths reveal intelligence to you?

I leaf through "Editorial Announcements"
a restive young camel doubling back on her tracks
a literary journal from twenty years ago
who requested who gave who "borrowed" who replied
who demanded who confirmed who designated who lectured
and who inspected the youngsters with a wink
without failing to feast their eyes
on the young men who were playing
who was thrown out who took a cut at the end of the year
who was anointed and appointed the one to wear the seasonal crown

who whored around who jerked off who lamented who did sorcery
who looked and was terrified and trampled underfoot
who harvested who snatched who caused blight who persecuted
and what kind of odor emanated from all this
who asked to be recognized in Hebrew letters
but was finished off and ended up in convulsions
or a chamberpot

and priests of beauty and the artists' brush
who dropped out tired of lice and lamentations

— *Translated from the Hebrew by Ammiel Alcalay*

BRACHA SERRI

BRACHA SERRI was born in San'a, Yemen, and now lives between Jerusalem and Berkeley. She studied Linguistics and Hebrew at the Hebrew University before going on to complete an M.A. in Linguistics and Education. She has worked in sociolinguistic research on Yemenite dialects with the prominent linguists Professors Haim Blanc and Haim Rabin, and taught in a wide variety of contexts, from university level to high school and adult education. Her often overtly political and feminist poetry also draws heavily on the linguistic and metaphoric tradition of the great Yemenite religious poets such as Shalom Shabazi. Serri has never shied away from bringing the full weight of judgement and traditional morality into the context of radical politics. A playwright as well as a poet, her play *The Tear* ran for over a year and toured twice, in 1985-86 and 1988-89. Her books include *Sacred Cow* (1991), *Red Heifer* (1990), and *Seventy Wandering Poems* (1983); her poetry has also been anthologized in *The Tribe of Dinah* (1989).

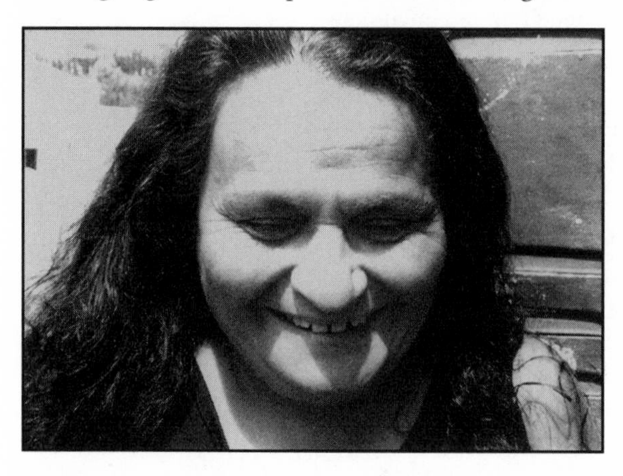

I AM THE DAUGHTER OF LOT

I am the daughter of Lot
you are all smitten with blindness
and I have not known a man.
You are men of Sodom.
Smitten with blindness.
Like a turbid wave raging
to break down the door
and know the messengers
instead of hearing the decree
and learning its lesson.
Pay heed to the warning
save yourselves from the epidemic.

I am the daughter of Lot.
I know the men of my city.
Smitten with blindness
and stupid.
Bursting to break down the door.
Striking the messengers
instead of drawing conclusions
to avoid disasters.
I am the daughter of Lot.
Alone. Understanding
no man will escape with me
from the valley of slaughter.
I am the daughter of Lot.
Silent as my mother who became a pillar of salt
such a dreadful pillar of remembrance.
I am the daughter of Lot
and you are smitten with blindness.

—*Translated from the Hebrew by Yonina Borvick and Ammiel Alcalay*

THE NOMAD IN ME

(returning from the Valley of Hinom)

The nomad in me
Churned up blood
Split heart
Beating in me
From the ancient days of Joshua.
Wandering the hills
The hill of Benjamin
To lament my youth in the mountains.
To lament my innocent virginity
Like the daughter of Jephtah the mighty.
To lament my love in the vineyards
Like Ruth who was torn away from her father's house.
To gather my limbs
Scattered throughout the land,
the land of the dozen tribes.
Snuggling in God's wing

Embracing the world and its fullness.
Torn between a husband I love
And a dear father far away
And the thousands of males
That are thirsty for
My blood
That swarm to my warm orifices
Tearing me to shreds.
Raped, torn, and loving
My body profaned and impure
Outlawed to my husband.
My jealous husband
Taking revenge
On my dozen limbs
Scattered throughout the land.
Nava Elimelech was not the first.
My churning blood
My scattered limbs
Lamenting my loves in the mountains
And cursing the earth forever
My blood boiling,
still unavenged.
Cursing the earth for the hatred of brothers.
My churning blood
My limbs scattered through the mountains
Seeking to reunite
Seeking to fuse
To the end of all generations.
Compressing the earth
And spewing forth its inhabitants.
My limbs scattered through the mountains
Dry the rains
Seeding tombstones and graves
My limbs scattered through the mountains
My holy loves that were desecrated
Churn up the hearts of young boys
My limbs scattered through the mountains
My churning blood
Reap boys from the grave.

—Translated from the Hebrew by Nava Mizrahhi

DISH

Mother cooked meat in the pot,
a tasty dish
to make you healthy.
They cooked me
in a song
- alive -
to make you happy.

Someone slaughtered me.
A ritual slaughter!
- make no mistake -
He cut me to pieces,
threw salt on the wounds
to draw the blood.
Oh, he kept strictly
to the rites!
Immersed me in water,
waited the set time.
Someone else came,
put the water to boil,
castigated my flesh.
Someone roasted me over a fire,
someone fried me in hot oil,
and added pungent spices.

May my spirit rise,
sweet incense
in your nostrils,
to awaken
your body's
senses.

— Translated from the Hebrew by Yaffa Berkovits

JERUSALEM AND SAN'A

Jerusalem on high
and San'a down below
are one.
One is my city
a patchwork of color,
a Babel of sounds
and smells.
The same openness
the same majesty.
An old woman's blessing
like a neighbor's.
The same yearnings
the same prayers.
God has moved
to Jerusalem the capital.
Old Jerusalem
not the young one.

I longed to kiss
these strangers,
our "enemies,"
to whisper my thanks
that they exist
as in days gone by
never to return.

I become a hovering dream
in the lanes of the Old City
a tiny spirit
from Yemen
which is no more.
Intoxicated by the scents
tipsy with the sounds
the perfumes, the spices,
aromatic coffee
dried figs and almonds
assorted raisins
saffron and myrrh
Sweet incense

Souvenirs
from the Temple.

— *Translated from the Hebrew by Yaffa Berkovits*

TO HOLD THE WORLD

To hold the world tight
In the palm of your hand
Crush it and squeeze it
As fine as sand
Toss it to the winds
Cast it to the deep
And then in silence
Lie down to sleep

— *Translated from the Hebrew by Yaffa Berkovits*

YEHEZKEL KEDMI

YEHEZKEL KEDMI was born in Jerusalem and still lives there; homeless for many years, he was last working as a cook and dishwasher in the kitchen of an elite school for artistically gifted children. As he recounts in the following interview, he spent much of his youth and a good part of his adult life on the streets and is a complete autodidact, expanding his range of interests while working as a night watchman at Hebrew University. His remarkable book-length poems are reminiscent of the work of Uri Zvi Greenberg; in terms of his use of language, the structure of his poetry, his thematic concerns and historical resonance, Kedmi is unquestionably one of the most essential and important of contemporary Hebrew poets. In one of the only articles written about him (published by Erez Bitton in his journal *Aperion*), the poet Hertzl Hakak wrote: "Kedmi sees himself as the speaker for those who have been made mute. The *mizrahi* house that he depicts hoards everything: the cold, the tempest, the alienation. . . .The *mizrahi* house is the last place to lean on—for faith, pain, values, for the very foundations of distress." The "house" where the following interview took place consists of a rented room on a strip of road between the Central Bus Station and Jerusalem's Convention Hall; like so many places in Israel and other parts of the so-called developing world, this strip contains the remnants of a few houses that once composed a neighborhood. On one side, there is a gravestone cutter's workshop, with stacks of gravestones lining the path, while on the other side—in another rented room—is a makeshift casino where the bottles begin breaking and the shots begin ringing out sometime after midnight. Even this very physical placement seems emblematic, not only of Kedmi's circumstances but of the irony of his prophetic voice at this particular moment in history. Most recently, a day prior to the assasination of Israeli Prime Minister Yitzhak Rabin, Kedmi telephoned to say that his rent had been raised and he was moving back out onto the streets of Jerusalem. Needless to say, Kedmi has been completely ignored by the literary establishment. Occaisonal news articles about him have

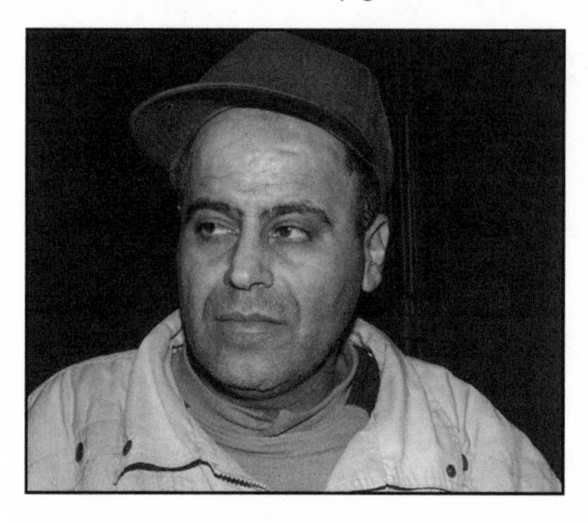

been relegated to the category of "special-interest stories," focusing on the incongruities and unlikeliness of his life rather than on the magnificence and urgency of his art. To date, Yehezkel Kedmi has published—at his own expense—one very large collection of poetry, *Eastern Ewe: Sister, Pillar of the City* (1991); his major new work, *Sodom, Gomorrah and Jerusalem,* still remains in manuscript.

MAKING A HOME FOR POETRY: AN INTERVIEW WITH YEHEZKEL KEDMI BY AMMIEL ALCALAY

Tell me about any responses you got before deciding to make this huge investment and publish your own work.

I wanted to bring out the book because of its painful, social theme; that was the strongest incentive that drove me on. And clearly a theme like this didn't draw me any supporters. I tried various official publishers. Rahel Idelman, for instance, who chairs the publishers' organization and is herself at the head of Schocken Publishers. In her letter of response, which I've kept, she wrote that she would be apprehensive to bring out the book as it stood.

Did she specify what kind of apprehensions she had?

No, she didn't. She wrote a very laconic letter whose brevity speaks for itself. If it was simply a case of a negative reaction, I don't think she would have taken the trouble to answer that way, she would simply evade it. At least she came out honestly by explicitly writing that she felt apprehensive. So I ended up going to private publishers and these publishers did what society here is accustomed to doing to people. I really didn't expect such great difficulties in bringing the book out. I thought that the theme would speak to the heart of many people. When the book was ready to be printed, I was convinced the poems would be of interest and I did send them off, primarily to the literary supplements of the major newspapers, and I got no response at all. I tried other ways, too. Yaron London, host of the literary TV show, wrote me that his "literary comprehension of this idiom is not profound enough to examine this book in any depth." That was his answer. In his case this already borders on a vulgar lie, because there's no other explanation for someone like that who is considered one of the most brilliant interviewers around. I also got the runaround from others; in the final analysis, almost all the responses had this form of evasiveness about them.

Since you are an autodidact, I'm interested in the quality of your Hebrew which is very complex, very rich, from your use of traditional materials to the integration of all kinds of other levels of language.

As I've said before, I really am an autodidact, but not out of choice. With me, there was another factor. The means were there, because I grew up on a kibbutz, from around the age of four. But during adolescence, at the age of twelve or thirteen, I went through the crisis that every kid that age goes through. It was more traumatic because I was cut off and didn't grow up in my natural environment; the transition from a *Mizrahi* society to an Ashkenazi society at that young age, without a family, was very difficult. We're talking about the mid-1950s, since I was born in 1951. The situation was not particularly bright, to put it mildly, for all the people of Israel; it was a period of austerity, when the state was being built. I had a sister who knew that the situation at home wasn't very good, so she arranged for me to go to a kibbutz. There I got a primary education. Your question was, how, despite this, did I get to the point where I could use Hebrew in such a way. The answer, I think, is first of all with some kind of inborn sense. I don't have another answer. Not because I think that's the ideal answer or the right answer. In stages, after I fell out with the kibbutz, I got to Jerusalem and I lived here in a way that, at least to me, reminds me of the Holocaust, or at least my own. Is it possible to compare this to the Holocaust of European Jewry? Of course not, because that happened to millions. You can't compare the Holocaust of a single person to millions. But to me, it was a Holocaust. I got to the big city from a greenhouse that was the kibbutz. And I didn't know the basics of survival. The kibbutz had abandoned me because I didn't measure up to the conditions or the kibbutz way of life in which you're supposed to fit into a certain mold. And of course I went through these problems without any family. Usually when you are confronted with a problem at that age, it's the family that keeps it within proportion. But I didn't have that safeguard. And I know many kids there who were problematic. And I know, and I could notice, even though I was a little kid, that their families gave them strength to pull through. When I got here, I had to fight, it was like being thrown into the jungle. The family here was doing very badly economically; I had no possibility of relying on them so I ended up on the street. That's how I found myself in the center of Jerusalem; in a cauldron that for me really was a jungle. And I really didn't know how to fight for survival, coming from such a protected place. In 1964, at the age of thirteen I started wandering around the streets all day, in Jerusalem, and I felt hungry. So I had to start learning from scratch, it took me a couple of years to understand, a couple of years of hunger and want, I didn't even have shoes. I didn't have a change of clothes. I would shower maybe once every half a year. I understood that I needed food. So I simply stole food in order to live. To grow. I understood that I had to grow. I understood that people grow at that age. That's also something autodidactic, which brings us back to the question. Like I understood that I had to steal in order to grow, that I needed physical nourishment in order to grow, something I was not so successful in doing, as you can see, I also realized that I needed spiritual and intellectual nourishment, something I was a bit more successful at. Libraries were accessible, literary supplements, journals, as I told you I was a guard at the university. So I persevered under extreme duress. I managed to write under the most elementary conditions—a desk, I never had a desk, no part of this book was ever written on a desk. I wrote while on duty at the Western gate of the University, with constant noise, I have no idea how I was able to manage. As far as the other things go, I simply learned, like at the university. On one of my rounds I encountered a philosophy book in one of the departments and I started looking through it; from there, I found my way to Spinoza, to Kant, to Nietzsche, to Plato. But everything was done independently. By then I had already found my trajectory, I only wanted the documentation. I wasn't a bookworm. My idea was to get as broad a perspective as possible. And it often seemed, though it might not be nice to say, that I had already thought through many of the things I read with my own common sense. For instance, I read, let's say, the existentialism of Sartre or the theology of Spinoza, or the writings of Plato or Aristotle—and I understood that you don't have to learn these things in an orderly way or in an academic way to be conscious of the problematic they dealt with since that problematic has to do with existence itself in all its various aspects. Today I'm aware of the fact that there is all kind of writing: prose, the novel, the lyric, all kinds of literary idioms. Then, I didn't know at all what poetry was. In the literary supplements I found poetry but most of it was modern poetry that didn't really speak to me, better yet, it distanced me from poetry. I had no sense of any kind of poetry, classical nor any other.

This is very interesting because, on the one hand, you grew up in the kibbutz, on the other hand, your poetry has things that are so deeply connected to the traditions of classical Sephardic poetry.

Maybe an answer to this can be found in the spiritual structure of the person. I suppose that the people who wrote those things, Saadia Gaon, al-Harizi, Yehuda Halevi, Ibn Gabirol, and the others, were gifted with the same spiritual structure that enabled them to imagine similar metaphors. And the language, of course, is taken from the sources, from the sources of Judaism which, despite everything, remained the easiest things for me to get to and to learn from.

It forms a kind of circle, because you drew from the sources and because of the structure of the soul, you've returned to those poets who also went into the sources . . .

The remarkable thing is that even if I was not aware of those great writers, there nevertheless is a great resemblance between me and them because of this aspect of internal structure and point of view. When I wrote the book I still didn't have any profound idea about poetry, except for Uri Zvi Greenberg, but even with him in a very marginal way because I didn't have access to his writings. All in all I saw only a few poems of his. With him, I didn't imitate or reproduce, I only saw one thing, I only saw what it is possible to do with the language. Except for Uri Zvi Greenberg, whom I encountered by chance, I didn't see very much other poetry. But of course I began to interest myself in all kinds of other areas, even medicine, everything; I studied a lot of history because I also saw that people who write have a wide spectrum of knowledge. And I understood, intuitively, that the further in depth I went, the greater capacity there would be for pleasure from the poetry since I would enter elements into it that would amplify its effects. Later, I began to read Saadia Gaon and Ibn Gabirol and particularly Yehuda Halevi.

Has this influenced you in terms of writing the second book?

The second book is called *Sodom, Gomorrah and Jerusalem,* and if you ask whether there is an influence, I don't think my poetry is influenced by anyone. Clearly, influence can be found in everyone's work, but I think that I have something distinct in my work. I don't say this to be arrogant. I just feel the distinct quality of my language. Finishing this book gives me the recognition that this is a language I acquired from no one else, it has accumulated within me, and I actualize it. I will always write in this language, I'm sure of that, no matter what I read.

The subject of your work is close to many people; yet, I don't think the work will get to those people. There is a contradiction here: this is something that I think many artists feel, that they are working for a particular audience, but that audience, for many reasons, has no access to it.

This is absolutely true. The conflict and the paradox is there. But I wrote this, first and foremost, from an inner feeling, as an expression of what I felt. Yet I saw constantly before me this paradox, that most of the people about whom I am writing would not read my work. So you know you are writing about them but they have constraints which prevent them from understanding the full trajectory of what you are saying about them.

Is this a question of understanding or a question of the "placement" of this genre or of these materials, within social and cultural hierarchies?

The best example of this is me. I was not a consumer of such things; had it not been for the autodidactic impulse and my success in reaching the information, the knowledge that would put me in a position to utilize the means, the ability to read poetry, to understand poetry, to even look at the diversity of things through a perspective that, naturally, I didn't have before. And I am the exception to the rule that proves the rule. The rule is not to be an autodidact, the rule is not to write books, the rule is not to go too far from a situation like mine, the length of whose path, from an intellectual standpoint, was preordained. What maintained my equilibrium was the idea of perpetuating something. In other words, I had a stake in creating a document, a literary document that would serve as testimony for this generation, of this time and of these events because the work was written on the great historical moment of the redemption of the Jewish people. But right alongside this were the darkest moments possible, that is, daily life in the state and, most importantly—and this is the emphasis in the book—the phenomenon of class segregation. One class for *mizrahim,* another for Ashkenazim. No one who has eyes in their head and speaks the truth doesn't see that there is a second Israel. And today, so many years after the establishment of the state, these things still hold true. All the prisons are filled with *mizrahi* Jews, most of the people who are uneducated, tracked in the school system, most of the people living in poor neighborhoods, almost all of them are *mizrahi*. There is a stigma, even on the daily level, if you're a little darker, if you have *mizrahi* features, things that nature cannot change. There is an immediate, negative social stigma. And people are related to through this. Like me, because I'm a little darker, I'm related to like an illiterate boor. So I assume that's how it is across the board, not just with me because I'm not the only *mizrahi* face in the state of Israel.

Do you think that if you had freer access to the media that the response would be better, that you could somehow meet in the middle with this audience or at least give them the tools to voice their feelings?

What you are saying is more apt for a public figure or a politician than for me. Because if I had the tools of a politician, a public figure, then I would of course reach a greater mass of people in a much easier way. And maybe even at some level I would be able to give them, through my own ways, the ability to discern to what extent—not how dire their situation is—but how much—in relation to the book—they could identify with it, if they were to identify.

—*Translated from the Hebrew by Ammiel Alcalay*

from EASTERN EWE: SISTER, PILLAR OF THE CITY

NOT EQUAL TO THEM THE EASTERNER . . .

My people, my people, my Eastern people, my people like a night I once
knew

and you are not like a single night of mine, I knew, not like one of my nights
but part of my people.
I wept and wept much the night I knew, the Easterner my night and my
people.
I loved you, my people -
I loved you, my night -
I loved you, my Easterner -
the Easterner, my night and my people.
Even then and always the night was like magic for me -
I never knew why.
Even then and always I loved the night -
I never knew why.
There was always magic in my night -
there was always a riddle in my night.
Someone gazing into the firmament at night -
gazes at the most beautiful of landscapes.
There is only one magic in the world, it comes with the hour of night, it is
night's domain.
The light of night -
magical.

Insofar as I go there and insofar as I come there, I come to night there.
Since I've known my soul sister is the night, night is my spirit's dominion.

Oh, how I have yearned for the havens of the night -
oh, how I have desired the sanctuary of night.
Then as always, the crystalline splendor overhead almost made me faint.
The splendor of the moon then struck me too as always, the waning
brilliance of the moon in the firmament.
Oh, the night is so lyrical -
oh what a lyrical night.
Oh such darkness -
oh this darkness.
How I loved to embrace the night, like someone being loved -
the course of a hand, the tone of voice, the closeness of spirit.
You will know the glowing nights and you knew them well for your luck has
surely been proven.
In the darkness of night is the wish of a man in pain, it is darkness itself.
Every night blacks out the senses,
every night the senses dull.

All the nocturnal prostrations are made as day turns to evening, so that night's black hour will come.

There are nights that blaze in the upper reaches of darkness and my lot is to be aflame.

On blazing nights with my spirit kindling, it was at such a time that I wept and wept much.
As far as I knew then—the Easterner my night and my people, the Easterner unequal to them.
Crying at night is the greatest human sadness that I had truly known.
There was great sadness in my night when I knew the Easterner, my night and my people;
great sadness in my heart when I knew of the Easterner, my night and my lament.

DAY BLOOD - NIGHT BLOOD

In the world this time is nighttime and I take my stand facing it alone.
This is the time blood floods through my soul and veins are not where the blood is.
And my body is drunk and my soul intoxicated and my senses more attuned than they were, higher.
In the world this is nighttime this time and facing it alone I take my stand.
Night of small light, sound of the cricket, the stillness good.
How my soul desires this hour of the night -
how my spirit covets this hour of night.
At night all the senses I have ever known arise within me.
A great darkness arises, the only tranquillity a person can know.
There is magic in the night, there is magic at night -
and intoxicated I stand facing it to forget.

To someone looking at night, it might seem as if a person's soul can be likened to the night.
There is rage and also fire in the nocturnal soul at such a nocturnal hour of night.

There is silence and there is blood rising in my spirit coursing through no veins it is blood.
And then I knew—night blood is the blood.

And then I knew—night blood is the blood.

And my body becomes drunk and my soul intoxicated and my senses higher
than they were before.
I have not known tranquil nights in my life, for my nights overturned my days.
There is a night wind that sings you a lullaby and you cannot sleep.
No surprises await you in this world, the ages to come are bereft of wonder -
none can be like nocturnal wonder, like the magic of the night.
Once, when I was still a child, I found myself near a tamarisk at night in the
desert -
and I will never forget that sight.
Once, when I was still a child, I found myself next to a beggar woman at noon,
on a street in the middle of Jerusalem -
and I will never forget that sight.
And then I knew—night blood, it is the blood flowing in the walls of my city.
And it too will come to the attention of my people in my day.

RAGING SOUL

With spirit raging I come to you at night
from the quiet there far from the city teeming with my inhuman cry.
From every sill and threshold within it the lament of my people swarms,
surging and billowing throughout all her streets, breaking upon all her
sidewalks and my cry -
my cry then is a beastly wail in the city of my savage lament.
My city then, it also expires in bestial grief,
my city swarms like a wailing lion and within her there is a pillory -
my Ewe is there, a pillar for my city, at her feet my living cry is embittering.
With soul raging my cry still mounts, it knows not it isn't wild,
my cry will not simply proceed there, my cry will not just go forth there
for there all the springs of lament converge and not just by chance,
since my cries have human eyes there—human eyes that see,
for a human cry holds all feeling, all spirit,
thus my cry goes forth, seeing like a man, the pillar my lament certainly sees.
Surely—indeed, most certainly—the pillar of my city, this my lament has
seen and laid its eyes on.
In raging spirit my city has been scattered into pillars and lament comes to it,
to a city dispersed,
my cry will not cease nor will it stand for a city in shards has no dam.

My cry goes out to fill the city inundating it to fill my country for it has seen
and sees the flood of my tears -
to learn to know the course of my land
for the city of my lament and my surging pillar stand to fill my country.
In spirit raging, my cry still intends to fully cover the Land of Israel,
in tempestuous spirit to still stand as her witness, to give cry to her lamentation.
Oh, Hebrew Ewe from Eastern exile,
how have my brothers given you over as a pillar to serve my city.
What kind of daughter were you, what kind of daughter were you
now that being a harlot at the threshold has made you rich,
now that being a whore at doorways has made you cheap.
Oh, my brother, oh my brother, look, even your own sister is here,
how my brother, how my brother, oh my brother, how?
How could you have given our sister over to serve as a pillar for the city,
how could you have degraded our sister so?
Oh, oh, my Jewish brother, oh, oh, my brother, Jew,
this time you cannot say this was the act of an alien nation,
for this is the Land of Israel and here the Jew is the ruler, the Jew.
With spirit raging, I come as evening falls and night begins
from there from a house far off to the city of my brother's wild hissing
at every threshold and open passageway.
With spirit raging I see there the darkened thresholds
and the face of my daughter affixed to the doors as if with nails.
Soul railing my brother still stands there her witness
and he shows no shame nor does he fear or flee
but stays fastened to the spot as if nailed to a cross
and he is a Jewish crusader
and he is a Jewish cross.
With soul raging
she is a Hebrew Ewe daughter of Eastern exile
she is my sister and she is your sister, too, my brother.
What kind of daughter, what kind of daughter
has now become a rich girl, harlot of the thresholds,
now a cheap girl, whore of the passageways
and she is my sister and she is your sister
how brother, how brother, oh brother, how -
how did you give your sister up to be a pillar of the city
this time you won't be able to say
that Titus is the man who did this to your sister,
for Titus no longer still dwells here amongst you.

MY PEOPLE, KNOWLEDGE, AND I

Over and above this the knowledge and over and above this my people and the chasm is unbreachable. In this I am.
The raging melody at evening time and you as one of the victorious conductors, but the troops are not before you.
Before you the world in its simple spirit, in its simple soil, with its simple tree.
Troops of warfaring soldiers will never emerge victorious, the simple world, wins so simply.
A shepherd with his pipe and herd, this is the world's kindness, a soldier his sword a bulwark, this is the world's anguish.
There is a lamentation which cannot be withstood, but to every army—there are those who stand up.
Human compassion, this is the great good I have seen, and its site is like one of the victors.

Over and above this my knowledge and over and above this my people, and the chasm is unbreachable—in this I am.
The lone house—my soul's yearning—was like magic whose meaning I could not unravel.
I knew no magic like the magic of the lit window of the house as we saw it from a distance.
The sight of the lone house at nightfall, it is and will remain in my heart as I weep over the sight of it.
The lone house at dusk, which no one as of yet has nor ever will go back to.
Turned topsy-turvy the lone house will revert to a wonder of wonders, in times at times,
evenings and nights, and each person will come back to it. Until there is no man or man.
Over and above this the knowledge and over and above this my people. And the chasm is unbreachable. In this I am.
Like the love of my very soul is my love for the hills of the Land of Israel.
As on a clear day in the Land of Israel I see the hills—hills.
All those thorns, all that vegetation, all those woods—a wonder.
All the watchmen's huts along the vineyards, all the solitary trees, all the planted trees—a wonder.
You cannot ever pass by all of this, you will always pass by all of this.

Over and above this the knowledge and over and above this my people, and the chasm is unbreachable. In this I am.
Another creature did I see and I wept, this was in my solitude -

there I saw the creature that is a man alone.
The way a person is abandoned with no one to embrace him, the way a person is abandoned and no one asks after his well-being.
There is no one to see the wounded soul but for the oppressed who also see the wounded soul.
Whoever has seen a solitary man in his lamenting and not wept with him,
has never seen a solitary man in his lament.
The solitary man has within him the sorrow of a child, the solitary man, he, truly, is a man.
And I saw another creature—that was the man leaving, by far the cruelest of creatures.

Over and above this the knowledge and over and above this my people and the chasm is unbreachable, in this I am.
In this I am—there is no scent in these gardens, there is no peace in this, the lilly of the sea will not appear this fall.
Fields of primrose blushing at sunset, the house at the end of the field,
the hyacinth garden sloping over the yield of Leah's land -
no matter what anyone says, only in the Land of Israel can it be like this.
Honey's warm nectar, mighty thistles in the wild fields, the scent of cinnamon in the marketplace -
I am enamoured by the sands of the Negev, I yearn for the hills of Israel.
I slept through *hamsin* nights in the Land of Israel, and I felt everything around me and I slept.
In all of this, a man's pain cannot be rectified,
by all this, the anxious furrows of his tribulations will not be made straight .

Over and above this the knowledge, and over and above this my people and the chasm is unbreachable, in this I am.
Whoever has not seen someone forgotten in the corner of a run down park -
the olive tree standing perpendicular through the seasons
before straightening its branches for winter, top to bottom -
then he has never truly seen the top of the bottom.
I am not in love with the olive tree nor is it up to me to sing its lament -
he who is in the park loves the olive tree
and it is he, more than anyone, whose lament overshadows that of the olive tree.
I am simply the one seeing this and commanded by the singer of songs to sing of it.
I knew of a thing that is not, and you will come to sense the knowledge of it,
that from a whirlwind of sorrow will the fringes of joy burst forth.

I knew that in sorrowful eyes, therein too is the good of the eyes
and that is the sole comfort of my people that I got to know by feeling it.

Over and above this the knowledge, and over and above this my people and
the chasm is unbreachable, in this I am.

from SODOM, GOMORRAH AND JERUSALEM

It's a pity rocks and boulders, traitors and satraps came not mysteriously to
pass judgement upon you father on your way to this city
or that a gang of highway robbers had not also welcomed you with drawn
daggers and violent cries and
stolen everything you had and banished you from their midst until you
became frightened and fled and never arrived to the city of Jerusalem
why couldn't a moon yearning for the world have arisen to kindle fear of the
night in you a silvery light to keep you afraid of the night
ages illuminated by silver rays fear of the moon in the great black ascension
on your way to Jerusalem
father had only a small fateful obstacle appeared on your way to Jerusalem
the city you so longed for in the dreams of your youth in your heart at
daybreak fervently aroused
in its yearning standing like a soldier ready to do battle unto the last drop of
blood in your veins just in order to arrive
and were you just felled by a rock your last drop of blood drained in the
battle and you found yourself martyred to the Name
you wouldn't have come to this city Jerusalem and your grave would have
been dug by Jewish gravediggers at a Jewish
funeral on the way to the last place of your heart's desire you would have lain
dead in battle outside the city of Jerusalem
I too would have heralded a great conflagration with a blessing in time to
come as I was about to be formed father
and I would breathe in an alien city distant from this city even then my keen
senses
would have uttered amen amen because there was a great fire on my father's
way to the city of Jerusalem
and my father would not have come and behold as I said in days to come
when I was born I would breathe and bless and rejoice
the joy of the Water Drawing Festival could not be greater than the
exultation of imagination in my brain kindling
now in the city of Jerusalem at the thought my father of you never having

gotten to Jerusalem
even at the high price of having had a disaster befall you on your way to Jerusalem
had you only gone astray on the road and been led by your legs to some other place -
the very heavens and fate's path would have done well for you not to bring you to your heart's desire -
the city of Jerusalem, even miserable stray dogs who had never testified to any wonders
in the world would come to block the way with their howling and corrupt the road in your eyes leading you to rebel against it.
An earthquake why was there none that time then my father when you marched
on the road rising Jerusalem way and were the earth to tremble beneath you then you would have returned gone back
and never have arrived to the city of Jerusalem and your desire for her the city of Jerusalem would have still prevailed
oh father my father if you only knew your fate and the fate of your family to be in the city of Jerusalem
you wouldn't have come to her even if on the way you murdered the dream you dreamt
all the days of your exile upon the nocturnal banks of the Tigris and the Euphrates to the light of a glittering moon
even if you betrayed all the harsh decrees you betook upon yourself beneath the yoke of heaven
just not to come to this city, oh father, my father if you only knew your bitter fate.
Why didn't you, father, bind yourself in exile by your own hand with phylacteries to the city of your birth
why didn't you bind the phylacteries you bound around your head to also make a like binding around the city of your birth
for the sake of the Name and in the name of the Name blessed may it be just not to have come to this city
for the beauty of the Euphrates should have blocked you its magic at evening stars and moon in the sky
the haughtiness of its sparkling clear waters in the rays of the lesser light at night
cleaving the darkness and illuminating the hurtling waters in the darkness of night with the brilliant splendor of the moon's silvery light
and you also used to play like our ancestors at twilight upon a harp at the

banks of the Euphrates
and at nightfall you would hang your harp and thus things followed from one day to the next
had even the violence of the Nations in Iraq preceded the dawn of your departure to barricade
the road from Iraq to Israel with your blood so you would not have come to this city Jerusalem
how come brigands and vagabonds plundering and pillaging to their heart's content didn't raid
the train you boarded from Baghdad on your journey to the city of Jerusalem and rob
and loot and burn the wagons and tamper with the steel tracks holding you on your way at another city
it's not even important which city just as long as it wasn't the city of Jerusalem you came to
it would even have been better had you been stopped by Beduin at the point of a sword upon their tempestuous mounts
so you would be gripped by a great fear and go back the way you came to that city
and you would never ever have come to this city again
cursed be that morning as the rising light of the sun's resplendent disc shone yet again as is
the way of the world from day to day. Why wasn't the sunny orb's splendor extinguished for just one day that day
a pity a real pity father that the roads were not destroyed that cities did not succumb a pity such a pity my father
such a shame that the road to the Land of Israel greeted you in expectation that the Jews welcomed you in the Land of Israel
it's such a pity father that the moon lit your path at night on your way to Jerusalem
if only the moon had fallen to the ground so you couldn't see your way to Jerusalem to the earth
of the Land of Israel and you would have gone every which way the wind blew except
in the direction of the wind leading to the city of Jerusalem
had even the Land our Land the Land of Israel the Land of Abraham Isaac and Jacob been conquered by the Nations
the land of our ancestors the land of the Jews and had they established in this Land holy to us a sovereign Arab land ruling over us
had even such a disaster taken place it would have been preferable to me and

to you had such a thing as this
happened to my father for a disaster befalling our nation would be better than the disaster me and my father went through
why didn't my grandfather stop you from going that grey day because I'm sure it was gray then the day you arose upon the route that is
no path from an Arab land to the Land of the Jews the Land of Israel the Land of the Gazelle
for my grandfather did not come to it and perhaps his senses were as keen as those of a prophet
as it had been told to me that with them my grandfather could have foretold the great evil that
would befall us in our innocence when we arrived to the Land of Israel to this city Jerusalem
oh grandfather if you had only seen us your beloved family as we were brought to utter devastation
you would have arisen from your grave to lament and place ashes upon your brow and a covering upon your head
and begin to mourn and sit over us for seven days of mourning as is the custom among the Jews but I am sure grandfather
that my blood is just like your blood because I too have been graced with senses as sharp as yours
and these words I write are acute as your prophesies for you would not have sat in mourning over us in the city of Jerusalem
but in the city of Babel our most glorious and holy place of exile among all the exiles of
our people Israel beneath the skies of the Sovereign of the universe our Lord our King who sits on high
why didn't you cry mother my holy mother like all the holy Jewish mothers
oh mother why didn't you cry with your eyes and your mouth clasping your two black braids to your neck
falling from the kerchief covering your holy head oh mother why didn't you cry
why didn't you become bitter with tears mother with the cries of a Jewish woman which is like no other cry
so the Jewish men of the family would hear and stop and go no further upon the road
for which Jewish man would dare take a chance with the tears of a Jewish woman.
Oh my father if you arose now from the grave your grave in Jerusalem and gathered

the severed limbs of your family which were cut piece by piece the soul
severed from the flesh in this city Jerusalem
and you went all the way back against the Jewish will that is in you against
the Jewish blood that is in you
against the Jewish vision that is in you and you returned to the land of your
exile the land of Babylon
and we too returned with you a family of severed Jews a family of refugee
Jews
a family of dead Jews of our own free will well-versed in the knowledge
aware of the disaster for which there is no atonement for which there is no
repentence
for which there can be no mending and which cannot be denied
as it happened to us here in the heart of the Land of the Jews in the heart of
the Land of Israel in the heart of this city of Jerusalem
and I say to you Jerusalem the inferno.

★ ★ ★ ★ ★

Oh Mother, how I longed for your humble likeness nights in the Land of
Israel
alone among human animals in a Land that devours its inhabitants, this state
of grievious
existence, of calm and melancholy nights that follow from bitter days in the
Land of Israel. And in this great darkness in my weeping imagination I saw
in my weeping heart with my weeping eyes. Your head with a brocade
kerchief and two black braids. Woven through with silver after such efforts
were made
to adorn you with a crown of suffering. And I longed for you at night oh
how I longed for you
and I saw you always always your unassuming figure. Why were you so meek
while in me
you gave birth to the heart of a lion. A shame you too didn't have a heart like
the one you
created in me so you wouldn't have fallen like a bird falling from a tree into
the barren woods
you had the heart of a quiet gray swallow no one even notices in the
abundance her voice
her lament her songs amongst her fledglings but gray like the color of your
hair mother
the way you chirped and raised your young like the black braids under your
kerchief

calm not witholding any secrets a greater good than life you were like that swallow greater
than life and small so small a little Jewish woman in the heart of Jerusalem oh mother and
Jerusalem has no heart whatsoever and there was no one to come to you in heart so you thought thus
is the heart of Jerusalem. And even if it were so heartless had you only not felt so,
it would have been enough for me your son who grew up and knew that there was no heart to meet
your heart in Jerusalem the inferno. And who more than I who has grown up knows the neccessity
the need the want of a person in the inferno of Jerusalem for an encounter of the heart in the hell
of Jerusalem. Jews Jews Jews all around and all around desolation desolation desolation
for there is no heart in their breast just Jerusalem stone which in their stony wisdom they
so love to adorn their dwellings and houses of worship in stone like the stone in their heart
oh mother tell me for you said that when you came to this land that consumes its inhabitants
when you came from there you said the houses are the very same houses but the people are not
thus are there dwelling places and people in Jerusalem a city like any city human and home
and the discerning eye can feel in their heart and know that those houses and those crowded
streets are like cities in the world but the people are not the same people in this inferno Jerusalem.

—*Translated from the Hebrew by Ammiel Alcalay*

SHELLEY ELKAYAM

SHELLEY ELKAYAM was born in Haifa in 1955 and presently lives in Jerusalem. On one side, she is a seventh-generation native of Haifa; the other side of the family is from Salonica, one of the great centers of Jewish culture following the expulsion from Spain. In many ways, Shelley Elkayam set the tone for the range of possibilities available to younger Sephardi and *mizrahi* artists in the 1980s. This is borne out by both the formal and thematic range of her work as well as her other activities. A tireless activist in peace, women's, educational, and social issues, Elkayam pointed the way toward a new model of the engaged Israeli intellectual. One of the founders of *East for Peace,* she was also a delegate to international conferences in Nairobi and China. Her work (which includes a children's book set to the tone of traditional medieval Hebrew tales), embodies a sense of language that is remarkably seamless in its lack of conflict over the many historical and rhetorical levels employed. Markedly different from writers of the previous generation, Elkayam presents a paradigm of someone profoundly at home in the Hebrew language. At the same time, she has reclaimed enormous areas—conceptual and linguistic—for women's expression. The transparency of her language is highly illusive as one realizes the extent to which she has managed to forge new semantic and experiential space within fundamental and primary Hebrew terms and concepts. This is illustrated most visibly in "Yes Indeed I'll Answer God," where practically every line is both an integration and a possible rereading of key Hebrew words and ideas. From assuming the identity of God as the writer ("I will ever be what I now am inscribing letters in light") who cannot be identified, to reinstating the primacy of Moses' acceptance of the Book of the Law (The Torah) as a poem that will stand witness, Elkayam's text provides an exhilarating and dizzying example of embracing the tradition from within as a means of opening up new areas of inquiry. Her books include *The Essence of Itself* (1981), *Poems* (1983), *Simple Days* (1984), a children's fable for adults called *When the Snake and the Mouse First Met* (1986), and *Song of the Architect* (1987). The following text, "Writing: A dialogue with the World,"is an edited version of two

talks; one was presented in Nairobi at the youth meeting of the World Conference on Religion and Peace in 1984, and the other at an international writers' conference in the former Yugoslavia in 1985.

WRITING: A DIALOGUE WITH THE WORLD
The Public and the Secret Language of Literature

I was five years old when I committed myself to be a poet of the Hebrew language. I did not read Hebrew nor did I write it, but I played the piano and knew how to read notes.

My mother is writing a letter to her sister abroad. They correspond in Ladino. I only spoke Hebrew, which they understood but could not read. So I was writing a letter in the Latin alphabet that phonetically sounded like Hebrew. For human contact. To bridge distances. This discovery of self-expression that echoed within the family woke up my wish to further broaden communication. At that time the state of Israel was about ten years old. The collective mind was tuned to believe in survival. Everyone was excited. Many languages were spoken: Yiddish, French, Arabic, Ladino, mixed with broken Hebrew, in dozens of accents. The radio broadcast a dramatically serious Hebrew, to which everyone listened intently.

Immigrant consciousness. An immigrant is an exile of free will. In every big city in Europe and America you can tell an immigrant society. You call them "minority groups." In our culture, the majority had minority-immigrant characteristics. That is (so to speak), historically, statistically, politically, and culturally. The quality and content of the reality that was taking this very shape was of concern to my father. Member of a family that had lived in Zion for many years, he already had a Sephardic consciousness when I was born. At that time immigrant consciousness meant writing about greeny summers in what was a yellowish desert, about oriental people as exotic strangers, as if they did not live right near by, all around, nearly within.

Within the roots of the word "Hebrew" there is a meaning which says: the language that reaches beyond. Like going beyond to the other shore. But it tells nothing about that "shore" or whether there is a shore at all. Yet, it means the very fact, the active fact of going beyond. The Hebrew language itself is a concept. A way of thinking. A spiral muscle—every tongue is. The content of our investigations into creativity is shaped by our language and literature. While our parents and teachers were carefully massaging that muscle, we, like our ancestors, were simply living it.

I have developed love and trust with Hebrew first as a listener and reader, an intimate trusting reader of the most powerful Hebrew text. That is, "The

Bible." Nowadays, in the inflation of written books, we should see our ancient texts as a diamond whose value is not fully recognized. Like a diamond that shines and has the ability to cut. But to know the difference between a precious diamond and a piece of glass we need to know the wisdom of differentiation.

To seek peace is good. But it is not enough. As our prophets already said with a certain irony, you speak "peace, peace and there is no peace." Prophecy in biblical Judaism is misunderstood if it is made synonymous with prediction. It speaks about the future, as does prediction, but not about the unconditional future that must inevitably come (bringing either destruction or redemption). Rather its fulfillment is dependant on condition, for it is dependant on human behavior. Prophesy itself has fulfilled a continuous function—to keep alive the faithful national self-criticism, and to reawaken it again and again.

The concept of peace in Judaism is a holistic one, where social justice remains a fundamental element of the work involved in achieving peace. A holistic experience of peace in relation to the human family and its environment is not known yet, it is not recorded in our collective memory. As Maimonides said: "Man does not know how those days will be until they will be. As those things have not been made explicit by the prophets and the sages have no tradition in their hands regarding it . . ." Yet we know that peace is an enterprise no less courageous than war. The real hero, after all, is one who makes "enemy" into "friend."

Like light through water, poetry refracts, reflects and disperses. Inspired by "outer worlds" and through linguistic tools, it serves as an instrument attuned to the poet's inner voice, to the poet's inner growth and to human life on earth. As the usage of the language points to the collective state of mind, we can say that a language that does not have a poetic dynamic is asleep or dead. A society lacking this dynamic can be easily manipulated or hypnotized and become the victim or victimizer, either of violence, confusion or superficiality. The power of love manifests itself in every child we meet. But sometimes children are violent, especially when their young voices are suppressed or choked; when they encounter hate, untruth, and frustration. In Hebrew, violence and muteness have the same root.

It is the reader within myself who writes. The reader within me brings me impressions and signs while reading them. Those readings of the reader within me keep my consciousness busy. It is the writer within me who works on formulating these readings. The reader and the writer within me are peers, although they take nothing for granted. They attract each other, they may also collide. Some formulas cure, some guarantee a headache. Some are constructive, some destructive, some vital, some more. Each letter, word, sentence, is potentially a formula. Every poem, every book is a formula. The word you read and write formulates your attention, our state of mind, our body of senses.

The finest work in writing is at a point where the writer and the reader are working together as one. If you read a certain text every day, it becomes your active subconsciousness, like memory. A text, like a formula, is working all the time whether we, the readers/writers, are aware of it or not. Great indeed is the writing which can relate to consciousness and subconsciousness as one. Greater is that which makes you read it again and again, which makes you know it by heart, which can surprise you, challenge, and enlighten you. Great is the text that moves the reader to write. In the beginning there was an inspired reader who committed themselves by dedication to writing themselves down on paper, as a movement, as a gesture, as an homage. Amen.

SEVEN STANZAS TO AN INDIAN CHIEF

1 I am the date and the olive and the grenade
whose name was taken
whose dream was fleeced
and thrown back in my face.

2 I am the Family Tree Of The Field,
every tree in the field,
every tree
of the land,
I am the Family Root Of The Worship Of The Place.

3 So whatever the Great Spirit will be
I bow before It
wherever It is to be found.

4 I am The Stock That Knows
the harlot's fees, the held, the holders and the fiefdoms.
The Stock That Hears
what seeing eyes cannot envision.
That my voice is in my eyes,
that my dream was stolen,
that they work me over in broad daylight,
with stars and headlines.

5 But I planted branches according to the nature of The Stock
and Steel came to me from the country There
to engrave his name in the palm of the stem
to root out my branches for the issue of my race
and to call me, The Stock, by *its* name.
The speech of the olive whose oil was made by heaps of lentils.
The word now that the good Name is better than finest oil.

6 Whose hand is bloody or filled with steel
whose hand is dull
cannot exact truth's precious oil.

7 And what cannot be
I seek in the presence of the Great Spirit
wherever It is to be found.

THE CRUSADER MAN

The Crusader man paid the Land a visit
and that was
around
so and so many
years back.

The Crusader man did the country
in this
or that many days.

The Crusader became the landlord.
An enemy with holdings.
Full of trust,
sword-bearing, armor-wearing, with a coat of mail.

Kind of a jumpy guy, the Crusader man.

The Land is a witness,
she sees it from
the way he laid his
place out,
from the fact

that he never did make himself a home.
From the way he'd attack
and cut himself off on the mountaintops.

WITH HELP

From the midst of this Syrian-African rift
that rent her living flesh.
What flower will bloom
upon her face of marl.
And what amount of song shall I lay before her.
I'll leave her to
her gods.
That she be given a name. With the help
of The Name. A note, eternal,
and a blue flame.

And now, when she speaks violence to me, without
words, reckless at times,
to what can she be likened,
what can she be likened to?

I'm unfamiliar with the woods in her brain.

Within the clearings there
a mammoth illusion is nourished.

VESSEL OF FRAGRANCE

Just give her the chance to sleep within herself
and within her own power she rests,
preserving in her eyes the bitter
water I'll call the waters of disputation.
I shall call her the priestess of her violence,
to her very eyelids.
A vessel of spices, incense
for her reflections. After knowledge like a wolf,
preying upon the wisdom of her heart.

She goes out of there bleeding beauty
And the fullness of her spirit praises the Lord
And the the fullness of her spirit praises the Lord
And the whole spirit that celebrates the Lord
And the whole spirit that prays for her.

THE HOUSE HAS TO HAVE AN OPENING TO THE EAST

The house has to open to the East.
To let morning through
and drench the bones
of the building
in sun.

A KIND OF VAGUE YEARNING

And I saw a thorn
whose faith in the wind
weighed down its own flowering in the seed of seeds,
I saw knapweed, donned in blue,
tighten up in a kind of grimace, to believe.
And I saw an almond, blooming pink
wherever you tapped it, from
within the scar. And I saw

a hothouse plant bleached in light,
stained by the yellow assault,
wish itself a thistle's reveille.
Kind of a vague
yearning, out of character.

GARDEN TIME

A dimpled garden
and I am Honi Bat-Honi circling around to plant seed.
Garden.
Neither black nor
white.
The garden is a voice, calling.

Dimpled graced garden.
Black and comely
burn-
ished.
Winter has come.
The divination of the leaves conceived in earth.
The divination of leaves blooming in the air.
The garden fire makes flowers.
The garden fire makes fruit.
The garden fire offers itself up.

Now I've left the garden.
From a distance it looks like the doors are shut,
it's disorganized there, they say.
The companions linger on
even when they're away,
in the company of my voice,
their heavenly call trickling along the lock.
Round garden. A ringing tone.

Those stepping out of time
but staying in the assembly,
have to make other rounds.
Have to be made black holes.
Singular.

And between time. From one day to the next. In two camps. Forgivingly.
Between the ears and on the scales, in the great inequity.
Morning dew, take the dawn,
seize the dizzy time
between your eyes.
Dark and comely.
Winter has come.
Its divination conceived in earth.
The dimple in your smile thrives.
The garden fire offers itself up on the mountain.
And I shall call forth your love
and your joy
that it kindle.

YES INDEED I'LL ANSWER GOD

And this is the judgment.
I will ever be what I now am inscribing letters in light.
A small letter as a sign in a crown of light.
Peace unto the crown.
Peace unto the King and the Queen and peace, peace unto the Escort.

Don't take it to heart.
Wind hovers over the deep
and space is laid out between the lines from sentence
to sentence like
chess: black and white.
Like on a park bench: a sitting king's falling.
A parable, my beloved readers:
the garden's a song
and the architect's checkmate.

And whoever wants to come to the garden -
arise
and enter.

Bless this breach.
Peace to Yeshurun.
Welcome, Lord's favor.
And Bless the Name, naturally, day by day in Mahaneh Yehuda.

All kidding aside.
Believe me, the Gates of Grace are already open.
Right now, this minute, today and forever,
and this song a witness between you and me
alive this instance, all, like they say,
with love and awe and completion.

Please don't worry.
For right before your very eyes what's written
is written. And that's a fact.

To everything there is a season and this is the time
since that's how song goes -

a pillar of fire:
intransitory.

And whatever is distinct has intention -
in other words, perfection within perfection.
Whatever you decide.
I'm with you.

As for me,
And I took it upon myself for the sake of the song so
indeed I'll come back to God.

And I gave my word
to grow to the scent of a blossom of light.
To be kindled by the right aroma.
To be
Amen.

Truly, simply, with love.

And whoever is bound
and finds himself in the garden,
finds himself
in the garden:
sing to him.
Come, my pleasantly tied,
unlace yourself in the palm
of my hand.

Now I return to
the man among you who is fine and tender.
Now, since I was reminded, I remember now.
My blood my soul my heart and will are one.
One—regardless.
You are one.
One now.

Enough.
This is judgment.
And I take the verdict upon myself
at its word.

Therefore, for the sake of the liberty you gained:
All ceremonies of the covenant
are memorial.
In Remembrance, of course.
Like a garden bell. Accordingly, say,
I forgive my father for doing things without questioning my desire.
Look, after all, the ledger's open.
Ceremonial testaments inscribed in the body.
A man and his covenant
carved in his form.

Accept this, take it upon yourself
and look at the voice
how
suddenly the body's stone.
The body suddenly ape.
Ape.
The body suddenly blossoms.
At once the body's at the Gates of Grace,
and someone utters—live, now
and who
ever wishes to enter the garden
arise
in fragrance
whoevever among you is a man of fine and tender
scent.

—Translated from the Hebrew by Ammiel Alcalay

RONNY SOMECK

RONNY SOMECK was born in Baghdad in 1951 and now lives in Ramat Gan. After studying at Tel Aviv University, Someck worked with street gangs; more recently he has taught literature and led writing workshops in a variety of contexts. He has published six collections of poetry and, in 1992, participated in the International Writing Program at Iowa. Usually seen as an astute observer of popular culture, The New York School, particularly Frank O' Hara, are often cited as influences in his work. Yet, critics ignore Someck's tragic vision and acute sense of almost prophetic testimony in his portraits of those marginalized by society. Just as others have laid claim to Jerusalem as the primary site of their work, Someck is the poet of Tel Aviv, a city overrun by imported goods, stark contrasts, and decay. Seemingly understated and matter-of-fact, Someck's poems are remarkably dense and often echo the laconic style of several medieval Hebrew poetic genres. The characters that inhabit Someck's world are constantly hemmed in by the utopian possibilities and intentions of the poem, as both form and desire. There is a looming sense of mortality in his work, just as there are frequent divisions between the terrestrial and the celestial; often the only interlocutors between these realms are birds, an unrequitable gaze or the human voice, as exemplified in the songs of great Arab singers like Umm Kulthoum or Fairuz. These voices, also, limn the barren spaces presently erected between Jews and Arabs. Someck's great project is to catalog the real, to rename and reclaim a world that has been categorized and stigmatized into oblivion. For this, he seeks out all the unofficial moments that contradict ideology, such as when the Israeli soldier peeling potatoes on a desolate army base is rendered defenceless by the great voice of memory in the person of Umm Kulthoum's aching tone. In many poems, Someck works his way between language, image and metaphor to wipe the slate clean and effect a shift in meaning. In "Poverty Line," for example, Someck insists on a house and not a shanty, a neighborhood and not a transit camp, thus repossessing the very materials of memory on his own terms. His books include: *Exile* (1976),

Solo (1980), *Asphalt* (1984), 7 *Lines on the wonder of the Yarkon* (1987), *Panther* (1989), and *Bloody Mary* (1994). Most recently, *Jasmine* (1995), a selection of his poetry translated into Arabic by the Palestinian poet Samih al-Qasim, has appeared.

THE FIRST LAW OF THE JUNGLE. A POEM MISSING-IN-ACTION

to my uncle, m.i.a., Palestine, 1947

The first law of the jungle is that there are no laws.
And in the death valley of elephants, the turning blade of the wind
scratches along your body.

We never met, but the first words my father brought back from his language
lessons
were "unknown" and "soldier," and he scattered them along a battle line,
the unfastened longitudes of your life and of his.
Someone told him that he saw you once, in a passing blur,
in the planetarium at Beit Dagan.
At night he returned home carrying the burden of your name
like a sack of potatoes.

The knife that was needed to cut through the peel of his loneliness
lay in a drawer,
sharpened by fantasies in which I withdrew you from the jaws of a lion.
I was four years old, and the licking gaslight flame
was also the throat of a dragon.

— *Translated from the Hebrew by Henry Israeli*

POVERTY LINE

As if you could stretch a line and say: below it, poverty.
Here's the bread made black
with cheap make-up
and the olives in a small plate
on the tablecloth.
In the air, doves flew with a soaring salute

to the ringing bell held by the kerosene vendor in his red cart,
and there was also the sound of rubber boots landing in the muddy ground.
I was a kid, in a house they called a shanty,
in a neighborhood they called a transit camp.
The only line I saw was the horizon and under it everything
looked poor.

IN ANSWER TO THE QUESTION: WHEN DID YOUR PEACE BEGIN?

Ben Gurion's wind teased hair hung
on the wall of the cafe near the transit camp
and next to it, in a frame just like it,
the doughnut face of Umm Kulthoum.
That was in '55 or '56 and I figured if
a man and a woman hung side by side like that
they had to be bride and groom.

AND HER HUSBAND BLURTED OUT: BUCHENWALD

They stretched a sheet out and brought Madame Klara down from
the second floor to the ambulance.
What'd she die of, we asked, before hearing the rumor
she'd hung herself in the tub,
and her husband blurted out: Buchenwald.
Until then we'd heard of whooping cough and angina
and we had scars from our chickenpox vaccines.
The day before she found a snake in the courtyard
and the cop from 30 Sun City St. had a pistol
so the snake's body became a juggler.
Afterwards, when he'd emptied out the whole magazine, we crushed
its head with a rock.

NIVA

She was like a box of sweets that death had wandered about in.
—Irwin Shaw

I saw her take off her shirt once.
Her chest was the color of a shack in the transit camp.
To exaggerate, I'll describe her nipples like the crest
of a slaughtered rooster,
you could say she lost her virginity on a Jewish Agency cot.
They called her Niva. She was like a box of sweets that death had wandered
about in.
To this day I remember the chocolate left on the corner of her mouth,
the palm of her hand scattering crows through the broken window
and the finger marking flight away from there.

HANDCUFFS. STREET POEM

They put the cuffs on him because there's no love in the world.
He stole a sprinkler so the cops would go after him and find
him under the bed and show him
what it means to steal a sprinkler when you don't even have a lawn to use it on.
No father either, and his mother's a line in the social worker's notebook.
What white legs the social had
like the cream cheese they used to serve every morning at the home,
and the way she told him how well he drew crows
that day he went to the Armenian in the Old City
to get himself tattooed like that, right on the muscle, as if
his hand was a wall in an ancient cave.
What wings you could have seen there
and eyes
and head tilted to a sky that was
the ceiling of the lock-up.

SELF-PORTRAIT FROM THE MARINES

You need a block of ice for the perfect crime. A shard
to slice the jugular
and let blood melt the fingerprints.
Like fingers resting on a page that turns into a sentry's neck

before your legs jump the barbed-wire fence
to dance in the middle of the base.
At eighteen I chewed nails,
spit rust.
And it's only because of my glasses that the Marines didn't take me.
Sea was painted in the eyes of the Wave recruiting me
and motor boats putted along the shore of her lips.
"Get a camera," she wanted to tell me, "and take a picture
of your life.
If you ever lose it,
at least you'll have a copy
left."

THE GIRL AND THE BUTCHER'S WINDOW

Every morning, at seven or quarter past seven,
I pass the face of a little girl.
I almost know her whole wardrobe by heart
and I know that her red raincoat drips winter
just as her caped summer skirt is always fastened
with a thick leather belt.
Once I asked about her and they said she was waiting
for a taxi to pick her up and take her to an institution for the retarded.
From the picture window, a few meters from the place she stands,
you can see kilos of meat hanging and butchers in white clothing
nimbly chopping a rib, a breast, or
a shrunken chicken.
Maybe instead of praising the sharpness of the blade
you have to write about the wind that it slices like a fan
and the eyes of that girl fixed every morning
to the window, shedding a few drops of blood.

SEVEN LINES ON THE MIRACULOUS YARKON

Soon the city of Tel Aviv will be drawn like a pistol.
What'll come from the sea starts with the hot wind and
on the street you can already hear the kind of quiet talk
that follows a shooting. Too bad there's no circus in this
town, too bad there's no sword swallower, no magician, no

elephants, no dragon; too bad just one dingy floats by right
as I show someone not from here the miraculous Yarkon.

STREET OF THE WELDERS. WEDDING SINGER

When history judges her, she'll go down on a stretcher.
Then her guitarists will play some other wedding
and promise the table of honor a bottle of champagne.
"One of your friends," she says, "once sang about
a guy who took the pipe. When I'm good to myself
that's the kind of woman I am but when I'm bad
I'm just a microphone whore."
On another street I might have fallen in love with her,
but here they change carburators on used cars in the morning
and at night they get married.
When she puts on that blue dress at twilight she
knows that from that color God made the sea
but the drops she's left with barely
make up a puddle.

EMBROIDERED RAG. POEM ON UMM KULTHOUM

She had a black evening gown on
and her voice hammered steel nails
into the elbow leaning on the table
in the cafe on Struma Square.
"My eyes have gotten used to seeing you,
and if you don't come one day
I'll blot that day from my life."
I came with a sponge to rub out
a huge eagle drawn in chalk
on the edge of a cloud.
An embroidered rag that years later the cook at
the base at Be'er Ora hooked to his belt loop
fluttered under its wings.
I asked him for a couple of potatoes
and on the cassette player her gown darkened again.
He shut his eyes to the steaming lunch and kept peeling potatoes.
Who's that singing, I started, Umm Kulthoum?

He nodded.
For all he cared, I could have cleaned out the whole kitchen.

HAWADJA BIALIK

An Arab girl sings a song by Bialik
and the wings of the bus shade the olive trees
by the curves of Wadi 'Ara.
No mother, no sister, and her eyes roll
from blink to blink at the idolatrous deceits
of *Hawadja* Bialik.
Once I read that the first sign heralding
the imminent extinction of a star
is pronounced swelling
and redness at the exterior.
A red carpet spreads over the mountains of her lips
and the heels of the song strike "do," ring out "la."
The collapse lasts millions of years until the star
becomes a molten ball
whose leftover heat is beamed at the space
of an unfinished house.
The sun singed to a blade punctuates the blue
T-shirts of the workers with sweat
and the distant voice of the muezzin's prayers
stretch out like an unstitched carpet over the back of a donkey
who's run out of gas.

THIS IS THE POEM ABOUT THE YOUNG WOMAN WHO WANTED ME TO WRITE A POEM ABOUT HER

She leaned the mop against the door to the toilets
at the Jaffa branch of the Savings and Loan and wrung it out
with her damp fingers.
I knew her will and aching back, her family's pride
and the number of times she'd sewn buttons on her shirt.
I knew she came from Klansawa and if there *were* a poem for her
I'd call it Fatma Morgana.
Years have gone by since then. The wings of song I'd promised have been
stitched

onto the back of a bird referred to in her dreams as
The Eye of the Happy Prince
when we meet I'd fly her over the head of Muhammad Ali
who when they screamed "dirty nigger" at him in the street
and his friends egged him on to answer with a punch asked:
"And if Arthur Rubenstein was going by here and
someone called him a "dirty Jew," you think
he'd hit him with a concert?"

BLOODY MARY

And poetry is a bimbo
in the backseat of an American car.
Her eyes squint like a trigger, the revolver of her hair
firing blonde bullets that cascade down her neck.
Let's say her handle's Mary, Bloody Mary,
and words gush out of her mouth like juice from the belly of a tomato
who's had its face rearranged
on a salad plate.
She knows grammar's a language cop
and the antenna on her earrings
picks up the siren from a long way off.
The wheel veers the car over from a question mark
to a full stop
and she opens the door
to stand at the side of the road like a metaphor for the word
whore.

NELSON. TRAFALGAR SQUARE

The admiral's statue is closed for repairs.
They covered it with a tarp
that once might have been the sail of a battleship.
The wind swirls down below,
with the wings of birds embarking from the bread crumbs
near the gentleman with the bowler hat
to the bread crumbs of a guy who shaved his head
and painted his mustache red.
Oh, death by the sword, waves of the sea, scent of burnt powder

and the sailors' whores on shore.
All history can be
cast into a bird fountain.

HISTORY'S BLOWOUTS IN THE VALLEY OF YEHOSHEPHAT

The English called the Valley of Yehoshephat—Josephat
the Arabs shortened it to Wadi Joz
and the Jews turned it into Nahal Egoz.
From this surplus of names the waters soaked into the earth's belly
like fragrances showered by an abundance of lovers
over a woman's body
that rests, in the meantime, like a spare tire
in the very heart of the trunk
waiting for history's next flat
to remind us she's around.

JASMINE. POEM ON SANDPAPER

Fairuz raises her lips
to heaven
to let jasmine rain down
on those who once met
without knowing they were in love.
I'm listening to her in Muhammad's
Fiat at noon on Ibn Gabirol Street.
A Lebanese singer playing in an Italian car
that belongs to an Arab poet from
Baqa' 'al-Gharbiyye on a street named
after a Hebrew poet who lived in Spain.
And the jasmine?
If it falls from the sky at the end of days
it'll stay green for
just a second at
the next light.

—*All translations, unless otherwise indicated, by Ammiel Alcalay*

TIKVA LEVI

TIKVA LEVI was born in Ashkelon; after studying literature at Hebrew University, she moved to Tel Aviv and became active in various groups dealing with social and political issues. She presently works at HILA, a grass roots activist group concerned with the institutional discrimination faced by *mizrahi* Jews in the Israeli school system; in addition, she has been instrumental in forging a place for *mizrahi* women within or, in some cases, outside of the Israeli feminist movement. Written from both a working class and a woman's perspective, Levi's "Purim Sequence" makes completely new areas available to younger Israeli writers. The staple issues of so much Hebrew writing that is more familiar to western audiences—the question of borders or relations between Jews and Arabs—are given a completely different dimension in Levi's work. Here the borders are not between nationalities but between the haves and the have nots, not between the Arab and the Jew out there but between the Arab *in* the Jew and in him or herself. The poem literally remaps not only the borders of the city she is traveling in but also places that city and its internal divisions within the greater global context of cultural, political, and economic divisions between East and West, North and South, the First and the Third Worlds, the rich and the poor, this side of the tracks and the other. Her overtly political poems, while seemingly antithetical to questions emerging from literary theory, are a direct means of confronting the very biases that dictate what is or can be considered a theoretically sound literary text. Indeed, they seem to operate within the paradoxical terms set by the Salvadoran poet Roque Dalton in his *Ars Poltica 1974:* "Poetry/Forgive me for having helped you understand/you're not made of words alone." While some of Levi's work has appeared before in English, her poetry remains unpublished in Hebrew.

FIGHTING AT THE BORDERS WITHIN: AN INTERVIEW WITH TIKVA LEVI BY AMMIEL ALCALAY

I am interested in hearing your thoughts about the relationship between poetry and politics, particularly in terms of whom a writer imagines their work is addressed to; maybe you could begin by talking about the study on Palestinian and Israeli poetry you had been working on.

Getting the materials and studying this in the context of Hebrew University was difficult enough. A lot of the material I gathered was in Arabic; some things were only available to me here in English, which is part of the whole problem. At the beginning, I had thought of using work from 1967 and going backward but then the intifida started; the idea was to concentrate on the poet's relationship to the land and to landscape. But as I found more and more material, this was already in the second year of an M.A. program, I found myself more interested in poetics, in the place of the poet within the poem, in the poet's function itself. I was also drawn to a kind of Palestinian political poetry that I was already familiar with, poetry that did not remain in a select, intellectual audience but is enormously popular. Like Marcel Khalife, for instance, whose poetry is set to music and which everyone sings, from three-year-old kids on. Besides the poetry itself, I gathered every piece of critical work I could get my hands on, mostly in Hebrew but also Arabic texts published in Cyprus which I translated. I was astonished by the awareness, the level of consciousness that went into a critical writing written hand-in-hand with poetry, and the direct linkage between the two. A lot of the critical work I was looking at was written on poetry that emerged from the intifada, which I was less familiar with. This in itself kind of pulled the rug out from under my study because the intifada radically changed the whole face of Palestinian poetry. There was a lot of garbage written, of course, but the fact that it was written, the fact that every eighteen-year-old felt the need to express themselves through poetry, was quite a phenomenon in and of itself.

In referring to "political poetry" maybe it makes more sense to change the terminology and think in terms of the audience, who it gets to, to whom is the work addressed, and how the poets see themselves in relation to this audience.

Many of the Palestinian poets see their function as primarily a political one, and their poetry does reach everyone.

On the other hand, this can also be a conflict, in the work of Mahmoud Darwish, for example, where always being "the voice of the people" can be confining.

This is always the problem of a "minority," this conflict between collective duty and personal expression. In Israel, though, you don't see poets who also fulfill concrete political functions or offices, like Mahmoud Darwish, Samih el-Qasim, or Fadwa Tuqan. These are people involved not simply as part of a critical public but within the political process itself. So there is a huge difference, not to mention the fact that the point of view from which this consciousness arises is that of a repressed minority.

This relates to your own position; you started pursuing academic studies, you have been translating and writing poetry, but now you find yourself in a very public, political role. Although it might seem completely removed, you are still very involved in using your writing, in having to present and state things for very specific purposes. How do you define yourself now, how do these things go together, are they in conflict?

This is an extremely complex issue. I wouldn't say that I left the university because I wanted to write poetry and I took a leave from poetry because I wanted to work in the community, in HILA, as an activist involved in changing the face of education for *mizrahim* in Israel. I left the university for other reasons entirely.

Was it from a sense of solidarity with the need to see culture become something else, since the culture that you are part of, that your poetry is a part of, is not a culture that finds any outlet in the academic settings available here?

Precisely, and this was reflected very specifically, in my clash with Gershon Shaked, for example. I was one of the few students who came into the M.A. program with a subject already in mind and material in hand in order to write my thesis. For the M.A., though, you are supposed to complete a requirement in another foreign language and he was unwilling to accept Arabic as my other language except under the condition that I follow through with my subject. He suggested I study French since he said no literary criticism had been written in Arabic. This is someone that, without knowing half a word of Arabic, can come along and decisively determine what is and is not legitimate. That was only the beginning. After that, I had a thesis director who didn't know any Arabic but at least she was fair enough to suggest that we find a codirector. But everything was so dragged out, every little thing was a battle. The subject fascinated me, though. I kept gathering things and got to where I was drowning in material; at this point, I have enough to write a doctorate. Then I decided I knew enough about the subject and the idea of breaking my head and struggling with all those academics and going through the defense just didn't appeal to me. The thought of standing up in front of people like Gershon Shaked or Dan Miron just made me lose my appetite. During my first year I finished most of the courses in the M.A. program; the second year I had already moved to Tel Aviv and become active in the Oriental Front, I was editing and writing for a newspaper called *Pa'amon* that dealt primarily with social issues, working at HILA, so I saw that there was a life after the university. All in all, I had spent six years at Hebrew University, so it was a real change. In the final analysis, you have to figure out where to put your energy. You can't write a thesis and struggle with all the Ashkenazim in academia, try to earn a living, be politically active, and on top of all that continue writing poetry. There's a limit to what a person can do. So the move to Tel Aviv opened me up to other things entirely, to other people, another social situation, other ways of thinking, other ideas, books that I never had time to read, all these things led me to want to express myself more in the role of an activist, even though I never stopped writing poetry. During this period I wrote a lot and I found that things I might have expressed before in prose or in letters now found their form in poetry.

In the "Purim Sequence" you question the whole idea of audience, I think, when you echo the words of God to Abraham in poem 5 about how many just men would he need to find in order to save Sodom; you ask how many readers it takes to make poetry; was it important for you that this work reach someone?

I didn't really think about it at all. It was a need, to express things, experiences. One incident that remains incredibly strong for me has to do with a trip I took with a friend of mine to Sakhnin. We were traveling around the Galilee and went to visit his parents. There are thirteen or fourteen siblings in the family, and his mother is a very proud, noble woman. One of the days we were there happened to be Land Day, it was a Friday. Suddenly I saw her crying, tears just rolling down her cheeks. Then I found out that this was a ritual, every Friday she just sat and cried because one of her sons, when he was seventeen, had been shot and killed on Area Nine, the army firing range which had been part of this family's olive groves. Years had passed since this happened, but the very hour that the boy's body had been brought in for burial was the time she put aside for this private memorial. It really affected me, I just sat and cried with her too. Then, of course, it was Land Day, and she marched at the head of the crowd and you begin to understand where she drew all this strength from. This said it all for me, the public strength and the private grief, a direct parallel to the role of poetry. So I wrote a poem, I couldn't think of any other way to express my solidarity, to unload this experience somehow. Later on I thought about publishing work. This was the period I began to work full-time at HILA and the first year was simply learning about the issues and how to deal with them. Education wasn't my field, which was an advantage in this case because I hadn't been exposed to all the crap that passes for a degree in education at the university. So I had more time the first year, I initiated fewer projects. After the first year, all my energies have gone into this work and I find this to be fine, I can express myself very clearly through this work and I see the results. I see the way parents who began thinking about these issues through us three years ago are speaking now, I see what has happened to their children, how they've moved into educational frameworks that can eventually lead them into the university. I see the enormous strides in consciousness-raising that have been made. And there is a tremendous satisfaction in this. I also feel that, not everyone of course, but many of these people simply speak poetry. When a mother comes to me and says: 'They buried my son alive, they only let his nose come up for air, they turned him into a hostage of the Ashkenazim.' I'm just giving the idea, I can't even begin to duplicate her language which is just incredible, but this is the terminology she uses. For me this is a much more fertile dialogue, it's also in my language and expresses things that I have also felt need to be said. This is an alternative and makes much more sense to me than trying to adapt myself to something else. Now that HILA has grown, and the intensive period of writing letters, informational materials, slogans and the thousand and one other things we've had to do has somewhat died down, I have more of a chance to directly engage in projects concerned with other kinds of writing; I was asked to write, for instance, a series of portraits of parents and the processes they and their children have gone through, but not in a sociological way, simply as a narrative, a story that others could pick up and read and identify with. I am now also editing a long series of interviews with various *mizrahi* professionals who have succeeded in one field or another—doctors, lawyers, physicists, mathematicians, you name it. The interviews explore their experiences in the Israeli educational system and how, miraculously in most cases, they managed to survive intact and become whatever they became. We also want to turn this into a book which, I think, would be enormously useful. In terms of my own poetry, I'm not the type of person who has to go to some Greek island or to Paris and write in solitude. I have to be around the life that is my poetry, I can't distance myself from things in order to get some other perspective. I have to be within the landscape that I am writing about, be a part of it. I have to be with the people who inhabit my work. This is one of the reasons that I can't even begin thinking about living in some other country. Writing is extremely important to me, I love the very act of it, touching pen to paper. If I moved somewhere else, this would be completely silenced within me.

How do you see some of these issues about the role of culture in terms of what is going on in Israel?

To tell you the truth, I find myself so discouraged by the Ashkenazi monopoly over culture in general and, more particularly, over literature. It's gotten to the point that I hardly pay attention any more to what is going on out there. And

I used to read every literary journal and literary supplement with absolute devotion, simply to follow what was going on. But even if something good was published, it still came out within a ghetto and I can no longer even relate to that ghetto. It's hard for me to divorce myself from all that but I see no other way.

I think that there are definitely periods in the life of an artist or the cultural life of a certain group of people at a historical moment when it simply might be better off to keep quiet, rather than keep trying to get in the door of someone else's house.

Exactly. Because the people who play those games to get through those doors completely lose themselves once they're inside. I understand them fully, but I also see how they are pandered to in order to fulfill some kind of a function that mainstream Ashkenazi culture defines. So there is a tremendous need, not to fill a vacuum, but simply to create alternative means of expression, alternative places and publications and contexts, to give a forum to artists who have no chance of reaching any kind of audience so long as they continue being themselves, because of alternative ways of thinking, because of their personal identities.

I think the only place that some of this has really taken place is in music, maybe because it's simply more direct and easier from a technical standpoint.

If you take Zohar Argov as a phenomenon, you can see that what is called "cassette music" also began as the creation of an alternative. They simply created a whole new market. Those cassettes were never sold in the hip places in Tel Aviv; if an Ashkenazi wants the music of Zohar Argov, they have to go to the Central Bus Station and not The Third Ear, for instance. Even the performances comprise a whole other world. Things take place at completely different hours, you see announcements for performances in various languages, like Farsi, for instance. The music came out from underground, but it has a separate existence. If you go see Shalom Hanoch, the show starts more or less at 9 o'clock. But when I went to see Avner Gadassi, the Yemenite singer, his show started at 2 A.M. Until then the audience had to pay a price, as lip service of course, but they still paid: until 2 A.M. they sing songs of the Land of Israel, the usual stuff. But everyone is there to hear the other stuff. I call Street of the Welders, the atmosphere that Ronny Someck describes in that poem of his, the *mizrahi* Dizengoff. You go to some of these clubs and you won't see an Ashkenazi face; I've even been to Yemenite clubs where we looked different! The history of this begins much earlier. The *mizrahi* musicians of the 1970's went in the direction of what was then, for us at least, underground rock, garage bands that listened to Led Zeppelin or Deep Purple. We listened to this music in clubs in Ashkelon and Ramle way before the crowd in North Tel Aviv; I was thirteen when we listened to this stuff while they still did folk dances in youth groups. All those musicians were *mizrahim;* they didn't play *mizrahi* music but they certainly didn't play the standard Israeli fare, the usual Russian stuff. Then certain groups began to go back to traditional instruments or Greek-style music and things began to develop in another direction. There was recently an enormous article on this whole phenomenon of clubs and garage music of the 1970s and the word *mizrahi* wasn't mentioned once, it was quite remarkable but keeping in line with the complete negation of a certain history. Not only the musicians, but the audiences were all *mizrahi;* nobody came to those clubs from North Tel Aviv, they didn't even know they existed. All the groups developed in our neighborhoods, without exception. And this also took place with neighborhood theater, like in Katamon with people like Nafi Salah. What's interesting is that the new wave of *mizrahi* music that is so much a part of my generation but which my parents' generation, for example, considers artificial in relation to the Arabic music they love, has actually given some legitimacy to the older, more classical Arabic stuff. Now there is more and more fusion music, things that are incredibly interesting and we can come along—after hearing this newer music which harks back to its classical sources—and say, of course, we remember hearing things *like* that at home but we always told our parents to turn it off. By the end of the process, though, you begin begging your parents to start searching through their old stuff to see if they have any cassettes or records from back then. Suddenly all your friends start handing over lists to anyone traveling to Egypt, so they can bring stuff back that we can't get here. These processes are different amongst the Palestinians because they are a minority that was more or less under constant watch but you do see generational differences in the music of Sabrin, for example.

If you compare this situation in music to what exists in literature, you begin to see something very interesting. The classical literature, the Golden Age of Spain, has been kept as an academic preserve that presumes all kinds of knowledge simply in order to get to it. It is so natural for an Arabic writer, take Emile Habiby for example, to utilize all kinds of references and devices from classical Arabic literature. But despite a few exceptions this is not a general practice amongst mizrahi *writers. There is a tremendous amount of writing that is part of this culture but is simply unavailable. The fact that you cannot get hold of the work of Yehuda al-Harizi and so many other fundamental texts outside of certain libraries is absolutely astonishing. Imagine an Arabic student who couldn't go into more or less any bookstore and find cheap editions of the texts of al-Maari or Abu Nuwas. This would be unthinkable.*

I am lucky because I had a chance to get to this material at the university; not that it was particularly offered, but at least I got the tools that enabled me to find it. These tools, however, are practically unavailable to those who don't get to the university and someone who is working without an awareness of this material is really working in a vacuum. When I started getting interested in Palestinian political poetry and I read Shimon Ballas's book *Arabic Literature in the Shadow of War,* I began to more fully comprehend the process undergone by Palestinians within Israel after 1967, when all this Arabic literature started coming to them from all over the place, after they had been cut off for so many years; it completely changed the nature of their work.

What's amazing is that, in many cases, things that by any logic, right or historical tradition pertain to the mizrahim *themselves and which are actually available in a certain form right here, cannot be gotten to by the people who need to get to them. Even when they are gotten to, they are not "translated" into a context that makes sense, in order to be used.*

But given the situation, how can you expect people to get to this culture? At least with the Palestinians then, they were waiting for something. With us it's a lot more complicated because there isn't even any consciousness regarding the need for these things. You can take this analogy into many areas because the nature of repression here is such that you really have to keep your eyes open. It's easy for me to speak now because I find myself with the right people, that is, with people I don't have to constantly debate or explain anything to. I don't know what would have happened to me if I kept studying. Maybe I would have gotten a heart attack or lived with an ulcer, I just don't know. One of the mothers I encountered at HILA, and I am using her term here, defined what has happened here as a "covert Holocaust." That's precisely what she said. This is sometimes much more difficult to deal with than a wall with a closed border. Here the border doesn't appear closed. How come I didn't know about Yehezkel Kedmi's book, for instance? I need you to come from New York to tell me about this book. And I know that it never would have gotten to me otherwise. There are plenty of other things I'll never know about that are going on, that much is clear to me. When I interviewed Shlomo Bar once I remember asking him a kind of provocative question when he talked about the suppression of *mizrahi* artists; I said, "But look, you made it didn't you?"He answered me with another question: "But do you and I even know how many like me died? I don't and neither do you." Even if I talk about my own experience trying to publish my work, and I don't want to sound like the eternal underdog, I am not talking as myself, Tikva Levi, but in the name of so many others I don't even know about who I'm sure have had the same experiences I have and lived through the same frustrations I have. And I know that it is only through this frustration that they have chosen in which direction to go, to try and fit in under conditions dictated from above, whether in literary or political institutions. Everything here is institutional. Try to think for a second about what I or anyone else can try to do here in order to find a place to present such work. In music there has been a breakthrough, any *mizrahi* musician can find a stage now. That's not the problem, there are other problems, like the producers who screw them, running them ragged for three or four years, three or four shows a night until they completely run out of steam, get thrown out and the producers find new, younger talent. You won't find a *mizrahi* Shalom Hanoch, Erik Einstein or Hava Alberstein, people who've reached middle age in one piece; the producers simply use the *mizrahi* musicians to make money hand over fist. But this is our problem, something we have to struggle with, since the producers themselves are all *mizrahim*. While I've been able to find a forum to express myself, I know there are many, many others who haven't. Look at what happens in film, when you look at the garbage that comes out and then you sit with someone like Eli Hamo and you hear about the kinds of things he wants to do, it would simply be enough for him to have a camcorder and an editing table. He doesn't need much more than that but as it is he can't even work because he lacks this basic equipment. This is frustrating and depressing and you see it in every field. Wherever you throw a stone, you'll hit someone who's frustrated trying to do something, believe me. I am less frustrated because I don't let myself even get into situations that I used to get into, debates, arguments. If you talk about energy, I am simply unprepared to waste my energy arguing with Ashkenazim. I don't need to prove anything. The most I can say if something comes up is simply that I don't talk to racists and get up and leave. I no longer argue, debate or try to convince the endless string of well-intentioned people who come around and truly want to help but who simply have no consciousness at all of the issues involved. Instead of sitting around and trying to convince some Ashkenazi that I'm right, I would rather put my energy into speaking to a hundred parents from HILA. That's the choice I've made and I am very happy with it. It's not only me, but part of a larger process. Sometimes at a seminar, there might be a group of thirty or so *mizrahim* and Arabs but as soon as a single Ashkenazi walks in, all our fire would be spewed in that direction. All of a sudden, no one's interested in the lecture anymore; we have to justify and apologize and explain, give facts, look in books and, before you know it, two hours have gone by. I'm not prepared to do this anymore. Go read, the most I can offer at this point is a bibliography. This is a very important process, this looking within, this self-examination. It's very constructive, I feel much more productive, at peace with myself, confident. Also you get very different feedback in this context. Even people who might argue against you, their opposition comes from completely different motives. But there is some kind of starting point, whether it's cultural, biographical, based on class, there is something on which to base a dialogue.

FIG FROM THE '67 BORDERS

The fig -
a well-known motif in poetry
of the Palestinian diaspora
but this
is a real fig
picked by
an old Palestinian
from a refugee camp in Gaza
every year
when the season is ripe
he comes to the Erez junction
to feel with his toothless mouth
the taste of a fig
containing within it
the world of before
reviving it
for another year

How can you explain the world to come
in the '67 borders to an old Palestinian
from the refugee camps in Gaza
in the shade of his former fig tree?

May 1987

LAND DAY

for Ali's mother

Your smooth dark face
streams hot tears
when you speak of your son
and that accurséd Friday
when they brought his riddled body
back from Area Nine or,
to be more exact, from the family's olive groves
five years later
on Friday morning
you stammer

at your private memorial
every Friday
the pain and the rage and the longing
amalgamate into a great love, worthy
of the land
that land that nourishes you to give you
the power to go on
thus, at the head of the procession
on Land Day
standing straight in your long gown
imbibing from her the cry
bound to her by primal power
hovering over the head of the procession
with a clenched fist your sparkling eyes
uplifted
unto your son smiling down from the sky
his hands extending from mother earth
caressing the soles of your feet, lightening their step
at the head of the procession

March 1987

AND FINALLY

And finally we won't ask you
where you were
and we won't seek final mercy
now from the empty-hearted
with heads held high we'll watch
how our blazing pain
bleaches your cruelty
bares your teeth
singes your numbness

January 1987

TO THE LIFE OF PLANTS ON THE ROAD

I saw them hitting the cactus
laughing at the sight of the juice that spilled
rubbing their palms in delight
at every hewn leaf
competing between themselves to see who would
make the still unripe fruit fly higher
with their stick
finally getting off
just as they tore out the root
and crushed it with their heavy boots

they went off without seeing
how a seed-bearing cloud
slowly landed on the ground
much bigger than the one that
had served the butchered cactus.

I saw
and made a blessing

January 1988

DECEMBER '86
BY THE RIVERS OF BABYLON

On a park bench
they sit and also cry
in their transmigratory company
my elders
thirty-six years in the Land
still foreigners
some dare—refugees
from the rivers of Babylon
and the palm trees

Reader -
don't be mistaken and think
nostalgia
to Zionism's uprooted

from Babylon in Israel
and from Palestine in the refugee camps
this is no ambrosia
but a bitter cup
drunk daily
years upon years
of hope compounded
to return to their borders
to their country to their homeland

May 1987

THE EXTENT OF THE TRAGEDY

the extent of the tragedy revealed itself to me in Zurich
there at the airport on the moving ramp
I saw my parents lost
not going up and not going down
they are the ones who don't know how to ask
and in what language would they ask
and which currency would they let go of

September 1988

WE LIVE IN JESSIE COHEN

We live in Jessie Cohen in Holon
on Zionism Street for those who know it
sandwiched in by Aharonovich and parallel to Anilievich
trapped by these names
I have an uncle who lives in the Ben Gurion Housing by the graveyard
we moved from Ashkelon, from Zion Heights
once they just called them projects
before the UN decision equating Zionism with racism
and those who decided on the names
never lived in these neighborhoods
but on University Street in Spring Heights
yet we're inside Racism parallel to Holocaust
awfully close to the graveyard
there in Ashkelon and here in Holon

September 1988

POOR BERTOLT BRECHT

Poor Bertolt Brecht came from the black forest
a poet of the forest that chilled him to the very bone
but I want to tell you about Yona Damati
who came to the big city from a miserable neighborhood
her burning eyes remove the shades
of estrangement in a single gaze
the whiteness of her smile mediates disguises
the *'ayin* and the *het* is a source of living waters for an accent
Yona Damati in the big city
moving between the drops of ugliness and antipathy
at the touch her dark, warm hand
frozen buds open up sunflowers turn
if we tell Yona Damati of the sun she brings with her
and what she does to the big city
her eyes will open wide, she'll crack up laughing
and tell you: What are you talking about, man,
me, Yona Damati, I came from the neighborhood
I just want to work in the big city.

January 1987

PURIM SEQUENCE

1. At the Bus Station
   Purim Eve

   The woman in the red jacket
   at the next station
   looked like a mailbox
   I took the letters out of my bag
   invitations to a meeting of
   The Public Committee on Education
   in Neighborhoods and Development Towns
   and went up to put them in
   only realizing up close
   how far away I was

2. At the Bus Station
   Purim Eve

A girl on the other side of the street
by the stations heading North
dressed up like Alexis:
I saw Mali,
a friend from the neighborhood
who does Alexis
all year round

3. In the Bus
Purim Eve

Allenby, corner of Yehuda Halevi
Wieseltier and a girl wrapped up in each
other, lyrically kissing
in the middle of the crossing
the Arabs still haven't breached
the Yarkon which once belonged
to Sheikh Munis
but is now a cesspool
even romantics avoid
navigating
not to mention
Arabs.

Defending a cesspool
is a joke
but what's funnier
is that they don't even clean it up
just pollute it more and more.

4. In the Bus
Purim Eve

Little kids in costume
giggle happily
real flower children
and Margalit Sa'anani sings
on "The Honey 'n in the Groove"

and the kids get off at
Tel Kabir and Tel Giborim
and Jessie Cohen as it meets
the Cemetary
of the Central City
that's where they spend their time
and here's where they live

5. In the Bus
Purim Eve

a few stations
before mine
and what'll happen
to the poems in my head
if I get run over at one
of the three intersections
on my way home
what'll come of these poems
before they're written
and if I do get home
and write them
what will become of them
and if only one person
reads them
will that make them poetry
and what if two
or even ten
will that make them poetry
"Oh let not the LORD be angry"
literary critics
"and I will speak, yet but this once"
may these poems find
favor in your eyes

6. On My Way Home
Purim Eve

A long deserted street
with a mailbox in the middle

the letters from the first poem
still in my hand
now they won't
get to
Meir Buzaglio—a doctoral student of philosophy
and Ya'akob ben Ya'akob—parent from Shikun Vatikim

past the last intersection
from the previous poem
a golden dusty cloud
of neon cleaves
the fog
and in a doorway
a teenage couple
hug and kiss
completely unrelated
to the couple from poem three

7. At Home
   Purim Eve

Got to get organized fast
to write
what's spinning
in my head from the bus station
in poem one
I put on a tape by Nafas
and feel this music arouse
something in me
like someone far far off
within
summoning me
Rafi
grew up in Dimona
lived in Paris
now an actor in Tel Aviv
told me half an hour before the meeting
of the Popular Front for Oriental Liberation
just that we weren't that much of a front
not to mention popular or liberated

We're just shades
here and there in the Land of Israel
we passed through
Sheikh Munis on the way
after the Arabs
in the transit camp
before they decided
to make it Spring Heights
but stature and springtime
don't exactly go with colored folk
and the border is at the Yarkon
which they continue to pollute
at least from the end
of poem three

8. After Midnight
   Purim

In the morning I'll join my parents
who went to celebrate Purim with
the family in Ashkelon
on Purim Eve
in the afternoon we'll eat off the grill.
The uncle, a professor from Haifa
who's researching the history of the community
that came from the village of 'Ana in Iraq
along with all his research assistants:
the aunt who can recite dozens of poems
you'll never see on state TV
and the uncle who sings the immortal *maqam*
that the son, doing his doctorate in economics
in Chicago and maybe going to work in Peru,
won't hear, even from the distance
of the poem before this one
and my mother, who knows the family tree
back nine generations,
in other words,
the name of the grandfather of the grandfather of
my grandfather
whose picture is now before me

this family tree
won't be computerized at the Museum of the Diaspora
and this tree,
I just want to make clear,
has nothing to do
with any poem

9. Later Than after the Midnight
of the Last Poem
Purim

Side two of Nafas
is
music made by Iranians
living in the U.S.A.
a fusion of East and West
beginning in classical Persian
with a crescendo
every melody is colonized
by the West
Khomeini alone
holds the breach
but at the same time
arms deals
with Israel and the U.S.
flourish
as long as Iraqis die
there is joy and jubilation in The Land
at a conference organized
by The International Education Fund
a professor told a joke:
a fan cheers a boxer from the stands
Give it to him in the teeth, let him have it in the teeth
in the second round the same fan gives his
let him have one in the teeth cheer
to the other boxer
when asked why'd you switch to the other side?
he answers: what difference does it make
I'm interested in teeth
don't ask what a hand he got

only one woman shrieked I don't get it
I don't get it like crazy
but who pays attention to loonies
especially in an ivory tower

10. Cats Wailing Outside
during the Second Watch of
Purim

I put Nafas on again
I do just fine
with this music
beduin flute
drums follow
galloping horses
and the 'oud gets in too
each instrument attentive to the other
when one moves into a solo
the others assent from afar
and keep down when need be
now the husky plaintive flute's up front
the drums and the 'oud recede
till little by little the sorrow lets up
and the drums kick in
only to give the 'oud another slot
living in balance
unlike the conquerors
from the poem before this
and what kind of harmony can exist
between conqueror and conquered
only my tree
grows broader
and taller
four more generations
after my grandfather
always before me

11. I Get the Urge to Send Good Wishes
But Not For
Purim

Happy holiday to all the trees
here and there in the Land of Israel
from the seventh poem
and to all those
who aren't dressed up
and those not looking
for the high boughs
to grab onto
and those without noisemakers summoning
the name Haman hung in a happy ending
upon the highest tree in the Kingdom
this joke too
like the one in poem nine
has long ceased to be funny

12. Reflections on
Purim

Is Mordechai a righteous man?

The wrath of Ahashverosh upon
Vashti was appeased—parenthetically
a word in favor of Vashti whose only sin was
her refusal to be a sexual object
heaven forfend she serve as model "to all the women,
so as to make their husbands contemptible in their eyes"
for their sake, "King Ahashverosh commanded
Vashti the Queen to be brought before him,
but she came not" -
so he sought "fair young virgins"
a golden opportunity, thought the righteous man,
and brought Esther into the picture
"Now when every girl's turn
was come to go in to King Ahashverosh after she had been
under the regulations for the women,"
somewhere around the age of 11, 12, 13,
"twelve months, for so were the days of their anointing,
namely, six months with oil of myrrh, and six months
with sweet odors, and with other ointments of the women,"
and the King opened and returned the merchandise

and Mordechai knew like everyone else
except the piece
warehoused for a year
but who actually reads
The Scroll of Esther
they only wait for Haman
to pound the noisemakers
only wait for Purim
to put on a costume
and be whatever they want
according to the rules
but they just forgot or didn't read
in last month's paper
that at the end of *Dynasty*
Crystal turns into a vegetable
and Alexis fries in the hot seat
for bumping Blake Carrington off
in last week's paper
it said Israel was about
to take *Dynasty* off the air
my paranoia tells me
that someone's interest is at work here
that my friend from the neighborhood in poem two
will just go on doing Alexis
the whole year through

13. Third Watch of the Holiday
Purim

Kamilia from Sabrin's on the tape:
"He who says—the homeland is only land -
is a traitor -
the homeland's human"
I turn down the volume
so only I can hear
my paranoia is transmitted
to the door or the window
someone might think that whoever listens
to Arabic is an Arab
and come to kill me

I hate to wake up early
but tomorrow I'll gladly
do it to water
my tree

14. Still on the Third Watch of
Purim

it's my paranoia again
drawing me back to poem thirteen
which is bound to raise the ire
of those from poem five
but I know nothing can make
me go back on the last one
I still have the strength to cleave to it
and remain steadfast right
to the end of the line

—*Translated from the Hebrew by Ammiel Alcalay*

SAMI SHALOM CHETRIT

SAMI SHALOM CHETRIT was born in Qasr as-Suq in Morocco in 1960. He studied Hebrew Literature and Political Science at Hebrew University; afterwards he lived in Los Angeles and New York, where he studied at Columbia University. Presently, he lives in Tel Aviv where he is the director of the Tel Aviv branch of the newly established alternative school *Kedma.* Chetrit's poetry relentlessly interrogates two of the defining and formative constituents that have gone into what might be termed

"official" Hebrew poetry. These are, on the one hand, the ideology, imagery, and mythology of writing that emerged from what is known as the *Palmah* generation; and, on the other, the uses of certain biblical material by the writers of that generation. His own displacements add an immediacy to his project of regenerating the sources of language with an ethical dimension directly connected to particular social and political situations. A number of his poems, "Hey Jeep," for instance, dealing with the intifada, or "Acrid Memory" (dealing with his experience as a soldier in Lebanon), are completely unprecedented in Israeli writing for their willingness to openly confront issues that are generally avoided or justified in one way or another. "Acrid Memory," for example, presents a damning and elaborate subversion of the well-known Israeli army maxim regarding the "purity of arms," a kind of code of honor proclaiming to curb the unwarranted abuse of power. In Chetrit's poem, it is only the old man—armed with a cane—who can purify the soldier, by risking his life to spit in the soldier's face. Chetrit's poems constantly interrogate the price power exacts, as in "Bad Dream," when the narrator, pursued by soldiers beating and shooting, seeks refuge in East Jerusalem, where "A woman in an Arab dress whose face is the face of my mother and / the face of my grandmother, lays my weary head on her shoulder." Yet, in a seeming sign of hope, as the narrator wakes up to hear his son riding on his back and shouting in his ear, "Daddy, hold on tight! I'm the rocket man, / I'm taking you to Jerusalem . . . ," the reader realizes that Jerusalem is the place of nightmare, lost identities and summary executions, of power gone awry. Chetrit's first book, *Openings* (1988), was the recipient of a prestigious literary award; he has also published translations of Langston Hughes and Maya Angelou in Hebrew and is presently at work on an anthology of Hebrew translations of contemporary African-American poetry. A new book, *Freha is a Beautiful Name,* was published by Nur in 1995.

ON THE WAY TO 'AYN HAROD

On the way to 'Ayn Harod
I lost my trilled *resh.*

Afterwards I didn't feel
the loss of my guttural *'ayin*
and the breathy *het*
I inherited from my father
who himself picked it up
on his way to the Land.

On the way to 'Ayn Harod
I lost my *'ayin.*
I didn't really *lose* it -
guess I just swalled it.

QUICK TAKE

In a poem you can't see
that I've got a green card
with an instant shot taken
at the Armenian place on
Salah ad-Dinn Street near
the American Consulate in
disintegrating Jerusalem.

In a poem you can't see
the irony in my eyes.

In poems you don't see
the poetic restriction
of writing confined verse
in a country without borders.

In poems you don't see
deceitful art embroidering
hypocrisy, both essential
to my existence, just like
the mug shot from Salah
ad-Dinn Street on my
green card is now.

"AND THOU SHALT TEACH THEM DILIGENTLY TO THY CHILDREN"

I am teaching my son to play soccer
in a strange land
I diligently teach my son soccer
in the land of baseball
I bring up my son in soccer
the way we used to over there.

Me and my son
kick back and forth to each other in Hebrew
I'm cautious and weary
he's tough and quick on his feet

kicking a soccer ball
back and forth
as we remember Zion.

A NIGHT OF SCUDS

When the scuds fell on Tel Aviv,
I went over to the Greek diner on the corner of Broadway.
The Greek served me American coffee,
but I didn't pick up on his being Greek
until he asked: Where are you from? You have an accent like . . .
You too, I said.
He laughed, I'm from Greece, I'm already here twenty years.
We're neighbors, I told him.
From where? he asked.
The Middle East: I answered.

From the TV above his head the reporter from CNN
gave the first estimates of the damages in Tel Aviv
from a sealed room in Jerusalem,
and in the studio an American expert discussed
the deadly effects of mustard gas and nerve gas and I thought
of my mother and I remembered how shaken up she was at
the first air-raid siren during the '67 war, pulling
us kids along into the bomb shelter and whispering
prayers nonstop in Moroccan Arabic . . .
The Greek continued guessing in English: Jordan, Lebanon?
Yisrael, I said, in Hebrew.
You don't look Israeli, he said.
Depends, I told him.
He chuckled for some reason and added some hot coffee
to what was left cooling in my cup: Really,
you look more like an Arab.
On TV they were interviewing people on the street,
Israelis in the environs of sealed Tel Aviv,
and then I realized the Greek was right:
These Israelis are blond,
and they all speak perfect American English!
I thought I would write a sorrowful song,
but then I ordered a hamburger with lots of mustard.

VICTORY PARADE

There's a victory parade on Broadway for the
glorious heroes: routers of the Middle Eastern devil.
And tucked away in the corner of the paper is a picture
of a woman from that demonic country: her piercing eyes
bore into God's focused lens, from her hands she offers
her shriveled-up child as he swallows up the scene
with silence and an abbreviated gesture.
In small print, the headline reads:
a helpless Iraqi mother bears the corpse of her dead baby.

ACRID MEMORY

At the train station a rabid crowd
doles out yellow ribbons and flags,
asking passersby to pledge their blessings
and give thanks to the boys coming home.
As for me, I put down:
miserable, pitiful souls.
And a stinging memory comes back.
Homecoming memory.
Driving through the streets of a strange city at full tilt
(the streets there weren't at all unfamiliar to us),
an old Arab stood by the side of the main road waving his cane
(Now I think: that old man's grandfather once must have stood
by the side of that very road and waved that very cane).
We stopped to find the meaning of his wave.
The old man bent toward me (in his eyes I saw that he didn't
get the essence of human adulation,
the quality of victory or failure), and spit a yellow
glob of saliva in my face before turning back on his way.
And on that day, I was purified.
And not just for a fleeting moment was I purified.

WHO IS A JEW AND WHAT KIND OF A JEW?

1. The story is told:

An American Jew dies and he leaves no children.
In his will, the following is written:
"I hereby decree that all my money and property
be given over to the State of Israel and my last
wish is that I be buried in the Land of Israel.
The undersigned, Isaac Cohen."
The attendants sent the deceased and his money,
according to his last request, to the Land of Israel,
to eternal rest. The clerks of Zion collected
his money and transferred the corpse, as a matter
of course, to the burial society of the Ashkenazi Jews.
They turned his papers upside-down but found no authorization
to determine whether or not he really was an Ashkenazi.

Because of their doubts they deferred, sending him
on to the eternal resting place for Sephardic Jews.
The Sephardi sages sat down to take the matter
under advisement and, in conclusion, their answer
was formulated like this: "The name Isaac Cohen could
be either here or there, and given that this is so,
if he is a Sephardic Jew, then we have been privileged
to fulfill a wonderful commandment; and if he is
an Ashkenazi Jew, then we will gladly bury him!"

2. Getting to Know a Friendly American Jew: Conversation (translated into Hebrew)

Tell me, you're from Israel?
Yes, I'm from there.
Oh, and where in Israel do you live?
Jerusalem. For the last few years I've lived there.
Oh, Jerusalem is such a beautiful city.
Yes, of course, a beautiful city.
And do you . . . you're from West . . . or East . . .
That's a tough question, depends on who's drawing the map.
You're funny, and do you, I mean, do you speak Hebrew?
Yes, of course.
I mean, that's your mother tongue?
Not really. My mother's tongue is Arabic, but now she speaks Hebrew fine.
Oh, *'Ze Yofi,'* I learned that in the kibbutz.
Not bad at all.
And you are, I mean, you're Israeli, right?
Yes, of course.
Your family is observant?
Pretty much.
Do they keep the Sabbath?
Me, no, depends actually . . .
Do you eat pork?
No, that, no.
Excuse me for prying, but I just have to ask you, are you Jewish or Arab?
I'm an Arab Jew.
You're funny.
No, I'm quite serious.
Arab Jew? I've never heard of that.

It's simple: Just the way you say you're an American Jew. Here, try to say "European Jews."
European Jews.
Now, say "Arab Jews."
You can't compare, European Jews is something else.
How come?
Because "Jew" just doesn't go with "Arab," it just doesn't go. It doesn't even sound right.
Depends on your ear.
Look, I've got nothing against Arabs. I even have friends who are Arabs, but how can you say "Arab Jew" when all the Arabs want is to destroy the Jews?
And how can you say "European Jew" when the Europeans have already destroyed the Jews?

3. When I Left

It was only when I left that I remembered
I hadn't wanted to get so involved,
I really only wanted to tell her
that my first babysitter in Morocco was a Muslim girl
and that I have a black-and-white photo of her in an old album
sitting on the mosaic tiles in the courtyard
and that when I was a new Moroccan stiletto immigrant
I tried in vain to recall a little boy's conversation
with his babysitter in Moroccan Arabic.
And whenever we brought her up, my mother would say:
How she loved you, she never left you for a second.

BAD DREAM, PART 1:

The state, unlike an individual, has no conscience.
— George Kennan

A wild night,
someone turned me in to the guards.
Scrambling through a forest of concrete and glass towers,
they're here, there and everywhere,
riding on black horses and waving their truncheons
calling me to halt in Hebrew but I don't.

As they get closer I see my Hebrew teacher,
the justice from the rabbinate and a respected professor
wearing a cowboy hat.
The rest are in uniform.
I was caught like a rat in the corner of a dark alley.
(Shots in the air, sirens wailing.)
The password is halt, the old justice cries to me.
The Lord is my God, I mumble tearfully, as the
professor shoots the justice to death and rebukes me:
God is not the issue here! You overlooked us.
And the Hebrew teacher corrects him, You should say "let us down,"
my esteemed professor.
He shoots her as well before taking aim at me and shooting
and shooting . . . and shooting . . .
I wake up with a start, damn it,
the television's still on (you should say, "is still on")
(American cops are loading a young black guy
on to an ambulance, the lights whirling.
A tall man in a cowboy hat reveals the face of the deceased
for a second, lights a cigarette, and hisses through a jet of smoke: He sure was tough, the stupid bastard.)
Sweating, I make my way to the toilet
and expel all my dreamy fear.
I turn the TV off and go back to sleep.

BAD DREAM, PART 2

Here's the sign: "New Jerusalem," down in the darkened city.
I break an opening through the wall and cross over to the East.
A woman in Arab dress whose face is the face of my mother and
the face of my grandmother, lays my weary head on her shoulder.
You just had a bad dream. You're home now.
No, I scream, they've got uniforms and truncheons and guns
and they have no conscience, they're shooting at rabbis
and teachers, believe me, I saw it all with my own two teary eyes.
We got to the village. They washed my face and gave me
goat's milk, black olives and warm bread.
The milk is from your goat, my mother says,
the one we got especially for you when you were two,
so you would flourish and grow and give your mother's

weary breasts a rest. I gave my speech in the town square,
before an indifferent crowd:
Two old women, my mother, my grandmother,
two venerable old men in glowing *galabiyyas,*
a couple of mischievous kids, one goat,
an engorged cow, a dozing donkey and a lame dog.
I remember my closing line:
There is no new Jerusalem, all is vanity,
I saw it with my own eyes, just a sign on the wall,
don't follow them, they're all cops.
The police appeared on the hills,
led by a man in a cowboy hat.
They built me a gallows of the choicest wood,
I smoked my last American cigarette,
they put the rope around my neck
and the professor, reading the charges against me
and pronouncing my sentence, repeated and emphasized:
You overlooked us! You overlooked us . . .
And then suddenly a ball of fire careened towards
me from the sky and, to my surprise,
I see my son riding a rocket of fire—he grabs
the rope and pulls me on high:
Hold on tight, Daddy, I'm the rocket man . . .

I got up smiling with the morning light,
my lively son riding on my back
and shouting into my ear:
Daddy, hold on tight! I'm the rocket man,
I'm taking you to Jerusalem . . .

HEY JEEP, HEY JEEP

1. Eight kids in an army jeep
   Eight soldiers, one major:
   eight kids and one minor

2. *Hey Jeep, Hey Jeep*

3. And his son Ishmael was thirteen years old
   at the cutting of his uncircumcised flesh.

4. And eight of his sons in the army jeep
   and his son cries to the Lord but no one hears

5. And behold his father running:
   Run, Muhammad, run,
   your son's spirit is coming towards you

6. Lord, Lord, where is the lamb for a burnt offering?

7. Now these are the generations of Ishmael, Abraham's son,
   whom Hagar the Egyptian, Sarah's handmaid, bore unto
   Abraham: And these are the names of the sons of Ishmael,
   by their names, according to their generations: the first
   born of Ishmael, Nebaioth; and Kedar, and Abdeel, and
   Mibsam, and Mishma, and Dumah, and Massa, Hadad,
   and Teman, Jetur, Naphish and Kedemah . . .
   and Muhammad Said Qarada and Said Qarada whose years
   numbered thirteen at his death.

8. And these are the generations of Isaac, Abraham's son:
   Abraham begot Isaac; and Isaac begot Esau and
   Jacob; now the sons of Jacob were twelve in number;
   the sons of Leah: Reuben—Jacob's firstborn—Simeon,
   Levi, Judah, Issachar, and Zebulun; the sons of Rachel;
   Joseph and Benjamin; and the sons of Zilpah, Rachel's
   maid: Gad and Asher: these are the sons of Jacob
   who were born to him in Paddan-aram.

9. And eight soldiers in an army Jeep.
   One has officer's stripes on his shoulder,
   a Hebrew officer to the Kingdom of Israel:
   maybe a bleeding-heart liberal
   or a down-and-out reactionary

10. *Hey Jeep, Hey Jeep,*
    what a night it is!

11. Maybe his name's Itsik

12. And the seven under him:
    one's an eagle eye
    another's bound to ritual
    the third has his feet on the ground
    the fourth's got his head in the clouds
    the fifth's got to do it all
    the sixth replies stoically
    the seventh can't wait for liberty

13. And there are "dovish intellectuals" amongst them
    and there are "militant hawks" amongst them
    and God is there amongst them
    and an officer is there amongst them

14. soon there's neither
    affection nor innocence

15. Black combat boots on their feet:
    "that oppress the poor and crush the destitute"

16. Subject displayed the following signs:
    pallor, bleeding from the nose and left ear.
    Internal hemorrhaging in the vicinity of the left temple.
    Compound fractures resulting from a blow
    (not a projectile), on the left temple.
    Break in the left knee.

17. He was thirteen the day of his murder.

18. Thirteen: the age of obligation.

19. Theater of the struggle:
    As one they arose and came from the
    combines and the collective farms
    from the shareholder's settlements
    and their surroundings, from the towns and from the cities.

20. *Take her to the left a bit,*
    take her to the right.

21. And the boy cried to his father: Father, I'm choking

22. Eight pairs of heavy duty combat boots

23. Eight outstretched pairs
and there were white amongst them
and there were black amongst them

24. *Hey Jeep, Hey Jeep.*

25. Eight soldiers, one a Hebrew major:
eight soldiers, and one Arab minor

26. *Hey, everyone agrees: with a jeep*
the only thing you need is speed

27. They finally pitched him from the fleeting coach,
cast their spirit to the blinding night

28. *Like wind up in the sky*
we'll fly
right on by

29. but thou shalt love thy neighbor as thyself
but thou shalt love thy neighbor as thyself
but thou shalt love thy neighbor as thyself
but thou shalt love thy neighbor as thyself
but thou shalt love thy neighbor as thyself
but thou shalt love thy neighbor as thyself
but thou shalt love the neighbor as thyself
but thou shalt love thy neighbor as thyself
but thou shalt love thy neighbor as thyself
but thou shalt love thy neighbor as thyself
but thou shalt love thy neighbor as thyself
but thou shalt love thy neighbor as thyself
but thou shalt love thy neighbor as thyself

Jerusalem, December 31, 1988

AT AN AUDITORIUM OF A LOCAL UNIVERSITY

At an Auditorium of a Local University
Ammiel Alcalay (poet) reads an English translation
of poems by Tikva Levi (poet).
I'm moved and aggravated -
When, for once, will our
translated poems be able
to breathe in Hebrew?

TRANSLATORS

Ammiel Alcalay teaches at Queens College where he chairs the Department of Classical, Middle Eastern, and Asian Languages and Cultures; he is also on the Medieval Studies and Comparative Literature faculty at the CUNY Graduate Center. His *After Jews and Arabs: Remaking Levantine Culture* (University of Minnesota Press, 1993) was chosen as one of the year's top twenty-five by *The Village Voice* and also named as one of the year's notable books by *The Independent* in London. *For/Za Sarajevo* (New York: Lusitania Press, 1993), a bi-lingual English and Serbo-Croatian collection that he edited, was named by *Art Forum* as one of the year's ten choices. He has also edited and co-translated Zlatko Dizdarević's *Sarajevo: A War Journal* (Henry Holt, 1994) and *Portraits of Sarajevo* (Fromm International, 1995). In 1993, The Singing Horse Press in Philadelphia published *the cairo notebooks,* a collection of prose and poetry. His poetry, prose, reviews, critical articles and translations have appeared in *The New York Times Book Review, The Village Voice Literary Supplement, The New Yorker, The New Republic, Time Magazine, Grand Street, Sulfur, The Nation, Middle East Report, Afterimage, Parnassus, City Lights Review, The Review of Contemporary Fiction, The Michigan Quarterly, Paper Air, Paintbrush* and *Mediterraneans.*

He is presently working on a collection by the Bosnian poet Semezdin Mehmedinović.

Marsha Weinstein studied English and American literature at Brown University. She lives in Jerusalem where she has done graduate work in the department of Comparative Literature at Hebrew University. Most recently she has translated a book of essays by Shulamith Hareven, *The Vocabulary of Peace: Life, Culture and Politics in the Middle East,* published by Mercury House in San Francisco. In addition, she has translated texts by Yitzhak Ben Ner, David Grossman, and Amnon Jackont. She is presently working on a translation of Ronit Matalon's new novel, *The One Facing Us,* to be published by Metropolitan Books.

Susan Einbinder studied at Brown, Columbia, and Hebrew Union College; her focus has been on comparative medieval studies, particularly Hebrew and Arabic strophic poetry of Spain and North Africa. She teaches Hebrew literature at Hebrew Union College in Cincinnati, where she is the first woman on the faculty to both have a doctorate and rabbinic ordination. Her articles have appeared in *Prooftexts, The Hebrew Union College Annual,* and *Medieval Encounters.* She is presently researching images of Jewish and Christian women martyrs in medieval French and Hebrew texts.

COVER ARTIST

Jack Jano was born in Fez, Morocco in 1950 and emigrated to Israel in 1957. He studied at the Bezalel Academy of Art in Jerusalem from 1971 to 1975. After finishing his studies he traveled extensively through Europe and the Far East. During this period he also lived in New York. His work has been exhibited widely and he is the recipient of numerous awards; he presently lives in Jerusalem.

PHOTOGRAPHER

Eli Hamo was born in Jerusalem; he was an early participant in Nafi Salah's Neighborhood Theatre projects and has been an activist in a variety of *mizrahi* political and cultural movements. One of the founding members of *NUR: Fire & Light,* he is a filmmaker and presently lives in Tel Aviv where he works at the *Kedma* school.

Photograph of Shoshannah Shababo courtesy of Orna Levin.

Photograph of Jacqueline Shohet Kahanoff courtesy of Josette d'Amade.

Photograph of Simha Zaramati Asta courtesy of Yosef Dehoah Halevi.

Photograph of Nissam Rejwan courtesy of the author.

Photograph of Albert Swissa courtesy of *The Melton Journal.*

Photograph of Ilana Sugbaker Messika courtesy of the author.

Photograph of Lev Hakak courtesy of the author.

Photograph of Bracha Serri courtesy of the author.

Photograph of Ronit Matalon by Michal Heiman.

Photograph of Tikva Levi by Muki Kurtzman.

Photographs of Avi Shmuelian, Yitzhak Gormezano Goren, Moshe Sartel, Shlomo Avayou, Erez Bitton, Amira Hess, Yehezkel Kedmi, Shelly Elkayam, Ronny Someck, Shimon Ballas, Samir Naqqash, Uziel Hazan, Dan Banaya-Seri, and Sami Shalom Chetrit by Eli Hamo / *NUR: Fire & Light*. Copyright © 1996 by Eli Hamo / *NUR: Fire & Light.*